Thousand Autumns

QIAN QIU

5

5

WRITTEN BY
Meng Xi Shi

TRANSLATED BY
Faelicy

ILLUSTRATED BY
Me.Mimo

BONUS ILLUSTRATION BY
Gearous

Seven Seas

Seven Seas Entertainment

THOUSAND AUTUMNS: QIAN QIU VOL. 5

Published originally under the title of 《千秋》(Qian Qiu)
Author © 夢溪石 (Meng Xi Shi)
English edition rights under license granted by 北京晋江原创网络科技有限公司
(Beijing Jinjiang Original Network Technology Co., Ltd.)
English edition copyright © 2024 Seven Seas Entertainment, Inc.
Arranged through JS Agency Co., Ltd
All rights reserved

Illustrations by Me.Mimo
Bonus Illustration by Gearous

Seven Seas press and purchase enquiries can be sent to
Marketing Manager Lauren Hill at press@gomanga.com.
Information regarding the distribution and purchase of digital editions is available
from Digital Manager CK Russell at digital@gomanga.com.

Follow Seven Seas Entertainment online at
sevenseasentertainment.com.

TRANSLATION: Faelicy
ADAPTATION: Harry Catlin
COVER DESIGN: M. A. Lewife
INTERIOR DESIGN & LAYOUT: Clay Gardner
PROOFREADER: Vivica Caligari, Kate Kishi
COPY EDITOR: Jade Gardner
EDITOR: Laurel Ashgrove
PREPRESS TECHNICIAN: Melanie Ujimori, Jules Valera
MANAGING EDITOR: Alyssa Scavetta
EDITOR-IN-CHIEF: Julie Davis
PUBLISHER: Lianne Sentar
VICE PRESIDENT: Adam Arnold
PRESIDENT: Jason DeAngelis

Standard Edition ISBN: 978-1-63858-946-4
Special Edition ISBN: 979-8-89160-116-1
Printed in Canada
First Printing: July 2024
10 9 8 7 6 5 4 3 2 1

TABLE OF
CONTENTS

Caught Off Guard

YAN WUSHI HAD SEEN his fill of beauties in his time. All the same, when suddenly greeted with Shen Qiao dressed in women's attire, he was left with a feeling of indescribable amazement.

That was his first reaction.

The second was: *My venerable self truly has a good eye.*

The art of disguise was demanding and nuanced. Save for changing one's face directly the way Huo Xijing did, it was utterly impossible to suddenly change appearances completely. Therefore, even after dressing up as a woman, Shen Qiao's face remained roughly the same as before. However, the maid of the Huanyue Sect was clever, and she made some modifications in the details so that the contours of his face appeared gentler and more feminine. This made it difficult for even those who knew Shen Qiao to recognize him.

Shen Qiao had always been very good-looking, but now that he'd been powdered and painted, he naturally became only more outstanding. Even in maid's clothes, his head bare of any precious jewels or ornaments of gold and silver, others would find their attention drawn after only a glance.

Yan Wushi had also noticed this problem. "Make his face sallower."

After a moment, Shen Qiao's face and neck were darkened and made to appear wan, dulling his overwhelming beauty by one-third.

The maid was meticulous—even the color of his hands had been changed, so that nothing would appear abnormal.

However, neither Bian Yanmei nor Shen Qiao knew any bone-shrinking techniques. Although donning women's attire, they were still tall and thus too eye-catching. Accordingly, Puliuru Jian found two maids from the manor who were on the taller side as well. Northern women tended to be tall, so it wasn't that difficult a task. Though they were still half a head shorter than Bian Yanmei, the height difference wasn't too obvious after raising their soles. Onlookers only thought these four maids entering the palace were taller than average and didn't pay any special attention to the two men in disguise.

Once the arrangements were finished, it was time to enter the palace. Shen Qiao and Bian Yanmei took the gift meant for the empress from the Duke of Sui's residence, carrying it before them with both hands as they joined the other two maids. Together, they entered the palace.

In truth, Shen Qiao wasn't too worried about his own safety. With his level of martial prowess, as long as he didn't run head-on into Xueting, he would be able to escape from danger alone even if the imperial guards surrounded him. However, if he also had to bring the two young masters and an empress with him, things would get too difficult. If something went wrong, even if Puliuru Jian didn't blame him for it, Shen Qiao's own reputation would be scattered on the winds, and he wouldn't have the face to stay in the jianghu anymore.

His thoughts twisted and turned. It didn't show in his expression, but the moment he entered the palace gates he'd already begun calculating the shortest route out of the palace.

"Stop looking." Bian Yanmei seemed to know what he was thinking. Without moving his lips, he used Sound Transmission to tell

Shen Qiao secretly: "Yuwen Yun has bestowed the title of empress to five women. Though the empress we are going to rescue is the Grand Empress of the Central Palace, she is the least favored. Therefore, her palace is in the northwest. There's a long distance to walk between here and there."

Shen Qiao also silently transmitted back: "Aren't there gates in the imperial palace? What if we leave from the northern gate?"

"The northern palace gate is never open," Bian Yanmei replied. "The palace wall is high too; we might be able to leap over it ourselves, but there'll be many problems if we need to bring two or three more people with us. The guards under Yuwen Yun are not pushovers. If we are surrounded and their archers shoot at us, there'll be no chance of escape even if we sprouted wings."

Shen Qiao frowned a little.

Long before leaving, they had already agreed on how to escape: Shen Qiao and Bian Yanmei would meet the empress, then lure the imperial guards at the gate inside and defeat them. Then they'd leave with the empress and Puliuru Jian's two sons. If they could avoid the various patrol guards and martial experts along the way, there'd be people waiting outside the gates to receive them—at that point, they'd be safe.

Once the hostages were free from Yuwen Yun's hands, Puliuru Jian could directly launch a coup. Xueting was currently at Qingliang Temple, where Yan Wushi would go to impede him. Sang Jingxing and Yuan Xiuxiu weren't in the capital, leaving Hehuan Sect leaderless for the time being. This was an opportunity bestowed by the heavens. Puliuru Jian was already in secret communication with the troops defending the capital. If his plan succeeded, the rivers and mountains would see a new ruler, and the sun and moon would shine within a new sky.

But while plans could be perfect, reality was much more troublesome—even the most meticulously laid plans would contain mistakes. Moreover, the matter itself had been a sudden one, leaving little time for precision, and there were many variables involved. Only heaven could know whether they'd succeed.

Of course, because it was inevitable that Yuwen Yun would be alerted, if Shen Qiao and Bian Yanmei were unable to rescue the hostages, Puliuru Jian would launch the coup early anyway, but that would run contrary to their original purpose of entering the palace on a rescue operation.

At this point, however, worrying about the past or future was useless and would only make them overcautious and indecisive. Shen Qiao and Bian Yanmei followed the two maids, passing through the numerous halls. Step by step, they drew closer to Qingning Hall, where the Lady Puliuru lived.

The eunuch led them to Qingning Hall's entrance. His aged face was neither warm nor cold as he said, "Her Highness the Empress is right inside. Before you enter, please open the items you brought. The guards need to inspect them."

Of course, they'd already had an inspection in front of the palace gates, otherwise they'd never have been able to enter the palace. However, the emperor disliked Lady Puliuru, so everyone in the palace had followed suit in dropping rocks on the downtrodden. This was nothing new—for as long as humans walked the land, there would be people who flattered those above them while kicking the ones below.

The two maids had arrived at the palace with Lady Dugu earlier. When the demand came for the inspection, they took a step forward and placed a heavy embroidered bag into the eunuch's hands, saying,

"Just a small token of our appreciation—tea money for this chamberlain. We ask him not to mind its inadequacy."

The eunuch felt the contents through the silk fabric. It wasn't silver—it was a jade pendant even more valuable than silver. His smile finally became genuine, and he didn't ask the guards to inspect further. "The empress must be anxious from all the waiting. You should go in quickly and leave as soon as you're done. Do not linger."

The maids gave their assent, thanked the eunuch, and led Shen Qiao and Bian Yanmei inside.

The empress had heard the news that the emperor had given permission for her birth family to visit the palace, and she'd already brought her two younger brothers into the main hall to sit and wait.

Normally, the empress was head of the six palaces, so she shouldn't have needed to inform the emperor if she wished to grant her birth family entry. However, after the Jin Dynasty, the societal regulations had collapsed and fallen into disorder. And now that Yuwen Yun had the throne, he'd begun making his own rules, even establishing five empresses at the same time. Even if the Puliuru family held the highest position, who'd ever seen such a thing in all of history? Even Liu Cong had only elevated four empresses. Yuwen Yun's actions were truly unprecedented. Lady Puliuru was also from a rich and powerful family—although her face didn't reveal it, it was impossible she held no grievances at all.

After the continuous house arrest she'd suffered all this time, when she saw the people her birth family had sent, the rims of her eyes instantly reddened.

The maid bowed and said, "The Lord and Lady are very concerned about the empress and the two young masters. They have specially prepared them some clothes and food and have ordered us lowly maids to enter the palace and present them."

As she spoke, she made a gesture.

The empress immediately understood and took them to a side room within the inner hall.

"Someone is watching from outside," she said. "If we talk here, they won't be able to hear. It's secure enough. Father and Mother have asked you to relay a message, haven't they?"

The maid didn't answer but only turned sideways, letting the people behind her through.

When the empress had first seen them, their heads were lowered and their clothes had been identical to the other maids', so she hadn't paid them any special attention. But now, when she looked at them again, she realized something was off.

Surely, her birth family didn't have such tall maids? They seemed a head taller than everyone else in her palace.

"You are...?"

Bian Yanmei had no interest in superfluous words. He gave a simple introduction for himself and Shen Qiao, then told the empress about their rescue plan.

"This is far too dangerous," the empress protested, expression troubled. "You may not know, but though Buddhist Master Xueting has left the palace, his disciples are still here to recite scriptures for the emperor. There are also members of Hehuan Sect here. You'll still need to take us with you, and I fear that the two of you alone won't be enough. If anything goes wrong, all your efforts will be in vain."

She wasn't from the jianghu, and it'd been many years since she'd married into the palace. Even if she knew about Huanyue Sect and Xuandu Mountain, there was no way for her to know just how formidable a martial artist Shen Qiao was.

Bian Yanmei didn't have the time to explain further either. "The Duke of Sui has entrusted us with this task. If we didn't have any confidence of success, we'd never have used such dangerous tactics."

Lady Puliuru was still full of doubts. "These maids have suffered through many hardships with me. The moment we leave, they'll inevitably bear the brunt of the emperor's rage..."

"I heard that Your Highness is very close to Empress Zhu," said Bian Yanmei. "Once we leave, the maids you favor can take shelter with Empress Zhu. The emperor will be focused on us; he won't think of chasing a couple of maids."

The empress's two younger brothers recognized Bian Yanmei— they'd already stood up and walked over to him. Shen Qiao and Bian Yanmei each picked up one of the boys. Seeing this, the empress dropped all further protests and quickly got up, following after them.

But right at that moment, a trusted maid of the empress who'd been outside the door rushed in. "Bad news, Your Highness!" she said urgently. "His Majesty has people with him, and they're coming here!"

The emperor's visits were so rare, they might as well have happened once every couple of thousand years. The empress was stunned frozen.

If Yuwen Yun was coming, there must be experts from Hehuan Sect or the Buddhist discipline accompanying him. If Shen Qiao and Bian Yanmei wanted to bring everyone out now, things wouldn't be so easy.

The two of them looked at each other. They had no choice but to change their plans for now.

The empress only had the time to hurriedly tell her brothers not to reveal anything before Yuwen Yun and his men had already arrived.

Yuwen Yun's temperament was very peculiar—perhaps this was due to the highly strict previous emperor suppressing him for so long. When he'd been suddenly liberated, he must have rebounded to terrible extremes. There really was no other explanation. The empress Lady Puliuru, on the other hand, possessed a good temperament and handled matters fairly. She would lend a helping hand to the maids and concubines who were mistreated and punished by Yuwen Yun whenever she could. She got along well with everyone in the palace, and she silently bore Yuwen Yun's insults with equanimity. If even someone like her couldn't take Yuwen Yun's capriciousness, that just showed how terrible the emperor's temperament was. With Yuwen Xian and the others serving as lessons of the past, even if Puliuru Jian had carried no thoughts of rebellion, Yuwen Yun's behavior would have forced those same thoughts to burst forth.

In order to indulge himself to the fullest without being admonished by his ministers, Yuwen Yun had abdicated the throne to his son Yuwen Chan, but he did not take the title of Emperor Emeritus. Instead, he proclaimed himself the Tianyuan Emperor. The ministers of the Zhou Dynasty had never seen this kind of bizarre development before. Although they didn't voice their complaints out loud, they couldn't resist silently denouncing it as absurd.

Usually, Yuwen Yun rarely visited the empress. Whenever he did, it'd be to yell and take his anger out on her. Yet today, his expression was strangely amiable—he even had a smile as refreshing as the spring breeze.

The empress walked out of the palace gates to receive him, but Yuwen Yun grabbed her hand and pulled her inside again. Then he asked her two younger brothers, "Are the little brothers-in-law growing used to life in the palace?"

Puliuru Jian's eldest was slow to answer, remaining quiet, but the younger son was cleverer. He tugged on his brother and dragged him into a bow. "Thank you very much for the concern, Your Majesty. We are both doing very well."

Yuwen Yun smiled. "What nice things did Duke of Sui send to you today?" he asked.

As he spoke, his gaze fell on Shen Qiao and the others.

"It's all food and clothing, nothing worth mentioning," said the empress.

"The palace doesn't lack such things," said Yuwen Yun. "Your father is far too meddlesome, even having someone deliver them from outside the palace. Can it be because he believes I've been mistreating you within it?"

"Your Majesty speaks too seriously," the empress hurriedly said. "It's just because my younger brothers are accompanying this concubine within the palace. They've never left home since childhood, so my father and mother can't help but spoil them. Please don't blame them, Your Majesty."

"Why are you so anxious? I didn't forbid anything. If I did, they wouldn't be able to enter the palace at all!" Yuwen Yun chuckled lightly, then said to Shen Qiao, "You, raise your head."

Of course, Shen Qiao couldn't pretend not to hear.

"I thought that you possessed a decent profile just now. Though your skin is a little dark, if you take good care of it, you might be able to bring your appearance to the next level!"

Shen Qiao really hadn't expected that Bian Yanmei's inauspicious remark would come true. The emperor really was flirting with him!

Though he thought so, he didn't say anything. He put on a look of panic and took a step back, then lowered his head once more.

The empress quickly stepped forward and smiled gently at the emperor, saying, "Your Majesty hasn't been here in a while. This concubine has been waiting day and night, and now I am finally able to see your exalted face; my heart is filled with joy. I wonder if Your Majesty is willing to stay for a meal?"

A mere instant before, a pleased expression had still graced Yuwen Yun's face, but now it suddenly turned dark. "Who do you think you are! To dare to ask me to accompany you for a meal? I'm disgusted just looking at you! Who knows if you'd poison my food?!"

Today, Shen Qiao was finally able to witness for himself the emperor's reputation for being temperamental and erratic. Though Yan Wushi was also mercurial, this was completely different.

When it came to Yan Wushi's personality, others could say, "He's an unparalleled martial artist, and his arrogance is peerless as well." But what could you say about Yuwen Yun? If not for his position, he'd have been hacked to death already.

The empress was so shocked by these words that her face turned pale, and she quickly knelt to ask for punishment.

At this moment, Bian Yanmei suddenly moved. He jumped up and rushed toward Yuwen Yun with lightning speed.

Naturally, Yuwen Yun was surrounded by martial experts—there were several monks representing the Buddhist discipline, as well as several men and women from Hehuan Sect. Yuwen Yun might have been well aware of how hated he was, seeing as he brought those experts with him at all hours of the day. If Buddhist Master Xueting hadn't gone to Qingliang Temple today to pray for the imperial family, he'd surely make him stay by his side at all times.

Bian Yanmei had calculated incredibly well. Though there were many martial experts around Yuwen Yun, there were no outstanding ones, let alone anyone of grandmaster status. Xueting, Sang Jingxing, and Yuan Xiuxiu were all absent. To catch some thieves, one must capture their leader first. If he could grab Yuwen Yun, then, with him in their hands, he could rescue the empress and her younger brothers in as grand a fashion as he pleased.

In a single moment, he had reached a tacit agreement with Shen Qiao. Bian Yanmei would be responsible for taking Yuwen Yun hostage while Shen Qiao was to deal with the people around the emperor, to stop them from interfering.

It only took an instant. Just as Bian Yanmei burst into action, someone else next to Yuwen Yun flashed forward as well, matching his speed. He immediately shielded Yuwen Yun behind him, and wind from his palm blew forth, accompanied by a surge of true qi. First weak then strong, it flowed boundlessly, completely beyond expectations.

Before, this man's face had been covered in whiskers, and the dense hairs concealed most of his face. However, when he made this move, his hair and beard flew up, and Shen Qiao recognized his actual countenance.

Buddhist Master Xueting.

He'd never gone to Qingliang Temple after all, but had stayed by Yuwen Yun's side the entire time!

Perhaps he'd anticipated that on the eighth of April, Puliuru Jian would take advantage of his departure from the palace, so he'd specially concocted a plan to lure the snake from its hole, all to make sure that Puliuru Jian would fall short.

At the same time, the other experts around Yuwen Yun also attacked Shen Qiao one after another.

Though Yuwen Yun was already prepared, he was so scared that he took a few steps back and called all the guards beyond the door to come in, shouting loudly, "Kill them, kill them all!"

Xueting was the only outstanding character defending Yuwen Yun. Shen Qiao had the empress and her siblings retreat into the inner hall, then guarded the passage there himself. He could hold his own against the crowd of enemies; fending them off alone was no hard task.

However, back across the hall, Bian Yanmei was far from Xueting's match. If Bian Yanmei lost, Shen Qiao would have to spare the time to deal with Xueting, leaving the empress and her siblings unattended.

Buddhist Master Xueting also believed the same thing.

But when he sent out his palm strike, his expression suddenly shifted as he realized he'd made an enormous mistake.

The Escaped Fish

XUETING WASN'T A FOOL; he'd been expecting that Puliuru Jian would likely take advantage of his absence from the palace on the eighth of April to act. Therefore, he had someone disguise themselves as him and go to Qingliang Temple while he covered up parts of his appearance and stayed by Yuwen Yun's side.

He had the right idea—regardless of whether Puliuru Jian wanted to stage a coup or rescue his children, while he remained by Yuwen Yun's side, Xueting would be like a wall of steel, leaving most people unable to approach Yuwen Yun. And as long as Yuwen Yun was alive, the Zhou Dynasty would survive as well. There was no need to heed to anything else.

When Bian Yanmei had leapt to action, Xueting reacted at incredible speed. He had already noticed this person: as a maid, she was far too tall. When this tall maid had grabbed for Yuwen Yun, Xueting struck out as well. However, as soon as he did, he realized that he'd missed someone else nearby.

And it wasn't Shen Qiao.

There'd been four maids when they entered the palace, two of whom were the disguised Shen Qiao and Bian Yanmei. One maid had been selected by Puliuru Jian: a real maid who possessed a silver tongue and the ability to handle key situations. But what about the other one?

The remaining woman had an utterly unremarkable appearance, and she hadn't said a word when they entered the palace, merely holding the gifts as Bian Yanmei spoke to the empress. She was practically half-invisible as a person—that she kept a supremely low profile went without saying.

Even the emperor's ears and eyes that he'd planted outside the Duke of Sui's residence had been deceived.

However, "she" was the one who attacked Xueting!

Xueting and this "woman" were also old enemies. The moment they came to blows, he knew who this newcomer was. He immediately struck at Bian Yanmei while hastily attacking that unremarkable maid, shouting, "Yan Wushi!"

But he hadn't expected how deeply Yan Wushi's reputation had ingrained itself in the hearts of others. When the people around him heard that name, fear immediately colored their faces, and even their attacks slowed by a few beats.

The maid laughed; it was indeed Yan Wushi's voice. "That's quite a refreshing getup, you bald old donkey. Have you been craning your neck waiting for my venerable self? With you this eager, how could my venerable self not grant your wish and come to meet you?"

As he spoke, there was a spate of clicking noises that numbed the ears, and the limbs of that "maid" suddenly lengthened in the moment "her" palm met Xueting's. The maid's attire "she" was wearing instantly grew tight.

It was clear at once that Yan Wushi's previous claim of not knowing any bone-shrinking techniques was pure nonsense. He not only knew, he'd polished them to brilliance. As arrogant as he was, he'd perfect even minor martial arts to a point that was far beyond what any normal person could achieve.

As for his face, he naturally hadn't used Bian Yanmei and Shen Qiao's method, where they'd just trimmed some eyebrows and applied some powder. Instead, he was outfitted with a genuine human skin mask. Yan Wushi originally found this mask after Shen Qiao had killed Huo Xijing. Following the principle of "only a dumb bastard wouldn't grab a golden opportunity," Yan Wushi had wanted to give it to Shen Qiao, but Shen Qiao absolutely refused, so he could only regretfully put it on his own face. Coupled with his bone-shrinking technique, he'd become another person entirely, unrecognizable to anyone else.

With Yan Wushi impeding Xueting, Bian Yanmei charged toward Yuwen Yun. However, the other people around Yuwen Yun weren't slow to react either. Xueting's two disciples, Liansheng and Lianmie, immediately rushed forward to clash with him. Some others had figured out that Shen Qiao and his party had entered the palace on a rescue mission, so they rushed toward the empress and her siblings, hoping to take this chance to capture them so they could threaten Shen Qiao and others into not taking any reckless actions.

As these people had taken Shen Qiao for a soft persimmon, thinking he would be easy pickings, Shen Qiao naturally had to teach them a lesson on etiquette. Even if he hadn't brought Shanhe Tongbei with him to the palace, it didn't hinder his attacks in the slightest. He took on five opponents by himself immediately, flawlessly defending the door to the inner hall. Even water couldn't have slipped through, let alone a person.

But these five experts included those from Hehuan Sect, as well as Xueting's disciples. Compared to the rest of the jianghu, their skills would have been considered first rate—they weren't easy to deal with. They'd learned many shady techniques in their time at the emperor's side and didn't shy away from using poison and concealed weapons in their fights, as shameful as those were. Though they still couldn't overcome Shen Qiao, it was enough to obstruct him a little—he couldn't defeat all five people in such a short time.

Xueting was truly a long-renowned martial arts grandmaster. Even if Yuan Zixiao had ranked him behind Yan Wushi, it didn't hinder his profound martial prowess. At their levels, their cultivation was already harmoniously complete. It was impossible for Yan Wushi to subdue him in one fell swoop. They each had to search for the other party's openings during the fight.

Meanwhile, Bian Yanmei's goal of capturing Yuwen Yun had been foiled by Liansheng and Lianmie, both of whom were disciples of a grandmaster and were also two people working in tandem. For the moment, Bian Yanmei was helpless against them.

Shen Qiao weighed the situation and made a decision.

No longer would he guard the entrance of the inner hall. Instead, he turned around and swept toward Yuwen Yun, who was preparing to sneak away.

At this point, the commotion had already attracted the guards outside the door. They rushed in with their weapons but were swept away by a palm blast from Bian Yanmei that sent quite a few of them tumbling right back outside again.

Despite his outlandish behavior, Yuwen Yun still cherished his own life dearly. Seeing the place descend into such chaos that even Xueting couldn't spare the time to protect him for the moment, he quickly stumbled toward the door—but he hadn't been expecting Shen Qiao to leap forward and pounce on him.

Now a dark shadow fell over his head. With Shen Qiao's level of skill, Yuwen Yun only managed half a scream before he was captured.

Shen Qiao only said one line to Yuwen Yun, in a cold tone: "Your Majesty, make them stop."

Yuwen Yun shouted at the top of his lungs, "Stop! Everyone stop!" The five people who had originally surrounded Shen Qiao had immediately split into two groups when they saw Shen Qiao abandon them to grab the emperor. Three of them leapt toward Shen Qiao, while the remaining two had rushed toward the inner hall to capture the empress and her brothers.

But the three people who went for Shen Qiao had been a step too slow. As swift as their footwork was, it wasn't anywhere near the level of Xuandu Mountain's "A Rainbow Stretches across the Heavens." They could only watch as the emperor was taken hostage.

Bian Yanmei, Liansheng, and Lianmie had no choice but to stop as well.

Yan Wushi and Xueting, meanwhile, were locked in a fierce battle, and they had already brought the fight from inside to outside the hall. Beneath the might of two grandmaster-level experts, the roof was already half destroyed—it was impossible for them to stop so easily.

In the beginning, Xueting had allied with four great martial arts masters to ambush Yan Wushi outside the Tuyuhun royal capital, cracking his head open and almost killing him. Yan Wushi was too vengeful a person to let that incident go so easily.

Already, he'd used the conflict between Dou Yanshan and Yun Fuyi to secretly stir up internal strife within the Liuhe Guild. In the end, Dou Yanshan was poisoned and killed, and Yun Fuyi succeeded him as guild leader. However, a mere half month after Yun Fuyi's succession, several hall masters under her received evidence of her collusion with the Göktürks. These hall masters then banded together to drive Yun Fuyi out of the leader's position, causing the Liuhe Guild to split into several factions, with its power and influence divided between several hall masters. Thus the Liuhe Guild splintered completely. It became another major event within the jianghu, in addition to the fiasco at the Sword Trial Conference.

Those hall masters wanted to leverage Huanyue Sect's influence within the northern business community to increase their own. Huanyue Sect also needed to borrow the Liuhe Guild's advantages in escort and water transport services to expand their own enterprises. For a while, they took to working together like a fish to water. Though Huanyue Sect's name never surfaced within this entire tale, Yan Wushi knew just how many benefits Huanyue Sect had gained from a divided Liuhe Guild.

Of the five people who'd ambushed Yan Wushi back then, Guang Lingsan had seen the way the winds were blowing and had the foresight to ingratiate himself to Yan Wushi. He also collaborated with him, sacrificing to him many benefits so that Yan Wushi would set aside his grudge for the time being. Duan Wenyang went without saying; he was fortunate enough to have a great shifu, so Yan Wushi had no intentions of touching him at the moment. As for Yu Ai, Yan Wushi was planning to leave him to Shen Qiao to deal with, and so he didn't do anything there either. That just left Dou Yanshan and Xueting. One had lost his life due to Yan Wushi's torment, and now he'd finally met the other today. It was a small world, to meet an enemy on a narrow road like this.

Hindered by Yan Wushi, Xueting couldn't move to save the emperor. When he saw that Yuwen Yun had been caught by Shen Qiao, he silently sighed to himself and focused his entire attention on fighting Yan Wushi, ignoring everything else.

People like Duan Wenyang and Yu Ai might have been highly skilled martial artists, but they also had too many things on their minds. If they'd been met with a scene like this, they'd inevitably grow distracted, leading to their defeat. However, Xueting was one of the most eminent monks of his generation. He'd been able to leave Tiantai Sect and establish his own branch without relying on the influence of his former sect, and he'd been honored as state preceptor. He certainly was not an easy person to deal with—he saw that he couldn't save Yuwen Yun, so he simply ignored the matter completely. Even Yan Wushi couldn't help but appreciate that level of composure and willpower.

"Bald old donkey, Yuwen Yun is no ruler. My venerable self doesn't believe that you can't tell. In reality, your determination to stay at his side and assist him goes against heaven itself. Don't you Buddhists value karma and retribution? Aren't you afraid of facing retribution yourself by acting as an accessory to a tyrant's crimes?"

As they fought, Yan Wushi still did his best to provoke him with words. Yet Xueting paid no heed to him at all. They exchanged several blows, both parties suspended in midair, robes and sleeves flapping as their true qi roiled. Their battle was far more spectacular than any of the others. Even the guards, after seeing that the emperor had been taken hostage, couldn't help but keep glancing at Xueting and Yan Wushi.

But with the emperor under Shen Qiao's control, no one dared to act recklessly. Even the palace soldiers, who'd been so fierce and aggressive just a moment ago, were forced to stop in their tracks.

Shen Qiao brought the emperor out of the Qingning Hall and asked a maid to bring the empress and her brothers out as well.

As long as they'd safely extricated the people, they'd have fulfilled their purpose in coming here.

However, a few moments later, when the empress came out, she was pulling only one brother behind her.

Shen Qiao's heart sank.

Before he could ask, the empress hurriedly said, "Just now, some-one broke the window and took Erlang away!"

If their goal was to take hostages to force Shen Qiao to release the emperor, there'd be no need to take the person away. It was clear that whatever this person's goal was, it wasn't to save the emperor.

The current situation didn't afford Shen Qiao the opportunity to think too much, though. He asked no further questions and had the empress and her brother come to his side.

Though Yuwen Yun had been forced into temporary compromise on account of his life, he glared at the empress, his eyes about ready to burst into flames. "You bitch! I knew you were good for nothing. If I'd known you were the kind of treacherous dog who'd bite the hand that fed you, I would've abolished your empress position first and let dozens of strong men fuck you…"

The wave of vulgar words spewing from the emperor's mouth irritated Shen Qiao. He increased the force he was using and said, "Your Majesty's life is now in danger, and you still have the time to curse others? I suggest you restrain yourself."

The grip on his throat made Yuwen Yun's face turn red. "You… Someone as strong as you, why would you help a traitor and usurper like Puliuru Jian? If you come to my side instead, I can make you a state preceptor. How about it?" Seeing Shen Qiao's indifference, he increased the weight of his offer. "I will give you the position of marquis, peerless in wealth and honor!"

Shen Qiao said, "Your Majesty, do you want me to squeeze even harder?"

Yuwen Yun was strangled to the point his eyes rolled back into his head, and he spoke no further.

With the emperor in hand, their path was naturally smooth and free from obstructions. Outside the palace gate, Puliuru Jian's men were already waiting. When the empress and her brother saw their father, they grew so emotional they were practically beside themselves. The empress was especially moved; she burst into tears as she rushed into her father's arms and began to wail.

She'd come from a noble family. Yuwen Yong had picked this daughter as the wife for his son out of admiration for her gentleness and elegance, believing her worthy of great responsibilities. And Lady Puliuru indeed lived up to his expectations. Since becoming the crown prince's consort, she had been diligent and dutiful, striving to manage Yuwen Yun's harem. But perhaps she hadn't accumulated enough blessings in her previous life to have the misfortune of marrying such a husband. When he'd been the crown prince, Yuwen Yun was honest and well behaved, but after becoming emperor, he showed his true colors completely, turning horrendously outlandish. Not only were the state affairs in a complete mess, he even established four additional empresses within the harem while cursing out Lady Puliuru every couple of days. She'd suffered these grievances for so long, she was at her breaking point.

Puliuru Jian's troops, stationed outside the palace, had already been embroiled in battle with the palace guards for some time. As soon as Yuwen Yun appeared, though, neither side had any reason to fight—victory and defeat were already decided.

But Shen Qiao's face showed no sign of joy. "In a momentary oversight, your son was taken away," he said to Puliuru Jian. "Now I must find him and bring him back to the Duke of Sui's residence."

Puliuru Jian consoled him, saying, "Life and death are determined by fate. You've already done your best, Daoist Master. Even if something happens, that is simply my son's fate, and no one else is to blame. If not for Daoist Master Shen, Sect Leader Yan, and Bian-dafu's[1] utmost assistance, Jian wouldn't have been able to see his children today."

Elsewhere, Yan Wushi and Xueting were still engaged in fierce battle, completely immersed in their own world with no time to look around. Their true qi drew the glazed tiles of Qingning Hall's roof; from time to time they'd explode with a thunderous roar, their shards spraying every which way and orbiting around the two fighters in a swirling vortex. Though the palace was full of martial experts, faced with a battle between two of the current martial arts grandmasters, they could only watch from afar.

Accompanied by his troops, Puliuru Jian used the captured emperor to control the nobles, swiftly stabilizing the chaos within the palace. Meanwhile, Shen Qiao and Bian Yanmei searched everywhere in the palace for Puliuru Jian's second son.

As the coup threw everyone in the palace into a state of panic, it was difficult to quickly find this person trying to profit from the chaos. Both of them searched starting from different areas in the palace, but despite their efforts, they remained empty-handed. It was truly quite strange.

Bian Yanmei frowned. "What does this person gain from kidnapping Puliuru Jian's second son?" he said.

Puliuru Jian wasn't the emperor yet, let alone one of his sons. Having the child in hand could never have the same effect as taking the emperor hostage. Moreover, whoever this person was, they'd snuck into Qingning Hall unnoticed. First, this meant they were quite skilled, and second, it meant they were familiar with the palace routes, so they had to have a certain amount of status. Third,

---

1   大夫. *A general suffix for court officials.*

they'd captured Puliuru Jian's son, so it was possible they wished to use this to negotiate with Puliuru Jian.

Shen Qiao wasn't the ignorant person he'd been in the past. He'd grown a great deal from his long experiences in the secular world, and his naivete had completely condensed, granting him the ability to see these worldly matters with much more clarity. A flash of insight came to him, and he said to Bian Yanmei, "We need not search for him. The other party will seek us out of their own volition."

Bian Yanmei had clearly also realized this. He nodded, and they returned to tell Puliuru Jian their conclusions.

The person arrived even quicker than they anticipated. Yan Wushi and Xueting had yet to reveal the victor of their battle when Murong Qin arrived.

He brought a message from Chen Gong, saying that Puliuru Jian's second son was in their hands. Moreover, he'd allow only Shen Qiao or Puliuru Jian to ransom him.

Puliuru Jian had just launched a palace coup, so he naturally had to remain in place to oversee matters. The soldiers who followed him also needed a calming force with them to stabilize their morale; it wasn't easy for him to leave. Though he was worried about the safety of his second son, he still chose to stay behind. "Whatever the other party wants, gold or silver, it doesn't matter," he said to Shen Qiao. "If it can save my son's life, any amount of money is worth it."

Shen Qiao naturally agreed.

Bian Yanmei also wanted to go with him, but Murong Qin said frostily, "If even someone of Daoist Master Shen's martial caliber can't escape unscathed, what's the point of you going? Don't force our hand into directly killing the hostage. You'll only end up in a situation where everyone loses. You can forget about taking advantage of anything then."

Bian Yanmei sneered. "Very well."

But he secretly sent Shen Qiao a meaningful glance.

Murong Qin led Shen Qiao out of the palace, and they took a long and twisted route through the capital, before finally entering an inconspicuous house.

Chen Gong sat in the main hall with Puliuru Jian's second son, calm and composed. He smiled a little at Shen Qiao and said, "It's been a while."

When Shen Qiao and Chen Gong had first met, they were both in terrible straits. One was blind, his martial arts destroyed, while the other was a child from a poor family, who never knew when his next meal would come. The two of them had traveled together and developed a camaraderie born from shared tribulations. But the world and men were unpredictable, and, unexpectedly, as they circled round and round, they found themselves meeting once again.

Within the haze, all things seemed to have been predestined.

Shen Qiao faintly thought that this meeting with Chen Gong was meant to be.

Chen Gong's Death

C HEN GONG HAD A SWORD firmly within his grasp. Shen Qiao recognized it at a glance—it was Tai'e, from which Chen Gong had retrieved the *Zhuyang Strategy* scroll before gifting it to Yuwen Yun.

The blade of the sword was pressed against the throat of Puliuru Jian's second son. That sword was an ancient, famous weapon. Having been forged by Ou Yezi and Gan Jiang together, it was incredibly sharp. The blade was only lightly touching the boy's neck, but a line of blood had already scored itself into his fair, tender skin.

"Ah-Chuang, don't move," Shen Qiao said to him, using a nickname he'd heard Puliuru Jian use for his son.

Chen Gong smiled slightly. "Please don't worry. I have no intention of harming the Duke of Yanmen Commandery. As long as I get what I want, I'll immediately leave this place and travel far away. I will no longer dance about in front of you in the future, being an irritant."

"What do you want?"

Chen Gong made a gesture. "Please sit." He had a hostage in hand, but he wasn't anxious in the slightest. And if he wasn't, Shen Qiao naturally was even less so.

"Shen Qiao, we met in humble circumstances," Chen Gong said, "so we can be called friends forged through hardship. To be honest, I've always been grateful to you in my heart. Never could I have imagined that the first chance we could sit calmly across from each other like this would be in this kind of time and place." Chen Gong had thrown away all perfunctory pretensions. He no longer addressed Shen Qiao as Daoist Master Shen but by his name directly.

"I cannot afford the Duke of Zhao's gratitude," said Shen Qiao.

Chen Gong smiled. "I still remember that, back in that broken-down temple, you helped me drive away those local riffraff, and you even gave me donkey-meat sandwiches to eat. At that time, I thought, 'Where did this fool come from? He's so skilled, but he voluntarily gave me his sandwiches.' At that time, I was just a poor child who couldn't even feed himself. I didn't even know what the jianghu was, let alone reading or writing. It was a long time later that I realized that you'd once held such a high position in the jianghu, and such a formidable reputation but because you fought with someone, you lost everything and even had to drag your sickly body around as you roamed the jianghu.

"Our journey together was full of hardships, but we finally managed to escape to Huai Province's capital. Seeing that we were one step closer to joining the Liuhe Guild, I was filled with joy, but then you suddenly proposed that we should go our separate ways."

Shen Qiao hadn't wanted to speak, but when he saw that Chen Gong had stopped, he said, "I parted ways with you not because I thought you were a burden but because I was afraid of implicating you."

This was an explanation long delayed, and completely unnecessary to Shen Qiao. He'd experienced many betrayals, the treacherous hearts of many people, and became an even firmer believer of the phrase "clean hands need no washing." If Chen Gong doubted him, it didn't matter how many times he explained himself.

Chen Gong smiled and said, "At that time, I was indeed judging your upright character through the lens of my own moral failings. I thought you found me a burden and intentionally left me behind, so I was dissatisfied."

Shen Qiao said coolly, "Even if that weren't the case, you still wouldn't have hesitated to betray me to Mu Tipo if you met him. Isn't that right? Then what's the point of saying more?"

No matter how thick Chen Gong's face was, he couldn't help the hint of awkwardness that flashed through his expression when he heard these words. However, he quickly smiled again and said, "Anyway, I was just saying that I've always been grateful to you from the bottom of my heart. If you hadn't brought me out of that small county town, I might still be living that miserable life, toiling endlessly, unable to eat three meals a day. Perhaps I'd even have to continue suffering my stepmother's exploitation and harassment."

"Chen Gong, though you were illiterate, you never forgot what you heard, and you were much more sophisticated than I was when it came to the ways of the world," said Shen Qiao. "Your aptitude and martial talent are rare even in the jianghu. Even without me, you'd still have found a way out of your predicament. The reason you have fallen to this point isn't because your aptitude was inferior in any way but because you took the wrong path."

"No, you're wrong." Chen Gong shook his head. "The reason my plans fell short isn't because I took the wrong path but because I was unlucky.

"Shen Qiao, you fell from Banbu Peak. If Yan Wushi hadn't happened to pass by, could you have been saved? If it had been Yu Ai or Kunye who came down to search, you'd have died long ago, isn't that right? I heard that since your parents died when you were young, you were able to train under Qi Fengge. However, there are millions of people in the world with excellent aptitude. By what rights did you become the one Qi Fengge chose? When you and I met that day, you were blind, your martial arts destroyed. You looked no different from an invalid. If you hadn't obtained the *Zhuyang Strategy*, how could you have been revived anew and returned to the ranks of martial arts experts? In the end, you were simply luckier than others. If I had half of your luck, why would I worry about being unable to achieve great things?"

Shen Qiao was silent for a moment before saying, "Those who walk different paths must part ways. If this is what you wish to think, there's nothing I can do."

"Looks like you don't agree with what I say," Chen Gong said with a grin. "I know that you are an upright gentleman, so you'd never acknowledge someone like me, who used all sorts of tricks and back doors, as your equal. You see, if you hadn't helped Puliuru Jian launch a coup today, I would still be Duke of Zhao. If everyone had minded their own business, we'd have no problems. But there's nothing to be done. I know that once Yuwen Yun dies, I'll have no place in Zhou. Puliuru Jian is similar to Yuwen Yong. They're completely different from Yuwen Yun and Gao Wei—he'd never uplift someone like me. Perhaps he'll even kill a couple of 'sycophants' like myself in order to demonstrate the new dynasty's direction. That's why we have to sit here today and negotiate terms.

"I know that there was a volume of the *Zhuyang Strategy* hidden in the inner palace of the Zhou kingdom, but after Yuwen Yong's death, I obtained permission from Yuwen Yun to search around the palace and couldn't find it anywhere. I believe that someone must've taken the volume with them during the chaos. As the scrolls are useless to ordinary people, they must've been from the jianghu, so

Huanyue Sect is the likeliest culprit. You are close to Yan Wushi, so he must've shown that scroll to you, right?"

Shen Qiao said coolly, "That's right. The scroll is indeed with me, but Yan Wushi didn't give it to me—it was Puliuru Jian."

Understanding dawned on Chen Gong. "No wonder!" he said. "Puliuru Jian's daughter is Yuwen Yun's empress, so she naturally had the greatest opportunity! And the reason your martial arts recovered so quickly must also be related to the *Zhuyang Strategy*."

It wasn't a question, but a confirmation, as Chen Gong had also cultivated with the *Zhuyang Strategy*. In this sense, his martial arts shared a source with Shen Qiao's.

"So you wish to be given the *Zhuyang Strategy* in exchange for the Duke of Yanmen Commandery?" said Shen Qiao.

Chen Gong smiled. "Correct, but I not only want the scroll hidden in the Zhou palace but also the one from your Xuandu Mountain."

"The scroll that Puliuru Jian gave me is on me now. I can give it to you, but the one on Xuandu Mountain has already been destroyed by my master. I can recite it, but I don't have the original. I fear that you might suspect me of tampering with the contents."

"I may doubt someone else," said Chen Gong, "but I trust your moral character."

Shen Qiao's expression was indifferent. "Thank you very much for your trust."

He took out that copy of the *Zhuyang Strategy* and tossed it to Chen Gong.

The *Zhuyang Strategy* scrolls were all written upon strips of silk, and the ink had been mixed with herbs to ensure that it wouldn't fade over time. The strips were light and thin, making them easy to store. What Chen Gong received was light to the point of being insubstantial, but the material itself was incredibly rare. The moment he touched it, he knew it was the same as the scroll he'd retrieved from Tai'e—the genuine article.

He reached out to catch the scroll, then tucked it into his lapels. "Could I trouble you to recite the scroll that was hidden on your Xuandu Mountain? Once I've memorized it, I will release the Duke of Yanmen Commandery."

As the hostage was in Chen Gong's hands, he had complete control over the situation, so he was naturally emboldened.

Shen Qiao saw that the complexion of the child in his arms was still rosy, so he recited Xuandu Mountain's volume of the *Zhuyang Strategy*.

Chen Gong listened attentively. Once Shen Qiao finished his recitation, he nodded. "I've memorized it. There are some words and phrases that I have yet to fully understand, but I trust that the palace situation has probably settled for now. Once Yan Wushi comes over, I'll be fighting one-on-two, and I probably won't be able to gain the upper hand; I don't have the time to consult with you any further. It's a bit of a pity."

"Yan Wushi is fighting with Xueting, so he'll be occupied for a while," Shen Qiao said. "Since I have already honored my side of the agreement, please abide by your promise as well and release the hostage. I will personally guarantee your safe exit from the capital."

"Forget it," said Chen Gong with a smile. "Even if you don't take action, that doesn't mean that others won't. I know that Yan Wushi has another disciple in the capital, a fairly skilled martial artist. With my current abilities, we might be evenly matched. I don't want to take any risks, so I'll have to wrong the Duke of Yanmen County and have him accompany me for a time. Once I leave the capital, I will naturally let him go."

Shen Qiao knew that it was useless to talk about promises and integrity with someone like Chen Gong, and that anger would be even more futile. As such, his face remained placid and unperturbed, and he only looked at Chen Gong for a moment before he nodded. "Fine. But if you refuse to abide by your agreement to release him, I will pursue you to even the ends of the earth."

Chen Gong chuckled. "Worry not. What would be the point in bringing such a burden along with me? Puliuru Jian has so many sons; I can't threaten him. I can only trade him for the *Zhuyang Strategy*!"

He stood up, still holding the hostage, and walked out of the manor. A carriage was already parked outside, and Murong Qin, who was acting as the coachman, was sitting at its front.

Though Chen Gong looked calm, in truth, every inch of his body was on full guard against Shen Qiao, deeply afraid that he might attack. Just as he was preparing to carry the hostage into the carriage, a slight movement came from behind him: something whistled through the air, the noise first distant then close. It shot straight at his head!

Murong Qin's figure moved as he immediately leapt behind Chen Gong.

It was only an instant, like a flash of lightning or blaze of sparks. But even though he knew that Murong Qin would come to his rescue, Chen Gong still couldn't stop himself from instinctively turning his head.

And in the time he took to turn around, Shen Qiao moved.

He was swift as a ghost. By the time he was in front of Chen Gong, his opponent hadn't even fully seen what was happening behind him. He felt a pain in his wrist, and Tai'e fell from his hand. His arms were suddenly empty—Shen Qiao had already picked up

Puliuru Ying, then slammed his other hand into Chen Gong's chest. Chen Gong felt a dull pain throb there and flew backward like a kite with its strings cut. He came to a stop when he crashed into a pillar, then fell heavily to the ground.

Shen Qiao's palm strike had used seven or eight-tenths of his true qi—naturally, it wasn't a weak blow.

Chen Gong spat a mouthful of blood onto the ground. Before he could react, Shen Qiao had already sealed the major acupoints all over his body. Tai'e flashed, and Chen Gong screamed despite himself, his eyes going wide in disbelief. No longer could he return to his previous composure from when he'd had everything under control.

"You! Where's my internal energy! Shen Qiao! You destroyed my martial arts!" His eyes bulged, and all the refined phrasing that he'd gradually cultivated along with his swelling status seemed to vanish like ashes and smoke. Right now, he seemed to have transformed back into that impoverished young man who could only rely on a broken-down temple to shelter himself from the wind and rain. "You dared to destroy my martial arts?! What right did you have?! What right?!"

Shen Qiao threw Tai'e to the ground. "All of the changes to your fate began when you met me in the broken-down temple. Since that's the case, I will bring it to a conclusion as well. You have a twisted disposition. For you, your martial arts are only a tool for climbing higher, but for others, they are likely to be a calamity of calamities." He shook his head. "Chen Gong, you don't deserve to practice martial arts."

"It's not up to you to decide whether I deserve it or not!" Chen Gong gritted his teeth. If looks could kill, Shen Qiao would have been reduced to fragments. "Just who do you think you are?! You're nothing but a dog under Yan Wushi, pitifully wagging your tail, using sex appeal to trick him into giving you the *Zhuyang Strategy*. How are you better than me?!"

A continuous stream of foul language spewed from his mouth. Shen Qiao was about to tap his mute acupoint, but before he could act, he saw Puliuru Ying bend down and pick up the Tai'e sword on the ground. The child gripped the handle and flipped the sword upside down, before stabbing it right into Chen Gong's heart!

A stream of blood gushed out. Chen Gong's eyes remained wide open in death, his stare full of his grievances still.

Shen Qiao looked on in surprise. "You..."

His expression ferocious, Puliuru Ying spat at Chen Gong's corpse, "You piece of filth, how dare you take this Commandery Duke hostage!"

Even if Chen Gong had racked his brain until his skull burst, he would have never expected to end up dying at the hands of a young child.

Meanwhile, Bian Yanmei had also subdued Murong Qin, leaving him with serious injuries.

Palace Coup

HEN YAN WUSHI returned from the palace, Shen Qiao and Bian Yanmei were each holding a weiqi piece, both looking relaxed as they played. It was obvious that their business had come to an end.

Seeing that Shen Qiao had already changed out of his disguise, Yan Wushi couldn't help but feel some regret. He'd thought that Shen Qiao's appearance as a woman had been a rare, lovely sight, but these sentiments could just be kept inside his heart. No matter how good Shen Qiao's temperament was, he probably wouldn't be able to stand hearing it.

As soon as he saw Yan Wushi, Bian Yanmei put down his weiqi piece and stood up to bow, his expression filled with cheer. "Respectfully welcoming Shizun on his return! With that bald old donkey Xueting executed for his crimes, the Buddhist discipline is likely finished for good!"

Yan Wushi was still dressed in maid's attire, although his true countenance was revealed now that he'd torn off his human skin mask. The resulting appearance was somewhat comical. However, with his terrifying presence, no one would have dared to laugh at him even if he'd been dressed in rags.

Hearing Bian Yanmei's words, he said, "The bald old donkey is still alive."

Bian Yanmei was taken aback.

Yan Wushi smiled slightly. "With his identity, wouldn't it be a pity if he died? We should at least get something from it. Though he's a Buddhist, he is deeply attached to the material world. If he can learn to be self-aware after this, what's wrong with letting him keep his sorry life?"

Bian Yanmei didn't know what he wanted to do, but since Yan Wushi had said so, he must have a goal in mind, so he respectfully agreed.

"Puliuru Ying has been rescued?"

"Yes, this disciple has sent Puliuru Ying back to the Duke of Sui's residence," said Bian Yanmei. "Chen Gong is dead, and Murong Qin is seriously injured. He's been taken into custody, so we can question him for testimony later."

"Mm," said Yan Wushi. Buddhist Master Xueting's skills were extremely profound. Though Yan Wushi had won this match, he'd still suffered some injuries.

He covered his mouth and gave a low cough. Just as Bian Yanmei was about to say that he'd go fetch some medicine, he saw a hint of bright red seeping through the cracks of Yan Wushi's fingers.

Are his injuries that serious? Bian Yanmei was dumbfounded. "Master, are you all right?" he asked hurriedly. "This manor still has some Heart-Clearing Pills..."

Yan Wushi waved his hand, then sat down where Bian Yanmei had just been sitting.

Although he was almost certain Yan Wushi was putting on an act, Shen Qiao still couldn't resist saying, "Are Sect Leader Yan's injuries serious? Does he need this humble Daoist to take a look?"

Almost as soon as he'd asked, Yan Wushi conveniently extended his hand, placing it on the game board. "Then I'll be troubling Daoist Master Shen."

You extended it way too quickly! Almost like you expected me to ask this question! Shen Qiao thought to himself, then lightly rested three fingers of his right hand on Yan Wushi's wrist.

"Your internal breathing is a bit disordered," he said. "You must've sustained some internal injuries, though they shouldn't be too much of an issue. You should be fine after some time recuperating, both internally and externally." Though Yan Wushi sustained a couple of internal injuries, they weren't serious enough to warrant vomiting blood. *Sure enough, he was pretending earlier,* Shen Qiao thought to himself.

Yan Wushi covered the back of Shen Qiao's hand with his own, tightening his grip, and smiled a little. "I've troubled Daoist Master Shen. Even after how my venerable self treated you, you were able to cast aside past grievances and join me in such treacherous circumstances. Your sense of justice would move even the stoniest of hearts."

His hands were white and slender, and they felt like lovely jade that had been smoothed by years of constant stroking. Only the fine calluses between the thumb and forefinger revealed the fact that their master had been practicing the sword for many years.

If someone else had said this, Shen Qiao might have replied with a couple of courtesies, but he'd long grown immune to Yan Wushi. Furthermore, the man was still dressed as a woman, so Shen Qiao found it even more disturbing—almost enough for all the hair on his body to fall off completely.

Before he could pull back his hand, Yan Wushi withdrew his own first, as if he'd truly only wanted to express his sentiments.

The women's clothes he was wearing were ill-fitting too—forget about others feeling awkward watching him, Yan Wushi himself didn't feel all that comfortable either. Bian Yanmei had already ordered someone to prepare some hot water and clothes, and now he invited his shizun to take a bath and change.

The great and lofty Huanyue Sect Leader wearing a high-waisted skirt was quite an eyesore, but Yan Wushi himself appeared completely at ease. He calmly rose but didn't forget to glance at the cup in front of Shen Qiao and ask Bian Yanmei, "What's in the cup?"

"Honey water," replied Bian Yanmei. He didn't know why Shizun would bother with such a trivial matter.

"Change it to plum wine," said Yan Wushi. "A-Qiao doesn't like honey water—too cloyingly sweet."

Shen Qiao raised an eyebrow and looked at him, wanting to ask how Yan Wushi knew that he disliked honey water, but he felt that this was much too foolish a question. He immediately closed his mouth and looked down at the weiqi board.

Bian Yanmei was also slightly surprised hearing this, but he acted like nothing had happened. "Yes."

The moment Yan Wushi left, Bian Yanmei followed him out and humbly asked, "Shizun, this disciple wishes to ask: should I continue treating Daoist Master Shen the way I have in the past?"

"Treat him the way you'd treat me." Yan Wushi gave him a glance full of appreciation, like he was pleased with what a quick learner he was. It greatly shook Bian Yanmei's spirits, and he thought to himself that he'd guessed right.

Of course, demonic practitioners had never been moral gentlemen willing to suffer grievances. Bian Yanmei had seen Yan Wushi dote on many beauties in the past too, but those had been short-lived, like the night-blooming cereus. He'd once thought that the phrase "going through a thousand flowers, yet never touching their leaves" would be more in line with his shizun's temperament. He hadn't expected his master to actually take a liking to a high-mountain bloom growing in the midst of snowy plains and glaciers, unstained by the dust of the secular world.

Bian Yanmei knew some things about Shen Qiao's character and personality too. He didn't believe that his master could successfully pluck this flower because while Shen Qiao looked easy to persuade, he possessed an unbending core that even the winds and rains couldn't break. He absolutely didn't seem like someone who'd walk the path of cut-sleeves and homosexuals. But that was the way Shifu was. Once he'd taken a liking to something, he was determined to obtain it.

When he thought about this, Bian Yanmei didn't know who to sympathize with.

He coughed lightly and said, "Forgive this disciple for speaking too much, but I don't think Daoist Master Shen has such intentions?" *You two don't seem to be in love at all!*

Yan Wushi looked askance at him and said, "Do you have any ideas?"

Bian Yanmei smiled. "This disciple knows of countless ways to conquer a woman," he said, "but not only is Shen Qiao not a woman, he's also not an ordinary person, so ordinary methods naturally wouldn't work on him. However, there's a fitting adage for this: 'A devoutly chaste woman fears a persistent man.' Regardless of the situation, there must be some truth to it, no? It's just..."

"It's just what?" prompted Yan Wushi.

"Shizun has a demeanor beyond all others," said Bian Yanmei. "If the other party were an ordinary person, even if you only wanted a passing fling, they'd likely be more than willing to share your bed.

But if it's Shen Qiao...once Shizun grows tired, he might be unwilling to let the matter drop so easily."

The implication was this: If your esteemed self wished for a casual romance, the world had plenty of beauties and many who'd be willing to climb into your bed themselves. But Shen Qiao wasn't only difficult to chase; even if you did catch him, you might have a hard time getting rid of him. As the saying went, "Inviting gods into your house is simple, sending them away is hard." *Shen Qiao is a martial artist grandmaster—don't bring trouble upon your esteemed self!*

Yan Wushi smiled. "How do you know that I only wish for a passing fling?"

Don't tell me your esteemed self wishes to spend the rest of your life with him? Bian Yanmei was shocked, but he didn't dare ask and only said, "I understand."

In fact, he still didn't quite understand. Shen Qiao was indeed an extraordinary beauty, but beauties were plentiful in this world, and Shen Qiao was hardly the most dazzling or eye-catching one. Did the fact that he was also a grandmaster make him seem especially enchanting to Shizun?

By the time Yan Wushi had bathed and changed clothes, returning refreshed, Shen Qiao had already filled most of the weiqi board.

Yan Wushi sat opposite him and asked him casually, "You've already met Puliuru Jian's two sons. What do you think of them?"

Shen Qiao didn't mind this question, and he pondered for a moment. "The eldest is honest; dull but not foolish. The second is clever, and his excellent talents are apparent."

"Your evaluation is truly pertinent. 'Dull but not foolish,' a phrase that strikes at the core of the matter!"

"Forgive me for being blunt. Puliuru Jian has incredible resolve and remarkable forbearance. When he takes charge of state administration in the future, he may very well be a wise king. However, his two sons should've had their personalities reversed. If the second son surpasses the first in ability, it may not bode well for the dynasty and state in the future."

Yan Wushi smiled. "A-Qiao, you're thinking too far," he said. "Is there any dynasty that can last forever? Ying Zheng had a delusion of his dynasty lasting thousands of years, but it ended up collapsing after only the second generation. Who knows if those two sons will die prematurely before reaching adulthood? Who knows if Puliuru Jian can even remain the emperor for ten years, if someone more powerful won't replace him? I only need to know that the person I'm currently working with can keep a clear head and avoid foolish moves. That's enough. As for the Puliuru family's succession over the next generations, I'm not his father, so why should I trouble myself over it for him?"

"Since Sect Leader Yan already has his thoughts, I don't need to say anything more."

"Puliuru Jian wanted to find a shifu for his two sons," said Yan Wushi. "With what you just said, I can tell that you're displeased with them both. Once I get back, I'll help you reject him."

"Sect Leader Yan is a stronger martial artist than me," said Shen Qiao, curiously. "Why didn't they seek you out for an apprenticeship?"

Yan Wushi smiled and said, "If you dislike them, I naturally dislike them as well. Considering our relationship, if we don't present a united front, people will misunderstand, won't they?"

What relationship? And people won't misunderstand if you say it like this? Shen Qiao was stunned by Yan Wushi's ability to argue black into white. "Sect Leader Yan worries too much," he said. "This humble Daoist isn't a member of Huanyue Sect.

Even if Sect Leader Yan and I don't have a united front, no one will misunderstand."

• • •

The palace coup truly embodied the phrase "in warfare, speed is king."

With the help of Yan Wushi and Shen Qiao, Puliuru Jian quickly gained control over Yuwen Yun, and through Yuwen Yun, he seized control of the court as well. As an experienced politician, he didn't let this bloody conflict spread to the entire capital—or even beyond its borders. Before anyone could react, the palace had already returned to its previous calm.

Before this, seeking to indulge himself in pleasures without his ministers interfering, Yuwen Yun had already abdicated the throne to his son Yuwen Chan and proclaimed himself the Tianyuan Emperor. As a result, now that Puliuru Jian had seized control of the situation, there wasn't even a need to establish another puppet. The eight-year-old Yuwen Chan was still the emperor, just with another regent above him. Yuwen Yun had finally fallen into the pit he'd dug for himself.

After Puliuru Jian came to power, he did not hurry to ascend to the throne and proclaim himself emperor. Instead, he supervised the country as the Great Chancellor of the Left for some time before announcing that Yuwen Yun had passed due to illness. He also stopped the construction of the royal gardens, and the officials whom Yuwen Yun had exiled for voicing their objections were gradually recalled to the capital, their reputations restored.

Just these two decrees were enough to win over the hearts of the people.

With a new emperor came new ministers. Puliuru Jian taking power also signaled the end of the easy road for the Buddhist discipline and Hehuan Sect.

Hehuan Sect needed no mention—during the palace coup, neither Sang Jingxing nor Yuan Xiuxiu had been in the capital. How could their remaining members be any match for Yan Wushi and Bian Yanmei? Since Yuwen Yun's ascension, Huanyue Sect was forced to feign helplessness while staying incognito. After suffering came the rewards: Bian Yanmei didn't restrain himself any longer and immediately launched an attack. They captured all of Hehuan Sect's allocated forces, both within and beyond the court, in one fell swoop.

Now that Yan Wushi had destroyed his martial arts, Buddhist Master Xueting was imprisoned on charges of immoral governance and inciting the previous emperor. Once Xueting fell, the Buddhist disciplines within the imperial capital lost their backing as well, scurrying away like monkeys from a fallen tree. Gradually, the government seized their temples, and the Buddhist disciples either scattered to the winds or confessed their guilt to the court.

Yan Wushi had no intention of eradicating Buddhism completely. He knew that Confucianism, Buddhism, and Daoism had been passed down within the Central Plains for a long time—they were deeply entrenched within the hearts of the people. Each school had its own faithful believers; it would be impossible to uproot them entirely using only mortal strength. At most, they could only weaken them temporarily, like Yuwen Yong had done in his time, eradicating the discipline on a massive scale. He'd killed many monks, destroyed quite a few temples, and burned a fair amount of Buddhist scriptures, but the moment he passed, the spring wind had revived them anew.

All Huanyue Sect needed was the ruler's support and the right to speak their minds rather than eliminating Buddhism entirely. After all, even if Buddhism disappeared, there'd still be Daoism and Buddhism. There would be no end of targets to destroy. Instead, the best method was to have the major factions keep each other in check, a state where no party could do anything to the others. This way, there would never be a situation where a single faction dominated the rest. It was a relatively sustainable solution.

Yan Wushi's views coincided perfectly with Puliuru Jian's, so their cooperation was incredibly harmonious.

Taking into account Yan Wushi's and Shen Qiao's contributions, Puliuru Jian not only ordered the construction of a new Xuandu Monastery within the capital, appointing Shen Qiao as Xuandu Monastery's Perfected Master of Profundity and Discerning Subtleties, but he also generously entrusted some of the imperial family's business dealings to Huanyue Sect. Furthermore, some time after he established the three provinces and six departments system, he also appointed someone from Huanyue Sect to the most lucrative of positions for senior officials: the Minister of Public Works. The Sui Dynasty would forever maintain an excellent cooperative relationship with Huanyue Sect, at least until Yang Guang turned against them and reneged on his promise.

But those were all stories for later.

The February after the coup, shortly after the end of the Lantern Festival, the emperor of Zhou, Yuwen Chan, expressed that Puliuru Jian was of noble character and great prestige and thus possessed the qualities of an enlightened ruler. He also claimed that he was young and ignorant, thus unworthy of this position, and he announced his intention to pass the throne to Puliuru Jian instead. Puliuru Jian declined three times before accepting.

He took the throne at Linguang Hall and changed the name of the country to Sui, and the name of his reign to Kaihuang. He also claimed that he wished to recognize his ancestors, so he changed his surname back to the Han name of Yang. Then, he announced a general amnesty.

Henceforth, a new monarch sat upon the throne, the Northern Dynasties changed hands. Ever since the collapse of the Jin and entry of the five barbarian tribes into the Central Plains, there'd been hundreds of years of chaos and turmoil, but now a new chapter had finally begun.

For the common people, the storms in the court and the sudden upheavals within the palace had nothing to do with them. Their demands were simple: to be well clothed and well fed. However, the new dynasty's direction ultimately brought some changes. Leaving aside everything else, the amnesty alone was enough that everyone didn't need to pay taxes this year, so the people's lives became a little easier as well.

More extra money in hand brought more smiles to people's faces.

At last, having come so far, Shen Qiao could feel the emotions stirring within his heart.

"For the first time, I can say I no longer regret the decision I made that day."

The streets were lively and bustling as people came and went. Today, there was a temple fair, and so many people had come out to purchase the things they'd need for the Dragon Boat Festival. Pouches woven from colorful silk threads were hung all over the small stalls on the streets and alleys. It was a dazzling feast for the eyes.

Hearing Shen Qiao's words, Yan Wushi smiled. "It seems that A-Qiao has been rather jumpy, deep down inside, this entire time."

Shen Qiao nodded and spoke honestly. "I've been afraid lately that my involvement would result in the world welcoming a foolish ruler, making the lives of the people even more difficult."

The two of them passed by a stall and heard the owner's loud and enthusiastic hawking. Yan Wushi swept a thoughtless glance over his goods, then purchased a tiger doll woven from colored fabric. A looped cord was fastened to the tiger's head, while a silk sash was tied to its lower end. It had a charming, simple look; vivacious and lively.

Yan Wushi shoved the tiger doll into Shen Qiao's hands.

Perplexed, Shen Qiao asked, "For me?" Holding the soft doll in his hands, he fiddled with it, moving it back and forth. He couldn't help but smile, "Truly quite cute."

Yan Wushi chuckled and thought to himself, *Yes, like you. Big cats, small cats, they're all cats. My venerable self spends my days in the company of cats.*

After strolling through the market, the two of them went back. Yan Wushi's Junior Preceptor residence was already unsealed, and Yang Jian had bestowed upon him a new noble title, changing its name to the Duke of Wu's residence. Yan Wushi now lived here; meanwhile, the construction of Shen Qiao's Xuandu Monastery hadn't finished, so he could only stay here as a guest.

The steward saw Yan Wushi and quickly came over to report that the second young master had returned. He'd also brought someone with him, a person claiming to be Daoist Master Shen's shidi.

Shen Qiao thought this strange, and when he saw Yu Shengyan and the person who'd arrived with him, he couldn't help being even more shocked.

"Si-shidi?"

Sect News

THE NEWCOMER WAS Yuan Ying.

After Shen Qiao had fallen from the cliff, everyone on Xuandu Mountain had been unable to help their panic, despite Yu Ai's best efforts to suppress it. Yuan Ying ranked fourth among Qi Fengge's disciples, and neither his temperament nor martial arts were particularly outstanding; he'd always remained a rather obscure character within the sect. After taking over Xuandu's Violet Palace, Yu Ai felt that this shidi of his, being the most timid of their lot, would be unable to make any waves. Hence, he never paid much attention to Yuan Ying.

Neither Yu Ai's collaboration with the Göktürks nor his accepting the title of Yuyang's Bishop of Great Peace and Perfected Master were secrets. At that time, the Göktürk Khaganate had been incredibly powerful—both Zhou and Qi were forced to acquiesce to them. Yu Ai had seen the Göktürks' ambitions and wanted to use their power to restore Xuandu Mountain to its former glory, so both parties remained in close communication. Duan Wenyang had even invited Yu Ai to the group ambush on Yan Wushi outside the royal capital of Tuyuhun. The ambush had little overlap with Xuandu Mountain's interests, but Yu Ai had still intervened to help.

However, the Göktürks' plans for Xuandu Mountain didn't stop there. Xuandu Mountain had a long legacy, possessing extraordinary influence within the jianghu and even in Daoism itself. If they could turn Xuandu Mountain Sect into their puppet, they would not only grasp a crucial bit of power within the Central Plains' Daoist discipline, but they'd get their hands on the hundreds of years' worth of wealth and martial arts classics Xuandu Mountain possessed as well.

Xuandu Mountain had lost Qi Fengge and spent many years since with their mountain gates sealed, thus gradually falling into decline. Shen Qiao was already gone, and their members' hearts were scattered. There wouldn't be a second Qi Fengge, so in the eyes of the Göktürks, it'd been the perfect time for them to infiltrate the sect.

Duan Wenyang had trained under Hulugu, but due to his mixed heritage, his status among the Göktürks was far inferior to his shidi Kunye's. He urgently needed some major contribution to improve his standing, and, coincidentally, he hit it off with the Eastern Khaganate's Ishbara Khagan, who wished to be independent. Unfortunately, the situation didn't develop as they'd hoped. Though Yu Ai had accepted the title of Yuyang's Bishop of Great Peace and Perfected Master, he refused to let the Göktürk people interfere in the sect's administration, and he also refused to let Ishbara Khagan station his people on Xuandu Mountain. Thus the cooperation between the two sides remained superficial, with no possibility of growing deeper.

The Göktürks were naturally displeased. Xuandu Mountain was like a large, rich chunk of meat right before them and yet they couldn't eat it.

Yuan Ying didn't know much about these things. It was only after he'd left Xuandu Mountain to head to Qingcheng Mountain that he met Yu Shengyan, who was returning from the Sword Trial

Conference. Yu Shengyan had then told him about these matters one by one.

Up until then, Yuan Ying had felt the atmosphere within his sect growing increasingly dismal. He sought out his third shixiong, Yu Ai, several times, proposing that they should find their second shixiong, Shen Qiao, and bring him back to the sect, so that he could revitalize it. Yu Ai placated Yuan Ying gently a couple of times, then entrusted him with teaching young disciples. With Yu Ai having put his trust in him, Yuan Ying could only set this matter aside for the time being. But who'd expect that troubles would arise out of nowhere? Their shimei Gu Hengbo left the mountain without permission without so much as a farewell. Yu Ai flew into a rage; he was furious. However, Yuan Ying was shocked speechless by what Gu Hengbo had written in her farewell letter to him. Afterward, he began paying more attention to Yu Ai, looking for a chance to secretly investigate.

It was then that an elder in Xuandu Mountain privately approached Yuan Ying, expressing his willingness to support him and have him replace Yu Ai. The more Yuan Ying thought about it, the stranger things seemed. He pondered the letter Gu Hengbo had left him some more, then quietly found his opportunity to leave Xuandu Mountain.

Yuan Ying had rarely left home since childhood. Life on the mountain was monotonous, but he'd always been able to endure the loneliness. He spent his days either training or reading, and he lacked even a shred of a youth's characteristic liveliness or cleverness. Even Gu Hengbo, who was around the same age he was, couldn't bear it and instead became closer to Shen Qiao.

He originally came from a wealthy family, but he had a childhood speech impediment, and as the family itself had many children, his parents never favored him. Even the household servants would pick and choose whom to serve, and thus they followed his parents in snubbing this young master. Once, when Yuan Ying was taken out of the house, the servants' negligence resulted in him getting lost. Only then did he meet Qi Fengge, who brought him back to the Yuan family and returned him to his parents. His mother and father saw that Qi Fengge was a Daoist who knew martial arts, so they took the opportunity to ask Qi Fengge to accept Yuan Ying as his disciple. Qi Fengge saw that Yuan Ying possessed a fair amount of aptitude, so he agreed.

In the last few years, Yuan Ying had visited his family only once, never mind leaving the mountain for training. His slightly dreary personality made him one of the least conspicuous presences on Xuandu Mountain. Nobody even realized that he'd quietly left Xuandu Mountain until a few days later.

After leaving the mountain, Yuan Ying had no experience of the world to fall back on and no idea where to go. He wanted to find Shen Qiao but didn't know where he was. When he heard that Qingcheng Mountain was holding the Sword Trial Conference, he thought that Shen Qiao might attend. He made inquiries all the way to Qingcheng Mountain, yet ended up intermittently hungry because he hadn't brought enough money.

Unexpectedly, he was a step too late. He'd just arrived at the mountain foot when he saw people coming down, one after another. It was here that Yuan Ying heard about the spectacular events that had happened at the conference, and then that Yan Wushi had taken Shen Qiao. He was fretting over this when he encountered Yu Shengyan, who'd also been descending the mountain.

Yuan Ying's appearance wasn't anything remarkable, and he was dressed like any other passerby. Few people would pay special notice to him, but Yu Shengyan noticed that whenever Yuan Ying heard people talking about Shen Qiao, he'd always look up and listen. This piqued Yu Shengyan's interest. When asked, Yuan Ying declared his family and sect. Only then did Yu Shengyan realize that he was Shen Qiao's shidi.

After listening to Yuan Ying recount all this, Shen Qiao sank into contemplation for a long while. Finally, he asked, "Who was the elder who implied they'd be able to support you in becoming the sect leader?"

"It was Zhang Benchu," said Yuan Ying. "Elder Zhang."

Xuandu Mountain had continued to this day, passed from one generation to the next. Though the mountains had been sealed off for a long time, the sect had quite a few internal, branching factions. Taking Qi Fengge's branch as an example, one could call it the orthodox main branch, hence the position of sect leader was theirs. For the other elders, their martial arts could be traced back to the second-generation sect leader's fellow disciples. Though they all came from Xuandu's Violet Palace just the same, each of them had one or two secret techniques that were only passed down within their specific branches. Therefore, strictly speaking, most of the elders of Xuandu Mountain belonged to the same generation as Shen Qiao and the others, but there were also those from more senior generations—his martial uncles. Zhang Benchu was one of them.

"Yu Ai was able to successfully become the sect leader because seven of the elders supported him. I trust that one of them must've been Zhang Benchu?"

Yuan Ying nodded and said, "Yes."

"What about Da-shixiong?" said Shen Qiao. "You're ranked fourth. If he approached you, he must've approached Da-shixiong already, right?"

Yuan Ying was a bit flustered. "This... This I don't know. I spend all day...inside the house reading...and practicing the sword...or teaching those disciples...swordplay." Having said this, he looked ashamed and said, "Er-shixiong, I'm... I'm sorry."

His apology wasn't only because he'd been unable to answer Shen Qiao's question, but more to express his regrets on not being able to do anything for Shen Qiao when he fell from the cliff before.

But Shen Qiao wasn't angry. Instead, he patted Yuan Ying's shoulder, the way he had in the past. "No need to apologize. You dislike conflicts with others by nature, and you rarely leave the sect. But this time, you were able to realize that something was wrong and left the mountain to look for me. That's already incredible. So, after meeting Zhang Benchu, you didn't tell Yu Ai about the situation?"

Yuan Ying flushed a little. "No...I didn't. Previously, Wu-shimei told me...that he was involved in your fall...from the cliff...so I...I was wary of him."

Shen Qiao gave a slight sigh and said no more.

Yan Wushi's gaze paused for a moment on Shen Qiao's hand, which was resting on Yuan Ying's shoulder, and then he lazily said, "Since Yuan-shidi has arrived, he can stay here. Your complexion is sallow, and you appear malnourished. Let's have the chef build you back up."

Shen Qiao glanced at him and thought to himself, *Who is your shidi?* The words rolled about in his throat, but Daoist Master Shen was kindhearted by nature, so he ultimately said nothing.

Yu Shengyan, meanwhile, was stunned. He couldn't have imagined that his shizun—who, despite his warm act, possessed a cold heart—would look at Yuan Ying with special regard. And why would he lower his own seniority to talk to Yuan Ying as an equal?

Just where did this little stutterer borrow such a huge face from, to the point that my shizun has to honorably address you as "shidi?" And you're not even trembling in terror while shedding tears of gratitude?

Of course Yuan Ying wasn't trembling in terror—he had no idea who Yan Wushi was. When he heard the man say to let him stay, he quickly turned to look at his shixiong for his opinion. It was obvious that he was an obedient child who respected his master and his teachings.

Shen Qiao saw him looking over and smiled. "Since Sect Leader Yan has sincerely invited you, you should accept."

Yuan Ying had seen Yu Shengyan bowing to Yan Wushi earlier, so he should have realized Yan Wushi's identity then. Instead he'd been caught unawares, only understanding now. He quickly cupped his hands. "Thank you, Sect Leader Yan. Then, I'll be troubling you!"

In the past, forget just one Yuan Ying, even if there'd been ten Yuan Yings, Yan Wushi wouldn't have paid them any attention. However, today was not the past—Yuan Ying was Shen Qiao's shidi, which ultimately made him more unique in Yan Wushi's eyes.

However, it was clear that Qi Fengge was truly unconventional when accepting disciples. He had five disciples beneath him, each with different temperaments, and disciples as simple and dull as Yuan Ying were rare indeed.

After Yu Shengyan glumly led Yuan Ying away to settle him in, Shen Qiao looked at the weiqi board in somewhat of a daze.

Yan Wushi immediately saw through his thoughts. "Do you wish to go to Xuandu Mountain?"

Shen Qiao pulled himself together. "Yes, I want to go back and take a look."

He'd wanted to go back for some time, but his previous strength had been insufficient, and he didn't want to take risks. But things were different now—his strength had more or less returned. Even against exceptional figures like Buddhist Master Xueting, he'd still have a fighting chance.

In any case, Xuandu Mountain would always be the sect where he'd grown up. Even if Shen Qiao had no intention of taking the position of sect teacher, he would not allow anyone with ulterior motives to attempt to destroy the Pure Land of his heart.

If Zhang Benchu had sought out Yuan Ying, that meant that Yu Ai had failed to live up to his expectations. There must have been conflicts between the two, perhaps significant enough that Zhang Benchu wished to expel Yu Ai from the position of sect leader. Considering this along with the information Huanyue Sect had obtained, if anyone claimed that there was outside intervention involved, Shen Qiao would never believe it.

"That's fine," said Yan Wushi. "It's about time, anyway. With your current martial prowess, you might not be able to chop Yu Ai into eight pieces, but stabbing a sword through his heart should be doable."

Shen Qiao was left almost speechless. "Just because I'm going doesn't mean I have to kill someone!"

Can you not spout such bloodthirsty words all the time?

Yan Wushi gave him a playful smile. "I fear that you won't be able to help it. Xuandu Mountain is like a chunk of rich meat that's been locked in a cage. Now that the cage has an opening, do you really expect those beasts that have been eyeing it hungrily for so long not to pounce?"

Shen Qiao didn't like his description, but he also understood that he was right. This was Xuandu Mountain's current situation. Though Yu Ai was a skilled martial artist, people often lacked caution when it came to internal affairs—just like Shen Qiao himself in the beginning.

"Actually," added Yan Wushi, "I've received a message saying that, after Hehuan Sect lost a large chunk of influence in Chang'an, they grew very close to the Göktürks."

Shen Qiao frowned. "You're saying that Hehuan Sect will also intervene in Xuandu Mountain's affairs?"

"That I don't know. You'll be alone on this trip, so why don't I lend you one of my disciples to assist you? Which one would you like? Bian Yanmei or Yu Shengyan?"

"These are Xuandu Mountain's internal issues," said Shen Qiao. "How can I trouble them?"

Yan Wushi deliberately said, "You're saying that you want this venerable one to personally accompany you?"

Shen Qiao was an honest person. He'd never had such intentions; Yan Wushi's words stunned him.

Yan Wushi didn't wait for a reply but smiled and said, "Unfortunately, I can't fulfill your wishes this time. My injuries from the previous battle with Xueting have yet to heal. Even if I go, I may not be able to help."

Shen Qiao had personally checked his pulse last time, so he had a very clear idea of the state of his injuries. Yet hearing Yan Wushi now, for some reason, deep down, he was no longer sure.

"It's been so long," he said, reaching out. "Why has it yet to heal?"

Yan Wushi didn't move in the slightest. He maintained his posture, leaning against the pillow, and let Shen Qiao place his hand on his wrist.

After freezing for a moment, Shen Qiao's expression fell. "How can this be?"

Change of Sect Leaders

ORIGINALLY, SHEN QIAO had thought that Yan Wushi's injuries weren't serious. After so many days, even if he wasn't fully healed, they should have recovered by half.

But the moment he checked his pulse this time, he discovered that Yan Wushi's meridians were congested, his circulation sluggish. There was a faint evidence of blood stasis—if anything, he seemed even worse than before.

Was it Xueting? Could his martial prowess have achieved the level where his strikes only looked shallow but could actually penetrate deep within?

But if Xueting had reached this level of skill, how could he lose to Yan Wushi, let alone allow Yan Wushi to destroy his martial arts?

Yan Wushi covered his mouth and coughed twice, then solved the mystery for him: "It's because I've been busy managing the affairs of Huanyue Sect these days. Our power and influence have been dispersed, so first we must slowly regather. Thus, I've had no time to heal, though I didn't expect it to be this serious."

Shen Qiao frowned and said, "It concerns your own health. How could you be so careless?"

Yan Wushi smiled; he clearly wasn't taking it seriously. "Don't worry, it's not a fatal injury. I'll recover in five days at most."

Shen Qiao thought for a moment, then took out a porcelain bottle from his pocket and placed it on the table. "The foundations of our internal cultivation, the Dao and the demonic, are antithetical to one another, so I can't assist you. However, Xuandu Mountain has quite a few excellent medications for external injuries that have been passed down from generation to generation in Xuandu Mountain. This is one I recently had a pharmacy prepare, based off a prescription. If you're willing to trust me, try taking it now: three pills a day. It can alleviate your injuries."

Yan Wushi picked up the porcelain bottle. It felt a little warm against his palm, still carrying some of Shen Qiao's body heat. His thumb caressed the delicate porcelain bottle with an air of indescribable suggestiveness.

Shen Qiao didn't think much of it. He thought that Yan Wushi was suspicious and didn't trust him; that he'd accepted it on the surface but would secretly throw the medicine away later. That would be a huge waste. In any case, the bottle contained quite a few precious medicinal ingredients, likely enough to save a fair number of people. So he added, "If you're not going to take any, give it back to me. In any case, your injuries aren't anything serious."

"Why wouldn't I take it?" Yan Wushi was amused to see him staring anxiously at the porcelain bottle. He deliberately went against what Shen Qiao asked: he pulled out the stopper and tipped three pills onto his palm, then took the plum juice in front of Shen Qiao and swallowed them with the liquid.

"I feel like the stuffiness here is gone," he said, rubbing his chest. "Suddenly, it's completely clear."

"...This isn't a divine elixir."

Yan Wushi laughed. "I was talking about the plum juice! I heard that Daoist cultivators can add even their body fluids to medicine.

You just drank this plum juice, so doesn't it contain your body fluids?"

What could Shen Qiao say in the face of such vulgar language? Even though he'd heard plenty of shameless words constantly throughout the day already, he couldn't stop the faint flush from surfacing on his fair face.

Yan Wushi saw the shame and irritation in his gaze. Without a word, Shen Qiao braced his hand on the table to stand, ready to leave, but Yan Wushi held down his hand and smiled. "All right, it's the medicine that was effective, not the body fluids. When did you go and prepare the pills? How come I didn't know?"

Shen Qiao's face was stony. "Must this humble Daoist report everything to Sect Leader Yan?"

"Of course not, but I'm concerned about you. I'm worried that you won't have enough money and that someone will take advantage of you."

"So that's how foolish this humble Daoist appears, in Sect Leader Yan's eyes?"

Are you not? If you weren't foolish, could I have sold you to Sang Jingxing without you even being the wiser? But outwardly, Yan Wushi continued to smile and said, "That's not true. You've been improving day by day since you left the mountain. I've seen it myself—you're much smarter than you were in the past."

Shen Qiao had endured and endured, but he finally couldn't take it anymore. "Looking at Sect Leader Yan now, he doesn't seem like he has any internal injuries. Perhaps he'll be able to recover even faster if he talks some more!"

"That's not enough," said Yan Wushi with a smile. "Without the excellent medicine known as Daoist Master Shen, my recovery is destined to be slower. But I heard that Yang Jian sent you a sum of money?"

"He did," said Shen Qiao. "That money was used to build the Xuandu Monastery."

"So you're really planning on staying in Chang'an long-term?"

"That's hard to say. I wish to go back to Xuandu Mountain first, to see if that matter can be resolved. In the future, when Xuandu Mountain wants to re-enter the secular world, it'll have an additional foothold in Chang'an. I think Yang Jian will make an ambitious and talented emperor. He isn't one of those foolish, prejudiced rulers, and he's tolerant toward the Daoist discipline. Perhaps Daoism will have the chance to welcome a second rise."

"He only did this to win over people's hearts," Yan Wushi reminded him.

Shen Qiao smiled. "I know, but there's nothing wrong with that. Though I'm a Daoist practitioner myself, I dare not say that Daoism is wholly free from degenerates. Having hundreds of schools of thought all contending with each other is a blessing for the commonfolk. That way, we can avoid the kind of situation where an emperor plunders the citizens' assets in the interests of one discipline, leaving them destitute. Yang Jian is deeply influenced by Buddhism, yet he can still treat Confucianism and Daoism fairly. In my opinion, this is the magnanimity that a ruler should demonstrate. Most importantly, if Xuandu Mountain wants to enter the secular world, now is a good time."

Yan Wushi raised an eyebrow. "Didn't you admire everything about Qi Fengge? Why are you contradicting his opinion on this matter?"

"That was then, this is now," said Shen Qiao. "No such opportunity existed when my late master was alive. If he were still here, I'm sure he'd agree with my ideas."

"Oh, if you put it that way, this venerable one understands."

"Understands what?"

"Whenever you want to do something, you'll just say that Qi Fengge would agree. Whenever you don't, you'll just say that you're respecting Qi Fengge's will. Either way, he's dead; he can't jump out to refute you."

He'd worded this deliberately, but to his surprise, Shen Qiao didn't grow angry from embarrassment. Instead, he thought for a moment, then smiled slightly. "You're not wrong about that." As he smiled, his eyes sparkled, shimmering brightly until the room seemed to fill with light. Even Yan Wushi's gaze upon him couldn't help but still for a moment. "My late master was more reasonable than anyone else. He would've understood my thoughts."

Yan Wushi raised his eyebrow. He completely disagreed with Shen Qiao's constant praise of his shifu, but he'd always boasted himself as being graciously tolerant—naturally, he wasn't going to split hairs over a dead man.

From this, one could see that though Shen Qiao was righteous by nature, he was by no means a person bound by rules. This was precisely why, out of his five disciples, Qi Fengge had ultimately chosen Shen Qiao to be his successor.

"Since you accepted that title from the court, even if you're not obligated to obey his orders, you still have a nominal relationship with the court," Yan Wushi said. "As such, Xuandu Mountain's affairs can't be completely considered your own personal matters. With the current relationship between Huanyue Sect and the Sui Dynasty, if Yang Jian knew you were going to Xuandu Mountain, even if I said nothing, he would still ask me to help. I will let Bian Yanmei accompany you on this trip. He is more tactful and will be able to lend you some assistance."

Now that he'd mentioned this reason, Shen Qiao no longer declined. He nodded. "Thank you very much, then." He hesitated for a moment, then said, "You're injured. It's better for you to rest quietly the next few days. Don't keep jumping about everywhere."

Yan Wushi's smile widened. "A-Qiao, are you worried about me?"

"No," said Shen Qiao.

"You're lying," said Yan Wushi.

Shen Qiao said nothing. *Then why did you even ask?*

Yan Wushi sighed. "Although I am very moved, I am doomed to disappoint your expectations. Don't forget that the bald old donkey is still waiting for me to take care of him. In the end, he was still the grand and lofty state preceptor of Zhou, a leader of Buddhism. I can't give him the cold shoulder for too long, now can I?"

From what I saw, you had no problems doing so, Shen Qiao thought to himself. But he caught on to a specific word in Yan Wushi's reply. "You wish to kill him?"

"I'm going to exchange him for another astronomical benefit," Yan Wushi responded lazily.

As for what astronomical benefit that was, if he was unwilling to say, Shen Qiao wouldn't be able to pry it out of him, so he asked no further.

A few days later, upon hearing that Shen Qiao was preparing to return to Xuandu Mountain, Yuan Ying was delighted and came to ask when Shen Qiao would depart.

But Shen Qiao didn't plan on taking him, as Xuandu Monastery was still under construction and needed someone to supervise. Yuan Ying was undoubtedly the best candidate. Upon hearing Shen Qiao's plans, Yuan Ying's face immediately fell, his joy dissolving into disappointment. The change was so obvious it was almost unbearable.

Shen Qiao thought this odd. "Si-shidi, do you wish to return to Xuandu Mountain that badly?"

"No, that's not it." Yuan Ying struggled to explain his unhappiness. These days, Yu Shengyan had been toying with him whenever he had nothing to do. Yuan Ying couldn't outtalk him, and though he was stronger than Yu Shengyan, Yu Shengyan never made it physical. Yuan Ying was an honest child—there was no way he could strike first. He also thought that, as a guest, he couldn't make things difficult for his Er-shixiong, so he'd endured it all. He'd long ranked Yu Shengyan at the top of his list of most troublesome characters.

Shen Qiao patted him on the shoulder. "I know you've devoted yourself to cultivating the Dao, ignoring all external affairs, but I can't think of a more suitable person than you to supervise the construction of Xuandu Monastery. I'll try to come back as soon as possible, but I can only trouble you to help out first."

Yuan Ying hurriedly said, "Er-shixiong, you...you go ahead. I'll go every day to supervise...you don't need...need to worry."

"Thank you, A-Ying."

"Er-shixiong, you...you don't need to thank me. We trained under the same shizun, but I'm the most...most useless one. I've never been able to help much, and I always felt very...very uneasy inside. It's rare for you to give me a task, so I'm very excited!"

After such a long separation, this si-shidi, who'd always jumped to hide behind others, had also matured. Shen Qiao was quite pleased.

By the time he'd made proper arrangements, Yan Wushi had already left Chang'an, one step ahead of him. Now, Shen Qiao and Bian Yanmei also set off for Xuandu Mountain.

Bian Yanmei was a rather interesting person. The way he did things was interesting, and the way he spoke was interesting as well, but he had an excellent sense of what and what not to do—unlike Yan Wushi, who'd often embarrass Shen Qiao into a rage by going overboard. Traveling with such a person was naturally as pleasant as a spring breeze. Furthermore, Shen Qiao himself had never been hard to get along with and also made for an excellent companion. He didn't enjoy showing off and was willing to patiently listen to others. Not to mention, if they ran into danger, he'd become the most reliable of helpers—anyone would wish to have this type of friend.

Bian Yanmei hadn't interacted much with Shen Qiao, but he'd spent a great deal of time in the imperial court and possessed an acute insight into the human heart. People like Shen Qiao would never betray their friends, so Bian Yanmei was naturally willing to make friends with him. As the saying went, having one more friend meant having one more avenue of retreat. Though Bian Yanmei had been taught and raised completely by Yan Wushi, and was intrinsically quite similar to his shifu, he was a bit slicker and more sophisticated by several notches. In addition, Bian Yanmei had already realized how Yan Wushi felt, so he deliberately tried to make nice with Shen Qiao on the journey. So, of course, the two got along quite well.

They both possessed qinggong and had swift horses with them— if they traveled day and night, they'd arrive in three to five days. If they instead chose to travel by day and rest during the night, it'd still take only a dozen or so days. If Shen Qiao had been alone, traveling through the night wouldn't have been an issue. But with Bian Yanmei accompanying him, he naturally couldn't force him to rush toward their destination.

So, after about ten days, the pair finally arrived at Xuandu Town, at the foot of Xuandu Mountain.

Seeing the bustling town, Bian Yanmei couldn't help but smile. "In the past two years, Xuandu Town has become more prosperous," he said. "I also visited a few years ago, and I only remember that there were fewer people then."

Shen Qiao also hadn't been here for a long time. He looked around and said, "Yes, though the green mountains remain unchanged—things might be constant, but the people are not!"

He'd grown up in the mountains since childhood and was also very familiar with Xuandu Town. The feelings he was having at this sight were naturally much stronger than Bian Yanmei's.

At this moment, the two of them were sitting at the teahouse, resting and drinking tea. When the nearby waiter heard their words, he came over and interjected. "I fear that this kind of excitement won't last long!"

"What do you mean?"

The waiter sighed. "You two must also know that these fields below the mountain belong to the Daoist priests on Xuandu Mountain. The previous masters sympathized with our difficult lives and charged very little rent, for which we were grateful. Otherwise, Xuandu Town wouldn't have the bustle and liveliness it does these days. But I don't know what the new leader thinks. A few days ago, he suddenly said he would increase this year's rent, and by a very large amount! How will we endure this? Even those who run inns and restaurants, or tea houses like ours, have to pay rent. If this continues, who'd dare to continue with their businesses? Our boss said that once this month finishes, we should pack things up and return to our hometown!"

"The new sect leader? Yu Ai?"

The waiter shook his head. "I don't think his surname was Yu. I heard that he only became sect leader last month and that he was previously Perfected Master Qi's eldest disciple..."

"Tan?"

"Yes, yes! His surname was Tan!"

Shen Qiao and Bian Yanmei exchanged a glance.

"But I heard before that it was Sect Leader Yu," said Shen Qiao, suppressing the towering waves of alarm rising within his heart. "How did it change to Sect Leader Tan?"

The waiter scratched his head. "This lowly one doesn't know."

After a couple more idle words, he saw another guest enter for tea and quickly went over to greet them, putting Shen Qiao's table aside.

Shen Qiao slowly furrowed his brows and said, "How did Da-shixiong end up becoming sect leader? Where's Yu Ai?"

"We set out at the end of last month and arrived here at the start of the new one, so it's also possible we missed the news along the way," said Bian Yanmei. "We can ask someone about this later; Daoist Master Shen need not feel anxious. We can head up the mountain after we've clarified the situation."

"Very well."

To understand the situation, the two of them had to first find a place to stay—either a relay station or an inn, which were always good places to ask for news. Bian Yanmei was no stranger to this and took to it with the ease of a light carriage on a familiar road. He led Shen Qiao into an inn that was neither large nor small. "Merchants and the people of the jianghu all share a particular characteristic," he said. "Unless they come from a wealthy family, they will never go to places that are too high-class. On the contrary, most of them would choose average places like this. Asking for news here is the best option."

Shen Qiao naturally had no objection and nodded in agreement.

Xuandu's Violet Palace was also a major Daoist sect. Since Yu Ai had announced that he was opening the mountain gates, many young people had come here seeking a master to learn martial arts under. Some of these people were descended from people of the jianghu but came from families which had fallen into decline by the current generation. Others had heard many stories of martial heroes and yearned for the flash of steel and blades. There was no lack of people with good aptitude among them, but, without exception, absolutely none of them were from a wealthy family. If they were, their families would have naturally arranged better futures for them, so they'd have no need to come all the way here, crossing thousands of miles to seek a master.

However, it was as Bian Yanmei said: due to this, they would choose to rest at this kind of inn, neither too luxurious nor too shabby.

The main lobby on the first floor was filled with the clamor of various noises. Bian Yanmei and Shen Qiao entered and found a place to sit down.

Coincidentally, several young people with swords sat next to them, and there was no need for them to ask around more—the other party had already started talking about the recent events of the jianghu.

"Have you heard?" said one of the youths. "The Huanyue Sect Leader sent a letter of challenge to Hulugu!"

Shen Qiao was about to pick up his cup, but when he heard this, his heart shook and his body froze.

Care and Thought

THOSE WHO'D NEVER WITNESSED Hulugu's strength firsthand might not feel anything upon hearing this news. From their perspective, Yan Wushi had been able to come out unscathed after a group ambush from five great martial arts experts, so he indeed should have the ability and confidence to challenge him.

So as soon as this news fell, it was like a drop of water splashing into a pot of oil, and the surroundings immediately began to boil over. Surprise or excitement colored the faces of many, and they all began to ask for details.

"When did this happen?"

"Just a few days ago. They said that Sect Leader Yan issued a letter of challenge to Hulugu. Hulugu was eating at the time, and he was so shocked he leapt up and almost choked to death!"

"You speak as if you were watching right next to him. Who's Hulugu?"

"You don't even know Hulugu? Then do you know Qi Fengge?"

"Nonsense. Would I come seeking a master at Xuandu Mountain if I didn't?!"

"Then how come you haven't heard of Hulugu? More than twenty years ago, Qi Fengge fought the Göktürk master, then forced him to swear not to enter the Central Plains for two decades. At the

Qingcheng Mountain Sword Trial Conference, Hulugu defeated Shen Qiao with only a few moves. Many people said that while Liuli Palace didn't announce the identity of the number-one martial artist in all the land, Hulugu was exactly that, both in name and in reality. Yan Wushi must've been dissatisfied with this and that's why he sent him a letter of challenge!"

"Hah, don't bring it up anymore. I originally wanted to go to the Sword Trial Conference, but my nag of a mom wouldn't let me. She said it was too dangerous. Before I came to Xuandu Mountain to look for a master this time, I had to secretly discuss things with my father first and ask him to stall my mother. Only then could I come out..."

The cacophony of voices gradually faded into a murmur in Shen Qiao's ears—his thoughts were still stuck on the words from before. It wasn't until Bian Yanmei shoved the cup into his hand that he realized that he'd remained in the same position the entire time, completely still.

"Thank you very much." Shen Qiao took the cup and poured some green bamboo juice into it. "Before we left, did Sect Leader Yan bring this up to you?"

As soon as he'd asked it, he felt that this question was somewhat unnecessary. Yan Wushi's personality meant he often did unexpected things. Even he might not have seen this coming, had they still been alive, let alone his disciples.

But Bian Yanmei's answer was even more surprising. "The challenge letter is real."

Shen Qiao was stunned. "Isn't he still injured?"

Bian Yanmei pondered for a moment, then said, "I have a couple of thoughts about this matter. Shizun didn't do this on a whim or to make a show of doing something shocking. There is a reason behind it."

"I wish to know the details."

"I heard that while you were on Qingcheng Mountain, you and Hulugu fought."

Shen Qiao nodded. "We did. Hulugu has emerged from twenty years of seclusion, and he's even stronger than in the past. I fear that fighting him to a draw at my current level would be incredibly difficult."

Shen Qiao had always been honest, and he believed that victory was victory, defeat was defeat. He didn't find it difficult to talk about his own defeat. No matter how formidable the enemy was, he'd only tell it like it was—he'd never exaggerate or dress it up.

Bian Yanmei said, "In Daoist Master Shen's opinion, if Shizun and Hulugu fought, what would be his chance of victory?"

Shen Qiao frowned and thought for a moment, then said, "If he's injured, it might be fifty-fifty."

But this only held if Yan Wushi was in good condition, having abundant internal power and no injuries at all.

Hearing this reply, worry revealed itself on Bian Yanmei's face. It was a long time before he spoke again. "I'm certain the Göktürks will intervene in Xuandu Mountain's affairs," he said. "You killed Kunye, and Hulugu is doubtless unwilling to let that slide. He might even disregard his honor as a master martial artist and personally participate himself. But now that Shizun has sent this challenge letter, Hulugu won't be able to spare the time to concern himself with you, so it'd reduce some of the obstacles before Daoist Master Shen."

Shen Qiao froze.

He'd thought about many possibilities, and the one he'd considered the most likely was simply that Yan Wushi wished to conquer the throne of the number one martial artist in the world. Shen Qiao had never expected that the true answer would be this one.

Seeing Shen Qiao's reaction, a look of self-deprecation appeared on Bian Yanmei's face. "Does Daoist Master Shen not believe me? I don't blame you. Us demonic practitioners have always been selfish and self-serving, marching to our own tune. When have we ever made sacrifices for anyone else?"

Shen Qiao sighed softly. "That's not it. Please don't misunderstand."

But he couldn't say that he'd never thought that way before.

"Actually, that's not all," Bian Yanmei said. "The reason Shizun spared Xueting's life was so that he could take him to Tiantai Sect, to exchange him for the last volume of the *Zhuyang Strategy*."

Again, Shen Qiao froze a little.

The *Zhuyang Strategy* consisted of five scrolls, and only one of them was related to the martial arts of the demonic discipline. Yan Wushi had already read that one, and he'd fully repaired the flaws within his demonic core, and so the remaining scroll was of little use to him—one could almost say useless. Therefore, it wasn't difficult to guess why he wished to obtain the scroll Tiantai Sect was safeguarding.

With Shen Qiao's intelligence, he naturally thought of the answer.

"It is said that during his early years, Xueting's goals clashed with Tiantai Sect's," he said. "Therefore, after his master passed away in meditation, he left the sect and established his own. Why would Tiantai Sect be willing to exchange the *Zhuyang Strategy* scroll for Xueting?"

"Tiantai Sect regards Xueting as a traitor. Shizun spared his life so Tiantai Sect themselves could deal with him. They need to repay Shizun's favor somehow. Naturally, he won't be able to obtain the original, but a copy should still be possible."

Shen Qiao sighed. "Sect Leader Yan has put much care and thought into the matter."

It'd be a lie to claim that he wasn't shaken at all, deep down.

However, Bian Yanmei also understood that even if Shen Qiao was shaken, he had no need to express those feelings out loud, so he didn't pause for too long. He quickly continued, "No need to worry, Daoist Master Shen. Shizun's injuries aren't serious, and the battle with Hulugu is slated to be half a month from now. It's enough time for Shizun to recuperate."

Someone who could stay in seclusion outside the Great Wall for twenty years, remaining indifferent to worldly affairs, was bound to be a person without much ambition regarding the secular world. Hulugu was such a person. Though his status and standing among the Göktürks meant he couldn't completely sever himself from the movements of the Khaganate, he was still a warrior first and foremost. Hence, to Hulugu, Yan Wushi's challenge letter was more compelling than Xuandu Mountain and their ilk. Half a month was neither long nor short. If he chose to attend the engagement, he wouldn't spare any further attention for the matters at Xuandu Mountain.

With just a little bit of thought, Shen Qiao could understand all these reasons and consequences.

If Yan Wushi had pointed them out before him, one by one, he still might have been moved, and he might have politely declined, but the shock he'd receive couldn't be comparable to what he felt right now.

Eventually, Yan Wushi still wouldn't be able to avoid fighting Hulugu, even without Shen Qiao in the picture, but that would be in the future. He'd chosen to issue the letter of challenge right now, and that decision, undoubtedly, had been largely due to Shen Qiao.

A man so fickle and selfish had done something that even many sentimental people might be unable to. How could Shen Qiao not be moved?

Bian Yanmei stealthily observed Shen Qiao's reaction—he had gone completely silent. He wondered to himself if Shen Qiao had gone catatonic from all the emotion and called out to him, "Daoist Master Shen?"

But Shen Qiao didn't weep with gratitude the way he'd expected. After his initial silence, he appeared incredibly calm. "Whatever the case, we're already here. After all the help your shizun has offered, if I don't resolve the issues here first, how would I have the face to meet him?"

Bian Yanmei nodded. "Let's ask someone about the situation on the mountain first. Then we can ascend it tomorrow."

"Very well."

Both men exuded refinement and grace, especially Shen Qiao, who was still carrying a longsword and dressed in Daoist robes. Before long, he attracted the attention of the young men next to him, and one of the ones who'd just been talking loudly mustered the courage to speak to them. "May I ask if this Daoist Master is from Xuandu's Violet Palace?"

Shen Qiao had been hoping for an opportunity to find a disciple who'd come down the mountain, so he may ask his questions, but when he saw them, he had a new idea. "No," he said, "this humble Daoist is Shan Qiaozi. I came here to ascend the mountain and visit a friend. What about you, young friends?"

Hearing Shen Qiao's "no," the young man was somewhat disappointed, but since he'd taken the initiative to come and ask, he couldn't really just brush Shen Qiao off. "We came to seek apprenticeship. This one is Duan Ying, and these two are my friends, Zhang Chao and Zhong Bojing."

The three cupped their hands at Shen Qiao and Bian Yanmei.

Shen Qiao nodded and slightly raised his own hands to return the greeting.

Duan Ying didn't mind, but the other two were displeased when they saw how this Daoist had only nodded and raised his hands in a perfunctory greeting. He hadn't even stood.

In truth, with Shen Qiao's actual identity, no one would have criticized him if he simply hadn't moved at all, never mind only lifting his hands in greeting.

Duan Ying asked, "Since Daoist Master Shan Qiaozi is visiting his friends on the mountain, he must know the perfected masters of Xuandu Mountain, right? We have long admired the grace exemplified by Xuandu's Violet Palace, so we wish to join the sect. We heard that Xuandu Mountain only accepts disciples twice a year on the spring and autumn equinoxes, but the timing of our arrival was unfortunate. Could we ask Daoist Master Shan Qiaozi to introduce us?"

When he asked this question, his two companions also looked at Shen Qiao with expectant gazes.

Shen Qiao gave a laugh and said, "Actually, I'm not familiar with either the sect leader or the elders but rather with another Daoist priest on the mountain—one responsible for lighting the stoves. So I won't be able to help you."

Their expressions filled with disappointment. Seeing this, Shen Qiao added, "However, every five days, several Daoist priests will come down the mountain to make purchases. There's a pastry shop selling snacks next to the inn, which is a favorite of the priests on the mountain. If you keep an eye on it, you might be able to meet them soon."

Hearing him say this, Duan Ying and the rest glanced at each other, then said, "If this is true, thank you very much for informing us, Daoist Master."

Shen Qiao waved his hand. "No need to be polite. If you can enter the sect, this humble Daoist will have three more friends at Xuandu Mountain. Isn't that quite an honor as well?"

Duan Ying felt this Daoist priest was not only good-looking, but he also spoke in a kindly manner, so he instantly formed a favorable impression of him. He spoke quite a few words of thanks and started discussing Daoist classics with Shen Qiao. It wasn't until Zhong Bojing and Zhang Chao urged him that he bid farewell.

Bian Yanmei had spent the entire time watching dispassionately from the sidelines. Now he finally spoke up. "That Zhang Chao's aptitude is quite decent. The other two are only mediocre."

Shen Qiao smiled but didn't speak.

In fact, he preferred Duan Ying out of the three. It wasn't because he'd spoken with him the most but because Duan Ying had been respectful and courteous even without knowing their identities. This made him appear much steadier and gentler compared to the other two. A person's aptitude was naturally important, but their sense of martial honor was even more so. If it were up to Shen Qiao, he would pass over the better-qualified Zhang Chao in favor of the comparatively mediocre Duan Ying.

That night, Shen Qiao and Bian Yanmei stayed at the inn. As luck would have it, the room shared by Duan Ying and his companions was very close to theirs.

The trio heeded Shen Qiao's words—early the next morning, they began keeping watch at the pastry shop. Sure enough, they didn't need to wait too long before two young Daoists arrived at the shop. A glance was enough to tell them that the two had come down from Xuandu Mountain.

Duan Ying and the others were overjoyed and quickly went up to them, explaining who they were and why they'd come to the mountain. They asked the Daoist priests if they could take them up the mountain as potential disciples.

Unexpectedly, the other party refused. "Xuandu Mountain only accepts disciples on the spring and autumn equinoxes every year. You didn't arrive during the correct period; please wait until the next time."

Duan Ying pleaded. "We have admired Xuandu Mountain for a long time, and we're willing to accept hardships. It's fine even if we can only be accepted and enlisted as lay disciples. We ask these two Daoist Masters to please help us!"

The slightly older Daoist was somewhat friendlier and more good-natured. He said to them, "Some things have been happening at Xuandu Mountain recently. The perfected masters on top are all busy, and they won't have the leisure to accept disciples. You truly came at a bad time. Why not go to Qingcheng Mountain to try your luck?"

Xuandu Mountain and Qingcheng Mountain were nowhere near each other; with that distance, one couldn't just casually walk over. Hearing these words, Duan Ying and his companions' faces practically overflowed with misery.

They pleaded again and again, but the Daoists refused to waver, so the three youths could only leave, disappointed.

"Hah, Yun Chang-shidi, why did you answer them so resolutely?" the older Daoist said. "Perhaps when we go back and report this, Shizun would be willing to accept them?"

"The mountain is going through troubled times now, and Shizun is clearly unwilling to interfere. How could he possibly accept any disciples now?!"

"Then why not have them find the acting sect leader? I find them quite pitiful."

"The acting sect leader likely can't spare the time either. I heard that people from Hehuan Sect will arrive soon. Who knows if the acting sect leader will even be able to hold on to his position then?"

"Don't be so harsh with your words, Yun Chang-shidi..."

"What are you scared of? No one can hear me. I must say, times were better when Sect Leader Shen was here. Everyone was harmonious and friendly, unlike now, where everyone is suspicious of everyone else. Will we ever have peaceful days again?" The young Daoist known as Yun Chang-shidi curled his lips.

However, the next moment, his expression immediately transformed into one of shock.

"Sect...Sect Leader Shen?" Seeing the person in front of him now, Yun Chang, whose tongue was normally so agile, was shocked into stuttering.

Conference

THE TWO DAOIST PRIESTS were as dumbfounded as if they'd seen a ghost in broad daylight, but Shen Qiao took no pride in frightening them.

"It's been a while, Xiao-Yun Chang," he said. "You've grown quite a bit taller." Then his gaze shifted to the other person, his expression as gentle as it'd been in the past, almost unchanged. "Le An has also made great leaps in his martial arts. You noticed me even before I appeared."

Le An and Yun Chang exchanged a glance, and after their initial moment of panic, they quickly bowed. "Greetings to Shen-shishu! We hope Shen-shishu is well!"

"How has your shifu been?" asked Shen Qiao.

"Thank you, Shishu, for your inquiry. Shifu is in good health. Ever since Shishu left the mountain, his esteemed self would often talk about you. If he knew that your esteemed self was safe and sound, he'd be overjoyed."

Though their shifu was from the same generation as Shen Qiao, he was much older and had devoted himself to his cultivation on Xuandu Mountain—he rarely concerned himself with the mundane affairs of the sect. It was only during his later years that he had accepted these two disciples.

"I also miss Kong-shixiong very much," Shen Qiao said. "I was about to head up the mountain to say hello to him."

Upon hearing his words, the two young Daoists immediately showed completely different reactions: Yun Chang's face shone with delight while Le An's expression was filled with concern.

Shen Qiao took in all these shifts in emotion, then deliberately said, "Why, you're not coming with me?"

Yun Chang was an outspoken young man; before Le An could speak, he'd already said, "Shen-shishu is willing to return? We couldn't be happier!"

Shen Qiao smiled. "But I don't think your Le An-shixiong looks particularly happy?"

Le An quickly cupped his hands and said, "Shen-shishu speaks too seriously. It's just that Sect Leader Yu's whereabouts are currently unknown, meaning the situation is somewhat chaotic. We don't wish to be caught up in it, so we originally planned on going down the mountain and lying low until the storm passes. But we didn't expect to encounter you."

In the beginning, when Shen Qiao had fought Kunye and lost, falling from the cliff, the jianghu had been rife with rumors for a period of time. Some of those rumors made their way back to Xuandu Mountain, greatly impacting Shen Qiao's reputation. Though no one said anything, they'd all believed that Shen Qiao's loss to Kunye had caused Xuandu Mountain's standing to plummet precipitously, losing them a great deal of face. This attitude meant that afterward, when Yu Ai became sect leader, few people opposed him—they all thought that Yu Ai had the means and capability, that maybe he could lead Xuandu Mountain to best its revival.

But at that time, Le An and Yun Chang's shifu hadn't been optimistic about Yu Ai, so he forbade them from participating in sect affairs. This master and his two disciples stayed out of everyone's sight, maintaining a weak presence within the sect. Both his disciples were young and eager for achievements, so while they obeyed their shifu's orders, they couldn't help but silently criticize him deep down. However, recent developments had been beyond their expectations, proving their shifu correct: Yu Ai encountered a bottleneck in his cooperation with the Göktürks, and at this time, the situation in the Central Plains was already changing constantly and rapidly. With the changeover of the Northern Dynasties from Zhou to Sui, the Göktürks' hold over the Central Plains was gradually weakening, causing Xuandu Mountain's standing to become increasingly awkward.

And yet, right at this moment, the sect leader Yu Ai suddenly disappeared overnight. Xuandu Mountain was left without a head, and so Tan Yuanchun, the eldest of Qi Fengge's disciples, temporarily took over the position. But though Tan Yuanchun used to be an elder, his personality wasn't forceful enough to maintain a firm grip on the sect. Therefore, many people on Xuandu Mountain voiced their objections. Among them was Elder Liu Yue, who opposed him the most vehemently. Both parties were locked in a silent power struggle, and the two sides inevitably tried to win over others to increase their influence.

Le An and Yun Chang's shifu used his seclusion as an excuse to avoid seeing outsiders, but people came knocking for his disciples several times. This annoyed them to the point they were left with no choice but to swap errands with others, giving themselves the duty of going down the mountain to make purchases. In fact, they were using the opportunity to hide and obtain some peace and quiet.

After listening to them relate this sequence of events, Shen Qiao was silent for a moment. Then he said, "Yu Ai was the sect leader, so he possessed martial skills far beyond average. Furthermore, he was on Xuandu Mountain, so how could he just disappear overnight? Did the two of you hear any rumors?"

They both shook their heads. "Shifu gave us orders. We're still young, so we're not allowed to participate in sect affairs. However, just a few days before Yu-shishu disappeared, a Göktürk envoy came up the mountain, wanting us to do something, but Yu-shishu refused. The two sides parted on bad terms, so many people said that Yu-shishu's disappearance was related to the Göktürks!"

This matched most of what Yuan Ying had said.

Shen Qiao asked, "Did you recognize the Göktürk envoy from that day?"

Both Le An and Yun Chang said they didn't.

The two young disciples didn't know much, so at this point in the conversation, there was nothing more to ask them. "I wish to head up the mountain," Shen Qiao said. "Will you come with me, or will you stay at the foot of the mountain for now?"

The pair looked at each other, then Yun Chang said, "We'll go up the mountain with you, Shen-shishu, lest you end up at a disadvantage!"

Le An had no time to cover Yun Chang's mouth, so he could only remain silent—which could count as him tacitly agreeing with his shidi's words.

Shen Qiao smiled. Though Yun Chang spoke a little thoughtlessly, he was frank and straightforward. Le An was slightly more fearful, but he wasn't a bad person either, otherwise he would have spoken up and refused.

"Never mind, you finally found some free time to come down the mountain and play," he told them. "Stay at the foot of the mountain and enjoy yourselves. It won't be too late if you can return two days later."

Le An had seen that Shen Qiao's ascent up the mountain couldn't be a good thing. Perhaps he wanted to regain his position as sect leader, which would inevitably require the support of the elders. At first he'd thought that Shen Qiao was going to drag them up the mountain, using them to make their shifu stand in line, but to his surprise, Shen Qiao mentioned nothing of it. Le An had purely been judging his upright character through his own moral failings.

Shen Qiao's candid, straightforward manner made Le An feel a little embarrassed, so he quickly spoke up to express his opinion. "With the position of sect leader currently yet to be determined, Xuandu Mountain cannot have even a single day of peace. Shen-shishu, your esteemed self was the only sect leader who Perfected Master Qi personally designated."

The implication within his words was that though they wouldn't interfere, if they had to support someone, they were sure to choose Shen Qiao. This tiny bit of consideration was really too meager when placed before Shen Qiao, but it was obviously not Shen Qiao's style to quibble with a young man.

"Thank you very much." He patted Le An's shoulder and said, "Don't make mischief or trouble here below the mountain. Come back soon."

His tone was ordinary, as if this was just some everyday chiding. Any passerby would have thought that Shen Qiao was only hiking up the mountain for some exercise.

The two young Daoists stared blankly at Shen Qiao and Bian Yanmei's retreating backs for a while, then Yun Chang suddenly said, "Shixiong, we should've gone up the mountain with Shen-shishu just now! Shizun's words last time were full of self-blame that he hadn't stood up to speak out for Shen-shishu that day. If his esteemed self saw us shirking responsibility and cowering away, he'd be disappointed."

"Right now, Elder Liu wishes to become the sect leader so badly, I fear he won't easily hand the position over to Shen-shishu," Le An argued. "How do you know what the conclusion will be with Shen-shishu's trip up the mountain this time? If we accompany him and the others mistake us for part of Shen-shishu's faction, won't we be dragging Shifu down?"

Yun Chang hung his head and sighed. "I just feel like we weren't very virtuous..."

Ultimately, Le An couldn't bear to see his shidi so disappointed. "Why don't we secretly follow after him?"

"That's good too!"

Meanwhile, Shen Qiao and Bian Yanmei were on their way up the mountain, and when the disciples on sentry duty saw him, they all had the same reactions as Le An and Yun Chang—as if they'd seen a ghost in broad daylight. At first, they were tongue-tied, their expressions panicked, and most of them could only helplessly watch as the pair ascended the mountain, without daring to stop them. However, there were still a small number of people who came to block Shen Qiao's path. One such disciple said bluntly, "You outcast disciple of Xuandu Mountain, how dare you barge your way onto the mountain!"

Shen Qiao recognized him—he was one of Elder Liu Yue's registered disciples. "Lou Liang, several years have already passed, and you're still here on sentry duty?"

He spoke this sentence gently, as if it were a normal greeting. However, it managed to poke right into Luo Liang's sore spot, and his face immediately flushed red out of either shame or anger. "You, you... Shen Qiao, you disrespectful madman! There's no place for you on Xuandu Mountain anymore!"

Shen Qiao smiled slightly. "You're right. To rush up the mountain like this would appear a bit too rude. No matter what, we should have a guide to lead us there. I think you're quite suitable."

So saying, he reached out and placed his hand on Lou Liang's shoulder.

Lou Liang had clearly seen that it wasn't a fast movement, with no fancy tricks to it whatsoever, but all the same, he found himself unable to react in time and was seized. A piercing pain came from his shoulder, and he was unable to struggle free at all. His expression immediately transformed into one of terror.

Ever since Xuandu Mountain had reopened its gates, the arrival of news was no longer as delayed or obstructed as before. The disciples had caught wind of Shen Qiao's actions outside from time to time, but hearing about something couldn't compare to seeing it in person. Even if they'd heard a hundred rumors about how powerful Shen Qiao had become, seeing it with their own eyes was something else.

Lou Liang was no fool either. He immediately realized that he was a raft who'd delivered himself up and quickly conceded. "Shen-shishu, please spare me. This disciple is acting under orders to keep watch, to forbid anyone from going up the mountain. It wasn't to disrespect Shen-shishu!"

Shen Qiao's eyebrows rose a little, and he said, "Everyone is forbidden from going up the mountain? But what happened, up on the mountain?"

Lou Liang shared everything he knew, not daring to hide anything. "Yes, the elders are holding a conference on the mountain to discuss the candidates for the sect leader's position."

"Have all the elders gathered?"

"Only Elder Kong is in seclusion, so he is absent."

The Elder Kong he spoke of was Le An and Yun Chang's master.

With their master this fearful, it was no wonder his disciples were the same. Bian Yanmei was watching dispassionately from the sidelines, but these scornful thoughts filled his heart.

Meanwhile, Shen Qiao was thinking that the negative consequences resulting from Xuandu Mountain's multiple generations of isolation were finally emerging one by one. With the sect's gates closed for so long, people's hearts had closed as well. If there were ambitious people like Yu Ai, there would naturally also be those like Elder Kong who'd grown timid with the closure, believing that it was best to avoid trouble whenever possible and that the wise should play it safe.

"Perfect timing," said Shen Qiao. "I should go up and listen myself."

Lou Liang hurriedly said, "I'll guide Shishu there!"

In fact, even if he didn't guide Shen Qiao, he had to. It was such a slender hand, fair as snow, yet it gripped his shoulder like a pair of iron pliers. Lou Liang was in terrible pain, but he didn't dare to show a hint of it. He quickened his pace and even judiciously explained the situation on the mountain to Shen Qiao.

Seeing Lou Liang so wretched, the other disciples dared not come forward and block him. They all moved to either side of the road, letting Shen Qiao's party of three continue upward.

It wasn't only because they'd been intimidated by Shen Qiao's martial prowess. Back then, when Shen Qiao had still been sect leader, he'd treated all the disciples incredibly well and been fair in meting out rewards and punishments in public, all while never putting on any airs in private. Many disciples admired and respected him deeply. But after the battle at Banbu Peak, Yu Ai had joined with the sect's elders and forcibly taken over the position of leader, which caught everyone off guard. Though many disciples were too afraid to offend their seniors, it didn't stop them from having their own thoughts on the matter. Now, upon seeing Shen Qiao return, quite a few of their gazes even showed expressions of joy.

Lou Liang took in those gazes and made his own judgment. He whispered to Shen Qiao, "Shen-shishu, this disciple knows that you came back to seek justice. My shifu has always been loyal to Xuandu Mountain—it was only because he was dissatisfied with Elder Tan's insistence on being acting sect leader, despite his mediocre abilities, that he opposed him so fiercely. If this disciple may be so bold, he asks your esteemed self to be gracious and show his shifu magnanimity. Don't be too hard on him, please?"

Though this person was impudent and rash, he still had a bit of conscience. Shen Qiao smiled slightly. "What if I wish to be hard on him?"

Lou Liang was at a loss for words. He'd been at Xuandu Mountain for so many years yet remained a registered disciple. This was not only due to his aptitude being mediocre, it was also because his shifu Liu Yue was someone who judged people based on their looks, rejecting all potential disciples who were too unattractive. As Lou Liang was only average in appearance, he naturally had no luck here. But because he was already a registered disciple under Liu Yue, he couldn't apprentice under any of the other elders. His level of dejection over this needed no elaboration. He thought to himself that, since he'd said those words, he could claim that he'd already done his best. After all, he couldn't control what Shen-shishu chose to do.

With Lou Liang leading the way, Shen Qiao and Bian Yanmei met no further obstructions. Some disciples had only joined the sect after the battle at Banbu Peak, so they didn't recognize Shen Qiao. When they saw Lou Liang, they even greeted him and asked, "Lou-shixiong, didn't we have orders from above that unrelated persons are forbidden from going up the mountain?"

Lou Liang's expression was solemn. "Who said he's an unrelated person? This is our sect's Shen-shishu. He has come back to attend the conference!"

Stunned by his bluff, the disciples let them pass without much trouble, which also saved Shen Qiao the trouble of taking action again.

Considering this, Lou Liang was still quite useful.

As they watched Lou Liang's group leave, the disciple who'd just blocked their way turned to his companion in confusion. "I don't think we have a shishu with the surname Shen?"

His companion racked his brains—then realization struck him. "Surname Shen... Could it be...Shen Qiao?!"

As understanding dawned on them both, they instantly looked at each other in shock. But by now, Shen Qiao's group was already far away. There was no time to stop them.

Shen Qiao and Lou Liang walked until they neared the entrance of the Sanqing Hall. As they approached, they heard a shout from inside: "Tan Yuanchun! Before you temporarily took on the position of acting sect leader after Sect Leader Yu, we needed someone to take care of the sect's mundane affairs. That's why we had no objections. But the acting sect leader is different from an actual sect leader. You aren't the strongest martial artist in the sect, nor do you have any sort of reputation within the jianghu. So why should you take the sect leader's position?"

Lou Liang looked embarrassed, for this voice belonged to his shifu, Liu Yue.

As today's discussion was an incredibly important one, everyone present was an elder of Xuandu Mountain. Hence, they didn't assign any disciples to keep watch outside the doors. The three of them approached, but no one noticed for now.

In contrast to Liu Yue, the person who answered him used a much calmer tone, mild and steady. It didn't seem like he'd been angered. "Elder Liu, if you have something to say, please say it properly. Aren't we all currently having a discussion? It's true that I'm untalented, and my aptitude is also the shallowest among the elders. But I understand that everyone recommended me not because I was the strongest but because I've already been managing our general affairs year in and year out, so I'm more familiar with them. Ultimately, it doesn't matter who the leader is. What's important is that they can contribute to Xuandu Mountain. Don't you agree?"

Liu Yue sneered. "So according to you, it doesn't matter whether the sect leader's strong, as long as they're familiar with handling the sect's general affairs? Then what about my registered disciple Lou Liang, who deals with mundane affairs every day? Wouldn't he be even more suitable for the position?"

When he said this, not only did Lou Liang long to hide himself in shame, Shen Qiao also frowned slightly.

"Tan-shidi, one ought to have some self-awareness as a person," Liu Yue went on. "Why did Perfected Master Qi forgo making you, his eldest disciple, the sect leader, when by all rights you should've been? Why did he favor Sect Leader Shen instead? Wasn't it precisely due to your mediocre aptitude? If you're the only choice, I'd rather invite Shen-shidi back. I heard that Shen-shidi has made great martial advancements, that he's no longer how he was in the past. He's also served as sect leader before, so no matter the situation, he'd still be more suitable than you, right?"

Hearing this, Shen Qiao no longer remained silent and walked in. "I'm deeply grateful for Elder Liu's favor."

No one had expected Shen Qiao to silently appear outside, then silently walk inside as well. An eerie silence descended within the main hall.

After a moment, Tan Yuanchun stood up and welcomed him, an expression of surprised joy on his face. "Er-shidi, when did you return?!"

Shen Qiao said, "I ascended the mountain just now and heard that everyone was discussing the sect leader's position, so I came over. I trust that I didn't interrupt anything?"

Embarrassment washed over everyone's face.

After Shen Qiao had fallen from the cliff, Yu Ai stole the position of sect leader. If one thought about it, he'd had no right to do so. However, he'd joined forces with the sect elders and forcefully taken over, and everyone found themselves unable to object. Of course, everyone had their own thoughts on the matter, but in truth, Shen Qiao was still a member of Xuandu's Violet Palace. With Yu Ai now missing and Shen Qiao's return, no one else was qualified to contend with him for the sect leader's seat.

Not to mention, Qi Fengge's Shanhe Tongbei was still on his back!

Liu Yue stole in before the others and reacted first. "Since Shen-shidi has returned, all is well. Now that Yu Ai has vanished, Xuandu Mountain is without a leader, and we are hoping for someone to take the reins. Now that you're back, we've finally found our pillar!"

Tan Yuanchun also smiled. "That's right, A-Qiao. Everything is well now that you've returned. Would you like to rest a bit before speaking?"

Shen Qiao met his concerned gaze and politely declined: "Thank you very much, Da-shixiong. We've already rested at the foot of the mountain. I heard that something happened to Yu Ai?"

"Yes, Yu-shidi suddenly disappeared a few days ago. He was fine the previous night, but come the next day, he suddenly vanished without a trace. We searched the entirety of Xuandu Mountain, but he was nowhere to be found."

He paused then, and his gaze slid to Bian Yanmei behind Shen Qiao. "Who is this?"

Shen Qiao did not conceal any intention. "This is the disciple of Huanyue Sect Leader Yan, Bian Yanmei-daoyou."

As soon as this remark was made, all present looked at Bian Yanmei, who did not show any embarrassment or awkwardness but instead allowed others to assess him in a grand manner.

Tan Yuanchun was first surprised, then deeply distressed. "That day on the mountain, Sect Leader Yan took you away. Da-shixiong was unable to stop him in time because he was too useless. But I didn't expect that you'd still be consorting with demonic practitioners!"

Shen Qiao remained calm. "Shixiong speaks too seriously. Shen Qiao can't bear the burden of the word 'consorting.' Shixiong saw with his own eyes that day—I was almost captured by Yu Ai, but Sect Leader Yan fortunately saved me. And yet you didn't come looking for me afterward?"

Tan Yuanchun sighed slightly. "A-Qiao, don't be angry with your Da-shixiong. At that time, Xuandu Mountain was under Yu Ai's control. Where would I get the ability to mobilize disciples to look for you?"

Shen Qiao said calmly, "If even Yuan Ying and Hengbo could throw everything away in order to leave the mountain and look for me, I suppose I thought too highly of Da-shixiong."

"A-Qiao, I understand that you still have anger within you..."

"Da-shixiong." Shen Qiao interrupted him. "Everyone knows you've always been a good person who's kind to anyone. That's why each and every one of us martial siblings love you very much. But being a good person doesn't mean you should have no uncrossable lines when it comes to your principles. You were deceived by Yu Ai and were forced against your will. I don't blame you for this. But that day, I said that Yu Ai had poisoned me right in front of you. Even if you didn't believe me, shouldn't you have investigated it afterward? Yet the ones who didn't hear about it with their own ears, Yuan Ying and Hengbo, believed me. The two of us have just reunited after a long separation, but instead of inquiring about this matter, you used Huanyue Sect to challenge my character and conduct. That really disappoints me!"

Tan Yuanchun's expression finally shifted. "What do you mean by this?"

At this moment, the disciples on sentry duty barged in while panicking, blood staining their clothing. "Elders, this is bad! Hehuan Sect have stormed into the mountain, and there...there are also Göktürks!"

Enemies Meet

EVERYONE'S EXPRESSIONS fell at this news, and Elder Lian Shan said, "A while ago, the Göktürks came up the mountain, saying that they hoped Xuandu Mountain would form an alliance with the Turks, but then Sect Leader..." He'd thoughtlessly been about to say "Sect Leader Yu," but then he glanced at Shen Qiao and changed his words. "But then Yu-shidi rejected them. I trust that they're unhappy with this, so this time they allied with Hehuan Sect and came up the mountain looking for trouble! They're hoping to take advantage of our leaderless situation!"

"The Göktürks were unable to take control of the Central Plains," said Shen Qiao. "Since they're separated from Xuandu Mountain by the Zhou Kingdom, if they can't manage to control Xuandu Mountain directly, their only option is to cooperate with Hehuan Sect."

Liu Yue didn't wait for Tan Yuanchun to speak but took the opportunity to say, "So in Shen-shidi's opinion, how should we respond?"

"We'll wait and see what they do, then respond accordingly."

His answer was rather cursory, but the others couldn't maintain the same matter-of-fact placidity.

"They've already fought their way up the mountain—it's obvious they haven't come in good faith. If we cower here, our disciples outside will suffer for it. At this time, we should take responsibility and face the enemy head-on."

Naturally, no one objected to Shen Qiao's words. They were arguing because it was Xuandu Mountain's own internal affairs, but now that there were outside enemies invading them, they needed to unite against these foreign forces.

Shen Qiao had no intention of squabbling over such details, so he followed the others and walked out.

At this moment, the party in question had just finished coming up the mountain, fierce and majestic. They came face-to-face with Tan Yuanchun's group, who'd come to receive them outside Sanqing Hall.

Xiao Se was in the front, and he laughed brightly. "We've troubled all of Xuandu Mountain's elders in welcoming us! You're much too courteous!"

Liu Yue sneered. "You hurt our disciples and barged your way up the mountain. How dare you speak so shamelessly!"

With a fiery passion, he instantly drew his sword, prepared to go up and fight.

Xiao Se took a half step back and used his fan to shield himself. "You're only a mediocre martial artist; you're no match for my shizun. Why are you in such a hurry to humiliate yourself? I heard that Xuandu Mountain's Sect Leader Yu has disappeared for some reason, so now your honored sect has no leader. Looks like it was true, otherwise why would everything be such a mess?"

Tan Yuanchun frowned. "You need not trouble yourselves over our sect's internal affairs. Xuandu Mountain has declined all guests today, yet you still came uninvited. Such uncouth manners!"

"This distinguished master looks a little unfamiliar," said Xiao Se, smiling. "Which elder are you?"

"Tan Yuanchun."

Xiao Se raised his eyebrow. "I heard that Qi Fengge had an eldest disciple, and though he apprenticed early, there was nothing outstanding about him. So when Qi Fengge was on his deathbed and choosing the disciple to inherit his mantle, he skipped right over his eldest disciple and picked his second disciple Shen Qiao instead. Is that true?"

He'd clearly seen that Shen Qiao was present but had deliberately said these things to provoke. But Shen Qiao's attention was not on Xiao Se—he was looking at Sang Jingxing and Duan Wenyang.

Many people had come up Xuandu Mountain. However, compared to the contingent who'd come to the Sword Trial Conference, this current Hehuan group was smaller. Shen Qiao noticed that Yuan Xiuxiu was not among them, and the faces of several disciples of Hehuan Sect had also disappeared—Shen Qiao may not have known their names, but he had some impression of them still.

When Shen Qiao swept his gaze over Bai Rong, she even winked at him and smiled.

He looked away uneasily.

Bian Yanmei leaned in and whispered, "Everyone in Hehuan Sect, man or woman, is utterly ruthless, capable of consuming even the bones of those they destroy. They love men with abundant primordial Yang, like Daoist Master Shen, the most. You must control yourself with them!"

Shen Qiao was caught between laughing and crying. "I find Bai Rong to be all right."

Not to mention that he had no such intentions in the slightest.

Bian Yanmei didn't know what was going on inside his mind—he really was afraid that Shen Qiao might fall into her trap. "She might look all pure and innocent to Daoist Master Shen," Bian Yanmei tried to remind him, "but in truth, who knows how many young men she's pair cultivated with. I heard that even Sang Jingxing was once an intimate confidante of hers."

In truth, Shen Qiao had already known about this matter. Hearing it again, he couldn't help but sigh. "In this world, everyone would love to live and act without scruples, but there are always certain things that will stop them from doing so. No matter how vicious a person is, as long as they possess a little goodness, I don't want to deny that goodness because of their evil."

He always remembered how Bai Rong had immediately shown him mercy and given him reminders when he'd been in desperate situations. Though she wouldn't go out of the way to help him out of his crises, neither did she pursue and attack him when he was in trouble, even when carrying out important duties for her sect. For this, Shen Qiao felt that he should remember this small share of kindness.

Bian Yanmei had long known that Shen Qiao was a kind person, but he didn't expect that he'd also have such a special view of Bai Rong. He said under his breath, "With how softhearted you are, no wonder Shizun has you wrapped around his little finger."

They spoke in low voices for a few moments. Meanwhile, Xuandu Mountain and Hehuan Sect were about to turn their weapons on each other with the next disagreement. But it wasn't just Hehuan Sect's party in attendance—Duan Wenyang and a couple of unfamiliar Göktürks were there as well. And Xuandu Mountain was missing a leader, leaving their minds scattered. They were filled with apprehension, thinking that their chances of victory weren't high, so they didn't dare strike first.

The other party had clearly noticed this as well. Duan Wenyang smiled. "We heard that your sect is going to choose a leader today, so we came up to watch the fun. However, since the hearts of your honored sect are divided, I fear it'll be hard for you to reach a consensus. Why don't we help you decide?"

Tan Yuanchun resolutely declined. "We won't trouble outsiders to make decisions about the affairs within Xuandu Mountain! Please leave quickly, otherwise you can't blame us for being impolite!"

As soon as he said this, Liu Yue rebuked him. "Who knows how many of our disciples they injured on their way here? How can we let them go so easily?"

Duan Wenyang gave a laugh. "You're unwilling to let us go so easily, but what can you do about it?"

"Naturally, you can leave after leaving your lives behind!" This sentence wasn't spoken by anyone present at the scene. The voice was dull and hoarse. Though the speaker had used all his strength, his volume wasn't loud either. If the people present hadn't been martial artists, they probably wouldn't have heard it at all.

The crowd followed the sound and couldn't help their shock.

A person hobbled out from behind Sanqing Hall, his steps heavy, as if he were suffering from internal injuries, and his legs were wounded as well. He limped as he walked, his clothes were spotted with bloodstains, and numerous gashes covered his face. He was in a wretched state.

But no one on Xuandu Mountain would fail to recognize him.

"Yu Ai?!"

The new arrival was indeed Yu Ai.

He clutched a bamboo staff. Using it as a crutch, he walked toward the crowd, step by step.

Duan Wenyang's face also showed surprise. "I heard that Sect Leader Yu had mysteriously disappeared a few days ago. It seems that the rumors were false!"

Yu Ai looked at him coldly. "I'm sure you're devastated that I'm not dead, aren't you?"

Duan Wenyang chuckled and said, "What does this have to do with me? I heard that the moment you died, your Xuandu Mountain started squabbling over the position of sect leader. Sect Leader Yu should suspect your martial siblings first!"

Tan Yuanchun's voice was full of concern. "Yu-shidi, you're still injured. Hurry, go bandage yourself and rest for a bit first!"

Yu Ai sent him a glance. "I was wrong," he said.

Everyone was stunned by his seemingly random words.

"Wrong about what?" asked Tan Yuanchun.

"I was determined to build a lasting foundation for Xuandu Mountain," said Yu Ai coolly. "I thought that the last few generations of our forefathers were too stubborn, unwilling to open their eyes to look at the world outside. Therefore, I took great pains in plotting against Shen-shixiong, in working together with the Göktürks. I thought that Xuandu Mountain would be able to re-establish its position as the world's foremost sect under my leadership. But I didn't expect that I'd be wrong from the very beginning—working with the Göktürks is like asking a tiger for its skin. I refused to be their puppet or present them Xuandu Mountain on a platter, so they reacted with treachery, wanting to drive me out of the sect leader's position so they could support another person in becoming their puppet instead. Then they could use this to seize the foundations of Xuandu Mountain's centuries-old legacy."

Tan Yuanchun was stunned. "You're saying that your disappearance was related to the Göktürks?"

"I'd entered seclusion that night when someone mimicked Shen-shixiong's handwriting and sent me a carrier pigeon," Yu Ai said coldly. "They said they were waiting for me in the backyard.

But when I got there, I was ambushed by three mysterious people—they all covered their faces, wore black clothes, and were excellent martial artists. I was no match for them and was severely injured, and then I fell tens of thousands of yards from the cliff. Fortunately, a tree branch broke my fall, and I was able to survive and return to the world today. It seems that heaven took pity on me, allowing me to return to testify against the culprits!"

Liu Yue frowned. "So you're saying that someone impersonated Shen-shidi and sent you a letter?"

Shocked, Tan Yuanchun pressed his questions. "Who were those three mysterious people?"

Yu Ai shook his head. "I don't know. They never showed their faces even once, but I know that Er-shixiong was definitely not among them."

Shen Qiao said coolly, "Someone mimicked my handwriting and sent you a letter, and you immediately believed it. That alone is proof of your guilty conscience."

"Er-shixiong is correct," said Yu Ai with a wry smile. "Even to this day, everything I've done has been fruitless, yet I hurt you, caused you to…"

He grew so agitated he had to stop speaking. A moment passed before he managed to forcibly regain his composure. "I caused you to suffer so much misery. I'm sorry; it's all my fault."

If apologies could change anything, would people no longer need to take responsibility for their crimes? Shen Qiao was not moved by the phrase "I'm sorry."

"Your distinguished self speaks too seriously."

Was he unwilling to say even a single "shidi"? Yu Ai's face darkened, and he smiled bitterly, "This is also my retribution."

"Yu-shidi, a dire enemy currently stands before us. Can we leave your matters aside for a bit?"

"No! Because the reason I was schemed against is related to the Göktürks!" Yu Ai took a deep breath and turned to Duan Wenyang. "A few days ago, I'd just rejected your proposal and refused to be a puppet for the Göktürks. Then I encountered an assassination attempt. Not even a fool would believe that you had nothing to do with it!"

Duan Wenyang smiled. "Sect Leader Yu Ai, you must not accuse people unjustly. I'm not from your Xuandu Mountain. How would I be able to sneak in here without anyone the wiser? At the very least, wouldn't I have to injure a couple of disciples?"

Shen Qiao suddenly answered, "If there's a spy within Xuandu Mountain coordinating with you, you'd naturally be able to deceive everyone."

Upon hearing this, Liu Yue, Tan Yuanchun, and the others couldn't help but be stunned. "What does Shen-shidi mean by this?"

"Yuan Ying told me that the Göktürks were unable to coerce nor bribe Yu Ai," said Shen Qiao calmly, "so they turned to inciting others. The Göktürks told Yuan Ying that if he obeyed them without question, they would help him become the sect leader. Since he didn't agree, of course they'd look for someone else. There will always be someone who cannot resist the temptation."

Yu Ai coughed a few times and covered his chest, saying, "That's right. First, I was ambushed, and now, while the position of the leader is vacant, you all come up the mountain. How could you have known unless someone tipped you off? It proves that today's events were premeditated!"

Duan Wenyang and company choosing to head up the mountain at this time was naturally not just for the sake of verbally taunting Xuandu Mountain. Yu Ai's appearance was unexpected, but his survival couldn't affect much. On the contrary, it was Shen Qiao's presence that was more troublesome.

Duan Wenyang made up his mind and exchanged a glance with Sang Jingxing. He laughed. "Since Sect Leader Yu has said so, if I don't play the villain, I'd be betraying your trust!"

With a slight wave of his hand, several of the Göktürks behind him all followed his order—they each brandished their sabers and leapt toward Liu Yue, Tan Yuanchun, and the others, dragging them into battle.

The martial prowess of the elders varied, but even those with unexceptional aptitude like Tan Yuanchun were only so when compared with Qi Fengge's other disciples. They weren't so mediocre that anyone could walk all over them. However, the Göktürks who'd followed Duan Wenyang up the mountain were naturally not pushovers either. Both sides immediately became embroiled in a back-and-forth scuffle. Blades danced and flashed, making for a hectic scene.

Duan Wenyang watched the battle with his arms behind his back. He didn't participate and instead smiled brightly. "These people were all personally trained by my master and can be considered the Göktürks' most powerful warriors," he said. "They have long heard of the formidable skills of Xuandu Mountain's Daoist masters. Today, they have the chance to seek martial guidance—I ask that the Daoist masters not hold back!"

Liu Yue and the others were busy dealing with those people; how could anyone spare the attention to answer him?

Lou Liang saw Duan Wenyang's gaze sweep over him, and his heart chilled. He was terrified that the other party would turn his attention to an insignificant little disciple like him, and he couldn't help but hide behind Shen Qiao.

Liu Yue swung his sword and pushed the Göktürk man engaged with him back a few steps, then exclaimed loudly, "Shen-shidi, many on Xuandu Mountain have greatly wronged you in the past, but when Yu Ai declared you an outcast disciple that day, I also spoke up for you. Please, for Perfected Master Qi's sake, help us defend Xuandu Mountain! Don't give any advantages to these scumbags!"

Duan Wenyang sputtered a laugh. "I truly feel aggrieved on your behalf, Daoist Master Shen! While you were downtrodden, they didn't lend you a hand. Today they're met with trouble, and they want you to repay their enmity with kindness. If you don't nurse any grievances, I will nurse them for you! I say, you shouldn't bother with this matter. Once they all die, the position of sect leader will naturally become yours again. How about it?"

"No," Shen Qiao said calmly, "Yu Ai proclaimed himself the leader, but I didn't agree. He expelled me from Xuandu Mountain, but I am still Qi Fengge's disciple."

He drew Shanhe Tongbei from his back. Beneath the dazzling light, its blade sparkled with a rippling luster, and there came the faint sounds of howling winds and rumbling thunder.

"With me around, no one is allowed to have designs on Xuandu Mountain." His tone was even, without any kind of earthshaking power or intimidation, yet no one could dare to take his words lightly.

"Shen-shidi, allow me to give you a hand!"

Accompanying that shout, three figures swept over from another direction, one in front and two behind. The first was Elder Kong Zheng, and he was followed by his two disciples—the martial siblings Le An and Yun Chang, whom Shen Qiao had encountered at the foot of the mountain.

Those two had followed Shen Qiao from afar. At first, they'd only wanted to watch, but they didn't expect to encounter members of the Göktürks and Hehuan Sect ascending the mountain to look for trouble. They didn't dare to intervene in internal conflicts, but an invasion from foreign enemies was another matter. The two immediately went to find their master Kong Zeng, Elder Kong, then rushed back, following Elder Kong's lead.

Kong Zeng came to Shen Qiao and cupped his hands. "Kong Zeng is late. He asks for Sect Leader Shen to punish him."

Shen Qiao nodded and said, "Elder Kong was halfway through his seclusion and at a crucial moment. It's already fortunate that you were able to come. What punishment is there to give?"

It was unclear if he'd noticed the address of "Sect Leader," but Shen Qiao hadn't denied it.

Kong Zeng's face flushed red, as his seclusion was just a pretext. In truth, he'd simply been unwilling to participate in selecting their next sect leader.

He didn't know if Shen Qiao had already seen through this, so he could only clumsily gloss over it. "When faced with such a dire enemy, how can we afford to care only about ourselves? I'm enough to handle such petty riffraff. The sect leader need not trouble himself with them!"

Duan Wenyang stood with his hands behind his back. He obviously wasn't taking Kong Zeng seriously. "I'm afraid you're no match for me."

Kong Zeng sneered and said, "What use is your smack-talk? We'll only know after we try!"

So saying, he raised his sword and slashed at Duan Wenyang.

With this opening strike, Hehuan Sect and the others naturally couldn't just watch from the sidelines. With the sole exception of Sang Jingxing, everyone jumped in, and fighting broke out all around at once.

Le An and Yun Chang naturally joined the fight to help their shifu, but unfortunately, they were young and their martial arts unpolished. It was difficult for them to contend with Xiao Se and Bai Rong, and they quickly found themselves at a disadvantage, being countered at every turn.

As Yun Chang's sword technique revealed openings, Xiao Se crooked his fingers and reached through the wind from Yun Chang's sword, grabbing at his neck. The movement was as swift as lightning, leaving Yun Chang no time to react before his throat was seized. If Xiao Se squeezed just a little tighter, he would die on the spot!

This had happened in an instant. Even Yun Chang couldn't put up any resistance, let alone Le An next to him.

Just as Yun Chang thought his death was imminent, he heard someone chuckle next to him. "Xiao Se, you're also a person of repute. Why are you picking on the weak?"

At these words, Yun Chang suddenly felt the grip around his neck loosen, followed by the lingering terror that came with escaping certain death.

Bian Yanmei's palm strike meant that Xiao Se had to toss aside Yun Chang to fight him. His fan blocked the palm blast, then he poured his internal energy into it and swept back at him. Their robes and sleeves tossed and flapped, and in an instant, they'd exchanged dozens of blows.

"And I thought Yan Wushi's eldest disciple would be someone incredible! Turns out you're nothing special!" Xiao Se sneered. "Seems to me you're not that much stronger than Yu Shengyan!"

In front of Sanqing Hall, the fighters clashed in close quarters, their murderous intent overflowing. In an instant, everything had fallen into chaos.

Yet Shen Qiao didn't move.

Because another person had yet to move as well—Sang Jingxing.

Previously, at the Sword Trial Conference, first Yuan Xiuxiu had intervened, and then Hulugu had appeared, so Shen Qiao ultimately failed to fight Sang Jingxing.

But Sang Jingxing had also seen the changes within Shen Qiao as a result.

He was no longer the same. This was no longer the blind man who could only resign himself to the mercy of others.

He was far more handsome than ever before, yet, unfortunately, he'd turned into a thorny flower, something that couldn't be devoured so easily.

The regret that he hadn't been able to obtain Shen Qiao that day lingered unceasingly in Sang Jingxing's heart. Furthermore, he'd suffered severe injuries at Shen Qiao's hands, and new grudges combined with old hatred—he'd never let Shen Qiao off so easily. He also knew that, since he'd tormented Shen Qiao into destroying his martial arts, Shen Qiao would not let the matter rest either.

"Shen Qiao," he suddenly said with a smile. "When I see you, I feel that it's such a pity."

Shen Qiao looked at him silently. He didn't ask Sang Jingxing what he meant.

"The pity lies in how I wasn't the one who picked you up beneath Banbu Peak," said Sang Jingxing. "If I had, would Yan Wushi be at the top?"

This kind of beauty, this kind of a talent—he was meant for Hehuan Sect from birth. He should have spent his days behind the bed curtains, as a vessel for cultivating others' martial arts.

Shen Qiao was neither surprised nor angry but asked an irrelevant question: "Where is Sect Leader Yuan? After our previous farewell, I miss her deeply."

Sang Jingxing smiled slightly. "I forgot to tell you that the leader of Hehuan Sect has changed. If you are willing to visit Hehuan Sect, I may take you to see where her corpse is submerged."

Shen Qiao raised an eyebrow. "You killed her?"

"Surprised?"

Shen Qiao slowly shook his head. "I've long heard about the discord between the two of you," he said, "but Sect Leader Yuan doesn't seem like someone who'd just wait to be killed."

"She did indeed have a couple of petty tricks up her sleeve. If not for that, I wouldn't have waited so long to kill her."

"What a pity."

"Did you like her?"

"Though Sect Leader Yuan was a woman, she still conducted herself as befitting a sect leader. If you were to become the leader instead, I fear that after today, Hehuan Sect will need to find someone else to swear allegiance to."

Sang Jingxing laughed as he was seized with anger. "What do you mean?"

"I'm going to kill you. That's what I mean."

At these words, Shen Qiao sprang into action.

His wrist moved, ever-so-slightly, and his figure transformed into a phantasm. Swathed within the sword glare's innumerable rays, his silhouette faded until it almost vanished.

The body moves with the will, the sword moves with the heart, the mountains and rivers grieve as one, and the world fades into gray!

Repay With a Life

FACED WITH SHEN QIAO's boundless sword glare, Sang Jingxing naturally wasn't waiting for it to kill him, but what looked like an indestructible sword screen in the eyes of onlookers wasn't all that terrifying to him.

Shen Qiao's opponent was, after all, a martial arts grandmaster.

Sang Jingxing moved, swift as a shooting star. His robes billowed upward, and his entire person seemed to ride the winds as he soared into the air like an immortal ascending beneath the sun. In a split second, he was suspended in midair; there, he sent a palm strike at Shen Qiao, who was behind the interwoven sword screen.

The wind from Sang Jingxing's palm slammed into the sword glare. All at once, it was like the star-studded reflection upon a lake had been shattered: after a frozen moment, the sword glare began to tremble before fragmenting into shards. Sang Jingxing's palm blast had managed to punch a hole right through it!

Sang Jingxing hovered in midair with nothing beneath his feet, but in the eyes of onlookers, there seemed to be invisible stones there, allowing him to jump upward, step by step.

He'd always been a tall man, but now, soaring into the sky against the wind with his robes rustling and Carved Dragon Palms having reached the zenith of perfection, he resembled a dragon flying high in the sky. A dragon whose mighty roar was powerful enough to conquer all creation, frightfully imposing, as if it wished to charge right into the nine heavens.

Though the entire venue had been engulfed by the melee, there were still some Xuandu Mountain disciples unable to intervene due to being mediocre martial artists. They could only watch and give encouragement from the sides, holding their swords. When they saw how powerful Sang Jingxing was, their hearts immediately leapt into their throats. They watched helplessly as this giant dragon formed by the condensing true qi roared down toward Shen Qiao, controlled by Sang Jingxing.

In comparison, Shen Qiao looked somewhat feeble and weak.

"What sorts of demonic techniques is Sang Jingxing using?" one disciple couldn't help blurting out. "How can he walk in midair?"

Lou Liang looked up and watched, his mouth agape. But at the same time, seeing the sheer gulf between them, a sense of inferiority and shame welled up within his heart.

How many months and years would he have to train to obtain martial arts like Sang Jingxing's? Actually, he didn't need to be like Sang Jinxing—if he had even one-twelfth of that man's strength, he'd be more than satisfied!

But with the other party this powerful, would Shen-shishu be able to deal with him?

At this moment, Bian Yanmei and Xiao Se were engaged in a fierce battle while Le An was up against Bai Rong. As a martial artist, Yun Chang was a bit weaker, which left him unable to intervene. He also didn't want to give his shixiong more trouble, so he could only watch from the side, ready to lend assistance whenever needed. In truth, though, Bai Rong was far more skilled than Le An, and even Le An could tell that the demoness in front of him was unwilling to use her full strength. She effortlessly darted around the wind from his sword, as if she were half toying with him. This frustrated Le An, but he was helpless to do anything, so he could only su   ss his anger and continue fighting.

When Yun Chang heard that question about Sang Jingxing,   e explained to the other disciple, "Unless he's an immortal, how ca someone just fly in thin air? Take a closer look, he's actually usin, his own movements as leverage. Each step he takes has him pushing off the insteps of his own feet. He uses that tiny bit of force to propel himself ever higher, but because Sang Jingxing's movements are too swift, it looks like he's treading on clouds and flying! My shifu once said that there's a footwork technique in Hehuan Sect called 'Sixteen Steps Between Heaven and Abyss' which can achieve this, but it invariably requires the coordination of profound internal energy."

Everyone stared intently and realized that it really was the case—but even if they'd understood the mystery, they'd be unable to develop such qinggong overnight. With their aptitude, even a lifetime's worth of energy might not be enough to achieve this. Just looking at this display of skill was enough for despair to well up within them.

But if Sang Jingxing was so formidable, could Shen-shishu really withstand him?

In an instant, many thoughts had already flashed through their minds, but to the two fighters, it was no more than the blink of an eye. The giant dragon roared silently, carrying with it the ferocious howling of winds. It was already before Shen Qiao, inches away. Even his robes and sleeves were swept up by the violent gale, and it seemed like he'd be blown away entirely.

Sang Jingxing's attack was overwhelming, blotting out both the sky and earth.

That sword glare, once so brilliant and dazzling, faded as the Carved Dragon Palm's true qi enshrouded it. Little by little, it slowly disappeared, as if it'd been finally engulfed and crushed. The entirety of the sword glare was now extinguished.

Was this...defeat?

Everyone watching the battle silently asked the same question.

Seeing the situation, all the disciples of Xuandu Mountain, such as Yun Chang and Lou Liang, felt an emptiness in their hearts, as well as the thought that perhaps Xuandu Mountain had no future. But other than this, they also felt that this was a matter of course. After all, Sang Jingxing's martial arts were so powerful, it was likely that no one present today could be his match.

However, right at that moment, the sword glare that had already disappeared suddenly revived and appeared anew. And it swelled and swelled, until it finally drew together into a single ray of light.

No, not a ray of light. It was a single sword glare!

The sword glare was there, but Shen Qiao had already disappeared from everyone's sight. An arc of white light pierced straight through the giant dragon's bloody maw, and the dragon Sang Jingxing had condensed through his qi completely disintegrated, scattering in all directions.

The internal energy barrier in front of Sang Jingxing, constructed through his own internal energy, also suffered a great impact, and his entire figure wavered in midair.

It only took an instant. A white arc suddenly appeared. The person was an illusion, yet the sword was real. None of the onlookers had gotten a clear view of how Shen Qiao moved; they only felt one thing: fast.

As fast as lightning, leaving no time to react!

As for Sang Jingxing, his martial prowess was far above that of the onlookers, and he was close to Shen Qiao, so naturally, he could see Shen Qiao's movements. However, just because he was able to see him clearly didn't mean that he was willing to confront him head-on. The sword's sharp edge sliced right through his attacks, and in an instant, Shen Qiao had turned the tables on him. Sang Jingxing chose to evade the blade's edge for now, and his body flew back.

He flew with incredible swiftness, retreating several yards in one breath. Sanqing Hall lay beneath him, and Sang Jingxing landed on the eaves. With an insubstantial tap of his foot, he immediately reversed directions and swept forward again, rushing toward Shen Qiao.

This time, he used the full might of his Carved Dragon Palm, telling himself that his previous probing had already plumbed his opponent's depths. This time, he had a clear idea of them, and he wouldn't hold back anymore.

Duels between martial arts masters were never won through clever tricks. Ultimately, only one's true strength could determine victory or defeat.

Sang Jingxing loved Shen Qiao's looks, and he'd had countless sexual fantasies of him before, imagining the moving scene of the man laying between the bed curtains. The more unobtainable Shen Qiao was, the more he coveted him. He was even a little jealous of Yan Wushi's fortune in love and sex.

But he also knew very well that even when Shen Qiao had been blind and without most of his skills, he'd still been able to stake his all on a move in order to take Sang Jingxing down with him. This indicated that Shen Qiao carried a ruthlessness within his bones, enough that he'd fight to the death in even the most desperate of situations.

This could not be underestimated.

So this time, Sang Jingxing poured in eight to nine-tenths of his martial strength; he wouldn't show even the slightest hint of leniency or tenderness.

Both sides were determined to win, swathed in murderous intent.

His palm blast roared, even stronger than before. It was like a storm raging upon the sea, the towering waves about to sweep away the very sky itself. This was the might of a Carved Dragon Palm that had been trained to its zenith: nine dragons condensed and surged forth from Sang Jingxing's roiling true qi, all rushing toward Shen Qiao from different directions.

The second arrived before the first wave had even subsided.

Everyone held their breath as they watched this scene. Even those who were fighting unconsciously slowed their movements.

When two tigers fought, one must fall. Shen Qiao and Sang Jingxing, these martial arts grandmasters, who would win and who would lose?

The ranking of the world's top ten experts had long reached Yun Chang, Lou Liang, and the others—they knew that Shen Qiao was in it, and with a rank even higher than Sang Jingxing's to boot. However, one believed what they saw, not what they heard. Before they could personally witness it themselves, they dared not fully trust it because the battle on Banbu Peak that year, and Shen Qiao's defeat, was still vivid in their minds—it had left a deep impression.

The scene of Shen Qiao being knocked off the cliff by Kunye left such a deep impression, in fact, that even though times had changed, many people who hadn't witnessed Shen Qiao's great rise from the bottom of the chasm, his step-by-step ascent, couldn't help but doubt Shen Qiao's strength in their hearts, questioning whether he could truly defeat Sang Jingxing.

The true qi surged toward Shen Qiao from all directions, from all places, like a raging tide, practically cutting off every avenue of retreat. Then, it gathered around Shen Qiao before crashing down over the top of his head. This palm strike condensed decades of Sang Jingxing's highest achievements in the Carved Dragon Palm. Any martial arts grandmaster, even Yan Wushi, couldn't afford to take it lightly or feign effortlessness.

Shen Qiao moved.

With a tap of his toes, he leapt off the ground.

His sword swept upward, like a fissure splitting a mountain in two.

In an instant, the mountain collapsed, the earth ruptured, and internal energy powerful enough to suspend oceans burst forth, pushing forward. Each wave was stronger than the next, and the two blasts of true qi met head-on, accompanied by the imperious power within the sword. A giant roar sounded, then Sang Jingxing coughed up a mouthful of fresh blood. Completely unable to withstand it, he collapsed, his body slammed down by the heavy force engulfing him from the front. He was involuntarily sent flying back and fell right off the roof of Sanqing Hall.

Just as he was about to touch the ground, he slapped his palm behind him. Once again, he leapt upward and flew toward Shen Qiao, then sent him three palm blasts in a row.

Shen Qiao was about to lift his sword to dissolve them, but at that moment, a faint, whistling noise suddenly came from behind him. Though slight, the sound had already reached his ears.

That small noise came with great speed, straight at the center of his back, without giving him any chance to evade. No matter how fast Shen Qiao could move, he was still a human being, not a god. At this time, he'd already put his entire mind into the battle with Sang Jingxing; he couldn't spare even a shred of attention to deal with anything else. His sword was already mid-strike; there was no time to dodge, let alone turn around mid-action to block the attack.

Three palms before him had arrived!

Each palm was stronger than the last, never any weaker than the previous. Shen Qiao now realized that though Sang Jingxing had vomited blood just now, his injuries weren't actually that serious—he'd only wanted to induce Shen Qiao into underestimating him and revealing an opening.

Behind him, the whistling noise was close at hand; it was impossible for him to escape. Shen Qiao secretly gritted his teeth and was forced to leave his entire back unguarded, his whole focus on dealing with the front.

Suddenly, a dark shadow rushed toward him, and it just happened to shield him from behind.

Shen Qiao only heard a muffled groan, followed by the sound of a body falling heavily to the ground. Then, shocked exclamations of "Yu-shishu!" sounded near his ears.

His heart sank, but he couldn't look back at all. He could only raise his sword to meet Sang Jingxing.

Beneath the mountains and rivers' shared grief, the winds and thunder resonated, and the sun and moon overlapped. The sword glare transformed into a thousand pinpoints of starlight, more brilliant than the stars themselves. These tiny specks, as if falling from the sky, descended into one's eyes, descended even into one's heart. However, within this kind of magnificent scene, impossible to describe through ink and brush, was a terrifying murderous intent that only those in the thick of battle could perceive.

When Sang Jingxing realized that all three of his palms had been dissolved by Shen Qiao, he turned and ran without a second thought. He possessed absolutely no resolve to value his reputation over his life. As long as he still lived, there would still be hope—as long as the forested mountain still stood, there'd be firewood to burn. Sang Jingxing had snatched the position of sect leader from Yuan Xiuxiu—he hadn't indulged in it enough yet. There were too many things he refused to abandon. It was impossible for him to be like Shen Qiao and fight to the death in a hopeless situation.

Hence, in terms of fighting spirit alone, he'd already lost.

As he turned and fled, the sword glare swept toward his back with the airiness of "A Rainbow Stretches across the Heavens." It pursued him relentlessly, drifting.

Many had practiced the sword their entire lives, but they'd never seen such agile swordplay that bordered on the supernatural. Everyone stared at it, frozen, their hearts shaken beyond all measure.

Sang Jingxing first felt a chill in the center of his back, followed by a sharp pain. He couldn't believe that his "Sixteen Steps between Heaven and Abyss" had lost to Shen Qiao's "A Rainbow Stretches across the Heavens." His initial chances of winning had already disappeared, and all that was left in his heart was fear. He quickened his steps, desperately trying to push all his decades of qinggong achievements to the utmost. His body moved so swiftly, he transformed into a wisp of light smoke and vanished right before everyone's eyes, leaving only a bloodstain on the ground.

Bai Rong had been watching their movements constantly. When she saw this, her lovely eyes flashed. "Shizun, what's wrong?!" she cried sweetly.

Then she abandoned Le An and chased after Sang Jingxing, running in the direction he'd fled.

Xiao Se secretly hated Bai Rong's cunning, and he hated himself even more for being a beat too slow. In a moment of carelessness, Bian Yanmei's palm slammed into his chest, and he coughed up blood while backing up several steps.

Meanwhile, rather than pursuing Sang Jingxing, Shen Qiao turned around.

Only now did he see that there was a silver awl stabbed into Yu Ai's chest. The awl's shaft was only as thick as a twig, but most of it was pierced inside him. Blood trickled from Yu Ai's mouth, and his face was ashen. The situation looked grave.

Shen Qiao took Yu Ai from Yun Chang's arms and poured true qi into his wrist, but his heart sank.

Yu Ai had already been injured before the assassination attempt. Climbing the mountain had also exhausted his strength, and now he'd even blocked this blow for Shen Qiao.

His pulse was weak, like a lone candle flickering in the wind or an arrow at the end of its flight. Even the Daluo Immortal would likely be incapable of reversing this.

But channeling true qi into him ultimately still had an effect. Yu Ai's body trembled slightly, and he slowly opened his eyes.

When he realized that the person holding him was Shen Qiao, he grabbed Shen Qiao's hand and said feebly, "Er-shixiong...A-Qiao..."

"I'm here." No matter how angry Shen Qiao had been, most of his anger had dissipated when Yu Ai shielded him from the sneak attack. At this moment, he felt only sorrow, and yet he consoled him. "Don't push yourself to speak. Rest properly. I will treat your wounds."

Yu Ai gently shook his head and struggled to speak. "Just now, the person who attacked you...was Tan...Tan Yuanchun!"

Shocked and furious, Shen Qiao looked around. Tan Yuanchun, who was supposed to be fighting the Göktürks, had already vanished completely. As for Duan Wenyang, he was being held up by two other elders and couldn't extricate himself to cause more trouble for Shen Qiao for the time being.

"Don't worry," Bian Yanmei told him. "Elder Liu already went to chase after him. I will go and look as well!" Then he turned to Yun Chang and Le An's shifu, Elder Kong Zeng. "I'll leave this to you, Elder Kong."

Kong Zeng had arrived late and didn't know who Bian Yanmei was, but, seeing that he was familiar with Shen Qiao, he of course didn't ignore him but quickly said, "Daoist friend, please rest assured. I am here!"

Tan Yuanchun had colluded with the Göktürks in a plot against Yu Ai. Though Shen Qiao hadn't expected this, he wasn't too shocked either. Those who harmed others would end up harmed in return; what goes around comes around. Yu Ai had plotted against him that day, so he should have expected that one day others would do the same to him.

But Shen Qiao hadn't expected that Yu Ai would step forward when he was facing a critical life-and-death situation, and even sacrifice his life for him.

"A-Qiao, do you still hate me?" Yu Ai asked.

"I don't know." Shen Qiao didn't want to deceive him. "Back when Shizun passed the position of sect leader to me, I couldn't have imagined that these events would happen after. If I could have foreseen them, I wouldn't have succeeded him as the leader."

"I...didn't expect them either." Yu Ai gave a bitter chuckle, then coughed a few times. More blood trickled from the corner of his mouth. "I used to think...that everything I did was right, that Shizun was too conservative, and that you were too useless. However, I later learned...that the one who was wrong...from beginning to end...was always...me!"

"Xuandu Mountain's doors have been closed for a long time," Shen Qiao said sternly. "We sealed off our eyes and ears and isolated ourselves from the rest of the world. It has reached a point where reform cannot be avoided. Before that, I was wholeheartedly determined to protect the legacy Shizun passed down to me, but I never thought about whether this method was appropriate for Xuandu Mountain. You were only wrong to cooperate with the Göktürks, and to poison me. Your love and concern for Xuandu Mountain, however, are things that even I can't match."

"But in the end," said Yu Ai, "I was still...the one who was wrong. I should've believed you...and I shouldn't have been greedy..."

He coughed fiercely, and blood gushed forth with even more vehemence. Alarmed, Shen Qiao tried to channel him more internal energy but found that his energy entering Yu Ai's body was like mud sinking into the great sea—it left no trace.

"So now...I'll use my life...to repay you. Don't hate me anymore... all right, A-Qiao?" Yu Ai no longer seemed aware, yet he continued holding Shen Qiao's hand.

Shen Qiao's tears plopped one by one onto the back of his hand, making Yu Ai tremble from the heat, but the man still smiled. "You're...crying for me... It means you don't hate me anymore...right?"

"I don't hate you anymore," said Shen Qiao. "Once you're better, let's go visit Shizun together."

The warm and gentle touch was nostalgic to Yu Ai, and his thoughts couldn't help drifting far away due to this sentence. "How I wish..." he coughed, "...to return to when we were young...

You could teach Yuan Ying and I...swordplay...on Shizun's behalf. Your face was always so stiff...but it was always very cute...no matter how I looked. I chased after you...wanting you to call...call me Shixiong. You were so annoyed by me...that you could only keep hiding from me...so I searched everywhere, searching and searching..."

His voice grew quieter and quieter, until it finally faded completely.

The hand grasping Shen Qiao's slowly released its grip, and just as its owner's life had slipped away, it soundlessly slid to the ground.

Punishment

SHEN QIAO REMAINED MOTIONLESS for a long time. In that instant, the clashing blades around him dwindled into silence. He held Yu Ai's body in his arms, his head hanging slightly, as it gradually grew cold. It was impossible to tell what he was thinking.

Perhaps he was recalling the past, many years ago: times when the martial siblings had slept, ate, and practiced the sword together on the mountain.

However, old dreams couldn't be recovered, and though some things remain, men change. The events of the past could never return. Just as some mistakes couldn't be repaired, some cracks could never be filled in, and when a person died, they couldn't be revived.

Yun Chang couldn't help but shed tears of sadness at the scene, but in the end, he was but a bystander. He remembered their current situation and quickly came to his senses. "Shen-shishu, Shen-shishu!" he hurriedly shouted.

Seeing Shen Qiao remain motionless, he thought that the other party had gone mad from grief, and he grew anxious despite himself.

A quick look was enough to see that Xuandu Mountain's situation hadn't improved very much. Although the greatest individual threat, Sang Jingxing, had fled, most of the members of Hehuan Sect remained. Xiao Se had been injured by Bian Yanmei, but not gravely so. Moreover, as Bian Yanmei and Liu Yue had gone to chase after Tan Yuanchun, two of Xuandu Mountain's seven elders were absent, leaving only five. They had to hold up Duan Wenyang while dealing with the experts he'd brought, as well as Xiao Se and the rest. It was quite a strenuous task.

Though Kong Zeng was an elder, he was still a level below Duan Wenyang in terms of martial arts. At this moment, he was being forced back by Duan Wenyang's aggressive attacks, unable to hold on. Even his sword almost slipped from his hand. His footwork went awry, and he stumbled twice before falling to the ground. As he had to watch out behind him, he left his front wide open. Duan Wenyang infused his flexible whip with true qi, and it instantly became as straight as a sword as it shot toward Kong Zeng's chest, ferocious and roiling with murderous intent.

If it struck Kong Zeng, he'd likely find a new, gaping hole in his chest.

Seeing this, Yun Chang panicked and quickly raised his sword to help. However, his speed couldn't keep up with his eyes, so it was impossible for him to make it in time. He was more than three of four breaths too slow—Duan Wenyang's whip had already touched Kong Zeng's clothes, about to rip into his flesh. Yun Chang involuntarily cried out, thinking that he was about to witness his shifu's death with his own eyes.

Right at this moment, a shadow flashed in front of Yun Chang. Yun Chang blinked, thinking he must have seen wrong, then realized that Duan Wenyang had already retracted his whip and there was another person beside Kong Zeng.

"Shen-shishu!" Yun Chang couldn't help but yell, his tone filled with surprise and an emotion that even he wasn't aware of.

"Move your Yu-shishu to the side," said Shen Qiao. "Swords are blind—don't let anyone harm the body." Shen Qiao didn't even look back as he said this but reached out to help Kong Zeng up, then swept toward Duan Wenyang.

As Shen Qiao had just dueled Sang Jingxing, Duan Wenyang thought that his strength would be sapped, his abilities far below his peak. But that wasn't the case—Shen Qiao's true qi seemed inexhaustible as it flowed into his sword without pause, then spilled forth as sword glares from his sword qi, seamless and flawless. Despite Duan Wenyang's skillful whip technique, he was left unable to attack, and thus completely powerless.

"Daoist Master Shen, if you have something to say, say it properly!" Duan Wenyang called out. "There's no need for us to swing our weapons! I'm not like Sang Jingxing. There's no deep grudge between us. Today, we only came due to Tan Yuanchun's invitation. Yu Ai's death was also entirely Tan Yuanchun's doing. All debts have their debtors; Daoist Master Shen must judge fairly!"

Duan Wenyang was different from his master. Though he possessed remarkable talent and had become the disciple Hulugu valued the most, his mixed heritage meant that he could never receive the reverence his shifu did in the Khaganate. Hence, his way of handling matters was also completely different from Hulugu's: he would always consider whether the concrete benefits outweighed the costs.

It was said that the relationship between master and disciple was like father and son, but even the most capable of fathers could have useless sons; likewise, a formidable master didn't guarantee a formidable disciple. Qi Fengge, for one, was a hero of his generation, but his disciples all had differing personalities and walked their own paths. Even if Qi Fengge came back to life, he wouldn't be able to force them all to live their lives according to his ideals.

If Hulugu had been here instead, he'd likely have fought Shen Qiao until a victor emerged. Duan Wenyang, on the other hand, saw that he no longer had any chance to achieve his objective today, so he began thinking up ways to extricate himself.

Shen Qiao said calmly, "Tan Yuanchun isn't here, so you can say anything you want. Once I catch you, I'll extract testimony from Tan Yuanchun and see what the truth is."

So he said, but his sword did slow somewhat. Seeing that the situation was turning in his favor, Duan Wenyang was pleased. "My path has intersected with Daoist Master Shen's again and again," he said. "Though we're not friends, I still know that you maintain a clear separation between gratitude and grudges. You're truly benevolent and generous beyond compare. If we look at things carefully, the person who threw you off that cliff was my shidi Kunye, who's already died at your hands. Yu Ai has passed as well, so these grudges should've come to an end."

"So you're saying that the reason you chose to come up the mountain today wasn't to plot against Xuandu Mountain nor to invade us while we're weak?" said Shen Qiao.

Duan Wenyang smiled, remaining calm. "'The politics of a position should be left to the one in that position.' That's one of your Han sayings. You and I are on different sides, so how we act will also be different. I work for the Khaganate's interests, and no one can blame me for that—I'm quite certain you don't either. Had Tan Yuanchun not secretly notified us, telling us that you'd be electing a new sect leader, we couldn't have known. All in all, you must secure what's inside before you deal with the outside, Daoist Master Shen!"

By this point, even Shen Qiao couldn't help but admire how thick this man's face was. "Yu Ai said someone conspired against him, causing him to fall from the cliff," he said. "I take you had a hand in this?"

Duan Wenyang boldly admitted to it. "Yes, but that was also because Tan Yuanchun showed us the way. Thanks to him, I learned that there is a winding path behind Xuandu Mountain which is undefended. By passing through the array, one can arrive at the summit directly. To be honest, Tan Yuanchun reached an agreement with us in secret long ago. The deal was that Sect Leader Sang and I would bring some people up the mountain, kill all the elders of your honored sect who opposed Tan Yuanchun becoming sect leader, and then Tan Yuanchun would step forward and drive us away. After he secured the position, he'd divide Xuandu Mountain's wealth and classical texts with us. This plan should've been flawless—if not for the variable that was you, Daoist Master Shen, everything would've gone smoothly."

Shen Qiao had known Tan Yuanchun for decades, yet he'd never suspected that his gentle and kindhearted da-shixiong was actually a traitor beneath his guileless exterior. Though he'd already anticipated it, he'd held a glimmer of hope in his heart—he couldn't help but make excuses for him, thinking that perhaps Tan Yuanchun had some troubles he couldn't talk about. It wasn't until his shixiong had launched a sneak attack and killed Yu Ai that Shen Qiao realized: the Tan Yuanchun they'd known for the past few decades had perhaps never been the real Tan Yuanchun at all.

Duan Wenyang seemed to notice what he was feeling, and he even comforted him. "You can know someone's face but not their heart. Daoist Master Shen need not grieve so much. In fact, that day when Yu Ai obtained Xiangjian Huan from my shidi and poisoned you, Tan Yuanchun also added fuel to the flames. I dare not say that Yu Ai only made up his mind to hurt you because of him, but words meant to sow dissension, once spoken enough, will undoubtedly have an effect."

"What evidence do you have?"

"Naturally, I have none." Duan Wenyang smiled. "Kunye and Yu Ai are already dead; do you expect me to go to the underworld and bring them back to testify? These are just the things my shidi told me back then. Whether they're true or false, Daoist Master Shen should ask Tan Yuanchun himself!"

With that, he withdrew and let out a whistle. The Göktürk masters seemed to have received his orders, for they followed right after him, and the small group quickly left in the direction they'd come from.

Duan Wenyang didn't look back, but his voice came from afar. "While we were heading up the mountain, two Xuandu Mountain disciples died, but they were both killed by Hehuan Sect. I didn't kill anyone; I only injured them. Daoist Master Shen can tell by looking at their wounds—don't lay this debt on me!"

Xiao Se was furious. "Shameless bastard!"

They'd come together, yet when it came to leaving, everyone had run off separately in the face of disaster. Most despicably, Duan Wenyang had even made sure to throw his allies to the wolves before departing.

Sang Jingxing and Bai Rong had already made a clean break for it, and now even Duan Wenyang had left with his people. How could the remaining Hehuan Sect disciples still have the will to fight? One after another, their minds became scattered, allowing Xuandu Mountain's members to exploit their openings. They were soundly crushed and ran about in a panic—in the end, out of the thirteen people from Hehuan Sect, only Xiao Se and a couple others managed to flee while the enraged members of Xuandu Mountain forced the remaining ten to leave their lives behind.

Kong Zeng limped over and apologized to Shen Qiao. "Kong Zeng is incompetent; he failed to keep Duan Wenyang here."

Shen Qiao's gaze swept over the others, many of them showing expressions of guilt and embarrassment. Some didn't dare to look at him but averted their gazes one after another and lowered their heads.

Shen Qiao understood very well that these expressions weren't only because they'd failed to kill Duan Wenyang and Xiao Se, but also because they hadn't taken the initiative to support Shen Qiao back when he'd been met with misfortune. Instead, they'd sided with Yu Ai.

Now that time had passed and the dust had settled, many people naturally understood that Yu Ai's collaboration with the Göktürks in order to guide Xuandu Mountain into reentering the secular world and regain their position as the world's foremost Daoist sect was as impossible as plucking a flower's reflection from within a mirror. It'd been wrong from the start, an illusory goal and a mansion built upon air. It was natural that they'd found themselves walking step by step into an abyss.

But who could have imagined that Yuwen Yong, who hadn't believed in Buddhism or Daoism, would die of a sudden illness while in his prime? And who could have thought that the once-powerful Qi would be annexed by Zhou, and that Yuwen Yong's successor, Yuwen Yun, would not only fail to carry his father's legacy forward or expand on it, but instead present his nation to someone else on a platter? Thus, the north had changed dynasties.

Meanwhile Shen Qiao, due to his meritorious assistance toward the new dynasty, had been bestowed the title of Perfected Master of Profundity and Discerning Subtleties, thereby securing Xuandu Mountain and even the Daoist discipline a place alongside the Sui Dynasty. Henceforth, Daoism and its traditions would be passed on from generation to generation, never-ending.

The Sui Dynasty took the opposite of the weak stance Zhou and Qi had shown the Khaganate: they were immediately hostile to them, and they seemed to be on the brink of war. Yu Ai had wanted to borrow the Khaganate's power to realize his dream of Xuandu Mountain rising once more, but it hadn't come true. The world was constantly changing, and who could have foreseen this?

And it was because they hadn't foreseen this that many of them held a guilty conscience, too afraid to face Shen Qiao. Considering this, one could see that they weren't bad people.

Of course, Shen Qiao also knew that for Yu Ai to successfully take over as sect leader, he must have had a fair amount of support from several of the elders. In fact, even most of the disciples on this mountain must have felt that Yu Ai was more suited to being the sect leader. If he pursued this matter, he'd probably have to expel all these people, which would be far too great of an impact on Xuandu Mountain. As the saying went, those who were too observant would have no disciples. It was better to turn a blind eye to certain things, when possible, than to excessively take everything to heart.

No one in this world was flawless or perfect in every way. Shen Qiao had gone through many ups and downs, but he held little resentment toward his fellow disciples or juniors and had no thoughts of seeking revenge or bragging about his achievements.

Back then, he'd inherited the position of Xuandu Mountain's sect leader from his shizun yet failed to hold on to it. This had been due to his negligence in the first place. To lay the blame on others without reflecting on his own mistakes first wasn't Shen Qiao's style.

Hence, he said to Kong Zeng, "When Yu Ai poisoned me that day, his actions were naturally intolerable to the sect's rules, but he has already died. A person's death is akin to a lamp going out—they come to nothing. Therefore I won't pursue these matters; I will bring his body before the memorial tablets of our forefathers and plead for forgiveness."

Having said this, Shen Qiao changed the topic. "However, from now on, I hope that everyone on Xuandu Mountain, from top to bottom, will be of one heart, our wills as unshakable as a fortress. If anyone colludes with outsiders again in the future, they will be dealt with according to the sect's precepts. No one will receive any leniency."

Shen Qiao was no longer the man he'd been before. His words carried a foreboding chill, his presence forceful and cold. Everyone's hearts trembled with fearful awe, and they quickly responded with their agreement.

At this point, there was no need to hold a succession ceremony again; everyone had already tacitly acknowledged Shen Qiao as the leader.

The outside of Sanqing Hall was in complete disorder. Many had already begun cleaning up the aftermath. Shen Qiao asked Kong Zeng to take some people down to search for those disciples who should have been on sentry duty near the mountain's foot. The injured were to be treated while the ones who'd been killed would have their corpses collected for burial on another day.

As Shen Qiao had once been the sect leader, he handled these matters with ease, his arrangements methodical and organized.

It was then that Bian Yanmei returned. "Tan Yuanchun has been captured," he reported. "Elder Liu has sent him to the punishment hall where you keep your prisoners. He awaits your judgment."

Shen Qiao saw that his figure was spotted with blood, and there was even fresh blood trickling from the corner of his mouth. "Are you injured?" he quickly asked.

Bian Yanmei waved his hand. "It's no issue. Elder Liu's injuries are even worse than mine."

He was too embarrassed to admit that, though he was Yan Wushi's disciple, he hadn't even been able to defeat Tan Yuanchun.

Shen Qiao took out some medicine for wounds. "My internal cultivation runs contrary to yours. It'll be difficult for me to heal your wounds through qi circulation."

Bian Yanmei took the medicine and thanked him. He then smiled and said, "No matter. The injury isn't serious. It'll recover once I circulate my qi for a couple of days. You should go and see Tan Yuanchun. I assume you have many things to ask him."

Shen Qiao did indeed have much to ask, up until he walked into the punishment hall. As he approached, he saw Tan Yuanchun in a wretched state, tied to a pillar. Suddenly, he felt that there was no need to ask anything.

Instead, Tan Yuanchun was the one wearing a cold and indifferent expression. When he saw Shen Qiao enter without speaking, he couldn't resist letting loose a cold laugh. "You must be very pleased to see the state I'm in?"

Shen Qiao remained silent for a while, then said to the disciple beside him, who was keeping watch, "Untie him, then bring another seat cushion here."

The disciple was a little apprehensive. "Sect Leader...?"

"Don't worry," said Shen Qiao. "With me here, nothing will happen."

Disciples on both sides came forward and untied Tan Yuanchun according to the instructions, and then brought another seat cushion and set it down.

Shen Qiao waved them away, then sat opposite Tan Yuanchun.

Tan Yuanchun had originally made up his mind not to speak, but after waiting for a long time, Shen Qiao still hadn't said a single word. This was making him somewhat anxious. "What did you want to say to me? I'll be taking the same knife regardless of whether I lean my head forward or cower away, so just get it over with!"

"I don't know what to say," said Shen Qiao.

"Winner takes all," said Tan Yuanchun. "What's the point of feigning compassion?"

Shen Qiao remained unmoved and calmly said, "Da-shixiong, we've been martial siblings for decades. Ever since I entered the sect, whenever Shizun wasn't at my side, you were the one who took care of me. We spent more time together than with Yu Ai, Yuan Ying, or anyone else. I thought I knew you well, and though it turns out that wasn't true, you should still know me well. You should also know very clearly if my compassion is an act, so why are purposely trying to anger me?"

Their eyes met, and Tan Yuanchun was able to easily look into the depths of Shen Qiao's eyes.

They were dark yet clear, as if one could see through them with a glance. The same as in the past; it'd never changed.

The barbs he'd been ready to erect at any moment gradually receded, one by one, and his cold and unyielding expression disappeared, leaving only a pool of stagnant water in its wake.

Tan Yuanchun closed his eyes. "What are you going to do with me? Will you kill me as compensation for Yu Ai's life?"

"Before he left, Duan Wenyang told me that you spoke words to incite Yu Ai that day, ultimately prompting him to poison me," said Shen Qiao.

"That's correct."

He simply admitted to it, causing the hand Shen Qiao had on his knee to tremble a little.

Tan Yuanchun's eyes didn't miss this detail. The corner of his mouth lifted in a sarcastic curve. "Don't tell me that, even now, you still harbor expectations of your Da-shixiong? I heard you suffered a great deal of hardships outside. I can scarcely imagine what a blind man without any of his martial arts would encounter. However, not only did you overcome them all, you even regained your martial arts. That was something I didn't expect. Congratulations, A-Qiao. Shizun once said that the martial path is nothing more than gradual, step-by-step advancement. However, there is an exception to this situation, wherein one dismantles everything and starts anew. When someone obtains this rare opportunity, one's mental state and martial arts can advance by leaps and bounds—but of course this is not the norm. I trust that you have already comprehended this special state that Shizun spoke of. His esteemed self will be able to smile and rest peacefully in the underworld."

"Why?"

Tan Yuanchun knew that Shen Qiao was asking about his previous comment. "Why not? From the moment Shizun handed the position of sect leader to you, I have been discontent. The matter with Yu Ai just happened to be an opportunity. I didn't need to do a thing myself; I only needed to push the boat along the current. So why wouldn't I do it? You see, even Yu Ai failed to realize that I was deliberately stirring up the dissatisfaction he held deep down toward you. If you hadn't shown up today, I would've already succeeded as sect leader with full legitimacy."

In his anguish, Shen Qiao couldn't conceal his anger. "You and the rest of our martial siblings have known my personality for so many years. When Shizun wished to hand the position of sect leader to me, I was worried you'd be unhappy. I even asked you about it before, but you showed no signs then. Even after I became the leader, if you wanted this position, I would've given it up so that we martial siblings could keep the harmonious accord between us. Why did you have to do this?!"

Tan Yuanchun gave two icy laughs, then suddenly grew agitated. "Why?! You're actually asking me why?! I entered the sect earlier than you, but Shizun valued you more! I am the eldest, yet Shizun taught you everything! You're more talented, and you have better aptitude. For the sake of the sect's long-term interests, Shizun naturally had to show you bias. That I can understand, but why was it that even in ordinary, private, and trivial matters, his entire heart was also on you?! Within his heart, only you, Shen Qiao, were his beloved disciple. How could there have been space for even a shadow of anyone else?! If he disliked me, he should've just expelled me. Why use our existences as foils for the love he showed you?!"

Shen Qiao's heart was ice-cold, and he stared at Tan Yuanchun in disbelief. "Is that how you saw Shizun?"

"Shizun doted on you and loved you. He was biased toward you in everything. So in your heart, he'd naturally be perfect in every way, with no flaws to speak of! But what about to the rest of us?! Yes, if I wished to be sect leader, you would've let me. Yes, you loved your siblings, you're benevolent, righteous, and loyal. But what's the use of that? It wasn't something Qi Fengge gave me himself, so why should I care?! What's the point of you giving me a hundred sect leader positions? I wanted to prove that his actions were wrong, that you couldn't afford his regard and trust. I wanted to prove that handing Xuandu Mountain over to you was wrong. I wanted him to open his eyes in the underworld and take a good look, to see he was wrong! I wanted him to remember that he has another disciple! A disciple named Tan Yuanchun!"

Shen Qiao remained silent for a long time. This ferocious Da-shixiong in front of him didn't have the slightest resemblance to the meek and kindly man he had known for so many years.

At last, Shen Qiao only gave an exhausted sigh. "Yuan Ying and Hengbo didn't have these thoughts."

Tan Yuanchun sneered. "That's because they entered late. Shizun neglected them from day one. Even Yuan Ying and Hengbo's martial arts were mostly taught by you; of course they'd never have any expectations. If you ask someone who's never tasted congee what its flavor is like, would they be able to answer?

"You now know that the kindly Da-shixiong in your mind has always been a lie. I took great pains in putting on this act for decades. While Shizun was alive, I was terrified of disappointing him, and after he died, I was terrified of revealing my thoughts too early. Now I finally don't need to pretend, and all I feel is unspeakable joy!" He looked up and burst into laughter. "I feel great! Just great!"

Shen Qiao watched him laugh, and the anguish in his expression gradually faded into indifference. Without saying anything, he stood.

"What are you going to do to me?" asked Tan Yuanchun. "Will you simply kill me? Or will you destroy my martial arts, blind me in both eyes, and then toss me out so that I can experience the suffering you went through in the past?"

Shen Qiao looked at him for a moment before suddenly drawing his sword from its sheath. He stepped forward and flicked his hand toward Tan Yuanchun.

Tan Yuanchun only had time to see a few flashes of sword glare, then his entire body exploded in agony. When he tried to circulate his qi, he found that his body was already completely empty, lacking even a shred of internal energy within it.

As expected, Shen Qiao really did want him to experience a fate worse than death! Tan Yuanchun couldn't help but sneer.

But then he heard Shen Qiao say, "You conspired against your martial siblings and violated the rules of our sect. You should be executed, but while on his deathbed, Shizun told me to love my siblings like my own hands and feet, to protect their health and happiness. Furthermore, he told me to treat you with great respect, that I must not slight you just because I've become the sect leader. Today, Yu Ai has already passed, and Shizun would certainly not wish to see another disciple accompanying him in the underworld. From now on, you will go to Qunling Peak and guard Shizun's tomb. Whether it's winter, summer, spring, or autumn, you are not allowed to take even half a step out of Qunling Peak. And I too will consider you dead."

Without looking back, he gradually faded into the distance, until his silhouette had vanished entirely. Yet his voice lingered in the area, reverberating.

Tan Yuanchun knelt on the ground, completely unable to feel the agony within his body. He only stared at Shen Qiao's back in a daze.

A long moment later, he suddenly burst into sobs.

The sound of crying drifted far from the punishment hall, and Shen Qiao paused in his steps, then looked up at the sky.

The clear and boundless sky stretched overhead, without a single white cloud to mar it. That pellucid blue that would never change despite the sorrow or joy of the lives beneath.

Shen Qiao closed his eyes, then looked down at Shanhe Tongbei in his hand. Out of nowhere, he remembered the scene in the cave, of Yan Wushi scaling fish using his sword.

And without him realizing, the sadness in his heart slowly, slowly dissipated.

122

Leading Xuandu Mountain Once More

THE DUST HAD SETTLED, and the crisis came to an end.
But Xuandu Mountain had paid a heavy, painful price.
Yu Ai was dead and Tan Yuanchun's martial arts had been destroyed. He'd spend the rest of his life guarding the tomb—a fate not that different from death. Among the other six elders, four were suffering from serious wounds, including Liu Yue. Due to his previous confrontation with Tan Yuanchun, his organs were damaged, and he'd likely need to recuperate in seclusion. The two remaining elders were also injured, more or less.

The ordinary disciples didn't need mentioning. Le An and Yun Chang were fortunate—when Sang Jingxing and the rest had come up the mountain, they went to notify their shifu and had only returned with Kong Zeng halfway through. They hadn't experienced the most brutal incident: the slaughter of the guard sentries at the foot of the mountain. Le An had suffered some injuries during his fight with Xiao Se, but due to the latter's lack of battle lust, his injuries were not serious. The remaining disciples were all severely wounded. One of them had taken a palm strike from Sang Jingxing and fallen off a cliff. His sternum had been shattered, but fortunately a tree branch had broken his fall, and he'd hung there by his last breath until someone rescued him.

At a glance, they resembled a company of infirm soldiers more than anything else, their anguished wails ringing all around.

But it was precisely thanks to this incident that those who'd still held fantasies about working together with the Göktürks were ultimately able to see the Göktürks' true faces. Now, they finally realized that if Xuandu Mountain wished to re-enter the world and rise again, they could never rely on external forces. No matter how powerful that assistance was, it would only be extraneous, like embroidering flowers on brocade. Ultimately, you could only rely on yourself.

Shen Qiao took control of Xuandu Mountain once again—a completely uncontroversial move at this juncture. He didn't even need to mention anything; apart from Liu Yue, who was still in seclusion, the other five elders came to him voluntarily and asked him to take over as leader. They also expressed their deepest regrets that they'd believed Yu Ai's words so easily in the past.

Before, when Yu Ai had disappeared, Liu Yue and Tan Yuanchun contended for the position of leader. Now that Shen Qiao had returned, this matter naturally lost any controversy it'd once had. Even if Liu Yue left seclusion, the position could never be his.

Shen Qiao listened to them, then fell silent for a while.

When everyone saw this, they were all somewhat uneasy. They wondered if Shen Qiao resented them. Now that their enemy had retreated, it would naturally be time to settle debts.

When Shen Qiao finally spoke up, his words surprised them. "The Sui Dynasty has built a new monastery in hopes of building friendly relations with the Daoist discipline. The Emperor of Sui granted me the right to build a monastery in Chang'an, and even allocated funds for the construction of Xuandu Monastery. When I left the capital, the monastery was almost complete. In the future, it'll be a branch of Xuandu's Violet Palace. My energy is limited, and

I cannot keep an eye on two things at once. Therefore, I plan to have several elders take turns every year in managing Chang'an's Xuandu Monastery. What do you all think?"

The people looked at each other. They hadn't been expecting Shen Qiao to talk about this.

Though Yu Ai outwardly cooperated with the Göktürks and ordered for new disciples to be recruited during spring and autumn, the results of opening Xuandu Mountain's gates hadn't been satisfactory. Only a few well-qualified people came to join the sect, which caused the elders great distress. They didn't know how to expand the Xuandu Mountain's influence in the minds of the Daoists, much less the world.

If they could obtain the Sui Dynasty's support and establish some doctrines at Xuandu Monastery in Chang'an, all their problems would naturally be solved. Not only that, Chang'an was full of talented people, so if a few elders could take turns visiting Xuandu Monastery every year and oversee things there, they'd no longer need to worry about recruiting good disciples.

Watching their sect flourish, knowing that it'd be passed down through future generations... They couldn't help but be happy.

Lian Shan was abashed. "The Sect Leader is magnanimous to not mind past grievances. However, we cannot simply gloss past it and act like nothing happened. About the matter of taking turns to oversee Chang'an, you need not include me. I am willing to spend the rest of my life teaching disciples and helping to manage general affairs. I won't take another step off this mountain."

Among the four elders who'd previously supported Yu Ai becoming sect leader of Xuandu Mountain, Lian Shan had been the friendliest with Yu Ai. In the end, it'd been due to selfish motives—he'd hoped to gain more influence himself by borrowing Yu Ai's power.

But Lian Shan wasn't a treacherous or evil person either. To put it another way... Xuandu Mountain had been passed down from generation to generation, and their selection of disciples was incredibly strict, with heavy emphasis on personality and character. There was the occasional exception, but it was rare. Faced with such a situation, Lian Shan had also realized his mistakes. Seeing Shen Qiao's magnanimity, he felt even more ashamed, so he took the chance to say these words, expressing his true feelings.

Kong Zeng came forward too. "If we wish to speak of mistakes, I was an elder, yet I stayed out of the matter and paid no attention to the rise and fall of my own sect. I stubbornly avoided everything, so I'm even more guilty of dereliction of duty. I wish to ask the Sect Leader to punish me—I'd be willing to spend the rest of my life guarding the tombs of our forefathers!"

Several other elders, upon seeing this, also spoke out and confessed their wrongdoings, one after another.

Shen Qiao knew that there were some things he had to say. "I also made mistakes regarding Yu Ai. If I hadn't been negligent and overlooked things, he would've never had his opportunity. I can also admit that his intentions for Xuandu Mountain weren't wrong. His mistakes were in asking a tiger for its skin and in harming his shixiong. Since he's already dead, expounding further is pointless—and since you all have the desire to mend your ways, you should consider my words all the more. Unless you believe that wallowing in your past mistakes and self-blame is more important than following your sect leader's orders?"

Naturally, everyone said they wouldn't dare.

"Since that's the case, there's no need to say more," said Shen Qiao.

Only then was everyone certain that Shen Qiao had no plans of settling old scores. They all breathed sighs of relief, and at the same time, they couldn't help but feel grateful.

Unlike before, when he'd inherited the position from Qi Fengge, this time Shen Qiao had become the leader through his own strength and reputation. There was no longer anyone who was dissatisfied or felt that he wasn't worthy of his position.

"I heard before that the Sect Leader accepted some disciples while outside the sect," said Lian Shan. "Now that you've returned, should we have someone bring those two shizhi back?"

He'd always been impeccable when it came to his conduct and duties. Before these matters had even crossed the minds of others, he'd already taken them into consideration.

Shen Qiao had been so busy, he had almost forgotten. "Thank you very much for the reminder, Elder Lian. Shiwu and Qilang should be staying at Bixia Sect as guests at the moment. I think Elder Kong's disciples, Le An and Yun Chang, are dependable in handling affairs. Why don't you ask those two to go and fetch them?"

Kong Zeng nodded. "It's time for them to head out and gain some experience."

Everyone discussed a few more things, mainly on what the direction and decision-making at Xuandu Mountain would look like in the future. Finally, Shen Qiao established some policies for rebuilding the sect and admitting disciples, then allotted duties to each elder. Finally, only two elders responsible for evaluating new disciples remained behind.

"When I came, I met three people at the foot of the mountain," Shen Qiao told them. "They traveled thousands of miles for the purpose of finding a master, but for some reason, they weren't allowed up the mountain. Could these two shishu please send someone down there to take a look? If they're still here, bring them up and evaluate them according to the rules. Moreover, from now on, we need not limit accepting disciples to only the spring and autumn equinoxes. Anyone who wishes to seek a master can be evaluated at any time. But in the future, the number of people who show up for our reputation will only increase, so the evaluation must be made stricter, especially when examining their characters and temperaments. I don't wish to see a second incident where our sect's members end up hurting each other."

The two elders agreed, and Shen Qiao informed them of Duan Ying and his companions' names, as well as the inn they were staying at.

Once he'd sent the two of them off, Bian Yanmei came over. "Daoist Master Shen is so busy, with thousands of matters to handle every day! Don't end up hurting your own health by overworking!"

"Thank you very much for your concern," Shen Qiao said with a wry smile. "I've seen you as a court official, socializing and politicking with many others, handling everything with composure and ease. I envied you greatly. If you became Xuandu Mountain's sect leader instead, you'd be a hundred times more suitable than I am!"

Bian Yanmei smiled. "Daoist Master Shen is too kind. I've spent so much time dealing with people over the last few years that I've neglected my martial arts and made no progress. Shizun was quite dissatisfied. So there's a trade-off to everything—how can anything in this world be flawless and perfect?"

"Are your injuries better now?" Shen Qiao asked.

"Thanks to Xuandu Mountain's wound medication, they have improved a lot. Now that this matter is over, I won't impose on you anymore, so I'm here to bid farewell."

Shen Qiao knew that Bian Yanmei still had much to attend to in Chang'an, so he said, "Shen Qiao is endlessly grateful for the assistance you provided this time. If you need anything in the future, please let me know, and I will do my best to help."

"Daoist Master Shen need not be so courteous," said Bian Yanmei with a smile. "If your esteemed self wishes to thank me, thank my shizun. If not for his honored orders, how could I have taken the liberty to make those decisions?"

"Do you know where Sect Leader Yan's battle with Hulugu is scheduled to take place?"

Bian Yanmei shook his head. "I don't know either. I'm afraid I'll have to send someone to make inquiries later."

Shen Qiao frowned a little despite himself. "Then, in your opinion, what are your shizun's chances of victory?"

"I didn't personally attend the Sword Trial Conference that day, so I haven't witnessed Hulugu's skills for myself. But I heard that he's outstandingly powerful, and few people in the world would be his match."

"Yes, I fought him myself at the Conference. Even if I exhausted my full strength, I have no doubt I would lose within fifty moves."

Bian Yanmei looked horrified. "He was really that powerful? Then what should we do? The flaw in Shizun's demonic core isn't fully repaired yet!"

"How can that be?" said Shen Qiao hurriedly. "Last time, I clearly heard him say that he's fully recovered, otherwise how would he have defeated Xueting?"

Bian Yanmei sighed. "Did Shizun actually say that to your esteemed self? In truth, Shizun's primordial qi was damaged during his battle with Xueting that day. His demonic core, which had almost fully healed, has begun to show flaws again. He will need a year and a half of rest to recover. But then the crisis at Xuandu Mountain happened, and if no one had stalled Hulugu, he certainly would've assisted his disciple Duan Wenyang when he came up the mountain to make trouble. Therefore, Shizun was forced into making this unwise decision. This battle..."

Bian Yanmei didn't continue, but his worried, apprehensive expression had already conveyed what he felt: it didn't bode well for the upcoming battle.

Shen Qiao's heart gradually sank.

"I trust that you have a way to communicate with Sect Leader Yan?" he asked. "Can you try to find information on his current whereabouts?"

"I can, but what would be the point? This battle is imperative. Daoist Master Shen doesn't have to feel guilty about it. My shizun only decides to do something if he's perfectly happy to do it. No one can force him."

Shen Qiao was silent for a moment, then whispered, "I know, but unless I see him, how can my heart rest?"

Bian Yanmei sighed. "In that case..."

Before they could finish speaking, a disciple from outside arrived to give a report. "Sect Leader, there's someone at the foot of the mountain calling himself Yu Shengyan, a disciple from Huanyue Sect."

Before Bian Yanmei could respond, Shen Qiao had already said, "Invite him up, quickly!" His face lit up with joy, and even his tone had inflected upward.

Bian Yanmei also smiled. "Perfect, now we won't need to make inquiries or contact anyone. Shidi must know Shizun's current location!"

After a while, Yu Shengyan followed the escorting disciple inside to meet him. Seeing him enter, Shen Qiao personally stood up to greet him.

With his martial prowess and seniority, it was unnecessary for him to pay his respects like this. Bian Yanmei hadn't planned on standing up, but seeing Shen Qiao, he had no choice but to follow his lead. He thought to himself that he'd probably greatly disturbed

Daoist Master Shen with his words earlier, and now the sect leader's mind must be confused.

On the way here, Yu Shengyan had seen that though everyone was wearing dreary expressions, all was still in perfect order. It was clear to him that Xuandu Mountain had just weathered a great calamity, and the crisis had already been resolved. When he saw Shen Qiao and his own shixiong personally welcoming him at the door, though, he was a bit astonished and flattered both.

"Congratulating Daoist Master Shen on regaining his position as sect leader," he said. "I trust that I'm the first to come and offer my congratulations? Daoist Master must give me a huge red envelope!" He didn't put on any airs but quickly cupped his hands, and even cracked a small joke.

Yet Shen Qiao couldn't bring himself to laugh. "Thank you very much. Where did you come from?"

Yu Shengyan saw the glance Bian Yanmei shot him from behind Shen Qiao, and for the moment, he was confused as to what was going on. He didn't dare to answer thoughtlessly. "From... From Chang'an!"

He remembered the purpose of his trip and removed a small bamboo tube from his lapels. "Shizun took Xueting to Tiantai Sect and exchanged him for a copy of the *Zhuyang Strategy* scroll from the Tiantai Sect Leader. He tasked me with bringing it to Daoist Master Shen."

Shen Qiao took the bamboo tube and unscrewed it, then pulled out a piece of silk from inside, covered in writing.

The silk piece weighed very little, but for some reason, Shen Qiao felt like he was holding a hundred pounds of gold, so heavy he could hardly lift his hand.

He squeezed the silk tightly, and his heart was a mess of emotions, impossible to describe.

"Do you know where your master is now?" he asked. "Or where his duel with Hulugu is scheduled to take place?"

"This battle is scheduled to take place at Banbu Peak," replied Yu Shengyan.

Shen Qiao was stunned.

His own duel with Kunye had been at Banbu Peak. Afterward, he fell from the cliff, grievously injured, and Yan Wushi had saved him. Everything began from there.

And now, everything had come back to Banbu Peak once more.

"Huanyue Sect has a villa not far from Banbu Peak," Yu Shengyan added. "I expect Shizun will arrive early and stay there first."

He didn't need to elaborate more about the villa, for Shen Qiao also remembered resting there after Yan Wushi and Yu Shengyan had brought him back from Banbu Peak.

Mysteriously and inexorably, everything had come full circle.

Yu Shengyan was still a little embarrassed about that incident. After he'd seen that Shen Qiao had lost his memory, he deceived him into thinking that he was a Huanyue Sect disciple and coaxed him into calling Yu Shengyan "Shixiong."

Yu Shengyan wasn't Yan Wushi's match when it came to cultivating shamelessness. If Yan Wushi were here, not only would he fail to be embarrassed, he'd also have brazenly said something to embarrass Shen Qiao instead.

Shen Qiao held that thought, finding it a little amusing, but he still couldn't bring himself to laugh. Clutching the silk piece in his hand, he'd already drawn up a plan within his heart.

Though Duan Ying and his three friends had come all the way to find a master, they'd been met with rejection. They hadn't even been allowed to climb Xuandu Mountain and were struck with dismay. After wandering about for a day, Zhong Bojing left first. He planned to try his luck at Qingcheng Mountain; after all, Chunyang Monastery was also a renowned sect.

The remaining two, Duan Ying and Zhang Chao, didn't know whether to go or stay. While they were hesitating, someone came to their door. The newcomer was dressed in the Daoist robes worn by Xuandu Mountain disciples, and they claimed that they'd come to guide the two up the mountain to undergo the entrance evaluation.

The pair were skeptical but also unwilling to give up on this glimmer of hope. They quickly followed the newcomer up the mountain. After overcoming all the difficulties presented to them, they finally passed the evaluation, and an elder of Xuandu Mountain even personally came to meet them. They were already ecstatic, thinking that their fortune had finally seen an upswing. Unexpectedly, though, after a shixiong from the sect had taken Zhang Chao away to his arrangements, another elder brought Duan Ying to Shen Qiao.

Shen Qiao had already packed his luggage and was about to set off, but he also had to leave the sect's disciples some instructions on a couple of matters. He managed to eke out some time in his busy schedule to meet Duan Ying and ask him, "Would you like to apprentice under me and become my disciple?"

Duan Ying had already been knocked into a daze by this astronomical, golden opportunity. After the elder's reminder, he finally realized that the even-tempered, friendly young Daoist the three of them had met at the foot of the mountain was actually Shen Qiao, the Xuandu Mountain Sect Leader and one of the top ten experts in the world!

Seeing his blank stare, Shen Qiao repeated his words, then added gently, "If you don't want to, it's perfectly fine to apprentice under another elder instead."

"Yes! I want to! I absolutely want to!" Duan Ying regained his senses, his face flushing red. He was practically leaping to say these words at least a hundred times.

Yu Shengyan was nearby, and when he saw this scene, he couldn't help but curl his lips, thinking to himself that Daoist Master Shen truly lacked a good eye for disciples. Just look at that idiotic response—he was far inferior to Yu Shengyan.

He'd just thought this when he saw his shixiong Bian Yanmei rolling his eyes at him.

Yu Shengyan was perplexed. *What did I do this time?*

Goodwill Abounds

SINCE HE'D JUST ADMITTED a new disciple, as the shifu, he couldn't just up and leave. Shen Qiao personally introduced Xuandu's Violet Palace's sect rules to Duan Ying, then briefly explained the situations of Shiwu and Yuwen Song. Duan Ying took note of everything, listening intently.

"I'll be away," Shen Qiao told him, "but you must not neglect your studies because of it. I'll have Elder Kong teach you the internal and mental cultivation techniques of our sect, as well as the Azure Waves sword technique. Every morning your martial siblings will wake up to practice the sword, and you should participate as well. I will check on your training upon my return. If you make good progress, I'll teach you the next stage of martial arts. Aptitude is indeed important for martial arts practitioners, but diligence can make up for any shortcomings. You must remember this. Though you're not the strongest when it comes to talent, it's still above average—if you can study and practice diligently, great achievements may very well be in your future."

"Yes!" said Duan Ying respectfully—but then he hesitantly asked, "Shizun, earlier, I heard my martial siblings say that the disciples can leave the mountain and head home during the new year and festival celebrations?"

Shen Qiao said, "That's right. If your home is in the towns near the foot of the mountain, you can even go back every month—no need to restrict your visits to just the new year and festivals. If your home is farther away, then it's fine to go back once a year."

"What if I don't have a home to go back to?" mumbled Duan Ying.

Shen Qiao was surprised. "As far as I know, aren't both of your parents still alive?"

Duan Ying gave a pained smile. "I won't deceive Shizun. My blood mother was my father's concubine, and she passed away early. All my brothers and sisters are children of the main wife; I'm the only exception…"

"If that's the case, you don't need to go back if you don't wish to return," Shen Qiao said gently. "In addition to you, I have two disciples who started earlier than you, though they're younger—when you see them later, you should address them as shixiong. But they are both orphans without any parents. In the future, you must get along well with them. You have many martial siblings on the mountain as well, so in the future, even if you don't go back home during the holidays, the mountain will still be very lively. Don't worry."

He didn't have much experience as a shifu, and the two disciples he'd admitted previously were still adolescents. As a result, he'd unconsciously used a half-coaxing tone, the kind one would use for children. Duan Ying found this both amusing and touching, and his heart grew even warmer.

Duan Ying was originally from the Southern Kingdom. Though the Luling Duan family couldn't be considered a wealthy family, they were still a martial arts family of some renown within the local area. He shouldn't have needed to seek distant opportunities, even running thousands of miles to look for a master. But as Duan Ying had told Shen Qiao, every family had its own circumstances. Duan Ying was unwilling to endure their bullying, nor was he permitted to learn the martial arts reserved for the family's legitimate children. Instead, he simply bid farewell to them and left to search for a famous master.

He'd gone to Linchuan Academy first. After all, Confucianism was prevalent in the Southern Kingdom, and many regarded Linchuan Academy as a sacred place for martial arts, especially the Academy Master, who was also the shixiong of the Southern Dynasty's Empress Liu. Linchuan Academy was even more prestigious in the south, with as many followers as clouds. But the more renowned the sect, the higher its standards. Duan Ying lacked both background and accomplishments—his aptitude wasn't particularly outstanding either—and so he was quickly eliminated in the initial examination stage. Still, he didn't give up, and after going to great pains, he finally got the opportunity to personally meet with Academy Master Ruyan Kehui and speak a few words with him. However, though Ruyan Kehui treated him kindly, he ultimately didn't agree to accept him as a disciple. Duan Ying understood that the man must have found his physical qualifications unsatisfactory.

Before he encountered Shen Qiao, Duan Ying thought all martial arts grandmasters in the world were like Ruyan Kehui and deeply valued talent and aptitude above all else. Therefore, when he came to Xuandu Mountain, he no longer held any unrealistic hopes. He thought he'd be satisfied as long as he could become a disciple of Xuandu Mountain and honestly learn some martial arts. He hadn't expected to end up receiving such a joyous surprise.

The loss Duan Ying had experienced led him to cherish this hard-won opportunity all the more, and he understood how rare a shifu like Shen Qiao was. So as not to disappoint his shifu, he would devote practically all his energy to martial arts. No one, least of all his parents, could have expected that this lowborn son whom they neglected would, in a few years, become a martial arts grandmaster of his generation whose reputation shook the world itself.

But that was a tale for later. At this moment, Duan Ying had just joined the sect, and he revealed a smile tinged with bashfulness at Shen Qiao's words. "Thank you very much, Shizun," he said. "Your esteemed self can rest easy and leave. This disciple will be sure to train properly and never disappoint your expectations. Please take care on your journey!"

Shen Qiao patted his shoulder, gave a few more words of encouragement, and then let him leave.

Due to this newly accepted disciple, he had to delay for another day, but things always came one after another. Not long after Duan Ying left, two more people arrived, each bringing him a message.

The first was from Chunyang Monastery on Qingcheng Mountain. Yi Pichen didn't know that Shen Qiao was already the leader of Xuandu Mountain, so the message was simply addressed to the sect leader. Aside from some routine greetings, its contents were mainly about the scheduled duel between Yan Wushi and Hulugu. He invited the Xuandu Mountain Sect Leader to watch the battle together with him.

For the jianghu of the Central Plains, this battle would not only herald the birth of the world's number one martial artist, it also signified a showdown between the martial arts of the Göktürks and the Central Plains. If Yan Wushi were defeated, his face wasn't the only one that would be lost. News of the battle at Banbu Peak had already spread. When the time came, many people would come to watch the battle in person. Even Yi Pichen had been swayed into watching; others needed no mention. It was likely that all the renowned martial experts of the Central Plains would gather on Yinghui Peak to watch the battle on Banbu Peak.

As a Daoist sect in the Central Plains, it was natural that Chunyang Monastery would get involved. Moreover, Hulugu had ruined the last Sword Trial Conference midway through. Though Yi Pichen hadn't said anything, he wasn't happy about it.

Yi Pichen had personally witnessed how terrifying Hulugu was. He'd thought to himself that his odds of winning against Shen Qiao were fifty-fifty, and yet Shen Qiao was defeated by Hulugu. This meant he would not be his match. No matter whether it was Ruyan Kehui, Guang Lingsan, or Yuan Xiuxiu, he believed that none of them would be able to match Hulugu either.

The frightening part wasn't the idea of Yan Wushi alone losing to Hulugu but the knowledge that, henceforth, no one in the Central Plains would be able to subdue Hulugu.

Now that Qi Fengge was gone, there'd never be another Qi Fengge.

Yu Shengyan had been in high spirits the day Shen Qiao and Kunye dueled on Banbu Peak, but Yan Wushi had no interest whatsoever. When an expert reached his level, it wasn't difficult to infer who was stronger based on the information one had obtained beforehand.

Of course, Yan Wushi wasn't some godly immortal either. Not even he could have expected that Shen Qiao would fall from the cliff, grievously injured.

But this battle was completely different. On one side was the Göktürks' great master who'd lost by just one move to Qi Fengge, who'd been the number one martial artist in the world. On the other side was the leader of a demonic sect who'd crushed Buddhist Master Xueting, someone who'd ranked second on Liuli Palace's rankings, and who'd also fought Qi Fengge once, many years ago.

The two should have had no relationship whatsoever, but now, due to the words "Qi Fengge," a subtle connection had appeared between them.

Who would win and who would lose?

Perhaps no one, including themselves, knew the answer.

Many people had the same thoughts as Yi Pichen, so this battle was sure to shake the world itself and draw all its eyes to the participants.

The messenger Yi Pichen had sent was Su Qiao. When he saw that Shen Qiao had shown up on Xuandu Mountain, he was first shocked but quickly righted himself and congratulated Shen Qiao. Then he apologized. "My master has yet to learn that Daoist Master Shen has regained his position as sect leader, otherwise he'd have sent over a congratulatory gift."

Shen Qiao smiled. "Thank you very much, but there isn't much to congratulate on this matter. Please go back and tell your master that I'll meet him at Yinghui Peak on the fifteenth of March."

Banbu Peak was treacherously steep, and the summit's terrain was even more cramped and rugged. Just fighting upon it was already a great test of skill—there was no space for anyone else to watch the fight. Those who wished to spectate would have to do so across from it, on Yinghui Peak.

After saying this, Shen Qiao thought about Madam Qin and her background, so he added, "Will Madam Qin also be going to watch the duel on Banbu Peak?"

Su Qiao shook his head. "My mother said that the past is past—she doesn't want to see her old acquaintances anymore. When the time comes, I'll go with my master. My mother probably won't be there."

"I see," said Shen Qiao. "Then please pass my greetings to your mother and brother."

Su Qiao smiled. "Of course."

The two of them chatted for a while. Su Qiao understood that he must be terribly busy now as the sect leader, so he took the initiative to bid him farewell. However, he'd rushed all the way here from afar, so sending him back right after he'd delivered the message would be rather rude, so Shen Qiao asked him to stay for the night. He also called over the disciples in charge of welcoming guests, asking them to entertain him properly.

The second message was delivered by an ordinary-looking girl. She claimed to be a Hehuan Sect disciple who'd come on their sect leader's orders.

Shen Qiao felt absolutely no good will toward Sang Jingxing. He'd only just severely injured the man on Xuandu Mountain, and now he had sent a messenger up the mountain. It was obviously not going to be anything good. However, Shen Qiao didn't want to embarrass a woman, and it was already too late for him to set off today. He decided that he might as well meet with the envoy from Hehuan Sect.

Unexpectedly, the first words out of her mouth were: "This one is Bing Xian, a disciple of Hehuan Sect. I came here on orders for two things. First, to congratulate Daoist Master Shen on returning to power on Xuandu Mountain. Second, our sect will be holding a grand succession ceremony for our new sect leader in ten days. The Sect Leader sent this one here to invite Daoist Master Shen to attend the ceremony."

Shen Qiao was surprised. "Succession ceremony?" he asked. "Isn't your leader Sang Jingxing?"

Bing Xian pursed her lips into a smile and said crisply, "Sect Leader Sang has already passed away, so the position of sect leader was succeeded by Sect Leader Sang's disciple. Sect Leader Bai said that she has a deep and unbreakable friendship with Daoist Master Shen; so, for this succession ceremony, even if she invites no one else, she absolutely must invite you!"

With this smile, even her previously ordinary eyes shone with a hint of charm.

For members of a sect, the death of their leader was naturally not something to be happy about, but this girl seemed jubilant. Although Shen Qiao also felt that Sang Jingxing's death was more than deserved, he found Bing Xian's words and actions somewhat odd too.

Bing Xian seemed to sense his question. "I dare not dirty Daoist Master Shen's ears, but before joining Hehuan Sect, Bing Xian was a woman from a good family who was kidnapped by Sang Jingxing and brought to Yichixue Temple," she explained. "We were set free only after Sang Jingxing's death, and Sect Leader Bai saw that I wished to learn martial arts and had decent aptitude and qualifications, so she let me officially enter the sect. On Xuandu Mountain, Sang Jingxing suffered grievous injuries due to Daoist Master Shen, and he passed away from his wounds not long after returning. The sect was left leaderless and in a panic. The Sect Leader considered the overall picture and chose to shoulder the responsibilities of leadership, taking on this heavy burden for the sake of the sect."

She was extraordinarily silver-tongued. Everyone had been contending for the position of Hehuan Sect's leader, yet she'd described it like an inconvenience everyone was desperate to avoid, and thus Bai Rong taking over as leader became a great act of benevolence instead.

Shen Qiao knew very well that though the injury Sang Jingxing had suffered was severe, the fact that he'd still been able to flee, combined with his abilities, meant that it shouldn't have been fatal. There was no reason he shouldn't have survived, unless...

His heart jolted and he met Bing Xian's quick-witted gaze. "Though Sang Jingxing is dead, there are other elders within the sect," he said. "Leaving aside the rest, Yuan Xiuxiu's disciple Xiao Se should also be able to contend for the position. Didn't he object when Bai Rong became the sect leader?"

Bing Xian smiled. "The sect leader's position belongs to the capable. Those elders aren't as capable as the Sect Leader, so they can only obey her orders. If they refuse, that means they're defying the Sect Leader and must be punished according to the rules of the sect. As for Elder Xiao, a wise man will submit to his fate. Since he is willing to devote himself to serving our sect, the Sect Leader will naturally elevate him."

These words implied that Bai Rong had already seized complete control of Hehuan Sect, to the point that even Xiao Se was unable to stir up any waves and could only bow to her.

Not only was Shen Qiao surprised, he also couldn't help but marvel at Bai Rong's strength.

Once, he'd seen a pitifulness buried with her cruelty and had only thought she'd be better off if she could leave Huanyue Sect. Little had he known that her intentions had lain elsewhere and that she'd rather swallow her humiliation and bide her time, waiting for an opportunity to spring from Sang Jingxing and Yuan Xiuxiu's internal conflict. Secretly, bit by bit, she'd seized power for herself, and, in the end, she finally emerged as the victor.

"The Sect Leader still has some things to say," said Bing Xian. "She ordered me to tell them to Daoist Master Shen."

"Please speak."

Bing Xian cleared her throat. When she spoke again, it was in a voice that resembled Bai Rong's. "Shen-lang, I know you don't like the practice of pair cultivation within Hehuan Sect. I wasn't able to change it in the past, but now that I'm the leader, I will naturally remove these practices, one by one. I've even freed all the beautiful girls Sang Jingxing captured and violated, and I'm letting them stay if they wish to do so. Are you satisfied with this? However, since the pair cultivation secret technique is a shortcut to martial arts training, many people are unwilling to give up the rich meat already in their mouths. I can't completely abolish it overnight. After all, there are still quite a few people in the sect waiting to see disaster befall me, so I must take it slowly. You must not look down on this one for this nor find other excuses to avoid talking to her anymore!"

Her tone was sweet and agreeable, as if Bai Rong was right before him, vivid and lively. If he closed his eyes, he might have even believed that Bai Rong was the one speaking to him.

Ever since Shen Qiao had entered the secular world, he'd begun to properly understand the ways of the world and its people. He wasn't made of wood, so how could he miss the feelings hidden within those words? But Shen Qiao knew very well that, though he was softhearted toward many people and many things, the only person he couldn't show that softness to at all was Bai Rong.

Otherwise, it would only harm them both and increase the injustices she'd received.

"Please tell her this in my stead," he said. "Xuandu Mountain congratulates Sect Leader Bai on her succession. However, this humble Daoist is leaving tomorrow, so he's afraid he cannot attend her succession ceremony in person. He hopes that Sect Leader Bai can forgive him."

Bing Xian looked at him for a moment, then suddenly sighed, "The goddess has affection, so why is King Xiang's heart like a stone?"[2]

---

2   神女有心, 奈何襄王心如铁石. A play on "襄王有意神女无心," which comes from Shennü-fu, the Song of the Goddess. In the original, King Xiang has an unrequited love for the goddess, but Bing Xian reverses it.

She'd been held captive by Sang Jingxing, so she naturally wasn't a naive maiden who knew nothing about the world. Due to her eloquence, Bai Rong had sent her to pass on her words. She'd thought that her sect leader's tremendous beauty and martial prowess, combined with the Sect Leader's admiration for her beloved and how she was willing to change the sect's tenets for him, would move any man in the world without fail. Even if he refused the invitation with righteous justifications, it wouldn't mean that his heart was completely unaffected. But this Daoist really did seem to have a heart of stone—he wasn't moved in the slightest.

Even Bing Xian couldn't help but silently sigh for Bai Rong. These sentiments were destined to be unrequited.

"If I'm indecisive, or my words ambiguous, I'd only be wronging her instead," Shen Qiao told her.

Bing Xian had wanted to call him a hypocrite, but as she watched Shen Qiao, his Daoist robe free of mortal dust, his face serene, just like an immortal from a painting, she suddenly couldn't say it anymore. Instead, within her heart, she faintly understood, just a little, why Sect Leader Bai would like this man.

It was love at first sight, and it will be my last. Now the world is but cold and gray.

Perhaps, she thought, there would always be some people, some things, in this world, that were worth waiting and making sacrifices for.

The next morning, Shen Qiao bid farewell to everyone on Xuandu Mountain and headed to Banbu Peak with Yu Shengyan.

Bian Yanmei had to leave for Chang'an to take care of the Huanyue Sect's affairs, so he couldn't accompany them. No matter who won this battle, Huanyue Sect would have to carry on.

Naturally, swords were blind—in a life-or-death battle like this one, it was highly likely that it'd conclude with someone breathing their last. If Yan Wushi died, it was hard to say whether Huanyue Sect could even survive.

Both Bian Yanmei and Yu Shengyan all but refused to entertain this kind of possibility—but, as the eldest disciple, Bian Yanmei had no choice but to prepare for the worst possible outcome.

True Thoughts

S HEN QIAO HAD NEVER imagined that he'd meet Yan Wushi again in this kind of situation.

After listening to what Bian Yanmei had said earlier, though Shen Qiao said nothing, his mind couldn't fail to make the connection.

When Yan Wushi had been at the peak of his martial strength, he might have been slightly inferior to Hulugu, but this slight gap didn't mean that the result was certain. The battlefield could change a thousand times in an instant—when experts fought, the likes of timing, terrain, and the people themselves were all the more influential. Sometimes, one careless move or lapse in judgment might determine the outcome. But if the flaw in Yan Wushi's demonic core had yet to be repaired, this slight gap would widen, and his chance of defeat would increase.

Shen Qiao thought and thought, pondering it for a long time, but he couldn't think of any way to guarantee Yan Wushi's victory.

Such a thing would be impossible in ordinary circumstances, let alone against someone like Hulugu. Even if his shizun Qi Fengge came back to life, he couldn't be certain of his victory.

In this way, he arrived outside the spare villa in Funing County, his mind full of worries. As he stood near the unlatched courtyard gates, he heard a lazy voice coming from inside. "No, A-Qiao, don't bite that."

A-Qiao? Don't bite?

Shen Qiao was baffled; he pushed open the gates and entered. There he saw Yan Wushi half leaning against a soft mattress inside the hallway, holding a jade jug filled with wine in one hand, propping himself up on the elbow of his other hand. His face oozed with satisfaction and leisure. Having heard the movement by the door, he raised his head and saw Shen Qiao and Yu Shengyan enter.

In front of him stood a fawn, the kind that couldn't yet walk steadily. It was making little bleating noises, like a lamb but slightly deeper. The fawn craned forward and bit the jade jug, playing a game of tug-of-war with Yan Wushi.

Shen Qiao stood there blankly for a moment. He'd never expected that someone who'd scheduled a duel with the world's number one martial expert would have so little sense of urgency that he'd actually have the leisure to...play with a fawn.

"A-Qiao?" Seeing the two new arrivals, Yan Wushi ignored Yu Shengyan and waved to Shen Qiao. "You came just in time. I had someone open a jug of mulberry wine, one that I buried ten years ago."

The fawn thought he was calling it, and it released the jade jug to lean in. Yan Wushi pushed its head away, and its dark, moist eyes seemed a bit hurt.

Shen Qiao reached out and stroked it. The fawn didn't fear strangers; it leaned with its neck and rubbed against Shen Qiao's palm. Shen Qiao suspected that he'd just heard wrong—he couldn't stop himself from asking, "Does it have a name?"

"Yes, its name is A-Qiao."

Shen Qiao was speechless.

Yan Wushi smiled. "Don't you think it looks a lot like you?"

Shen Qiao glanced at the fawn. It was a sika deer, still too young for its antlers to have grown in. Its ears were fluffy and pliable, and there was a tuft of white fur at the back of its neck. And there were its eyes, pure and innocent, full of trust and reliance on humans. But while it was adorable, Shen Qiao couldn't see how it resembled himself at all.

Putting that aside, he went straight to the point. "I heard that you challenged Hulugu to a duel?" He phrased it as a question, but since he already knew the answer, these words were no more than an opening statement.

"I did." These words were spoken very casually as well, as if Yan Wushi had agreed to go watch the flowers or snow rather than face a decisive life-or-death battle.

Yu Shengyan had the good sense to not involve himself. After bowing to Yan Wushi, he went somewhere else in the villa, leaving only the two of them in the courtyard.

Plus a deer.

Shen Qiao had rushed here, worn and covered in the dust of travel. At this moment, however, he found himself unconsciously influenced by Yan Wushi. His emotions gradually settled, and he sat down next to him, but his upright posture cut a clear contrast with Yan Wushi's casual one.

Yan Wushi seemed a little amused. "Are you worried about me, A-Qiao?"

The fawn thought he was calling it, and it trotted toward him on its little legs. Shen Qiao watched in silence as Yan Wushi doubled over in laughter.

"I have a proposition for Sect Leader Yan," Shen Qiao said helplessly.

Yan Wushi stopped laughing, and his eyes shone. "Oh? Sect Leader Shen is now a man of exalted status. What matter would require you to use the word 'proposition'?"

Shen Qiao said slowly, "About your duel with Hulugu: how about I go in your place?"

It was rare for anything to freeze Yan Wushi in surprise, even for a moment.

He quickly recovered and said, "You already fought him last time. And you lost."

"I know," said Shen Qiao, "but twenty years ago he fought against my late master. Twenty years have passed, and my master is no longer here; logically, I should be the one to continue this battle in his stead."

Yan Wushi suddenly smiled. "In truth, you believe that I sent him that challenge letter in order to lure him away, to prevent him from heading up Xuandu Mountain and causing you trouble?"

"I heard that the flaw in your demonic core has yet to be repaired," said Shen Qiao, "and that the last fight you had with Xueting only aggravated it further."

A hint of confusion flashed over Yan Wushi's face. "Did Bian Yanmei say that?"

Shen Qiao nodded.

Yan Wushi sank into contemplation, pondering whether it was better for him to admit to his disciple's words or to simply claim that Bian Yanmei had been lying. If he admitted to it, Shen Qiao would grow even more insistent on fighting Hulugu in his place. But if he said his disciple was lying, Shen Qiao would get angry...

For the first time, Yan Wushi felt that having an overly capable disciple might not actually be a good thing. However, when issues arose, it was time for the disciple to work. And when blame was slung, it was of course for the disciple to carry.

So he said, "Last time, you checked my pulse as well. My injuries aren't serious."

He extended his wrist.

Shen Qiao smoothly placed his fingers upon it and briefly took his pulse. His expression was bewildered. "If I look only at your pulse, your wounds do seem more or less healed. However, it's impossible to tell whether your demonic core has been repaired through this method."

"It's already healed."

That confused Shen Qiao even more. "Then Bian Yanmei doesn't know that you're already healed?"

"Perhaps."

"You could've avoided this battle, or at least delayed it for a little longer." In the end, it would still be for his sake.

Yan Wushi smiled. He suddenly raised his chin by a fraction, then nodded at the begonia flowers nearby. "What do you think of those flowers?"

"They're splendidly beautiful," said Shen Qiao. "The rich crimson is enchanting."

Yan Wushi casually picked up a fallen leaf beside him. He flicked his finger, and a begonia blossom plopped to the ground. Another flick, and another begonia fell. "Flying flowers and falling leaves could all become sharp weapons capable of harm." Yan Wushi's actions fully and incisively embodied this saying.

After a few more flowers fell, Shen Qiao couldn't bear to continue watching. He grabbed the other man's wrist. "What are you doing?!"

"Destroying the flowers!" Yan Wushi's tone was still languid, his posture unchanging. But instead of shaking off Shen Qiao's hand, he let him hold it.

"The flowers were blooming perfectly well, and they've done nothing to provoke you. So why must you hurt them?"

Yan Wushi laughed. "Look, A-Qiao. This is the biggest difference between you and me.

"In my opinion, those flowers have already bloomed into their finest form. If they continue to bloom, they'll only start wilting one by one. I'm sending them off; that way, their most beautiful moment will be the one that remains in your heart. Isn't that a good thing?"

His tone was careless, his wrist unmoving, letting Shen Qiao continue gripping it. Then he closed his fingers into a fist, made a squeezing motion, and those fallen leaves immediately crumbled into dust that fell through the cracks between his fingers.

"Many spend their days like dogs, baying at the slightest hint of profit. They struggle and plot for the smallest of benefits, inviting trouble upon themselves again and again. This is the tragedy of the insignificant. People in the jianghu speak of repaying kindness with kindness and enmity with enmity, but in truth, they do it to rid themselves of that tragedy. What is the point of living in this world if one cannot live grandly and splendidly, following one's heart's desires? People and flowers are the same.

"Back then, I was able to challenge Cui Youwang and Qi Fengge, so now, I can naturally challenge Hulugu as well. Of course, the outcome of victor and defeated is uncertain, but it's precisely this suspense that makes it exciting. If the outcome was determined from the beginning, how would it be any different from a pool of lifeless, stagnant water? So though you are a factor in this battle, ultimately, it's mainly for myself."

At this point, Shen Qiao naturally had no way to persuade him further.

He knew very well that he and Yan Wushi had always been two people with completely different personalities—he valued steadiness and doing things step by step, while Yan Wushi loved the unexpected, to the point that he wouldn't hesitate to risk himself to pursue it. However, Yan Wushi did not consider his actions risky.

He greatly enjoyed the process. Even if he were to die at Hulugu's hands, it wouldn't matter. This was how he wished to live his life.

To many people, this attitude would seem overconfident to the point of wild arrogance, but this was precisely who Yan Wushi was.

Just as Shen Qiao was thinking this, he heard Yan Wushi say, "A-Qiao, do you know?"

"Mm?" Shen Qiao returned to himself.

"In the past, I classified all humans into two categories."

"Mm," said Shen Qiao. He knew this. "They were either your opponents or insects."

Opponents were those who could stand on equal footing with him. Insects were the ones not worth his attention.

In the past, Shen Qiao had been an insect in his eyes.

"But now," Yan Wushi said leisurely, "I've changed my way of thinking. A-Qiao, you're different from most people in the world. You have compassion for all mankind carved into your bones, to the point that you're willing to give yourself up for others without asking for anything in return. In the past, I thought you were the same as everyone else: you might start out good and innocent, but the world is fickle, and in the end it'd teach you to change as well. But you went completely beyond my expectations. Human affairs are like a stream, yet you are a rock. No matter how the stream flows, you will never shift."

Shen Qiao gave a brief laugh. "It's rare to hear Sect Leader Yan praise me. How remarkable! This humble Daoist is greatly honored."

"Do you still hold a grudge against me in your heart?"

Shen Qiao shook his head. "No, it's the exact opposite. I admire you greatly. There aren't many people in this world who can live so willfully, but Sect Leader Yan is one of them. Before I left the mountain, the only world and jianghu I knew was the tiny little space that my late master had told me about. I'd never seen it with my own eyes. If not for Yan Wushi's instruction, I wouldn't be alive listening to you say these things now."

Yan Wushi found that solemn, serious expression and tone of Shen Qiao's incredibly adorable. He didn't suppress his desire to reach out and pat Shen Qiao's head. "So you still won't admit that it's like you?" he said. "Turn around and look at it."

There were many intelligent people in the world, but those with self-awareness, who were able to see their own flaws, were much less common. And those who could discover their flaws and were also willing to speak out about them, to change themselves, were rarer and more precious still.

Shen Qiao possessed an almost crystalline transparency.

In truth, he understood completely, yet he was willing to view everything and everyone different from him with kindness and clemency.

Shen Qiao was caught off guard by Yan Wushi's attempt to pat him on the head. His first instinct was to avoid it, then he subconsciously looked back at the fawn.

The fawn's round, glossy eyes met his gaze, and their dark, moist surfaces reflected his figure within them clearly.

Shen Qiao's heart suddenly softened. He reached out and touched its neck, and the fawn lowered its head and licked his palm in response. Shen Qiao couldn't help but laugh.

"Thank you very much, A-Qiao."

Who in the world would be fortunate enough to hear Sect Leader Yan express his gratitude? Shen Qiao started a little, then turned to look at him.

Yan Wushi smiled brightly as he gazed back at him. "Thank you for repaying my enmity with kindness, thus saving me. I've already lost count of how many times you saved me, so shouldn't I say a word of thanks?"

"You've saved me many times as well. There's no need to thank me."

"So, our friendship has reached the point where we don't need to thank each other?" Yan Wushi said meaningfully.

Shen Qiao only felt that this statement seemed somewhat off but couldn't quite put his finger on why.

Yan Wushi suddenly reached out and grabbed him, then pressed him beneath his body. Only an expert would move so swiftly!

Before Shen Qiao could react, he heard Yan Wushi say, "You also know that I have countless enemies. You're the only person with whom I've shared any deep relationship. In this fight with Hulugu, it's hard to predict whether I'll survive, so I wanted to find someone I could entrust my orphans to, and you're the only person I could think of."

His warm breath, only inches from Shen Qiao, puffed right against Shen Qiao's face, and he was left completely confused. He didn't know what to do first—push Yan Wushi away or respond to what he'd said. At that moment, his mind was completely blank.

"What...what do you mean, entrust your orphans?"

Before the Battle

Y AN WUSHI'S QUESTION had caught Shen Qiao's complete attention, and for a moment, he failed to realize that they were still locked in a bizarre position. But there was no one to remind him—Yan Wushi was even less likely to do so than the fawn was.

Yan Wushi's grave and solemn expression didn't help matters either. A smile had always lingered on his lips, all year long, whether it was the small shadow of a smirk or wild, unrestrained laughter. It made it plain to see that he was a willful man who did as he pleased. Now, however, there was no trace of a smile on his face, and this absence imparted an imperceptible sense of intimidation instead. Unconsciously, the listener would restrain their other thoughts in order to focus on his words.

"Huanyue Sect accepts disciples based on quality over quantity," Yan Wushi explained. "So far, we only have two within our sect: Bian Yanmei and Yu Shengyan. In terms of martial aptitude, Bian Yanmei isn't exceptional—only above average. His brilliance lies elsewhere."

Shen Qiao agreed with this assessment. Bian Yanmei's ability to handle various worldly, people-related affairs was indeed remarkable. Over the years, Huanyue Sect had laid down extensive roots both within and beyond the court. Yuwen Yun had tried with all his strength to attack and eliminate them, but now, with the establishment of the new dynasty, Huanyue Sect had been able to quickly rejuvenate themselves, and Bian Yanmei's contributions had been key to this achievement. Even if Yan Wushi had the ability to do the same, he might not have had the patience.

"As for Yu Shengyan, he possesses talent in martial arts, but he's too young. If I die, the two of them will be alone and isolated. If that happens, I want you to help watch over them a little..."

Shen Qiao was stunned.

If I die...

Hearing these words, an unfamiliar feeling welled up within his heart, delicate and subtle.

Outside the royal capital of Tuyuhun, Yan Wushi had been ambushed by five great experts. Despite rushing, by the time Shen Qiao arrived, he'd already been lying unconscious on the ground. Shen Qiao had believed he was dead, but...

...But at that time, although Shen Qiao had lamented his passing, it'd only been due to his desire to settle the grudges and kindness between them and to mourn the death of a master martial artist of his generation. It was different from how he felt at this moment, with all these inexplicable emotions flooding into his heart.

Yan Wushi saw his expression and sputtered a laugh in response. "Are you feeling sad for my sake?"

Shen Qiao collected himself. "The flaw in the demonic core you spoke of has already been repaired, so you can go all-out in your battle against Hulugu."

Yan Wushi smiled. "That's right. But all things have their exceptions, and even more when the opponent is Hulugu. Or, based on your understanding of me, were you hoping I'd arrogantly announce that I will definitely win?"

Shen Qiao smiled back. "If Sect Leader Yan said that, I wouldn't find it surprising at all."

He finally realized that their poses were rather inappropriate, and he couldn't help extending his arm to push Yan Wushi away, wanting to prop his body up.

But Yan Wushi didn't budge at all. Not only did he refuse to move, he also pinned Shen Qiao in place. He did this with incredible skill—Shen Qiao was left completely unable to move, but at the same time, there was no feeling of being constricted or stifled.

Shen Qiao, thinking he was still waiting for his answer, said, "I understand what Sect Leader Yan has entrusted me with; I will do my best to protect them. If anything happens to Huanyue Sect, as long as they don't do anything immoral or unethical, I will shield them with all my strength."

In the jianghu, a person's word was considered as valuable as a thousand gold—with Shen Qiao's character, this vow of his was even more priceless than that. The only thing that could prevent him from carrying out this unshakable spoken promise was his death.

He thought about Yan Wushi's wording just now, though, of "entrusting his orphans" to him, and immediately laughed a little at the irony of it.

Bian Yanmei and Yu Shengyan, what about either of them came even close to being "weak" and "alone"? Even if you turned them loose in the jianghu, the vast majority of people would just end up bullied by them.

But even after Shen Qiao's answer, Yan Wushi remained motionless. He asked, with a sincerity and warmth that Shen Qiao had never heard before, "A-Qiao, how can I repay you for your kindness?"

"One should always treat friends with sincerity," Shen Qiao replied. "There's no need to repay me."

Yan Wushi went on as if he hadn't heard him. "Fame, wealth, and glory—those magnificent treasures that others can only dream of are all worthless in your eyes."

Shen Qiao corrected him. "That's not true. In fact, I also love fame, wealth, and glory."

"Mm?"

"It is impossible for Xuandu Mountain to remain aloof from the world, and I wish to protect it. Therefore, I cannot remain aloof from the world either. In the jianghu, strength is the most reliable of all, but Xuandu Mountain is also a Daoist sect. Since it is a Daoist sect, it's impossible for it to avoid all associations with the court. You helped me connect with Yang Jian, which allowed Xuandu Mountain to gain a foothold in Chang'an. I'm very grateful to you."

Yan Wushi smiled slightly. This person had truly understood everything.

"So fame, wealth, and glory are still useful," Shen Qiao said. "As long as one remains clear-minded and avoids being ensnared by them, that's enough."

This concept was familiar to everyone, but avoiding ensnarement by these things was easier said than done. The Yu Ai and Tan Yuanchun of the past might have believed in such ideals as well, but which of them had been able to hold on to them in the end?

"That's why you're special," said Yan Wushi. "These things are truly worldly possessions that you see as external to you. I've thought about it for a long time, but I couldn't think of anything that I can repay you with, so I can only repay you with myself. What do you say?"

Of course not! Shen Qiao was dumbfounded. When he saw Yan Wushi about to lower his head, he slammed a palm into his chest without hesitation.

Yan Wushi grabbed for his wrist, but that meant he couldn't maintain his center of gravity and had to lean a little to one side. Shen Qiao's other hand chopped at his shoulder, and in an instant, the two of them had exchanged a couple of strikes. Shen Qiao took the chance to counterattack and flipped them over, pinning Yan Wushi beneath him.

Yan Wushi looked stunned. "So you like this kind of position. You should have said so earlier!"

His expression was truly as innocent as could be.

With all of Daoist Master Shen's life experiences, even if he didn't understand precisely what Yan Wushi was talking about, the suggestiveness within those words was clear. Now he fully believed that the man's demonic core must have been repaired long ago. Otherwise, how could he have the leisure to mess with others when there was such a huge battle looming ahead?!

Shen Qiao reached out to seal his acupoints, but Yan Wushi naturally wouldn't let him. Hands flew. In the blink of an eye, they'd exchanged a couple more blows, each move carrying a bloodless edge.

They were both experts who ranked within the top ten. Shen Qiao might have been a little weaker, but not by much. Yan Wushi simply gave up resisting and left himself open to Shen Qiao's palm strike.

Sure enough, Shen Qiao started and couldn't bring himself to attack. Yan Wushi seized the opportunity and pinned Shen Qiao beneath him again.

There was a beauty in his arms, and it'd be difficult to find another one like him even if he scoured the entire world. But what enthralled Yan Wushi wasn't his appearance. All those who'd interacted with Shen Qiao knew that this man had a heart that was tolerant and broad-minded, like an ocean that embraced the rivers. It was a heart that remained unshakable despite being buffeted by the many storms of life. However, he never inflicted his own pain on others either. Normally, he'd be the gentlest and most amiable of friends, yet in critical moments, he was the most trustworthy and reliable of companions, one who'd live and die by your side.

Shen Qiao hadn't been wrong. In the past, Yan Wushi believed that, aside from his disciples, there were only two types of people: opponents and insects. However, Shen Qiao's presence within his heart now clearly excluded him from these two categories. Not only that, it was far, far weightier, to an extent that even Bian Yanmei could never imagine.

It didn't matter when his mindset had changed. What was important was that Shen Qiao had slowly dropped his guard and was willing to treat him as a friend, to the point that he'd even be willing to make such a heavy promise to him, for him. But this wasn't enough.

To Yan Wushi, it was far from enough.

What he wanted was to be peerlessly special, one of a kind in all of heaven and earth, and he didn't want the kind of standing that others could easily imitate or seize. He'd always been an imperious person—if he wanted something, he must have the best, and no one could be capable of replacing him.

But Yan Wushi did not display these thoughts excessively. Forget using force to get his way—compared to the methods he'd used in the past, his current actions were overflowing with tenderness. All of this was because he knew Shen Qiao too well.

This man looked soft and gentle, but he possessed a core more unyielding than anyone else's. Even slightly excessive methods might make Shen Qiao disdain him and push him further and further away. Look at Yu Ai—his mistakes couldn't have made for a clearer lesson on this.

So Yan Wushi had deviated from his usual behavior. He'd slowly, gradually lured Shen Qiao into his trap. Not only was he not intense, he hadn't even sealed Shen Qiao's acupoints during their short fight just now—if he sealed them, he could force Shen Qiao into a passive position, make him listen, but what would be the point of that?

Naturally, there'd be no point.

Therefore, as Shen Qiao was amenable to coaxing but not coercion, losing the advantage to Yan Wushi again was completely reasonable.

"You don't want anything, so I can only give you myself," Yan Wushi said. "Is even that still not enough?" With their current poses, Yan Wushi should have been arrogantly looking down at him and oozing with superiority, but Shen Qiao could actually see a hint of hurt and compromise in his grin. He was instantly both annoyed and amused.

Yan Wushi slowly lowered his head, his tone soft and gentle. "Do you remember what happened back in the cave?"

Shen Qiao only remembered two incidents involving caves. The first was when Yan Wushi had fought Ruyan Kehui. Shen Qiao had thought he was injured and followed him into a cave, and Yan Wushi almost strangled him. The second was when Yan Wushi had used his Shanhe Tongbei to scale fish.

When he recalled these memories, Shen Qiao's expression darkened.

"Please let go, Sect Leader Yan. I'm not used to speaking to others like this."

"There aren't any outsiders; don't worry." Yan Wushi smiled and picked him up, half pinning him against the wall. This moved

Shen Qiao from a lying posture to a sitting one, but he was still half trapped in Yan Wushi's arms.

He said nothing.

Yan Wushi hadn't sealed Shen Qiao's acupoints either. The important thing was that if he wished to break free, he'd have no choice but to fight Yan Wushi. If he went easy on him, Yan Wushi would easily negate his attacks. If he used actual force, Yan Wushi would simply give up resisting and leave himself at Shen Qiao's mercy. That considered, Shen Qiao wouldn't be able to bring himself to attack. This was truly...

Dead pigs were unafraid of boiling water; if someone was shameless or unscrupulous enough, they'd have nothing to fear.

"I'm already about to die," said Yan Wushi. "Do you lack even the patience to listen to a few words from me?"

Shen Qiao sighed and gave up struggling. "Say them, then."

Yan Wushi smiled. "But just now I thought about it: no matter how much I say, it won't compare to just doing it."

He kept hopping from one thought to the next, and Shen Qiao couldn't keep up at all. "Huh?" he said blankly.

Then he was unable to make any sounds. His voice cut off suddenly as a shadow obstructed his line of sight. Something hot and soft landed on his lips. Yan Wushi pried his teeth right open, then dove straight in.

A short yell came from the side. Yu Shengyan stood in the doorway. The fawn stood behind him, biting into the corner of his robes. As a result, when he tried to back away and leave, he almost tripped over the fawn.

Shen Qiao slammed a palm into Yan Wushi's shoulder, his waist straightening a little as he leapt up gracefully, no longer restrained.

But his lips were slightly red and swollen, and the hair at his temples was mussed. Even his complexion looked unnatural, with shame overlapping with anger. It was impossible to discern if he was more humiliated or more furious. But with his current appearance, even if he wished to be dignified, it was impossible.

Yu Shengyan saw his shizun's airy gaze slant over to him, and he longed to just bash his head open against the pillars of the colonnade. Normally, with his martial prowess, he wouldn't have made such a mistake. He could only blame his own terrible timing.

He'd just been strolling around the villa, thinking that the two of them should have already finished their conversation and he could go and greet Shizun—but who knew that he'd just happen to run into a scene that shouldn't have been seen?

What...bad luck!

Yu Shengyan gave a dry chuckle. "Um... Can we just pretend that I was never here?"

He no longer had the courage to greet his master. He turned around and quickly fled, running as far away as he could.

Da-shixiong, is it not too late to go back and seek refuge with you in Chang'an? Wah!

126

Gambler

L ESS THAN TWO DAYS remained until the decisive battle. The fight had caught almost everyone's attention. The inns in Funing had long been filled as countless people from the jianghu flocked to this small, normally unknown town. It was just like it had been when Shen Qiao and Kunye had dueled.

There was one difference, though. Shen Qiao had been renowned back then, but it hadn't been due to his martial arts. The reason his battle with Kunye had attracted attention was because, on a certain level, it represented the continuation of Qi Fengge and Hulugu's brilliance. Everyone had searched for the radiance of the two greatest martial arts masters in the land within their successors.

However, to many people, the battle between Yan Wushi and Hulugu was seen as a confrontation between the martial arts circles of the Central Plains and the Göktürk Khaganate.

Buddhist, Daoist, and Confucian sects, and even numerous other kinds of sects, both large and small—of those who heard the news, nine out of ten had rushed right over.

It was said that one inn had been completely booked by Linchuan Academy. Even Academy Master Ruyan Kehui himself had personally come to witness this battle.

Buddhist Master Fayi from Tiantai Sect, Yi Pichen from Qingcheng Mountain's Chunyang Monastery, Xuandu's Violet

Palace, Fajing Sect, Hehuan Sect, Liuli Palace, Bixia Sect, and even the Kosa Sage from faraway Tuyuhun... All these people either came themselves or sent their disciples. It was plain to see that they didn't want to miss this exciting, once-in-a-lifetime, and decisive battle.

This level of attention—practically the entire world was watching! It was far more dazzling a spectacle than the match between Shen Qiao and Kunye had been. But a battle capable of drawing this many eyes must also be a battle that carried tremendous risks.

To succeed would mean becoming unparalleled in the world.

To fail would be akin to falling into the abyss.

This wasn't only a duel of martial arts, it was also a duel for their reputations—and their lives. No one was naive enough to believe that the battle between these two would be just some friendly spar. Everyone knew that twenty years ago, during the duel between Qi Fengge and Hulugu, Hulugu had been grievously injured and almost died. He had been forced to swear not to enter the Central Plains for twenty years. Instead, he left for lands far beyond the Great Wall and entered a death seclusion. Qi Fengge himself hadn't gotten off too easily either—many people privately whispered that Qi Fengge had sustained serious wounds in that duel as well, and it'd left a lurking peril within him that had later led to Perfected Master Qi's death. Naturally, though, this statement was but a rumor; no one could confirm it.

Whatever the case, many people in the jianghu were only average practitioners who were unlikely to glimpse the martial summit for their entire lives. Just showing up here was already the chance of a lifetime for them, even if they couldn't climb the precipitous Yinghui Peak and could only wait at the foot of the mountain in Funing County.

"I heard that Funing County's largest gambling den, Tongfu Gambling House, has already opened its doors. They're taking bets on who will win in the Sect Leader's match with Hulugu." The villa's steward respectfully reported the situation to Yan Wushi.

These days, Yu Shengyan hadn't dared to appear in front of Yan Wushi. No one knew where he'd run off to.

Though they were staying at the spare villa on the outskirts of town, that didn't mean they couldn't get any news. On the contrary, the steward would send people to inquire about the latest information each day such as which new sects had arrived in the county, which inn they were staying in, where the people from Linchuan Academy had gone today, and so forth. All this news quickly reached their ears.

Despite being one of the parties involved in the decisive battle, Yan Wushi was more leisurely and composed than anyone could have imagined. He was currently holding a walnut shell—the maid had left it on the side after cracking some walnuts—which he tossed to the fawn. "A-Qiao, come here."

The fawn was currently snuggled up to Shen Qiao in a bid for affection, its head lowered as it drank water from his cup. The walnut shell smacked it in the head, but rather than fuss about Yan Wushi's attack, he simply continued to drink calmly.

It was Shen Qiao who couldn't bear such actions. Leaving aside that this man had chosen his name for the fawn, which clearly carried no good intentions, the fawn was perfectly well behaved and never provoked anyone, yet Yan Wushi was always bullying and teasing it.

Another walnut shell flew over, but this time it didn't hit the fawn, for a leaf knocked it away. It instead grazed past the steward's ear, then embedded itself into the pillar behind him.

The steward broke out into a cold sweat.

Shen Qiao was apologetic. "I'm sorry, did I scare you?"

The steward shook his head repeatedly. How was he worthy of accepting this apology? Yan Wushi couldn't help but burst out laughing.

Shen Qiao wanted to roll his eyes at him, but that would make him look far too ridiculous. He patted the ignorant fawn, thinking that he'd find a chance to give him a new name.

Yan Wushi suddenly asked, "How are the betting odds?"

The steward looked on blankly for a moment before realizing that the question was for him. He quickly said, "1-10."

Shen Qiao had never gambled before, but he too knew what that "1-10" meant. He was astonished despite himself. "On who?"

"On the master's victory," said the steward.

"Then what about the bets on Hulugu?"

The steward gave a light cough. "1-2."

Shen Qiao was speechless.

Yan Wushi wasn't upset; instead, he smiled. "Seems like they're not optimistic I'll win!"

When Hulugu reappeared in the jianghu, his stunning debut had been on Qingcheng Mountain. First, he'd defeated Yi Pichen, then Shen Qiao. They were two of the world's top ten, both grandmaster-level experts, yet they'd lost to Hulugu in a blink of an eye. These battle records were enough to astound the whole world.

On the other hand, there was Yan Wushi. Though he was indeed formidable, Hulugu's display of strength before this match had been enough to dull his shine. Moreover, Hulugu was from the same generation as Qi Fengge. His martial arts had already achieved a level where age wouldn't serve as an obstacle or restrict his physical power. Instead, it signified his experience.

Shen Qiao's tone was flat. "Seeing what you're like right now, I'm not optimistic either."

Yan Wushi raised an eyebrow. "What is my venerable self like?

Just because there's a major battle upcoming, I have to act all lost and bewildered, unable to sleep and eat? Or should I burst into tears while hugging your thighs and cry, 'A-Qiao, I don't want to go anymore'?"

Shen Qiao shot him a look but didn't speak.

"I don't think there's anything to worry about," Yan Wushi consoled him. "You needn't worry either. I've already entrusted Huanyue Sect to you. At worst, I'll just get another crack in my skull. It's not like it's never been cracked open before."

Shen Qiao was speechless once again.

Yan Wushi smiled brightly and shrugged. "If it cracks, Xie Ling might be able to return again. Then the two of you can enjoy your lovers' talk once more."

There was absolutely nothing Shen Qiao could say to that.

He was a person of the jianghu, and one with exceptional martial prowess. Furthermore, he'd personally fought with Hulugu, so he naturally understood what this battle meant. And because he knew, he'd spent these days constantly thinking of methods to help Yan Wushi, to give him a greater chance of victory.

But when it came to the martial path, finding shortcuts was easier said than done. Even if Shen Qiao had managed to rebuild his bones and muscles, he'd lost all of his martial arts first. Though you couldn't build the new without destroying the old, who'd want to "destroy" something that was working perfectly well? The fact that Yan Wushi had been able to repair the demonic core's flaw was already incredibly fortunate. If he hadn't obtained that *Zhuyang Strategy* scroll from Chen Gong, his chance of victory against Hulugu might have dropped even lower.

Worries plagued Shen Qiao's heart, and his mind spun without pause as he rummaged through his memories. These last couple of days, he'd been silent more often than usual.

Right now, he pondered for a long time, though he didn't forget to block two more walnut shells for the fawn partway through.

"I've been thinking a lot, but I recalled something," he said at last. "After that battle between Shizun and Hulugu, I had some realizations. It's been many years, and I was young then, so I don't remember them too clearly. I only recalled a little after this long. Perhaps it won't be of any help to you, but it's still better for you to know a little rather than heading in completely unprepared."

"Mm," said Yan Wushi. He quietly waited for the rest.

Shen Qiao took some time to organize his thoughts. "Shizun once said that Hulugu is a martial arts prodigy. He's trained with practically every weapon and is proficient in all of them. But in the end, he didn't choose to use any weapon, relying on his bare palms instead. It wasn't just because his internal cultivation was exquisite, to the point that a weapon would be merely a superficial touch, but more because he's already integrated all those weapons into his every move and stance. But everyone has their strengths and weaknesses. Other than the heavenly Dao, there are no perfect existences in this world. That's just as true of Hulugu as anyone else; he must have his own weaknesses. Twenty years ago, he lost to Shizun because his abilities and internal energy both were slightly inferior to Shizun's. But this time, if you pit your internal energy against his, you might not have a chance of winning, so you'll need to search somewhere else for more weaknesses."

Saying this, he realized something himself: "In truth, these words might not be useful to you at all, and you can only use them as reference."

When two people fought, they'd experience many feelings that were mysterious and profound. These feelings couldn't be expressed in words—only those fighting the battle could experience them.

Even if Shen Qiao's tongue had been cast from silver, he still probably wouldn't be able to explain them clearly. But as he clearly wanted Yan Wushi to win, he'd struggled to pull these out from his memories.

Yan Wushi looked at him with a tender gaze. "Even though I'm the one who's going to fight Hulugu, you're the one who's about to collapse from anxiety. It's been hard on you."

Shen Qiao was caught between laughing and crying. "This battle is no trivial matter. You can tell just by looking at the number of people in Funing County! You're the only one who's this carefree! I won't mention your disciples, but haven't you realized how on edge everyone in the villa has been the past two days?"

Yan Wushi gave a laugh and rose to his feet. "I know that you're the most worried about me. Why drag other people into it? Sitting around like this all day is so boring. Come, I'll take you out to play."

Shen Qiao frowned a little, but Yan Wushi had already walked out, so he could only follow after him.

Yan Wushi led him into the county town, but instead of visiting any particular grandmaster at an inn, he walked into a gambling den with practiced ease.

Shen Qiao looked up.

Tongfu Gambling House.

The place was packed. A fair number of jianghu practitioners were present, contributing to the bustling atmosphere. As the battle had yet to start, many had come to while away their time by gambling. The betting boards for Hulugu and Yan Wushi naturally attracted the most people—the crowd clustered so densely that it seemed almost watertight. But Yan Wushi only called over one of the dealers in the gambling den, laying down a bet for himself, then he pulled Shen Qiao elsewhere.

"This is the game 'Large or Small.' It's very easy to play: There are three dice, and if their combined sum is less than or equal to ten, it's small. If it's greater than or equal to eleven, it's large," he said to Shen Qiao. Seeing the confusion on his face, he couldn't help but smile.

This was a different world, one that was entirely unfamiliar to Shen Qiao. Shouts rang out everywhere; some people were cheering in joy after winning money, while others were wailing and moaning, having lost it. In his Daoist robes, Shen Qiao looked obviously out of place. Considering his robes and his exceptional, eye-catching appearance, someone would have recognized him long ago if not for the fact that most of the people milling in and out were but lower-ranking members of the jianghu.

And Yan Wushi needed no mention. His sheer presence already left those near him unable to breathe—absolutely no one dared to look twice in his direction.

Here, what determined victory and defeat wasn't martial arts but luck. It was impossible to say how many people had staked their fortunes here and ended up destitute. Year after year, the gambling den continued to thrive, yet how many batches of visitors, milling in and out of then den, had it done in?

As he stood within, Shen Qiao, who wouldn't have flinched even if a mountain collapsed before him, now found himself at a bit of a loss.

Perhaps Yan Wushi thought that this kind of Shen Qiao would be incredibly adorable and that this trip to the den hadn't been in vain. He tugged at him while smiling. "Qi Fengge would've never brought you to a gambling den, would he?"

Shen Qiao frowned, his answer clear: *How could Shizun ever bring me to a place like this?*

Yan Wushi brought him to the dealing table and spoke in a coaxing tone, the kind you'd use on a child: "It's very fun. Look, even in a game like Large or Small, these people are fully engrossed, terrified they might overlook even the slightest detail."

Shen Qiao swept a glance at the faces of the people around him. Sure enough, they all seemed deeply enthralled, their eyes completely fixed on the porcelain cups in the dealer's hand.

Once the porcelain cup was raised, the result was clear and everyone's expressions transformed in an instant: originally taut, one group's beamed in elation while the other's dropped with dejected frustration.

But Shen Qiao couldn't understand their agitation. He was a character who'd wandered into this place, a dispassionate onlooker. He couldn't empathize with their feelings.

Yan Wushi placed a wooden gambling chip he'd traded for earlier into Shen Qiao's hand. This represented ten taels, enough money to cover over half a year of an ordinary family's expenses. Here it also counted as a fairly large wager, but Huanyue Sect was incredibly wealthy, so Yan Wushi didn't even blink. "Give it a try."

"Finalize your bets! Finalize your bets!" yelled the dealer as he shook the porcelain cup, then placed it upside-down on the table.

Shen Qiao hesitated for a moment—then he flicked his finger. The wooden chip soundlessly landed on the area where the word "small" was written.

That move of his was extraordinarily beautiful; though the dealer was incredibly busy, he looked up to see it was a good-looking young man with a sword on his back. He wondered to himself if this man had come to trash the den.

The porcelain cup lifted. It was "small."

The odds for this table were 1-1, so Shen Qiao won another wooden chip. This meant that he now had twenty taels.

During the second round of bets, he chose "large."

The results were announced. It really was "large." Several consecutive rounds came and went; Shen Qiao bet correctly each time. Even the patrons nearby had taken notice of him, wondering, *Do even Daoist priests like gambling nowadays?* But it didn't stop them from placing their bets together with Shen Qiao.

The dealer couldn't take it any longer: he secretly reported the matter to the owner. The owner came out with several people and saw that the man in question was from the jianghu, not someone to be trifled with. So he quickly presented Shen Qiao with a generous sum and respectfully requested that they leave. He even told them that there was another Sifang Gambling House in the county and that it was also very large.

The moment they left the den, Yan Wushi began to laugh. He laughed until he'd stooped over, supporting himself on Shen Qiao's shoulder.

Shen Qiao said nothing.

Yan Wushi laughed almost to the point of tears. "This is the first time I've been kicked out of a gambling den. I truly owe it to you. Were you using your internal energy to listen to the dice?"

"...How would I know that such a thing was forbidden?" Shen Qiao's tone carried a hint of unconscious indignation.

Yan Wushi prodded at him. "These are the rules. Even if Qi Fengge had come, he'd be forbidden from using his internal energy. Otherwise there wouldn't be a single gambling den that'd allow him inside."

Surprisingly, Shen Qiao quickly grew relieved at this. He even smiled. "In any case, if you hadn't dragged me here, I never would've gone in."

He looked at the heavy purse in Yan Wushi's hand and asked curiously, "You won quite a bit. You didn't use your internal energy?"

Yan Wushi laughed. "This gambling den has a good reputation. The dealer doesn't cheat, so everyone relies on their own luck. That makes it a bit more fun. Don't you feel that using your internal energy to listen to the dice and obtain the result beforehand actually makes things boring instead?"

Though Shen Qiao didn't enjoy playing such games, he still understood what Yan Wushi was saying. He nodded. "Leaving a little bit of suspense is a way of making things more enjoyable."

Yan Wushi played with the purse, tossing it up and down. A blink of an eye later, he'd tossed it into the cracked bowl of a roadside beggar, his aim unfailingly true. The beggar hadn't expected that a fortune would descend on him from the heavens one day—he was stupefied.

In contrast, the person who'd tossed him the money didn't even spare him a glance, as if all he'd tossed aside was a rock.

"That's right," he said. "Life is all about gambling. Reincarnation is gambling. Some people are born into good families, never having to worry about food or clothing. Others are born as children of beggars and into a life of poverty. Marrying is also a gamble on whether the couple will be harmonious and if their family will be stable. It could be an ordinary, market-side family, a wealthy, extravagant family, or even the emperor's imperial family itself. Are these not all full of gambles?"

Shen Qiao thought of himself. If Qi Fengge hadn't taken him in as a disciple, it wouldn't have mattered how talented he was. Within this turbulent world, he'd likely have become a lone ghost wandering the wilderness long ago.

Yan Wushi had used gambling as a metaphor, and there were indeed comparable aspects. Shen Qiao couldn't say it was wrong.

He shook his head. "Yan Wushi, you are a gambler to the core."

To bring himself the greatest enjoyment, he could stake even his life as the bet. In the whole world, there perhaps was no gambler crazier than him.

Yan Wushi smiled. "A-Qiao knows me well. If I was sure to win against Hulugu, what would be the point of going? Things are only interesting when my victory is uncertain! If this suspense were missing, life would truly be so dull!"

A faint smile tugged at the corner of Shen Qiao's mouth. "In this world, people as willful as you are seldom seen."

"Come, since I won some money, I'll treat you."

"You gave your winnings to a beggar just now," Shen Qiao reminded him.

"I win money for pleasure, and if someone's pleased, they should treat others. What does that have to do with gambling?"

In short, he was happy.

Yan Wushi dragged the speechless Shen Qiao away.

127

One Question

"SAY, WHERE WOULD MY SHIZUN take someone?" Yu Shengyan asked. He lay beneath the colonnade, bored out of his mind as he teased the deer with a tuft of cogon grass. He still found it rather strange. Shizun wasn't the type to love small animals; why would he suddenly procure a deer and raise it here?

The steward smiled. "If your esteemed self is curious, you can follow them and take a look. Then you'll know."

Yu Shengyan quickly shook his head. "I'm not interested in doing things that'll get me killed. But the duel is tomorrow, and Shizun doesn't seem worried at all. Truly a case where the emperor is unconcerned, but his eunuchs are in a tizzy. You've been serving Shizun since before I became his disciple, so you must understand him better than I do, right?"

The steward half rose from his seat in a short bow. "I dare not accept Erlangjun's praise. The master's thoughts are as inscrutable as the sea, not something this lowly one can fathom. However, the master has always looked ahead before moving: for every step he takes, he's planned three in advance. I trust that his match with Hulugu this time is no exception. The master is blessed with great fortune, so I'm sure he'll return safe and sound."

Yu Shengyan couldn't stop himself from smiling. This steward held his shizun in extremely high regard; he could tell just from his words. In the steward's eyes, everything about Shizun was good, from the top of his head to the tip of his toes.

"Tell me honestly," he said. "Did you make a bet in the county town?"

The steward's eyes snapped wide open, then he gave a quiet cough, covering his mouth as he mumbled, "I bet a little."

Yu Shengyan pressed him. "How much is a little?"

The old steward looked helpless. "Around twenty taels or so."

"So little? Didn't you say that Shizun would definitely win just now?!"

The steward also laughed. "It was just a small bet to lift one's mood. Must I stake my entire fortune? If you're bored, you should take a stroll through the county town. Quite a few people from the jianghu have gathered there now; it's a perfect chance to spar."

"With the big battle so close, I'm not going to stir up any trouble."

In truth, he really wanted to follow Yan Wushi and Shen Qiao to see the excitement, but he'd already offended Shizun earlier with his poor judgment, so he could only cower in the villa like a turtle and chat idly with this old steward.

The steward saw how listless he was and took the initiative to continue the earlier topic. "Then in your esteemed view, where would the Master and Daoist Master Shen go? Why don't we make a bet?"

"What are we betting?"

The steward smiled. "The jade set of jug and cups from the Han Dynasty that this lowly one recovered earlier. Hasn't Erlangjun been enamored with them for a while? I'll wager those."

Yu Shengyan's spirits lifted, and he flipped upward into a seated position like a carp leaping from the water. "Then I'll wager the glaze weiqi set that Shixiong gave me. But when they get back, I don't dare go up to them and ask, so how can we know the results?"

"That's easy. Daoist Master Shen is very amiable; when they get back, just ask him."

"If they go out, they'll certainly have a meal outside, so we can't count that. And if Shizun specially brought Daoist Master Shen outside, it wouldn't only be to have a meal."

The steward nodded. "Then this lowly one guesses that they went to visit some friends. Right now, experts have gathered like storm clouds in Funing County—even Academy Master Ruyan has come. Perhaps the Master and Daoist Master Shen wished to meet with some old acquaintances."

Yu Shengyan laughed. "Uncle Zhang, I fear you're going to lose to me!"

The steward also smiled. "Erlangjun hasn't made his guess yet; how does he know I'll lose?"

"From Shizun's personality, he'd never take the initiative to visit someone. He's already fought with Ruyan Kehui, so Shizun won't look for him again. Besides, the decisive battle with Hulugu takes place the day after tomorrow, so at this time, he should conserve his strength."

The steward wasn't unconvinced. "Then what are you referring to?"

"There are four pleasures in life: eating, drinking, sex, and gambling. So my guess is that this time, they're either at a gambling den or a brothel."

The steward was speechless.

It was news to him that the four pleasures of life were these four pleasures, specifically.

"There are countless beauties who'd throw themselves into the master's arms," said the steward, "and the villa also has many beautiful singers and dancers. Why would he take Daoist Master Shen somewhere like that?"

"This is what you don't understand," said Yu Shengyan. "Daoist Master Shen doesn't get these things yet. He's kept his heart pure and free from desires since childhood—like a block of wood. The only place in the world that can help someone understand these things is the pleasure district. Even if he doesn't experience it firsthand, as long as he gets a look, his mind will be opened. So Shizun must first take Daoist Master Shen to a place where he can experience the differences between men and women. Once he has a mode of comparison, he'll be able to understand true earthly bliss!"

The steward was confused. "Mode of comparison for what?"

"Oh," said Yu Shengyan. "For the difference between Shizun and a woman..."

He suddenly cut himself off as he silently thought, *That was close.* He'd almost said something he shouldn't have. He must forget the scene he'd witnessed as quickly as possible.

He kept things vague and hurriedly waved it off. "In short, it's either a gambling den or a brothel. Take a good look when they get back. If Daoist Master Shen's cheeks are flushed, or if he looks bashful, they definitely went to a brothel—it's the only place that'd give him that kind of expression."

The steward said nothing but thought, *You seem to know a lot about it.*

Yu Shengyan noticed the steward's odd expression. "Are you betting or not? Or could it be that you can't bear to lose your jade jug set, so you want to go back on our deal?"

The steward quickly replied, "The word of an upright gentleman is like a swift horse: once released, it cannot be returned. How could I renege? Of course I'm betting!"

Yu Shengyan stood, tossing the cogon grass at the fawn's head. "Then I'll wait to collect my winnings! Don't be heartbroken once it happens!"

His mood had finally lightened quite a bit. After taking a few steps, he looked back and waved at the deer. "Come here, I'll take you to have some barbecue."

Then he asked the steward, "Did Shizun give it a name?"

"...He did."

"What is it?"

"A-Qiao."

Yu Shengyan froze. "Which Qiao?"

The steward suppressed his smile. "The one you're thinking of."

Their eyes met, and they simply stared at each other blankly. Yu Shengyan suddenly said, "Is it all right if I change my guess of them going to a brothel?"

The steward laughed. "So you're reneging?"

Yu Shengyan was left with no recourse. "Forget it, forget it."

He waved to the fawn again. "Daoist Master Shen, shall we go have some barbecue?"

The steward said nothing.

The fawn returned Yu Shengyan's gaze with a guileless look.

Meanwhile, Shen Qiao was not eating barbecue, nor was he in a brothel. He was by the lakeside.

The lake wasn't far from the villa, and they were sitting within the pavilion there. Yan Wushi had some people marinate freshly caught prawns and fish in wine, creating a dish of drunken prawns and fish, which they then served. Together with some quality aged wine, it truly was the picture of an ideal life, one that would satisfy even the immortals.

Yan Wushi had always known how to make his life more pleasant.

Though he often spent days in the wilderness, dining and sleeping amid wind and dew, if there was a chance for something better, he'd never make himself suffer pointlessly.

"Where did you find these ready workers?" Shen Qiao thought it somewhat odd.

"There's a relay station nearby. Originally, it didn't get much business, but I purchased it and moved some of the villa's staff over. When more sophisticated guests come to fish, you can make some money off serving them food. At night, they can also stay at the station—no need to rush back to the city."

Shen Qiao smiled. "I fear that only you would do such a thing."

"With all the treacherous, precipitous mountains nearby, like Banbu Peak and Yinghui Peak, many scholars and learned men will naturally come this way. It's not a place people are completely uninterested in."

Shen Qiao understood what he was saying. The main purpose of this station was to gather and relay news. After all, it was located on an official road, so many people would stop there. As for the skilled chef who did the cooking, or the maids who served the food and wine, those were mainly for Sect Leader Yan to enjoy. Whether or not they turned a profit didn't matter.

The dishes before them were almost all cooked in wine; the aroma was so rich and strong that one could grow intoxicated from the scent alone.

Shen Qiao wasn't someone who abstained from wine, but when he saw the full cup of aged wine before him, he looked embarrassed. "To be honest, I'm not a good drinker."

It was the type of wine that could get a person drunk immediately. He could tell that at a glance.

Yan Wushi filled his own cup to the brim and downed it with a gulp. "I'm about to die, yet you won't even drink a cup of wine for me."

Shen Qiao didn't reply. Though he knew perfectly well that Yan Wushi was being insincere, Shen Qiao still picked up the cup and drank the contents in two gulps. After a wave of burning heat flowed down his throat, he immediately felt his entire person start burning up, the warmth traveling from his stomach outward.

"This is shaojiu?"[3] He was a little surprised.

Yan Wushi shook his head. "Not really. It's only a little pungent due to the addition of cornelian cherries and Sichuan peppers. However, since fish and prawns are cool by nature, they balance each other out."

A maid came forward to peel the drunken shrimp, then she placed the tender meat on the plate in front of Shen Qiao.

Shen Qiao put it in his mouth. The sweetness from the freshwater prawn together with the rich aroma of wine indeed left an endless, lingering aftertaste. He set down his chopsticks, and when he saw the maid about to step forward to refill his plate, he waved his hands. "I'm afraid that I'll get drunk if I eat too much. I've finished."

Yan Wushi shook his head. "After this meal, after you return from Banbu Peak, you don't even know if I'll be sitting in front of you still, yet you even find moving your chopsticks to be that much of a bother? I'm heartbroken."

"Can you stop bringing this up?" said Shen Qiao. "Hulugu is indeed powerful, but you're no pushover yourself. How can you lose your life so easily?!"

Yan Wushi waved the maid away and personally filled Shen Qiao's cup with wine. "The world is ever changing," he said coolly.

3   烧酒. A type of colorless Chinese liquor. Very popular to serve.

"I might be arrogant, but I dare not say I'm sure to win. With this battle, Hulugu needs to defeat me to prove to the world that he's long surpassed Qi Fengge and to raise the Göktürks' prestige even more. If he has the chance to kill me yet doesn't, he'd be betraying his illustrious reputation. And if I get the chance to kill Hulugu, it wouldn't be my nature to avoid taking it either."

Shen Qiao sighed quietly. He couldn't bear to go against Yan Wushi any longer and finally stopped refusing the cup of wine.

Yan Wushi's actions hadn't been in good faith. Normally, he'd never have the chance to make Shen Qiao drink, but now, the precious chance to admire a drunken beauty had appeared, so he'd looked for his weak spot while pouring him one cup after another. He hadn't expected that Shen Qiao's words about being a poor drinker were really true, though—after drinking a mere three cups of wine, a faint red had already bloomed over his cheeks, and his eyes were no longer as clear as before.

How many times could one see such a scene in their lifetime? Next time, it would be much more difficult to make Shen Qiao drink. He ought to have someone paint this later. As Yan Wushi reached his hand out to stroke his companion's face, he thought that it felt quite warm.

Shen Qiao held his forehead. He didn't throw a drunken fit; only his reactions had slowed a little. Suddenly, and without knowing why, he raised a hand to rub his face. He dazedly stared at that hand for a long time afterward, then a pained expression slowly surfaced on his face.

Yan Wushi hadn't expected his alcohol tolerance to be this bad. He watched him teeter around, about to fall over, and had no choice but to sit himself closer and hold Shen Qiao in his arms. "Nauseated?"

Shen Qiao shook his head and covered his face with his hands. For a long moment, he said nothing. Even with how capable Yan Wushi was, he couldn't guess what this action meant right away. However, his solution was very direct: he reached out and pulled the hands covering Shen Qiao's face away.

Yan Wushi was truly very sharp—he instantly felt some slight moisture on his fingers.

He looked back at Shen Qiao's eyes and found that they were wet. He couldn't tell if it was due to the alcohol fumes or if Shen Qiao was actually crying.

At last, Yan Wushi dropped that teasing, leisurely smile, and his expression grew visibly emotional.

He'd only wanted to appreciate a drunken beauty; he hadn't intended to make the beauty cry. While Shen Qiao had wept a few times in the past, every single one of those times had come from a place of deep emotion and heartfelt sorrow.

Shen Qiao's personality tended to be soft and gentle, but he was also firm and unyielding on the inside. He certainly wasn't the kind of weak person who'd burst into tears at the drop of a hat. He frowned a little now, as if he hadn't expected that Yan Wushi would do this, but the moisture within his eyes remained just moisture; it didn't gather into tears and trickle down his face.

"A-Qiao, you are sad for me. You're afraid that this battle with Hulugu is one I won't return from, right?" Yan Wushi said gently.

Shen Qiao sighed. Because of the wine, he couldn't stop himself from expressing his melancholy. Otherwise, he'd at most be a little quieter than usual. He propped himself up, as if trying to shake off Yan Wushi's embrace, but his drunkenness made his body soft and limp—he'd temporarily lost his agility as a martial arts practitioner, leaving his body unable to keep up with his will.

Forced to give up, he said, "It's strange. If I were the one fighting Hulugu instead, I'd only feel that this day was inevitable, and with a heart overflowing with heroic spirit, I'd stop thinking about anything else. But when it's a friend who's doing this, all that's left inside me is worry."

"Friend." Yan Wushi played with this word in his mouth, then said, "If it were Li Qingyu battling Hulugu instead, would you also be this worried?"

Shen Qiao considered the question seriously, and his brows pinched tighter and tighter. But even after a long while, he still hadn't given him an answer.

And what answer did Yan Wushi need? He smiled, stroking the hair at Shen Qiao's temples.

Shen Qiao rubbed at his temples. "Mm?"

"A-Qiao."

He buried his face into the crook of Shen Qiao's neck, then gently crumbled this name into pieces, letting it reverberate endlessly in his heart.

It didn't occur to Shen Qiao how suggestive their poses were. He only felt Yan Wushi's hair rubbing against his neck until it itched, and he couldn't help but push the man away. He rose and staggered over to the lakeside, then bent down to splash some lake water onto his face. The ice-cold droplets jolted him, and a good portion of his mental clarity returned.

Yan Wushi came over to support him. "Let's go back."

Shen Qiao nodded and couldn't resist complaining. "I'll never drink wine ever again."

Yan Wushi ribbed at him. "You're such a terrible drinker, so you should train yourself."

Shen Qiao's head throbbed. "Next time, only if someone else wishes to fight Hulugu again. Otherwise no one will be able to make me drink anything, no matter how grand the upcoming event."

Yan Wushi burst into loud laughter.

Shen Qiao circulated his qi to relieve some of the alcohol's effects. Though his mind was still a muddled mess, he could finally walk on his own.

It was almost evening when they returned to the villa to find the fawn grazing in the front yard. Shen Qiao's thoughts were still foggy and shaky, so he became somewhat childish. He stepped forward and wrapped his arms around the fawn's neck, whispering, "I'll pick a new name for you, all right?"

Across the yard, Yan Wushi beckoned to him. "A-Qiao, come here."

Before Shen Qiao could figure out which one he was calling, the fawn had already shaken Shen Qiao off and was happily bounding toward Yan Wushi.

Shen Qiao suppressed his displeasure and leaned against a pillar, rubbing his head. He wondered why on earth he'd been so worried for that man earlier. It was truly unnecessary.

Afterward, he couldn't recall when he'd fallen asleep, or how he'd made it back to his bedroom. Everything seemed like it was part of a dream, separated from him by a veil, hazy and unreal, like a flower within a mirror or the moon in the water.

After sleeping for a very, very long time, Shen Qiao woke, feeling refreshed and invigorated, as if he'd slept through the four seasons entirely.

He washed up before summoning a maid to ask about the time and date.

"You've already slept for a full day and night," she told him. "It's dawn now. I believe that the master and Hulugu are already fighting on Banbu Peak."

Shen Qiao was flabbergasted, completely unable to believe that he'd slept so long. On second thought, he realized, Yan Wushi had probably done something, like press his sleep acupoint during his drunken slumber.

But there was no time to speak further. He grasped Shanhe Tongbei, and with a flash, he swept toward Banbu Peak.

128

A World-Shaking Battle

ANBU PEAK was still the same Banbu Peak.

It had towered here for hundreds and thousands of years. Neither the rise and fall of the world nor the changing of dynasties had any effect on it at all.

Thanks to the recent rainfall, many clouds cloaked the sun and vapor steamed above the river surface, transforming into mountain mist. Even Yinghui Peak opposite it had become wrapped in white. It looked like an immortal realm.

But those standing within this scene lacked the mood to admire it, and they certainly didn't feel like they were in the realm of immortals.

After several days of consecutive rain, the mountain roads had become unusually slippery. Combined with Yinghui Peak's already rugged terrain, when common people simply stood beneath the mountain and gazed upward, they'd be unable to stop themselves from gasping. There was even less to be said about climbing it—it was like trying to tread on thin ice. Even for martial arts practitioners with their qinggong and internal cultivation, each step would take much slower than usual.

Furthermore, today's Yinghui Peak was especially exuberant and lively.

Normally, there'd only be a smattering of woodcutters or poets on the mountain roads, but today, from time to time, one could see people of the jianghu carrying swords and sabers as they ascended the mountain. However, the roads leading to the summit had been formed not through excavation but rather through years and years of feet treading upon it. As such, the parts where few people walked were filled with steep cliffs that resembled swords, perfectly straight and vertical, with no safe place to pass. Those with extraordinary qinggong could continue upward, but the mediocre martial artists would be forced to stop there, then look up and heave a sigh.

From the foot of the mountain to the summit, there were nine areas, or natural hurdles, that were incredibly difficult to climb. These nine obstacles became methods to test one's martial arts, so much so that only a scant number, countable on one hand, could make it to the summit. The number of people who ended up able to stand atop Yinghui Peak and view the match were the few among few.

But many people had traveled here from thousands of miles away, all so they could observe this ultimate, once-in-a-lifetime battle, even if it was only so they'd have something to boast to their grandchildren in the future. How could they be willing to stop at the foot of the mountain? No matter how difficult the climb, many were still willing to face those difficulties directly, to tread forward on those mountain paths.

"Xiongzhang, this Yinghui Peak is so hard to climb. Why don't we try climbing Banbu Peak instead? Yan Wushi and Hulugu are fighting their duel on the summit of Banbu Peak, aren't they? Even if we reach this summit, we'd have to watch the battle from across the river. It wouldn't be as clear compared to watching it on Banbu Peak, especially when it's so foggy today!"

The one speaking these words was Wang Zhuo from Kuaji Commandery's Wang family. Back at the Sword Trial Conference, he'd almost been wounded by Duan Wenyang, only to be rescued by Gu Hengbo.

Young men had always been weak to beautiful young ladies, and Wang-sanlang was no exception. Within his heart, he secretly held a torch for Gu Hengbo, and he wished to find a chance to talk to her. But Gu Hengbo completely ignored him, and after the Sword Trial Conference ended, she went chasing after Yuan Zixiao. Wang-erlang couldn't bear to see his little brother moping around all day; when he heard that two of the greatest martial arts experts had scheduled a duel atop Banbu Peak, he brought his little brother along to watch the fight.

The two of them were good enough martial artists to be considered rising stars of the jianghu's younger generation; however, when faced with the nine hurdles of Yinghui Peak, they were ultimately forced to stop at the last one.

There were no stairs before them, only a pencil-straight cliff face around five yards high. If they wished to reach the summit, they'd have to overcome this wall first, and there was no foothold to use as leverage in the middle either. The previous night's rain had caused a rockslide, making the scarp even smoother, and it was slippery from rainwater. The only way onward was by clearing it in a single leap.

The Wang brothers stared at the wall in a daze. Seven or eight other people had found themselves stymied here, the same as them. They had all been preparing to go up the mountain to watch the fight. Just like the Wang brothers, they'd passed the first eight obstacles but were now stumped.

Wang-erlang shot his brother a glance. "Do you think everyone else a fool? If Banbu Peak was that easy to traverse, everyone would have gone there already. Why would they come here? They say that Banbu Peak's summit spans only several feet. Just finding a place to stand is difficult. Those who can fight upon it must be exceptional. How could it accommodate onlookers?"

Wang-sanlang froze, stunned. "Then what should we do? We came all this distance just to stand here?"

He looked in the direction of the distant Banbu Peak but was disheartened to find another mountain solidly in the way. Even craning his neck, he could glimpse nothing more than a stretch of white clouds, never mind the people on the mountain.

Wang-erlang hadn't expected to be met with this kind of situation either. He said regretfully, "You know that there's always a better person, always a higher sky. Li-shaoxia and Su-shaoxia from Chunyang Monastery went up just now."

Wang-sanlang thought about Gu Hengbo, and his spirits fell even lower. "The duel on Banbu Peak should've started by now," he sighed. "I wonder how the battle's going?"

He didn't say it, but Wang-erlang also sorely wished to know. That group of ten people, the two brothers among them, stared at each other, at a loss. One person refused to admit defeat and decided to try again. He walked to the mountain wall, drew in a deep breath, and leapt upward. His figure rose like a white crane spreading its wings or a wild goose soaring high in the sky—it made for a lovely scene.

Ten or so pairs of eyes fell on that person, watching as he reached the apex of his jump. He was already more than halfway up the wall, but he'd exhausted this breath, and he had no choice but to kick at the cliff wall, trying to use it as leverage to leap up again. But the surface beneath his foot was incomparably slippery, and he couldn't find even the slightest bit of traction. His body immediately dropped, and the breath he'd struggled to keep was released as well. Unable to go any higher, he was forced to fall back to the ground.

He'd made a fool of himself before an audience, so he couldn't help but feel awkward. "My skills are lacking," he said. "I've embarrassed myself before you."

If any of the others had possessed the ability to scale it, they wouldn't still be standing here, so they all immediately began to comfort him. "This brother is too modest; your qinggong is already amazing, but it rained yesterday, so it's even more difficult to climb than normal. Otherwise we'd already all have made it over!"

Everyone commiserated with each other and chatted together for a while. Wang-erlang couldn't help but ask, "My brother and I only arrived just now; how many people have already gone up?"

One of the others answered, "There aren't that many, but it wasn't that few either. Experts like Palace Master Ruyan, Monastery Master Yi, and Duan Wenyang are naturally a given, but there were quite a few from the younger generation who made it up there too. I only recognized Li Qingyu, Su Qiao, and Xie Xiang. I'm not familiar with the remainder."

Someone else added, "I did recognize one—there was also Chao Yu from Chixia Sword Sect."

Wang-erlang was taken aback. He'd fought Chao Yu before, and the man had been a step above him in skill, but he didn't expect that he'd be able to leap up there. That showed that Wang-erlang was still below him.

At this time, another person attempted to head up again, but unsurprisingly, he too returned with his wings clipped in the end. Everyone else was growing somewhat discouraged.

"It should be almost seven by now. An hour has already passed. I fear they must've started fighting long ago—it's just the outcome isn't decided yet. In my opinion, we might as well head down the mountain and wait for news. It's better than being stuck here, unable to go up or down."

Even so, when there was only the final hurdle left, who'd be willing to throw it all away and turn back?

The person who'd tried leaping up just now sighed. "Hah, I can only blame my past self for thinking qinggong useless and refusing to put in the effort to learn it. Being trapped here now is really infuriating..."

Before he finished speaking, he made a sound of surprise. "Everyone, look. Another person's coming up. I wonder if he can get up here?"

Everyone quickly followed the sound and looked. Sure enough, a figure came sweeping up toward them from below at great speed. In the blink of an eye, this person was right before them.

The Wang brothers recognized the newcomer, and they couldn't help but exclaim in surprise. "Esteemed Daoist Master Shen!"

Shen Qiao didn't know when his address had changed from just "Daoist Master Shen" to "esteemed Daoist Master Shen." He also wasn't in the mood to scrutinize it carefully—the only thing he cared about right now was the battle on Banbu Peak. So even though he recognized the brothers, he only nodded at them in greeting. He had no plans to exchange pleasantries.

Half of the ten or so people there recognized Shen Qiao due to the incident at the Sword Trial Conference. The remaining half hadn't gone, so they didn't recognize him—but all the same, upon hearing him being addressed as the one and only "esteemed Daoist Master Shen," it should have been clear who Shen Qiao was. For that half of the group, their gazes on Shen Qiao instantly changed. Now they carried some admiration and worship as well.

Wang-sanlang saw that Shen Qiao didn't stop, and that he was about to continue upward, so he quickly called after him. "Daoist Master Shen, please wait!"

Shen Qiao's brows furrowed slightly, but he ultimately did stop, turning back to look at him.

"If I may ask," said Wang-sanlang hesitantly, "has Daoist Master Shen seen your shimei?"

Hengbo? Shen Qiao shook his head. "I haven't seen her since the Sword Trial Conference ended."

Hearing this, Wang-sanlang couldn't conceal his disappointment.

"Do you all wish to go up?" asked Shen Qiao.

Wang-sanlang was a bit embarrassed. "Yes, but it's too high, and there are no footholds, so..."

Shen Qiao glanced at the brothers and said, "I'll take you over this stretch, then."

"Eh?" said Wang-sanlang.

"Coming?" asked Shen Qiao.

Wang-erlang recovered faster and quickly agreed, "Coming, coming! Thank you, esteemed Daoist Master Shen! But there's two of us, so I fear your esteemed self will need to make two trips..."

"No matter," said Shen Qiao.

Wang-erlang barely had time to wonder what this "no matter" was referring to before he felt his shoulder being tightly grasped in Shen Qiao's hand.

Before he realized what was going on, the scene before him blurred and his feet had already left the ground. Wang-erlang felt like his entire person had been lifted like a wrapped bundle.

Shen Qiao was actually carrying a person in each arm, and he didn't even need a second kick-off point or to catch his breath in the middle. He leapt right onto the stone wall!

It wasn't just the Wang brothers; the entire crowd below them watched as the three vanished from their line of sight. They stared, eyes round and tongue-tied, completely speechless.

Earlier, the crowd had personally witnessed Li Qingyu and the others jumping up there, and you couldn't say their qinggong was poor. But if they wished to bring two other people up with them, they might not have succeeded. One could see just how incredible Shen Qiao's qinggong was.

For a long time, the crowd was unable to collect themselves. Several of them felt regretful and despondent—regret that there hadn't been time to make acquaintants with Shen Qiao so that he could have taken them there as well.

After a long time, someone finally gave a deep sigh. "Always a better person, always a higher sky. If Shen Qiao is already that formidable, what state have Yan Wushi and Hulugu achieved? I don't need to watch the battle anymore. Better to go back and train for a couple of years first!"

After saying this he shook his head, then headed down the mountain, dejected.

The remainder weren't as pessimistic as he was, but they too had suffered a harsh blow seeing Shen Qiao's qinggong just now.

Meanwhile, after traversing that mountain, there were no overly precipitous hurdles left. Shen Qiao said to the two brothers, "I'll be leaving first. You can take your time to catch up."

"Thank you for helping us, esteemed Daoist Master Shen," said Wang-erlang hurriedly. "We can walk the remainder ourselves. You go ahead first!"

Shen Qiao inclined his head slightly, then quickened his steps, as expected. A moment later, he'd reached the summit.

At this point, there were quite a few people standing at the summit. Shen Qiao gave his surroundings a quick scan and saw a number of familiar faces. Everyone was completely engrossed as they watched the two figures on the opposing Banbu Peak. They hadn't noticed Shen Qiao's arrival.

Banbu Peak and Yinghui Peak weren't very far from each other as the crow flew, but there was a river in between, separating the two peaks. Though mist was currently swirling around the peaks, the cold mountain winds would disperse the thick fog from time to time. Everyone who'd made it here was naturally first-class in terms of both martial arts and eyesight, so it wasn't difficult for them to see the situation on the opposing peak.

Shen Qiao didn't have the mind for pleasantries any more than the rest of them did. From the moment he'd arrived, his attention had been completely drawn to the other side.

Both Yan Wushi and Hulugu were barehanded and weaponless. However, with every move and stance they made, their robes would rustle, their sleeves flapping. It was difficult to tell if it was the mountain winds that were buffeting them or the true qi that washed over them. Even the mist and clouds shrouding the peak gradually cleared as they fought. This allowed those on Yinghui Peak to watch the battle with perfect clarity.

When Shen Qiao arrived, the two of them had already been engaged for almost an hour, and neither of the two had any intention of finishing the fight. As their palms rose and fell, the stones split, and clouds scattered. The sheer force involved was so great, the audience could hear the sounds all the way on Yinghui Peak.

As a martial expert, and especially as a grandmaster-level martial expert, Shen Qiao noticed something right away: neither side showed any sign of reserving themselves. If this continued, there was no way this could end like a spar, where the fight finished once someone tagged their opponent. Instead, it was a battle that would only end with someone's death.

If Shen Qiao could see it, the people around him, like Ruyan Kehui and Yi Pichen, could naturally see it as well.

At the summit of Yinghui peak, the mountain winds screamed and the fighters' robes danced madly. Xie Xiang and several other martial experts from the younger generation were even forced to circulate their qi to stabilize themselves. The opposing Banbu Peak had even less vegetation than Yinghui Peak, so the wind would only blow harder there. But neither Yan Wushi nor Hulugu seemed to be affected in the slightest. Instead, the roaring and howling wind ended up being guided by their true qi. Under their control, it formed into a series of cyclones that revolved around the two combatants, and the winds transformed from wild and unruly to docile and obedient.

Xie Xiang was an outspoken man. After a while, he was unable to hold on to his composure the way Li Qingyu and the others did. Seeing the situation, he couldn't help but ask his shifu, "Shifu, in your esteemed opinion, who has the greater chance of victory?"

He didn't ask who *would* win but instead who had the better chance of winning. This showed that he believed the current situation to be deadlocked and difficult to discern. It was a tricky situation.

Ruyan Kehui wanted to test his disciple, so he asked a question back. "What do you think?"

Xie Xiang frowned as he thought for a long moment. Then he said, "It's probably Hulugu?"

"Why?" asked Ruyan Kehui.

"Both of them are unparalleled martial experts, and right now, it's impossible to tell who's stronger. But if we're talking about the profundity of their internal cultivation, Hulugu should have a slight edge."

As Duan Wenyang was present, Ruyan Kehui refused to uplift Hulugu for him, so he didn't say more. But within his heart, he was of the same mind.

Yan Wushi was indeed extremely formidable, with a terrifying force and might behind his attacks. But, after all, Hulugu was still Hulugu. On Qingcheng Mountain, he'd been able to defeat someone like Yi Pichen as easily as snapping bamboo. This level of martial arts was probably something even Yan Wushi hadn't achieved. Hence, in this battle, the outsiders might have found it quite suspenseful, but for grandmaster-level martial experts like them, they might have been able to faintly glimpse the outcome from the beginning.

Though Ruyan Kehui had no fondness for Yan Wushi, they were ultimately both still martial artists from the Central Plains. If Yan Wushi lost, the Central Plains' martial arts world would lose all face, so Ruyan Kehui and the others naturally wished for Yan Wushi to win.

The chance of victory for him was slim, but that didn't mean there was none.

In contrast to the watching crowd, who each held their own thoughts and calculations within their hearts, the two people on Banbu Peak made for a completely different scene.

Hulugu had never fought Yan Wushi before, but before their duel, his disciple Duan Wenyang had already long gone to various places to gather all the information he could find about Yan Wushi. Hulugu also knew that this man was egotistical by nature. Back then, before he'd made any great achievements martially, he already had the courage to challenge Cui Youwang and Qi Fengge. It wasn't strange that he'd written a challenge letter to Hulugu and set up a battle with him. But above all, he was passionate about martial arts—fighting a duel with an equally matched opponent was a dream one could ask for but rarely receive.

On the summit of Banbu Peak, jagged stones jutted skyward while bowed trees crept forth. If one calculated the amount of standing space, it would measure only a few square feet; at best it could hold three men sitting cross-legged. To fight upon this kind of surface while braving the fierce high winds—that was undoubtedly an incredible test for one's martial arts.

But neither party's moves were flashy nor embellished in the slightest. Their attacks slammed into each other head-on in a direct confrontation. Hulugu had claimed to have mastered dozens of weapons that he'd integrated into his palms themselves. Every move and stance secretly coincided with a sword, spear, saber, or halberd technique. When he attacked, it was with a force capable of toppling mountains and overturning seas, like a great river cascading forth or the sea waves rolling in. It rushed forward in a first strike, determined to crush Yan Wushi beneath it.

At this moment, the high winds came screaming in from all directions. Guided by Hulugu's true qi, it was only aggravated further. It tightly engulfed Yan Wushi, tearing inch by inch through the defenses he'd constructed with his true qi, roaring and wailing as if it wanted to rend him to pieces entirely.

It was as if there were only one person left between all of heaven and earth. Yan Wushi's internal energy was imperious, but it couldn't contend with the power of nature itself. Once his internal energy was exhausted, Hulugu's offensive would surge over him and devour everything. There would never be any chance of escape again.

Hulugu's internal energy worked in tandem with those high winds to perfectly trap Yan Wushi in a watertight grasp. If he tried to advance or retreat by a few steps, he'd find himself suppressed by the other party's qi and unable to make a move.

But if Yan Wushi could surrender this early, he wouldn't be Yan Wushi at all.

The winds were piercingly cold. Sometimes they blew in from the southeast, at other times from the northwest. Banbu Peak was surrounded by empty space on all four sides, and so the wind would never stop. All things came with their trade-offs—this was a law of this world. Since Hulugu had wanted to harness the wind's power, he needed to exert more internal energy to coordinate with it.

Yan Wushi was at a clear disadvantage, yet his face remained placid, his feet planted in place and unmoving. He lightly closed both his eyes and his entire body's internal energy swelled forth, transforming into a barrier strong enough to temporarily hold back Hulugu's attack. But against Hulugu, this kind of feeble defense couldn't last more than a short moment. Once that moment passed, his defense would collapse, his entire person buffeted by the powerful qi pouring in from all directions, and he'd suffer a grisly death.

But Yan Wushi didn't need that much time. The reason he'd closed his eyes was so that he could listen closely to the direction those high winds were blowing in.

Heaven and earth were ever-changing; these high winds were also unfathomable. But human movements had a pattern one could follow. No matter how much Hulugu wished to become one with heaven, in the end, it was impossible for him to truly fuse with it— eventually, a gap would be found.

A moment was enough!

Yan Wushi's eyes opened wide as he thrust a palm toward Hulugu's left side, then quickly leaped into the air before launching another palm strike.

The desperate situation he'd been in crumbled entirely, and that wasn't all: he'd even counterattacked, switching from the defensive to offensive!

The hour they'd spent on the previous exchange had given Hulugu a thorough understanding of just how troublesome his opponent was. However, he hadn't expected that he could defeat Yan Wushi in such a short amount of time, so he was mentally prepared. He immediately raised his sleeves, and he drifted backward to land on the needles of a pine tree, swaying in the wind as if he were weightless.

But with this tiny bit of leverage, he abruptly swept upward by a great many yards. His figure was suddenly enshrouded within the white mists, disappearing, and several people almost thought they'd seen the work of a ghost.

Of course, there was no ghost.

Hulugu was using several of the blind spots within human vision to confuse his opponent. Using his incredible speed, he seemed to flit about without a trace, managing to fool the onlookers' eyes for a time, even in broad daylight. Once the veil of night descended, this skill would be enough to terrify anyone.

Even the spectating crowd couldn't stop their faces from shifting a little. Some of them had already begun to silently ponder whether they themselves could handle this situation upon encountering it.

The Wang siblings needed no mention, but the likes of Li Qingyu and Xie Xiang were young, bright, and talented, and they'd grown proud and arrogant because of it. But when they asked themselves this question, they also realized that if they'd been the one in that situation, there was a nine out of ten chance that they'd fail to break free.

How many years would it take to achieve what Yan Wushi and Hulugu had?

This question surfaced almost simultaneously within the hearts of these onlookers.

Meanwhile, Yan Wushi remained still.

He knew that moving was useless. Since his opponent was already swift enough to deceive everyone's eyes, any attempt to chase after him would be a waste of his effort.

Yan Wushi knew this very well, so he waited for his opponent to come to a complete stop first. And that would happen the moment Hulugu put his full strength into a strike. So he chose to answer Hulugu's movement with stillness. The hand concealed within his sleeve was already mobilizing the internal energy all over his body as he gathered his true qi.

He was gathering his lifetime's worth of skills into this palm strike.

Hulugu attempted to crush him first using an early strike, but in doing so, he realized something that secretly shocked him: Yan Wushi had no openings!

No matter how skilled someone's martial arts were, even if they'd already achieved a state of complete harmony, it was impossible for them to lack any openings or flaws. All things in heaven and earth, vegetation and creatures alike, even people—all of them had their flaws.

Yan Wushi couldn't be an exception.

Hulugu understood that if Yan Wushi appeared to have no flaws, that meant he simply wasn't able to perceive them, not that Yan Wushi was a perfect, flawless being on par with the heavenly Dao itself. He realized with surprise that the resolve within that man's nature, as well as the craftiness within his actions, were superior to even the Qi Fengge from the past.

Given enough time, perhaps this man might really be able to attain the state of Great Completion. Perhaps he could even glimpse and break through the absolute summit of martial arts itself and ascend directly to heaven as an immortal. This kind of ascension was different from the way the soul would depart from the body after death. It was comprehending the heavenly Dao itself, to glimpse the mysteries of the ultimate primordial universe.

Hulugu had cultivated his martial path for decades. Along the way, he'd suffered a defeat at Qi Fengge's hands, then willingly stayed outside the Great Wall for twenty years, living in seclusion. He'd never been a person who lacked patience or endurance. But when he faced Yan Wushi now, he couldn't help the trace of envy that suddenly, involuntarily rose from the depths of his heart.

That's right: envy.

Envy that Yan Wushi was younger than himself, that he wasn't necessarily more talented yet still possessed the opportunity to break through to the supreme martial path. This golden opportunity wasn't something anyone could forcibly obtain.

All humans had envy within their hearts. Hulugu wasn't a god or an immortal, so naturally he did too. But this wisp of envy, so tiny it was almost imperceptible, was quickly flung to the back of his mind.

He decided to attack.

Hulugu's fingers were long and slender but not fair. He was a Göktürk and a martial arts practitioner, so his palm carried those commonly seen calluses, the skin a little yellowed. But within these two hands was concealed a thunderous power, a strength enormous enough to horrify anyone.

The true qi surrounding his body made his sleeves billow high, and he pressed his fingers together. At first, they resembled soft emerald ripples, but in an instant, they'd transformed into a razor-sharp blade of ice, and he sliced downward at the crown of Yan Wushi's head.

And at almost the exact same moment, Yan Wushi leapt into the air. While suspended, he turned around and met Hulugu's palm blast.

When the strong met the strong, one was destined to become the weak.

Hulugu could acknowledge that Yan Wushi was incredibly powerful. He could also admit that when he'd been Yan Wushi's age, he probably couldn't have attained the level Yan Wushi was at right now. But that didn't mean that he'd present him this victory on a platter.

They were both well aware that a duel between the two was inevitable. Even if it hadn't been today, sooner or later, it would have come. Because with Qi Fengge gone, there was only one Yan Wushi in the world, and he was the only one capable of matching Hulugu. To each other, they were something like fated nemeses. Today's match could only end in death.

Their palm blasts met, and their true qi scattered in all directions. All at once, branches snapped and rubble flew with a loud rumble, and even the mist and clouds shrouding the sky fled in terror, transforming into fine silken threads that drifted through the air. Their true qi had condensed into a barrier around the two combatants, preventing any debris or dust from entering.

Everyone stared with bated breath.

It only lasted an instant.

Powerful true qi collided in midair, and Hulugu drifted to the ground while Yan Wushi floated backward a little, only landing a moment later.

Wang-sanlang's mouth and tongue had gone paper-dry, and he found himself unable to say a word. He couldn't stop himself from tugging on his brother's sleeve as he forced several words out of his throat. "This…is Hulugu's victory?"

Wang-erlang didn't answer him. His gaze remained fixed on Banbu Peak, unable to shift it by even a hair's breadth.

The other people around them were much the same.

Hulugu and Yan Wushi were only a few inches from each other. They stood face-to-face, their gazes locked. From afar, it could look like a reunion between two good friends rather than two enemies about to fight to the death.

It's not finished yet?

Wang-sanlang had only just thought this when Hulugu made his move.

He swept toward Yan Wushi at a speed Wang-sanlang could scarcely comprehend, but Yan Wushi seemed to have anticipated it, and the two combatants lunged toward each other almost simultaneously. In an instant they exchanged another ten-odd blows. Hulugu had completely integrated the essence of dozens of years of swordplay into his palm techniques, and the fierce winds that surged madly from his palm strikes were like blades, eager to devour all in their path. They cascaded down upon Yan Wushi's body without the slightest reservation.

Suddenly, Yan Wushi laughed.

For hidden deep within this palm technique that was almost omnipresent in its might, this technique that left no trace to be found, Yan Wushi had detected a tiny sliver of a flaw.

Perhaps it was the shadow that Qi Fengge had left twenty years ago. Perhaps it was the urgency he'd felt seeing the great number of martial experts appearing one after another on the Central Plains.

Or perhaps it was because his eagerness to defeat Yan Wushi had given way to impatience.

But no matter what it was, it was something Yan Wushi was only too happy to see.

He recalled what Shen Qiao had said to him before: Hulugu had mastered multiple weapons and integrated swordplay, saber arts, and all the rest into his palm techniques, polishing them to near perfection. But just because they were near perfection didn't mean they were perfect.

All things had their flaws.

Yan Wushi suddenly extended a finger.

His opponent's palm blast had transformed into hundreds and thousands of afterimages, yet he'd extended only one finger.

And this finger was pointed right at Hulugu!

Hulugu's expression twitched slightly. He knew that Yan Wushi had discovered his opening.

It took only an instant. Hulugu's palm blast had already landed upon Yan Wushi's body, but Yan Wushi's single finger, with the decades of skills he'd cultivated gathered within it, effortlessly struck right against Hulugu's heart.

There was a huge bang, and Hulugu's whole body flew straight back. He agilely grabbed onto a branch suspended above the cliff, using that as leverage to return to the summit. He slammed heavily into a boulder and coughed up a large mouthful of blood. His entire face first turned a purplish-green, then such a deathly white that he looked almost transparent.

In contrast, Yan Wushi had remained standing in place from start to finish, completely motionless. The only exception was the hand he'd extended that one finger from just now—it now hung limply at his side, trembling slightly.

"You've...won." For every word Hulugu spoke, he coughed out a mouthful of blood. And with every mouthful of blood, his face grew a little more ashen.

Yan Wushi still didn't move.

But Hulugu had already moved his gaze from Yan Wushi and landed on the languid white clouds over him and on the profound blue sky above.

His lifelong regret wasn't that he'd failed to help the Göktürks enter the Central Plains, nor was it that he'd fallen to Qi Fengge and Yan Wushi. His only regret was that he hadn't managed to take one step further on the martial path.

After he died, if reincarnation existed, would he still have the chance to pursue that martial summit in his next life?

He slowly closed his eyes.

"Hulugu's...dead?" Wang-sanlang stammered. His gaze was practically frozen in place as he stared at Yan Wushi.

"He should be, right? Sect Leader Yan..." Wang-erlang's tone was a little uncertain; he was unable to see how Yan Wushi was doing.

No one proposed leaving the mountain. It seemed as if they'd yet to return to their senses after the battle they'd witnessed. Ruyan Kehui, Yi Pichen, and the others seemed even more affected: they remained standing in place for a very long time, as if they were comprehending an inexplicable mystery.

However, Yu Shengyan was terribly anxious. He thought that his shizun must have been injured, but he was far away and couldn't reach him. If he tried to get there by running down the mountain and ascending Banbu Peak from the bottom, who could say how much time that would take?

But the current situation didn't afford him the time to think.

He turned his head, about to head down the mountain, when a hand suddenly pressed down on his shoulder.

Yu Shengyan looked back. It was Shen Qiao.

"Daoist Master Shen?"

"I'll go." Shen Qiao only spoke those two words.

The next moment, Yu Shengyan's eyes went very round, disbelief written all over his face, as Shen Qiao did something no one could have ever imagined. He broke off a branch from a nearby tree, then tossed it into the air. Pumped full of true qi, the branch soared far away. Then, Shen Qiao drifted into the air before sweeping out in the direction of that branch. His figure was as graceful as that of a godly immortal.

Did Shen Qiao intend to jump from here to Banbu Peak? Surely... that wasn't possible?!

Wang-sanlang was dumbfounded.

The two peaks weren't that far apart, but even someone with exceptional qinggong would find traversing this distance rather taxing, as there was no place you could use to propel yourself forward in between. If you were just a little careless and fell, beneath you would be the thousand-yard cliff and torrential waters of the river.

He suddenly understood the purpose of the branch Shen Qiao had thrown.

Shen Qiao's qinggong was unparalleled; scant few in the jianghu would be his match. But even so, no one had ever attempted to reach Banbu Peak from Yinghui Peak like this. A natural chasm yawned in the middle—one would truly be risking their life if they dared try. Shen Qiao floated through the air until he seemed to have exhausted both his qi and strength. His figure sank a little, and Wang-sanlang couldn't stop his heart from fiercely jolting inside his chest.

But Shen Qiao didn't lose his footing or fall. He seemed to have accounted for the distance perfectly. With this drop, his foot just happened to land on that branch, and he lightly pushed off it. Once again, he soared into the air and continued gliding forward. After he'd pushed off it, the branch immediately lost its forward momentum and plummeted.

Everyone stared blankly at Shen Qiao's retreating silhouette. Even Ruyan Kehui and the other grandmasters revealed expressions of shock. This was far beyond their expectations. Wang-sanlang's gaze had already evolved from admiration into worship.

But Shen Qiao didn't have the mind to concern himself with their impressions. Right now, all his attention was on Yan Wushi. This battle had killed someone as powerful as Hulugu. Could Yan Wushi really be perfectly unscathed?

The Wang brothers' eyes might not have been good enough to tell, but Shen Qiao had understood with just a glance. Not only was Yan Wushi not perfectly unscathed, he wasn't doing much better than Hulugu!

But even knowing this, he still hadn't expected that he'd need to catch Yan Wushi's collapsing figure right after landing on Banbu Peak.

"Yan Wushi!" Shen Qiao's face fell in horror. Where his skin was pressed to Yan Wushi's, all he felt was a stretch of icy cold!

Yan Wushi's eyes were tightly shut, his face peaceful. A trace of dark crimson trickled from the corner of his mouth, slowly flowing down toward his chin.

Immediately, without another word, Shen Qiao pulled out a porcelain bottle. He tipped out a pill and carefully fed it to Yan Wushi, then placed his hand on the man's pulse. After taking it for a moment, even though he'd already prepared himself for this result, his mind spiraled into chaos, and his heart felt like it would shatter!

His life force was exhausted, his Yang energy gone. Everything seemed to have withered away—there was no sign of life.

No sign of life...

In an instant, Shen Qiao's complexion almost matched the nearby Hulugu's.

His hands trembled as he forced himself to suppress his roiling emotions. He pulled out another bottle of wound medication and tipped out many pills. He desperately wanted to feed Yan Wushi all of them, all at once.

Back when he'd heard news of the duel, Shen Qiao had already finished preparing the medication. He'd specially looked for a formulation meant to heal severe injuries that had been passed down through the generations at Xuandu Mountain. He'd done it to prepare for the worst, but he'd always hoped that he wouldn't have to use it.

You must not overdo things, the remaining part of Shen Qiao's reason told him. He forced himself to draw a deep breath, then counted out three more pills before again feeding it to the man in his arms.

He waited a long, long time, but Yan Wushi's complexion took absolutely no turn for the better.

Shen Qiao's heart was a field of ice.

He continued to support Yan Wushi's neck, but a numbness slowly crept up the rest of his body. Even as he knelt on the ground, the rocks stabbing into his knees through his robes, he did not feel a hint of pain.

Shen Qiao clutched Yan Wushi's wrist tightly, his grip so forceful that he almost shattered the wrist itself.

All around him, the high wind howled, the sound grazing past his ears. The people on Yinghui had yet to disperse, but at this moment, none of them could catch Shen Qiao's attention.

He closed his eyes, hoping that everything before him was just a dream.

However, when Shen Qiao next opened his eyes, that man who'd treated everything as a game, who'd always been egotistical and arrogant without compare, was still lying still in his arms. His eyes were tightly shut, and there was no life in him.

He'd never known this feeling before. Of sorrow and suffering swelling to an extreme, when the heart tangles into knots. So, it felt something like this.

"Yan Wushi." Shen Qiao's voice was quiet and hoarse as he spoke into his ear. "If you wake up... If you can wake up, I'll do anything you want. Even if you tell me that this is all just a hoax that you planned..."

Shen Qiao couldn't speak any further. With a shock, he suddenly realized just how heavy the weight of this man already was inside his heart.

It was heavier than a thousand tons; so heavy that he was completely unable to withstand it.

He shivered and dropped his head, then slowly pressed his lips to the other man's face, then forehead. He lightly caressed him before burying his face into the crook of Yan Wushi's neck.

Moisture gradually seeped through the collar's fabric. Then, Yan Wushi suddenly moved, just the slightest bit.

Shen Qiao almost suspected that he'd seen wrong. He didn't even have the courage to raise his head.

But the next moment, Yan Wushi's feeble voice drifted into his ear: "Just now, you said that you'd do anything?"

Shen Qiao was dumbstruck.

Epilogue–Part One

THE MOMENT HE SAW Hulugu collapse, Yu Shengyan was first ecstatic, then horrified, for he knew very well that Hulugu was no ordinary person. He was a peerless martial artist, practically the best in the world. No matter how strong Shizun was, there was no way he could have defeated Hulugu and escaped unscathed.

When this thought emerged, he was desperate to go check on Shizun, but the distance between here and Banbu Peak wasn't something he could traverse, no matter what he did.

Just as Yu Shengyan was going to descend the mountain, a figure moved even faster.

It was Shen Qiao.

Yu Shengyan stared agape as Shen Qiao leapt right into the sky and swept to the opposite peak, riding on the wind like a godly immortal.

The cries that'd been about to burst from Yu Shengyan died in his throat. Like everyone else there, he could only watch, eyes wide and tongue-tied, as Shen Qiao drifted toward Banbu Peak.

To be precise, Shen Qiao really was drifting.

The gales at the mountain summit were bitingly cold. Even if one stood still, their robes would thrash unceasingly in the wind. If the person wasn't a martial artist but an ordinary person, the wind would have blown them right off unless they clung tightly to a tree trunk. Even the Wang siblings, who stood among martial arts masters, were forced to secretly use their internal energy from time to time to secure themselves, lest they be sent flying in a moment of carelessness.

Yet, within those violent winds, Shen Qiao's clothes fluttered as he steadily drifted toward the opposite peak. He seemed to be moving slowly, but in truth it was incredibly fast. From one peak to the other, he'd managed to traverse a distance that no ordinary person could overcome.

In terms of qinggong alone, there were likely very few people in the world who could match him. It was possible that even Shizun would find himself slightly inferior. Yu Shengyan thought on this, but in the next moment, he abruptly returned to his senses and remembered his original goal to go down the mountain.

At this time, yet another person stole in front of him, his speed around one-third faster than Yu Shengyan's. It was such a steep mountain path, yet that person traversed it like it was flat ground. He soon vanished from Yu Shengyan's line of sight.

When he'd come up earlier, Yu Shengyan had sighted Duan Wenyang, but as their shifus were dueling, the two of them had no heart to fight themselves. At this moment, Duan Wenyang had seen Hulugu fall. With his heart naturally torn with anxiety, he hurried over.

Yu Shengyan had once heard that Duan Wenyang had suffered a great deal of contempt within the Khaganate when he was young. It was only after Hulugu had grown fond of him and taken Duan Wenyang as his disciple that his circumstances had drastically changed. So despite Duan Wenyang's overwhelming ambition, he was incredibly filial to his shizun.

But Yu Shengyan's current mood wasn't much calmer than Duan Wenyang's. They both ran down the mountain, one in front and the other trailing behind. Upon arriving at the foot of Yinghui Peak, they were about to start climbing when they saw Shen Qiao from afar, walking down with Yan Wushi on his back.

"Daoist Master Shen!" Yu Shengyan called, and he quickly rushed over.

He saw Yan Wushi, sprawled over Shen Qiao's back. His shizun's eyes were tightly closed, and his complexion was a deathly gray. Yue Shengyan's face immediately fell. "Shizun!"

"Let's talk later." Shen Qiao only spoke these three words.

"Daoist Master Shen!" Duan Wenyang called after him. "Please, how is my shizun?"

Shen Qiao sent him a glance. "Just now, I was only focused on bringing Sect Leader Yan down, so I didn't have the time to look after your shifu. I'm not too sure."

There was nothing Duan Wenyang could say. At that moment, he even suspected that Shen Qiao might have taken advantage of his shizun's predicament and killed him. At that time, there'd only been the three of them on Banbu Peak—no one would be able to know the truth. But Duan Wenyang immediately rejected the thought the moment it flashed into his mind. Even though they were on different sides, Duan Wenyang had to admit that, given Shen Qiao's moral character, he'd never do such a thing.

Some people were destined to never become friends, but some people's characters were such that even their enemies couldn't criticize them. Perhaps this could describe Shen Qiao.

So he said nothing in the end and simply watched as Shen Qiao and his companions faded into the distance. Then he turned and swept up the mountain.

Yu Shengyan had no time to spare Duan Wenyang any attention. He followed closely after Shen Qiao, all the way until they arrived at the spare villa.

Yan Wushi had always been incomparably powerful in the eyes of others—the steward had never seen him like this. He'd originally come out joyfully to greet them, but now he found himself greatly terrified as well.

Yu Shengyan mustered up the courage to touch Yan Wushi's hand, and his soul almost scattered in fright. "Why...why is he cold?!"

"His injuries are too severe," Shen Qiao told him. "I'll write a prescription. Grab three portions of the medicine, then add four bowls of water and simmer over low heat until there's only one bowl's worth left. Do this twice a day."

"Yes!" Yu Shengyan knew that Xuandu Mountain's knowledge had been passed down over hundreds of years, so they'd certainly have some life-saving recipes that weren't shared with outsiders. Even the remedies within the imperial palaces wouldn't be able to compare.

Shen Qiao carried Yan Wushi into his room before carefully laying him down. He checked his pulse, wrote down the prescription, and then fed him the medicine, all by himself.

Perhaps it was Shen Qiao's prescription that worked, or perhaps it was Yan Wushi's own cultivation of his internal circulation. Either way, three days later, he finally woke.

"Shizun!" Yu Shengyan had just entered the room with a bowl of piping-hot medicine. When he saw him, he couldn't help but shout in joy.

This caused Shen Qiao, who'd been dozing on the side with his forehead propped on his hand, to jump awake as well.

Yan Wushi opened his eyes and looked at his disciple, who was about to help him up to feed him medicine. "Leave."

"Ah?"

His wasn't a slow reaction; he quickly glanced at Shen Qiao.

Shen Qiao nodded. "You can leave. I'll do it."

Yu Shengyan gave his own shizun another glance.

Ever since Yan Wushi had woken up, his gaze had practically been fixed on Shen Qiao. He didn't look at Yu Shengyan once.

A sense of sorrow suddenly erupted within Yu Shengyan, something like "a rootless blade of grass battered by the cold wind and rain." He handed the bowl to Shen Qiao and silently took his leave.

Shen Qiao hadn't noticed Yu Shengyan's feelings. He scooped up a spoonful of medicinal soup and brought it to Yan Wushi's mouth. He'd done these same actions for three days; they were already very practiced.

"How are you feeling?" he asked.

"Not bad," said Yan Wushi lazily. Though his complexion was a bit pale, neither his posture nor his expression resembled an injured patient.

"Your pulse has been gradually stabilizing, though there's still some weakness," Shen Qiao told him. "You'll need to recuperate slowly. It seems like the flaw within your demonic core really has been fully repaired, otherwise..."

He shook his head and spoke no further.

Otherwise the one who'd been able to descend the mountain wouldn't have been Yan Wushi but Hulugu.

Twenty years ago, Hulugu had lost to Qi Fengge by a hair's breadth. Twenty years later, he could have only gotten stronger. Yan Wushi had taken an enormous risk with this battle—even if he'd managed to see through to his opponent's weaknesses at the very last moment, with how closely matched their internal energy was, a head-on clash could only lead to one conclusion: either the death of Hulugu or of Yan Wushi.

If Shen Qiao hadn't leapt directly to him from Yinghui Peak—if he'd first descended before climbing up Banbu Peak—that small sliver of lost time could have changed everything, and perhaps Yan Wushi wouldn't have been so fortunate.

Yan Wushi sent him a soft smile. "A-Qiao, do you still remember what you said before? You said that as long as I woke up, you'd do anything."

Shen Qiao's hand, extended halfway, froze in midair. "That's something I said out of desperation..."

"A gentleman's word cannot be repealed," Yan Wushi said icily.

Shen Qiao was helpless. "Then what do you want?"

"The medicine is too bitter."

Poor Daoist Master Shen was so pure and simple, he hadn't figured out what Yan Wushi meant yet. "Then shall I go and ask for some honey?"

Yan Wushi shook his head and took the bowl, tilted his head back, and drank it in one gulp. Then he suddenly grabbed Shen Qiao's lapels and pulled him close, pressing his mouth to the other man's with unerring accuracy.

Shen Qiao's eyes went wide. His first instinct was to push him away, but Yan Wushi's embrace was incredibly tight. If he used force, he could hurt him...

During this moment of hesitation, Yan Wushi had already thoroughly sampled the taste of that tongue and pair of lips. That long-awaited taste he'd yearned after—it was unforgettable.

"Ugh—"

An astringent bitterness tinged with medicine forced its way into Shen Qiao's mouth. His momentary softness had already given Yan Wushi full rein, and Shen Qiao lost all ground. Right now, both his hands were restrained, and his center of gravity tipped back while Yan Wushi insatiably pressed himself on top. Shen Qiao's waist was unable to support the weight of two people, and he was forced to straighten it, lifting his chin. Saliva overflowed from the corner of his lips, following the line of that beautiful, fair neck as it meandered downward.

By the time Shen Qiao finally came to his senses and shoved Yan Wushi away, he didn't realize just how pitiful his current appearance was.

The hair at his temples was mussed from all the rubbing, and his eyes were glossy with tears, like two pools of clear spring water. The flush of his cheeks had yet to fade, and his lips were also red and swollen. Combined with his current appearance...

It was clearly the picture of a person who'd been ravished by a lecher.

Yet the victim was unable to settle scores with the lecher, for the lecher was currently clutching at his chest, his eyebrows furrowed as he groaned. "It hurts..."

Shen Qiao was speechless.

Yan Wushi gave a sigh. "I used too much qi just now; even breathing in causes my chest to hurt. Looks like I'll need to rest for a very long time before I can recover."

He'd just taken advantage of someone, and now he was playing the victim! This man was completely and utterly devoid of any sense of shame!

Shen Qiao's face alternated between green and white. "How can you be so badly injured and still lack all self-respect!"

It would have been better if Yan Wushi had remained unconscious, the way he'd been the last few days.

"It was you who said that as long as I wake up, you would do anything," Yan Wushi said meaningfully. "And now a couple of kisses later, you're saying no? You're Daoist; you deeply value promises. Since you said 'anything,' and this doesn't go against your morals or ethics, then of course I can kiss you, can't I?"

When it came to debates, even a hundred Shen Qiaos wouldn't be a match for a single Yan Wushi. "...From what I see, you're about healed anyway. You don't need the medicine anymore. You can just recuperate quietly like this!"

An angry beauty held its own charm. Yan Wushi was all smiles as he admired Shen Qiao, thinking that everything about the man's body, from head to toe, was exceedingly lovely to look at.

Having been jerked around, Shen Qiao refused to feed him medicine up close ever again—this way, Yan Wushi wouldn't be able to find any further excuses or chances. Every day from then onward, Shen Qiao would only stand at the doorway and cast him a few glances before leaving.

Thus, several days passed. News from outside gradually began to trickle in.

Hulugu had indeed passed on. Duan Wenyang had taken his body back to the Khaganate to inter him, but there was another rumor circulating the jianghu—one that said Yan Wushi had also passed from the serious wounds he'd sustained in that battle. But because Shen Qiao had taken his body away so quickly, it was rumored that he'd died without anyone seeing his corpse.

Naturally, the people in the villa knew that he'd survived. Though he'd barely been breathing when Shen Qiao had brought him down the mountain, his powerful abilities combined with Shen Qiao's rescue efforts meant that the single step he'd taken across the bridge to the underworld had been retracted.

But outsiders didn't know this. A group of people had been waiting at the foot of Banbu Peak for the results then, and they'd seen Shen Qiao carry Yan Wushi down the mountain and Yu Shengyan's grieving face as well. No one from Huanyue Sect had stepped forward to clarify matters, so everyone logically assumed that Yan Wushi's life had flickered out as well.

Those who didn't believe ran to ask the martial experts with the good fortune to have witnessed the match, like Ruyan Kehui and Yi Pichen. Being grandmasters, their opinions naturally carried more weight. However, Ruyan Kehui didn't offer much opinion on their survival, or lack thereof. He only said that Hulugu and Yan Wushi were both one of the few martial arts masters in the current world and that he greatly admired them both.

Yi Pichen's response was much more explicit. He believed that both sides had been evenly matched, and thus they'd both suffered grievously—there'd be no good fate for either of them.

Guided by these words, many people grew even more convinced that Yan Wushi had died.

Then, if both the first-place and second-place martial artists had passed, who was the most powerful person in the jianghu now?

And more importantly, how would the gambling dens handle the betting results?

There were people who'd bet on both sides suffering severe injuries, or on both sides dying, but it'd been a third-option bet, so most people wouldn't think of choosing it. The odds had hit a high of 1-37, meaning that if you bet one tael, you'd end up receiving thirty-seven.

Rumor had it that many of Funing County's gambling dens suffered huge losses thanks to this result and declared bankruptcy one after the other. However, there was one man named Xi Xingke who'd made a huge fortune. In one night, he'd become a supremely wealthy man.

Who was this Xi Xingke? No one knew.

"Shizun." Yu Shengyan entered the room and presented Yan Wushi with their accounting log. "This is the money we won this time. It's more than fifty thousand taels."

These fifty-thousand taels had bankrupted almost all the gambling dens in Funing County. For at least one year, it was unlikely anyone in Funing County would dare to open another gambling den.

Yu Shengyan smiled. "Everyone is trying to figure out who Xi Xingke[4] is. It's actually not that hard to guess. Huanyue, 'Moon Cleansing,' and Xixing, 'Star Washing'—isn't it obvious if you think about it? Once your esteemed self shows your face again, people are going to be furious!"

Even if they were furious, there was nothing they could do. They'd set up the odds and laid down their wagers of their own accord. Surely they wouldn't have the guts to come running to Huanyue Sect looking for trouble—unless they were simply tired of living?

Yan Wushi grunted in response, but he wasn't too concerned with the amount of money. "Where's A-Qiao?"

"Daoist Master Shen is practicing the sword in the courtyard. I think he wants to go to Chang'an."

Yan Wushi beckoned him over. "No matter. Come here."

Yu Shengyan leaned his ear close and listened to Yan Wushi's instructions on how to proceed. Then he repeatedly nodded. "This disciple will go and do it now!"

"Also, take ten thousand taels out of that fifty thousand and deliver them to Chunyang Monastery."

---

4   洗星客. 洗星 (xixing) means "star washing" while 浣月 (huanyue) means "moon cleansing." 客 (ke) means customer.

"Yes!"

Were those words of Yi Pichen's really just him talking recklessly? Even a Daoist monastery detached from the secular world still needed to survive. Yi Pichen had just said a few vague words—words that had guided people into believing something false, which had helped Yan Wushi win the bet, and thus he'd earned his monastery ten thousand taels, to everyone's delight and satisfaction.

Epilogue–Part Two

SHEN QIAO INDEED WISHED to go to Chang'an. After all, Yuan Ying was still there overseeing the construction of Xuandu Monastery. He lacked experience, so Shen Qiao couldn't leave him there by himself for too long.

Once Xuandu Monastery was finished, the Sui Dynasty would issue an imperial edict, and the emperor himself might personally summon him. At that point, as Sect Leader, Shen Qiao would have to make an appearance. If he let Yuan Ying, with his clumsy tongue, meet with the emperor instead, Shen Qiao didn't need much of an imagination to know that it would be quite inappropriate.

After deliberating, Shen Qiao went to find Yu Shengyan, wanting to bid him farewell. However, for two days in a row, Yu Shengyan either left early or returned late, making it impossible for Shen Qiao to run into him. It wasn't until the third day that Shen Qiao managed to stop him by the door.

Yu Shengyan smiled. "Shizun is currently bedridden, so this disciple is taking care of anything that needs to be done. I have to run about on so many errands. Look here." He held up the letter in his hand. "I still need to help Shizun deliver this letter to Monastery Master Yi. If Daoist Master Shen needs something, it's better to tell Shizun directly. Shizun is sure to agree!"

Shen Qiao stopped him and coughed once. "Actually, there's no need to bother him. I just wanted to say my farewells. Telling you is the same as telling him."

"Daoist Master Shen, you and my shizun are very close," Yu Shengyan said earnestly. "If Shizun knew that you said goodbye to me in private, but not to him, I fear that he'd be angry at me! If you're leaving, it's better to tell Shizun yourself, lest I end up in a difficult position!"

But Shen Qiao didn't want to talk to Yan Wushi. That was why he'd come to Yu Shengyan instead.

In truth, deep inside his heart, part of him really didn't know how to face Yan Wushi; he could only choose this kind of method and avoid him.

Yu Shengyan was about to say something when someone ran out and whispered a few words in his ear. Yu Shengyan's expression shifted drastically in alarm. "How can this be? He was fine just this morning!"

When Shen Qiao heard this, his heart leapt right into his throat. "What happened?"

Yu Shengyan forcibly calmed himself down, and his demeanor flipped. No longer did he try to make Shen Qiao stay. "It's nothing. This one still has some things to take care of! Please forgive him for leaving first!"

After saying this, he immediately turned and hurried away with the newcomer without giving Shen Qiao any chance to reply.

Shen Qiao remained standing in place. The more he thought about it, the more certain he was that the conversation just now had something to do with Yan Wushi. And the more he thought about it, the higher his heart seemed to suspend itself. Thus, he turned right around and walked toward Yan Wushi's house.

Even before he'd arrived at the house, he could see people darting in and out. Some were carrying hot water while others carried laundry for washing. Shen Qiao's eyes were sharp—he caught the blood stains on the clothes right away.

His heart skipped a beat. He dropped all other considerations and barged right into the house.

Behind the folding screen was the bedroom. There was a person lying on the bed—undoubtedly Yan Wushi.

His eyes were tightly shut, his complexion a chilly white—right now, it looked exactly as it had the day Shen Qiao carried him down Banbu Peak.

At the sight of him, Shen Qiao's heart almost stopped. He quickly stepped forward and was about to grab Yan Wushi's wrist, wanting to thoroughly take his pulse.

But right at this moment, Yan Wushi slowly opened his eyes. "Weren't you leaving? Why are you still here?"

His tone was cold and indifferent, and there was no hint of his smile from before. Even the gaze he cast at Shen Qiao was akin to an icy spring, fathomlessly deep.

Shen Qiao was taken aback.

His words of farewell stopped in his throat, and he couldn't utter a single one.

Yan Wushi closed his eyes again. "I'm fine. If you're leaving, just go," he said coolly.

In the past, there'd been no method Yan Wushi wouldn't use, nothing he'd stop at when it came to things he wanted to do and the goals he wanted to achieve. Given that the two of them had been together for quite some time, Shen Qiao felt that he understood him rather well. Yet, at this time, the usual lighthearted demeanor Yan Wushi showed Shen Qiao had suddenly become cold and indifferent.

Shen Qiao could not feel a single ounce of relief or joy in his heart. On the contrary, he felt a vague and indescribable sense of unease.

Shen Qiao composed himself. "If I'm going to save someone, I'll save them to the end. Since I'm the one who carried you down Banbu Peak, I'll only leave once you've fully recovered."

He'd thought that Yan Wushi was already out of danger. Who could've known that this would happen now? Shen Qiao found his heart suspended once more.

But Yan Wushi refused to let him take his pulse. "Thank you, Sect Leader Shen. Several times already, you've done everything you could to save my venerable self. My venerable self will keep this within my heart. However, Huanyue Sect has excellent doctors as well, and I dare not trouble Sect Leader Shen further."

He hid his hand under the covers, closed his eyes, and pretended to fall asleep.

Yu Shengyan had been standing nearby. He likely couldn't take Shen Qiao looking so lost and dazed, for he said, "Daoist Master Shen..."

Shen Qiao returned to himself and asked, "Just before, I saw some blood on your clothes. What happened?"

Yu Shengyan said awkwardly, "I was peeling fruit and accidentally cut myself."

He raised his hand to show him. There was indeed a large gash along his palm, though the bleeding had stopped and medicinal powder had been applied to it. The dried blood mixed with the white powder gave off a slightly ghastly look.

But Shen Qiao had seen all manners of hideous wounds before. A small injury like this was nothing to speak of.

Yu Shengyan was talented and clever, and he showed much promise on the martial path—one could see a hint of his master there. All he lacked was experience, but a low-level mistake like cutting yourself while peeling fruit shouldn't have been made by anyone with any knowledge of martial arts, let alone Yu Shengyan. However, Shen Qiao was currently upset and distracted, so he'd completely failed to notice this ridiculous inconsistency.

Shen Qiao glanced over at Yan Wushi. His eyes were still closed; it looked like he'd fallen asleep.

With Shen Qiao's character, he'd never do a thing like shaking someone awake, but hurt suddenly burst inside his heart: *You were the one who kept provoking me, but now you're going to ignore me instead?*

Of course, Shen Qiao's thoughts weren't this straightforward, but this was the general idea.

Yu Shengyan was standing between the two, feeling that bizarre atmosphere around him. To save himself from further awkwardness, he tried to break the stalemate. "Daoist Master Shen, I also want to visit Shixiong in Chang'an. Why don't we go together?"

Shen Qiao shook his head. "You take good care of your Shizun. I'll head out first." He didn't look at Yan Wushi again, but he kept his voice very gentle out of consideration for the resting person.

Yu Shengyan rubbed his nose as he looked at Shen Qiao's retreating back. "Shizun, have we gone too far? Daoist Master Shen seems upset."

Yan Wushi opened his eyes, then said languidly, "If the medicine isn't potent, how can it be effective?" He sent another glance at Yu Shengyan. "I naturally have my reasons for treating him coldly. But you're forbidden from showing him even an ounce of disrespect."

"This disciple wouldn't dare!" Yu Shengyan hurriedly replied.

Where would he get the courage? Not only was Shen Qiao close to his own shifu, but he was also one of the top ten martial artists in the world, as well as a sect leader. No matter which point you brought up, they were all things Yu Shengyan respected deeply.

"But what if Daoist Master Shen actually leaves...?" *Your esteemed self shouldn't overdo it,* thought Yu Shengyan. *Shen Qiao is soft and gentle on the outside but hard and unyielding on the inside. If he really does leave out of rage, your esteemed self might not be able to coax him back.*

Yan Wushi smiled slightly. "Truthfully, he already feels the same way, deep within his heart; he just can't put down his pride. His Daoist core is all that's stopping him."

Really? Yu Shengyan thought to himself. *How come I couldn't tell at all?*

Yan Wushi seemed to have noticed what he was thinking. "You need to spend a couple more years learning from Bian Yanmei how to judge people."

His shizun had seen right through him at a glance. Yu Shengyan secretly stuck out his tongue, but he naturally didn't dare to say more.

Sure enough, Shen Qiao really did leave. Early the next morning, before Yu Shengyan had the chance to see him off, he received a message from a subordinate informing him of Daoist Master Shen's departure.

However, Shen Qiao didn't forget to leave behind a few prescriptions and pills for Yan Wushi's recuperation before he left.

He was kind by nature, but kind wasn't the same as foolish. Upon returning to his house, even if Shen Qiao hadn't been able to take Yan Wushi's pulse, he quickly guessed most of what had happened—that Yan Wushi had been faking his illness. He couldn't help but grow angry, and thus he'd changed his plans: his idea of leaving in two days became leaving early the next morning.

At first, Shen Qiao really did head for Chang'an, but when he reached Feng Province, he ended up running into Yuan Ying, who'd come looking for him.

After Shen Qiao had regained his position as sect leader of Xuandu Mountain, he'd sent two elders to assist Yuan Ying. Though Yuan Ying didn't know much about construction, he'd head to the site every day to do his inspecting, trembling the entire time. This continued all the way until Gu Hengbo traveled to Chang'an to look for Shen Qiao, whereupon Yuan Ying found that Gu Hengbo was far more meticulous and capable than he was when it came to supervising construction work. Meanwhile, news of Hulugu and Yan Wushi's duel had been spreading everywhere. Worried that Hulugu would win, and even more worried that Hulugu would go after Shen Qiao in the case he did win, Yuan Ying entrusted Xuandu Monastery to Gu Hengbo, then left Chang'an himself to look for Shen Qiao.

Among Qi Fengge's five disciples, only Yuan Ying was unfamiliar with management and administration. Instead he'd devoted himself to martial arts and his studies and, until recently, never took a step out of Xuandu Mountain. The other four disciples had their own individual strengths. Even Tan Yuanchun and Yu Ai had helped a lot when Shen Qiao first inherited the sect leader's position from Qi Fengge—Tan Yuanchun was adept at training disciples while Yu Ai was good with trivial daily affairs. As for Gu Hengbo, Shen Qiao had never discriminated against her on account of her gender; he taught her the same things he'd taught Yuan Ying. Though her personality was somewhat colder, she was swift and resolute when it came to handling affairs, and her procedures were clear and organized. Having her there to supervise Xuandu Monastery, as well as to make arrangements in the capital, naturally put Shen Qiao at ease compared to when Yuan Ying was tasked with it.

After the two martial siblings met, Yuan Ying saw that Shen Qiao was fine, which put him at ease in turn. Knowing that Gu Hengbo was handling things back in Chang'an, Shen Qiao no longer felt the need to hurry there so quickly. He sent Yuan Ying back first, then changed course to Yuan Province. He planned to head south into the Chen Kingdom to take a look.

Shen Qiao had only been to Chen once before. Yuwen Qing had been sent there as an envoy of Northern Zhou, and Yuwen Yong tasked Yan Wushi with escorting him. Shen Qiao was part of the company as well, but at that time his martial arts had yet to recover, and his vision was still very poor; to avoid causing trouble for others, he'd only left the guest complex once. Chen covered a vast territory, yet he'd only been able to see a tiny fraction of it, and he deeply felt that it was a pity. Now that he had the chance, he naturally wanted to see it properly using his own eyes.

At this time, Chen was in the south with Sui in the north. Aside from the Göktürk Khaganate, there was also a small country called Liang, with its capital Jiangling, as well as another small nation called Pubu, located southwest of Chen. Ever since the Jin Dynasty had migrated south, the common folk of the world suffered from war and displacement. Everyone hoped that an enlightened ruler could suppress both the north and the south, uniting the Central Plains and giving the people a relatively stable life. But as they continued to hope over the next couple of centuries, all their hopes netted them was the Uprising of the Five Barbarians along with the dynastic changes in the south and north both: from the Song Dynasty to the current Chen Dynasty in the south, and the Zhou Dynasty being supplanted by the Sui Dynasty in the north. In the end, their hopes of reunification weren't met. No one knew when that enlightened ruler would finally descend, and no one knew who among Chen and Sui would be more likely to unify the lands—or even if the Göktürks would ultimately take advantage of their situation to claim victory instead.

There were too many variables in these turbulent times. When it came to the question of to whom the world would belong, no knowledgeable person could give an answer that they'd be willing to stake their life on—not even Yan Wushi. He'd once favored Yuwen Yong, and yet due to the man's unworthy descendants, his dynasty had crumbled, and the nation changed hands.

Yang Jian, the current emperor of the Northern Dynasty, showed promise as a wise ruler. However, the noble families of the south held him in contempt. After all, this person had once served as a Xianbei official and had even used a Xianbei surname. Now that he'd usurped the throne and become emperor, he'd immediately changed his surname to a Han one, even linking his ancestors to a well-known clan within the Central Plains—how could someone this shameless be capable of unifying the lands?

The Confucians claimed their own practices as orthodox. Confucian sects like Linchuan Academy resided in the south, and they naturally regarded the Chen Dynasty as being chosen by heaven. As such, they believed that the Lord of Chen was the enlightened ruler who would unify the world.

For the time being, the Lord of Chen did well to preserve his ancestors' accomplishments and carried out his governance in a clear, orderly manner. So there was indeed a sense of peace.

Shen Qiao didn't support Yang Jian solely because he believed Yan Wushi's words; he did so because he'd truly seen that Yang Jian was intelligent and capable. It wasn't enough for a ruler of a country to be astute, they also had to be tolerant toward others, and Yang Jian possessed both these qualities.

However, these qualities alone weren't enough either, so he planned to visit Chen and take a stroll through the country. This way, he could relax while personally experiencing the local customs and practices of Chen. This method would be a hundred times more effective than hearing descriptions secondhand.

On the way to Jiankang, Shen Qiao met the Li family, who were traveling there from Jiang Province to seek refuge with their relatives. This family was both wealthy and large, and they'd even hired bodyguards to escort them. Upon encountering Shen Qiao and learning that he was heading to Jiankang too, they invited him to travel together with them.

Jiang Province was currently part of the Sui Dynasty's territory. Therefore, traveling from Jiang Province to Jiankang essentially meant crossing between the domains of the Northern and Southern Dynasties. Though the imperial courts didn't forbid their citizens from interacting, the split between the two kingdoms meant that there were areas without proper jurisdiction from either country. Quite a few bandits took advantage of this to cause chaos in those unmanned areas, so civilians, who were easy targets for looting, usually traveled together in large groups of horses and people.

The wife of the Li family was a widow, and now she wished to bring her daughter to Jiankang to take refuge with her birth family. Though she had servants to accompany her, as well as the guards she'd hired, she still didn't feel particularly safe. Meanwhile, Shen Qiao had an approachable appearance, and he carried a sword, implying he had some measure of skill. These days, when traveling long distances to meet your relatives, an extra person meant extra help. Shen Qiao also saw that the other party was made up of a widow and her daughter, and since they were going the same way, he agreed. For the rest of the journey, he rode astride a horse together with the escorts.

The escort agency had dispatched four guards in total, and the leader had the surname Liu. The Li family had paid a generous sum for those four guards, otherwise they'd have only sent two. After all, in the agency's eyes, protecting two delicate women didn't seem like a difficult task at all, especially when there were already servants with them.

At first, Escort Guard Liu was somewhat curious about Shen Qiao. He even inquired about his identity, but Shen Qiao didn't disclose much—only that he was a wandering Daoist with a couple of years of martial arts training and that he was now traveling the world.

There were many traveling Daoists these days. Escort Guard Liu traveled extensively, and so he'd met quite a few of them. After hearing what Shen Qiao said, he lost most of his interest, and even thought that this man might have been planning to use his good looks to seduce the Li family's young lady to swindle some money off her. Or even worse, he might possess ulterior motives and be coveting the young lady's beauty.

In truth, one couldn't blame him for these thoughts. The Li daughter was young and lovely, right around the age where she'd grow interested in men, and thus had few defenses against a Daoist priest like Shen Qiao, with his incredible poise. Though she couldn't approach him directly with everyone watching, she still sent people over several times to deliver him things: sometimes pastries, sometimes other items. Though Escort Guard Liu would also receive a portion in passing, how could he fail to see that her real target was Shen Qiao?

Shen Qiao had realized Escort Guard Liu's misunderstanding, but he knew that explaining would be useless. If anything, it could end up backfiring, and he'd make matters worse. Everyone would go their separate ways once they arrived in Jiankang anyway, and the journey itself would only take a couple of days, so there was no need to delve into the details.

After journeying together for a few days, they arrived at the foot of Qianlong Mountain in Huainan. There was still some distance left until the next town where they could stay overnight—they wouldn't make it there before nightfall. Thus Escort Guard Liu made a gesture, signaling to everyone that they'd be resting here for the night.

Epilogue–Part Three

THE TERRAIN WAS FLAT and spacious, apart from the mountain to the side, which would shield them from the wind at night. It was indeed a good place to rest. Escort Liu hadn't chosen their site haphazardly when he'd had them stop. Shen Qiao, however, possessed the keen intuition of a martial arts practitioner, and he noticed that something seemed off.

He couldn't help but scan his surroundings.

As the sun dipped low in the west, the world gradually dimmed. Shen Qiao's eyes had been seriously injured in the past, but with the recovery of his internal cultivation, his sight had essentially returned to its former clarity. However, he still failed to spot anything suspicious as he surveyed the area.

"Daoist Master." Escort Guard Liu had personally come to invite him. "My brothers have stewed some dried meat. If the Daoist Master doesn't abstain from meat, would you like a bowl?"

In truth, Escort Guard Liu wasn't particularly interested in this excessively good-looking Daoist. However, the man was carrying a sword, and it wasn't flashy, so it was evident he had at least some skill. In case anything happened during their journey, they could look out for each other. For someone like Escort Guard Liu, who traveled the jianghu for a living, an extra friend was naturally better than an extra enemy.

Shen Qiao didn't abstain from eating meat; he simply preferred lighter dishes. However, one couldn't be picky when out and about, so he didn't refuse the invitation. After thanking Escort Guard Liu, he walked over and sat down to eat the meat stew together with them.

Both the wife and daughter of the Li family remained inside the carriage. The curtains were drawn, walling off the space inside from outsiders. Surrounding the carriage were the Li family's servants and maids, and the escort party also made sure to be discreet. They didn't disturb them but rather kept a couple dozen paces between the two groups.

"I know the Daoist Master is heading to Jiankang, but do you have a place to stay?" asked Escort Guard Liu. "If you don't have one, you can go to Baimen Monastery in the city. I heard that the new emperor is very interested in Daoist alchemy. If it's you, Daoist Master, I'm sure he'll elevate you."

Shen Qiao was caught between laughing and crying. Though he was a Daoist, he wasn't the kind who refined pills or drew talismans. One must know that there were many kinds of Daoists.

He didn't shoot down Escort Guard Liu's offer, though. Instead, he asked, "I thought the Chen Dynasty believed strongly in Confucianism. Why is the new emperor interested in Daoists?"

It was only after Shen Qiao crossed the border into Chen that he'd learned that the previous Lord of Chen, Chen Xu, had passed away not long ago. The new emperor was Chen Shubao, and he was the first son of Chen Xu and Empress Liu Jingyan, as well as the rightful heir to the throne.

But Shen Qiao also knew that Chen was Linchuan Academy's territory. Liu Jingyan was the empress dowager, but she had another identity too: Ruyan Kehui's shimei.

Escort Guard Liu shook his head and smiled. "How would I know something like that? Perhaps the emperor was taken by impulse and ended up interested in alchemy? Since ancient times, all emperors have pursued the path of immortality. Even people within the jianghu itself claim that reaching the martial summit is to reach the realm of immortals, don't they?"

But an emperor ignoring national affairs to pursue an interest as illusory as alchemy? Even if one spent a lifetime refining pills, they might not achieve any results. Doing something like that was truly putting the cart before the horse.

Shen Qiao also knew that Escort Guard Liu wouldn't know too much, given his position, so he didn't ask further. Everyone chatted for a while until the sky turned completely dark, and then they got up one after another, heading to rest for the night.

"Daoist Master Shen isn't going to rest?" Escort Guard Liu couldn't help but ask upon seeing Shen Qiao sitting cross-legged beneath a tree.

It was currently summer. People weren't too picky when it came to the great outdoors: even without tents, many would sleep directly on the ground or on top of the two-wheeled transport carts. A robe as a blanket was enough to pass the night. Escort Guard Liu and the others were long used to this kind of lifestyle, so they didn't find it harsh.

"I'm used to meditating for rest, even at night. Liu-xiong doesn't need to worry about me." Shen Qiao smiled.

Escort Guard Liu was a little envious. "Hah! Back when I was studying martial arts, I too would often meditate in place of lying down to rest. Unfortunately, I've been running around constantly these past few years. I get tired during the day, and the moment I lie down at night, I'm dead to the world. Don't even know north from south! Over time, even the internal cultivation skills Shifu taught me have gone to waste!"

"Which sect is Liu-xiong from?" asked Shen Qiao off-handedly.

"I'm a disciple from Zhongnan Sect."

Shen Qiao made a sound of surprise. "Then you're from the same sect as Zhangsun Sheng?"

Escort Guard Liu was dispirited. "Zhangsun-shixiong is the sect leader's personal disciple, and he's from a noble family in the Northern Dynasty. I'm only a son from a humble commoner's family and am but an external disciple. Being so coarse and un-refined, how can I dare to claim that I'm from the same sect as Zhangsun-shixiong?"

Only after Shen Qiao consoled him a little did Escort Guard Liu's mood take a turn for the better. He watched Shen Qiao meditate and recalled his own long-abandoned training. His heart ached, so he also sat down near Shen Qiao, ready to meditate for the night.

In truth, Escort Guard Liu also practiced qi circulation while meditating on most days, but the majority of people regarded qi circulation and breathing exercises as something completely differ-ent from actual sleep. Though Escort Guard Liu had the desire to copy Shen Qiao, he couldn't even hold out until midnight. With his back against a tree trunk, he fell into a deep slumber.

That very instant, Shen Qiao suddenly leapt to his feet and pounced forward.

At the same time, a whistling noise sounded before them. An arrow streaked through the sky like a shooting star, flying straight at the carriage with the Li family's wife and daughter inside.

No one had managed to react in time. Though there were people keeping watch, most couldn't stave off their fatigue by this hour, leaving their reflexes dulled significantly. Even Escort Guard

Liu, who'd trained at an orthodox martial arts sect, had only just managed to peel open his eyes, looking up in the direction of the sound.

But the arrow failed to pierce the carriage. Someone had caught it in their bare hands.

From the arrow in Shen Qiao's grasp there came a snap, and its shaft immediately broke into two halves. Then many more arrows flew over, all at once.

"Bandits! There are bandits!" Piercing whistles and shouts rang out over the open field. Even those in deep sleep snapped awake, one after another. They grabbed their weapons and prepared for battle.

By the time they'd fully reacted, Shen Qiao had already caught five or six arrows. The enemies obviously hadn't expected there would be someone so formidable with this procession. The ambush had failed, and they were forced to switch to direct confrontation. They bounded out from the shadows and charged.

This group wore black clothes, but a look was enough to tell that they were bandits. Escort Guard Liu had mentioned that this place was a no-man's-land, claimed by neither the north nor the south, and so bandits skulked around here. The Li family's wife and daughter hadn't thought that their luck would be "wonderful" enough to encounter such an event. They were screaming in terror inside the carriage, and the servants who'd been surrounding the carriage were sent scattering in every direction as they dodged and hid from the incoming arrows.

The scene erupted into complete chaos.

There were about thirty or forty attackers in total, all capable fighters who'd been trained through their long years of crime. They were tall and strapping, with fierce expressions. Once the escorts realized what was happening, they all came up to join the skirmish, but they lacked the bandits' ferocity and quickly found themselves at a disadvantage.

The Li family was wealthy. They were moving their entire household to Jiankang, so they'd brought all their belongings with them. Anyone with a bit of judgment could tell that this was a fat sheep, prime for slaughter. Naturally, the bandits were unwilling to let them go and had mobilized this many men accordingly.

But these bandits had never expected to face the likes of Shen Qiao.

For Escort Guard Liu, fighting one-to-two was almost pushing him to his limit. But to Shen Qiao, though these bandits were decently strong, none of them were worth taking seriously. If he drew Shanhe Tongbei here, they'd only be crushed even further. These normally undefeated bandits were no match for Shen Qiao.

Everyone was dumbfounded as they watched Shen Qiao take on hordes of bandits by himself. He injured some, knocked down others. Escort Guard Liu finally returned to his senses and hurriedly called people to come forth and help, sealing each bandit's acupoints one by one and tying them up.

"Aiya!"

From behind Shen Qiao, an arrow came piercing through the air, firing toward the back of his head. He hadn't realized that the bandits had left some within the shadows, but with his martial prowess, it wouldn't have been too late to react. He was about to turn and block the arrow, but someone had been even faster: that pained shout was from the person who'd blocked the arrow for him.

Shen Qiao was beyond stunned. He'd never expected that the Li family's daughter, who he'd seen only a few times, would risk herself to block the arrow for him. He lowered her to the ground, then ran into the shadows with his sword and defeated the shooter. Only afterward did he return to check on the injured girl.

It was obvious the Li family's wife too hadn't expected that her daughter would suddenly do something like this. She'd stumbled out of the carriage and was currently holding her daughter while crying. That arrow had struck the girl right on her shoulder, and blood quickly stained her shirt crimson.

Shen Qiao had no choice but to carry the girl into the carriage. He first sealed a couple of acupoints to stem the blood flow, then he broke the arrow into two, pulling each end out one by one. Then he personally bandaged the wound himself.

The Li family's daughter had lost a great deal of blood. She trembled and opened her eyes, her gaze darting around in search of Shen Qiao until she caught him right in front of her. "Daoist Master, am I going to die?" she asked in a daze.

Shen Qiao was caught between laughing and crying. "You won't."

The location of her wound was tremendously fortunate—it hadn't pierced any muscles or bones. Though it was clear she'd lost a large amount of blood, the injury itself wasn't serious. Shen Qiao had never needed her to risk her life and take the arrow for him in the first place, but as she'd already done so, he couldn't brush off her kindness.

He took out the wound medication he had on him and applied some to her, then had her take another portion orally. He then explained to the Li family's wife that she'd need to administer the medicine to her daughter three times a day.

The Li family's daughter tugged on Shen Qiao's sleeve. "Can the Daoist Master stay here a little longer?"

These days, the customs weren't as conservative or closed-off—though they still weren't as brazen as they'd been during the Qin and Han Dynasties, where people would make love in the wild and women could still pursue if they had someone they liked. As her own mother was right next to her, the implications of the Li family's daughter's words were more than blatant.

Shen Qiao shook his head. "This humble Daoist is but a priest, involved with the secular world. I'm grateful for the little niangzi's noble deed just now. But this humble Daoist's martial abilities are still enough for self-defense, so I must ask the little niangzi to not do such risky things in the future."

Little Li-niangzi sighed. "I've been admiring Daoist Master Shen this entire journey and secretly paying attention to him the entire time. I knew that the Daoist Master's heart is as hard as stone and that he holds no such intentions toward me. But life is short, lasting only several decades. Just meeting someone I like is rare enough. For something like this, what's wrong with losing some face? If the Daoist Master were to be moved, then naturally I'd be ecstatic. If the Daoist Master remains unmoved, then at least I haven't betrayed my heart!"

The Li family's wife hadn't expected her daughter to say such daring words. She yearned to cover her mouth. "Hold your tongue, my child!"

Shen Qiao was taken aback. "This little niangzi's words truly reach the core of Daoism. To do as your heart wishes, without restricting yourself."

Little Li-niangzi gave a weak smile. "Daoism is about simplicity. I didn't expect Daoist Master to be less straightforward than me."

Shen Qiao said no more to her; there wasn't much to say in the first place. He put down the medicine, gave the Li family's wife a couple more instructions, and left.

Outside, Escort Guard Liu and the others had already finished with the bandits and were now taking care of the aftermath. These days, it was useless to hand such people over to the government since they didn't want to deal with them either. As the ones in question were bandits whose hands had been stained with blood, the only options were to kill them or set them free. If they freed them, returning the tiger to its mountain, then when the next party would pass this road, these bandits would once again show up to plunder and murder. Of course, Escort Guard Liu would never choose that.

Once Escort Guard Liu had finished dealing with everything, he saw that a hazy glow was already starting to tint the sky. He was no longer sleepy either, so he prepared to have everyone take to the road again.

He saw that Shen Qiao was still standing beneath the tree and walked over to him. Shen Qiao's mind seemed to be wandering, and it wasn't clear what he was thinking about.

Escort Guard Liu couldn't help but smile. "The Li family is incredibly wealthy, and their daughter is infatuated with the Daoist Master. If the Daoist Master is willing to return to secular society and marry, you'll definitely secure an enormous fortune for the future."

Only then did Shen Qiao come back to his senses. He'd been plagued by his thoughts the entire journey, but now he'd suddenly been awakened by some words from little Li-niangzi, and it was as if he'd finally figured out a problem that had long perplexed him for a very long time. For a moment, his face relaxed, shining like jade against the faint light of dawn, clear and smooth. Even Escort Guard Liu was slightly stunned. He thought, *No wonder little Li-niangzi fell in love at first sight, to the point that she could disregard her life. This Daoist priest is indeed good-looking, not to mention his incredible martial prowess.*

"Liu-xiong, there's something I'd like to seek your guidance on, please," said Shen Qiao.

Escort Guard Liu quickly said, "This one is deeply indebted to Daoist Master Shen for helping me; this one has yet to even thank you for saving my life. There's no need to use the word 'please.' The Daoist Master need only ask!"

Shen Qiao's expression was very solemn. "May I ask if Liu-xiong has ever had a beloved?"

Escort Guard Liu looked stunned. "Huh?"

Epilogue–Part Four

"WHAT... WHAT DO YOU MEAN, 'a beloved'?" Escort Guard Liu stammered.

Shen Qiao shook his head, laughing despite himself. "No, that was too forward of me. I shouldn't have asked a question like that."

Escort Guard Liu returned to his senses and scratched his head. Thinking that he'd roughly figured out Shen Qiao's train of thought, he said, "Daoist Master Shen has been cultivating since a young age, keeping his heart pure and free of desires. I trust that this was your first time with such worldly matters, so little Li-niangzi must've given you a scare. It's normal to be a bit confused about what to do!"

After the battle they'd gone through, Escort Guard Liu had dropped his courteous, distant attitude from before for a much friendlier one. "Actually, about what your esteemed self was asking... I'm not really sure how to answer. It's not possible for that many loving romances and whispering sweethearts to exist in this world. I was fortunate to be able to learn martial arts at Zhongnan Sect; it wasn't until I was seventeen that I left the mountain and returned home. My parents arranged a marriage for me, saying that though the girl in question didn't know any martial arts, she'd been educated since she was young and was a woman of virtue and integrity. Since it was an order from my parents, of course I had to comply. I can't really say whether I liked her or not. However, since we married, my wife has worked hard to manage our domestic affairs, and I am incredibly grateful to her. Only bored scholars with too much time on their hands speak of loving romances, not people like us who travel the jianghu spending our days out in the elements facing life-and-death struggles, just like earlier. If the Daoist Master hadn't been here with us this trip, we really might've met our deaths here!" "Liu-xiong need not be so courteous," said Shen Qiao. "Since we're traveling together, it's expected we should help each other as well."

Escort Guard Liu responded with a laugh. "Once we arrive in Jiankang, I must treat the Daoist Master to a good meal. You absolutely can't turn me down!"

"I'd appreciate it," said Shen Qiao. "I'm not familiar with the area, so I look forward to Liu-xiong's guidance."

"Perfect!" said Escort Guard Liu. "I'll be honest, when I first saw how erudite and frail you looked, I was afraid you'd be like those scholars who only carry swords for decoration. I never imagined—" he tsked, "—that you'd be so strong! I fear that even my shifu might not compare!"

"Li-xiong is too kind."

"I won't treat Daoist Master Shen as an outsider, so I'll be straight with you. Jokes are one thing, but the Li family's young mistress is deeply attached to the Daoist Master, and I do think she's a good choice. This year has been rather chaotic. The Daoist Master is strong enough to protect himself, but instead of wandering alone through the jianghu, wouldn't it be better to take the young mistress as your wife? With the Li family's wealth, even if you can't become a great hero, you can still live as a rich and carefree old man!"

Shen Qiao didn't know whether he should laugh or cry. "Liu-xiong has misunderstood," he said. "I don't have any such intentions toward the Li family's young mistress, for my heart already belongs to another. It's only that before, everything was a bit of a mess, so I never gave it careful thought. Just now, the young mistress's words were the wake-up call that made me realize my feelings."

Understanding dawned on Escort Guard Liu. "So it's like that! No wonder you asked me that question! The Daoist Master's beloved... How does she feel about you?"

Shen Qiao frowned slightly. "That person used to be very aggressive, so I could only keep retreating. But later they seemed to have gotten angry."

Escort Guard Liu was a little speechless. "These years, women have grown even bolder than men!"

He gave it a second thought: This Daoist Master was so elegant and refined, and he was also a powerful martial artist. No wonder the girl had fallen in love with him. The Li family's young mistress had only seen him a couple of times, with how she spends all day inside her carriage, yet hadn't she disregarded all danger to herself and jumped in front of him to block that arrow?

Ultimately, Escort Guard Liu was a man with experience, so he began advising Shen Qiao. "Women are usually shy, so it's already rare for them to bare their feelings, yet you refused her. If this happened a few times, a woman with thinner skin would of course be too embarrassed to come to you again. If you take the initiative to explain things to her, that should resolve everything, easily!"

The corner of Shen Qiao's mouth twitched. "That person... Their skin isn't that thin."

Escort Guard Liu laughed. "If it's not thin, doesn't that make things even easier? I'll say it directly, with the Daoist Master's character and looks, if you do as I say, she'll definitely turn shy and agree! Afterward, you can have a matchmaker approach her family to suggest the engagement!"

Shen Qiao sighed. "They're terribly arrogant. I fear they won't yield now that they're frustrated."

"That's easy enough to deal with! Everyone has things they like. Just give her a couple of her favorite things and your situation will naturally improve from there."

"I must ask Liu-xiong to please advise me," said Shen Qiao modestly.

"How about giving her some hairpins? Don't women usually like jewelry and hair ornaments? If she likes plainer things, gift her peachwood hair sticks or jade hairpins. If she likes the fancier kind, you can give her the ones inlaid with gold, silver, or precious stones. I guarantee that it's foolproof!"

Shen Qiao considered how Yan Wushi's arrangements and attire had always been prepared by others. A single hair stick on his head probably cost the same as an average person's yearly spendings. He also hadn't shown any particular fondness for them either, so Shen Qiao shook his head. "The one I love doesn't really have much interest in accessories."

Escort Guard Liu frowned. "Then...what about food? Clothing, food, shelter, or transportation? Surely she must have preferences about those?"

Shen Qiao thought for a while, then hesitantly said, "They like tangren?"

However, it was Xie Ling who liked tangren.

Did Yan Wushi also like eating tangren? Shen Qiao imagined Sect Leader Yan licking a tangren in his arrogant and imperious manner, and his expression instantly contorted.

Escort Guard Liu also found it odd. "Isn't tangren usually enjoyed by young children?" After a moment, he seemed relieved again, and he gave an explanation that he found perfectly reasonable: "Daoist Master's beloved likely isn't too old, right?"

Shen Qiao lightly coughed, feeling a little uncomfortable. "Perhaps."

Escort Guard Liu thought to himself that Shen Qiao's appearance was indeed the kind that young maidens were attracted to. After all, little Li-niangzi had only seen him a few times and she was already head over heels. "That's even better. The younger they are, the less experienced they are as well, so a couple of words from you will be enough to make her happy. Say, Daoist Master Shen, since your affections are mutual, why didn't you try and find out what that little lady of yours likes?"

In truth, Shen Qiao did know what "she" liked, but knowing that was still useless. "I believe they like practicing martial arts the most. They also like competing with others in them."

There were a lot of women in the jianghu who were obsessed with martial arts, so Escort Guard Liu didn't find this surprising. "With the Daoist Master's prowess, offering her martial advice must be a simple enough matter."

Shen Qiao rubbed his nose. "I can't defeat them."

Escort Guard Liu was stunned. Women these days were really far too aggressive! No wonder Daoist Master Shen had rejected her multiple times before. He too wouldn't dare to marry such a tigress! "That, that…" He was running out of things to say. "In any case, just try everything you can. The ancient saying that 'with sufficient sincerity, one can split stone and metal' still has its wisdom. Since she likes you too, even if the things you give her aren't to her liking, she'll be able to understand your feelings."

Shen Qiao understood that he wouldn't be able to get any more answers. "Thank you very much, Liu-xiong. I've learned a lot."

Escort Guard Liu felt that though Shen Qiao was a powerful martial artist, he was completely clueless in romance. Hence he gave him a lot more advice, even including how, when in the boudoir, he'd pick up his wife and walk around during the daytime. "Don't worry about the way women act in public, where each one acts more proper and serious than the last. Once the doors are closed and no one can see, what's wrong with indulging her a little? Life is short—you only live a few decades! It's not easy to meet someone you like, so you should cherish her!"

Shen Qiao tried not to laugh. "All right, I'll keep this in mind."

By now, everyone had already finished packing. They all quickened their pace so as to enter the city as quickly as possible and rest. Shen Qiao and Escort Guard Liu fell to the end of the procession to protect the back of the carriage.

They galloped the rest of the way, the wind whistling past them. No one bothered to speak anymore, and they naturally didn't know that within the carriage, there was another conversation taking place, whispered and quiet.

Little Liu-niangzi, who was supposed to be unconscious, groaned as she stirred, then asked the person next to her, "What did you think of my performance earlier?"

The Li family's wife spoke truthfully, "It was a bit too exaggerated."

Little Liu-niangzi rolled her eyes. "I even had to deliberately injure myself to give Daoist Master Shen his wake-up call. But if Daoist Master Shen can see the light from this, this wound won't have been in vain!"

The Li family's wife was very sympathetic. "It must've been hard. You really took that arrow!"

"You don't say!" said little Liu-niangzi miserably. "It really hurt! But Daoist Master Shen is too capable. If I didn't make the act genuine and he saw through me, what would I do then?"

"Don't think about it anymore," the Li family's wife consoled her. "You know that this is a mission. The more thoroughly we complete it, the better off we'll be. The Sect Leader has always been generous, so he'll definitely reward you well."

After going through an attempted robbery, everyone's hearts were plagued by lingering fears. They couldn't wait to reach the town as quickly as possible so that they may avoid experiencing another raid.

Because of the little Liu-niangzi's injury, the group stopped in the next town for a couple of days. Paying for three meals a day on top of room fees wasn't a small expense, but fortunately, the Li family was wealthy enough that they weren't too concerned about the cost. The Li family's wife was willing to pay so her daughter could rest a few days longer. She also thanked Shen Qiao profusely for driving off the bandits; she never grumbled about Shen Qiao causing her daughter heartbreak or injury. She even insisted on giving him a large sum of money.

After about half a month, the group finally arrived in Jiankang. Upon entering the city, the mother and daughter reunited with their relatives. Everyone should have gone their separate ways at this point, but the passionate Escort Guard Liu enthusiastically dragged Shen Qiao all over Jiankang. He pointed out the local scenery and culture, then treated him to a meal. Afterward, he told Shen Qiao his address and invited him to visit in the future when he was free. Only after this did he finally take his leave.

After bidding farewell to Escort Guard Liu, Shen Qiao sought out the Baimen Temple the other men had talked about earlier, planning to stay there for a couple of days. Right at this time, an envoy just happened to arrive, bearing an imperial edict calling all eminent Daoists to enter the palace. Finding Shen Qiao's demeanor extraordinary, this envoy came to question him about his background. Shen Qiao answered each and every one of them using the exact same story he'd told Escort Guard Liu.

The envoy was very anxious about gathering enough people for the emperor's demands, so naturally he didn't question anyone too thoroughly. Furthermore, most people were easily influenced by appearances, and Shen Qiao's countenance aligned perfectly with how many imagined an "immortal" might look.

"May I ask the Daoist Master, do you practice alchemy?"

Shen Qiao had wanted to say no, but before the word could leave his mouth, his thoughts shifted, and he changed his tune. "The Dao I cultivate is the path of affection. When it comes to alchemy, I may know the surface concepts, but I don't comprehend their essence. However, I do have some experience with fortune-telling through facial features."

The envoy was somewhat disappointed to hear that he wasn't familiar with alchemy, but when Shen Qiao mentioned reading facial features, he cheered up again. "That means that the Daoist Master also knows divination?"

"A little bit," said Shen Qiao modestly.

"Today, His Majesty is interested in Daoism, and he wishes for guidance from all eminent Daoists. Would the Daoist Master be willing to accompany me to the palace? If the emperor is pleased, what awaits Daoist Master Shen will be fortune and wealth beyond your wildest imagination!"

Shen Qiao had come to Chen precisely so he could assess the Lord of Chen from up close and see how he compared to Yang Jian. He hadn't expected to be offered a pillow before even growing drowsy. As he wasn't on close terms with Ruyan Kehui, it'd be very difficult to find another honest opportunity to meet the emperor if he missed this chance.

Now that he was doing his cultivation in the secular world, he knew much more about how the world worked. If he rashly agreed, not only would he fail to demonstrate the proper poise expected of an eminent master, he'd even draw the other party's contempt.

Therefore, he looked hesitant instead. "This humble Daoist has sworn an oath before his Daoist forefathers to read the Daoist classics several times every day. He has yet to finish today's studies, so it seems that meeting with His Majesty isn't in his fate this time. Perhaps another day."

As Confucianism was enormously influential within Chen, there weren't many sizable Daoist monasteries in Jiankang. This Baimen Monastery was also not particularly conspicuous when compared to the rest. Having been suppressed for so long, when they heard that the emperor was summoning them, all of Baimen Monastery's Daoist priests grew incredibly excited, their faces glowing with joy. It was only this newcomer priest who held himself with such composure.

Sure enough, the envoy's opinion of him rose, and even Baimen Monastery's other Daoists began to urge him. "Daoist friend, you should accept. After all, you're a guest of our Baimen Monastery; if His Majesty grows angry and pursues this matter, we'll end up dragged into it!"

Only then did Shen Qiao sigh. "Then may I trouble the envoy to lead the way?"

Shen Qiao wasn't the only priest being summoned by the court. Once he agreed, his name was entered into a register. After three days, when the envoy had gathered around ten Daoists who seemed to fit the requirements, he finally led Shen Qiao and two other priests from Baimen Monastery into the palace.

The Chen palace wasn't much larger than the Sui palace, but it was far more exquisitely and beautifully designed, fully demonstrating the beauty of Jiangnan. Many of the Daoists had never seen this level of opulence in their lives. Even if they strove to keep it from showing up on their faces, they couldn't stop their gazes from betraying their awe.

Shen Qiao's party of three entered the palace and was led to Wangxian Hall.

Inside, there were eight seats on each side, and most of them were occupied. The remaining three seats, which were closest to the entrance, were naturally reserved for them.

Shen Qiao had no intentions of fighting with the other two priests for the right to sit first. He let them have the two seats in the front while he sat in the one closest to the entrance. The two men looked at him gratefully.

To sit closest to the door, of course, meant that you were the character of least importance.

"His Majesty has yet to arrive," the eunuch said. "Everyone, please remain quiet and wait for a moment."

Being Daoists, they naturally wouldn't dare to be too loud, but quiet whispers were still inevitable. Shen Qiao swept his gaze around the room, and when it fell on a particular man, all the hair on his body instantly stood on end. He almost thought that something was wrong with his eyes.

Originally, that man's eyes had been closed, as if he were drowsing, and had an air of haughty aloofness about him. Right then, his eyes suddenly opened, and he looked in Shen Qiao's direction.

Two pairs of eyes met, but the other party turned away, as if nothing had happened.

Shen Qiao was speechless.

Epilogue–Part Five

SHEN QIAO WAS no longer blind, so there was no way he could mistake a person for somebody else.

What astonished him was how daring the other party was. Other than changing into a set of Daoist robes, he hadn't even altered his looks at all. He simply sat there, inside the Chen imperial palace as the Emperor of Chen's guest of honor, with that face completely undisguised.

Everyone knew that Chen was Confucian territory. To put it more bluntly, to Ruyan Kehui, it was a forbidden domain that only he was allowed to access, or perhaps it could be called a choice cut of meat reserved only for his pleasure. As an example, the Buddhist Tiantai Sect was also located within Chen's borders, but Linchuan Academy had eclipsed it so much, it'd lost most of its radiance.

If it were a one-on-one duel, Yan Wushi naturally wouldn't fear Ruyan Kehui. However, even a powerful dragon would have difficulty defeating a snake on its own territory. If the great and lofty Huanyue Sect Leader had disguised himself as a Daoist in order to enter the palace and meet the Lord of Chen, plotting to wrest benefits away from the Confucian faction, and thus incurring the Confucian faction's wrath... If this spread to the public, it'd invite much disapproval and scorn. In Shen Qiao's opinion, Yan Wushi had no reason to bring trouble down upon himself like this.

But ultimately, Yan Wushi was Yan Wushi. If he moved according to other people's expectations, he wouldn't be Yan Wushi anymore.

Perhaps Shen Qiao had spent far too much time looking at Yan Wushi, for the Baimen Monastery priests beside him had taken notice. They leaned over and whispered, "Daoist Master Shen, do you recognize that Daoist friend?"

"I don't," said Shen Qiao. "I've also just arrived in Jiankang, and I was about to ask Daoist Comrade Zhang to introduce us."

Daoist Master Zhang said, "I only recognize the two priests across from you. One is from Lanshui Monastery, within the capital. Lanshui Monastery is even more dilapidated than our Baimen Monastery. I have no idea how they managed to bewitch the envoys into letting them through!"

Shen Qiao was caught between laughing and crying. People of similar backgrounds would disparage each other the most. Just because someone cultivated the Dao didn't mean that they'd necessarily carry themselves with the poise expected of an immortal. In truth, there were all types of people, never lacking in variety.

"I heard that His Majesty had already summoned some Daoist comrades," said Shen Qiao. "Was His Majesty dissatisfied?"

Daoist Master Zhang said, "His Majesty seeks immortality, so he naturally needs to seek Daoists out for guidance, but those Confucians are deeply against it. The largest monastery within the capital is Donghai Monastery. Initially, His Majesty sought priests from there, but it's said that partway through their discussion, the Confucians caught wind of it. That Ruyan Kehui was truly infuriating—he actually requested the Empress Dowager to pressure them. She exposed the immortal techniques of the Donghai Monastery's priests as a ruse, then had them expelled."

A hint of schadenfreude slipped into Daoist Master Zhang's voice as he went on. "Though if not for this, how would we have gotten our chance to distinguish ourselves? Those priests from Donghai Monastery wanted to take everything for themselves, and that's why it was so easy to drive them away. If all the Daoist priests in Jiankang could join forces, we might not need to fear Linchuan Academy at all!"

Shen Qiao thought, *I fear that even if you joined forces, you'd still be no match for Ruyan Kehui.* "If that's the case, why hasn't Linchuan Academy shown up with us at the palace today?" he asked.

"It's your first time here, so it's natural you don't know," said Daoist Master Zhang. "Not long after the emperor ascended, the Prince of Shixing revolted. Ruyan Kehui is currently with the army, assisting with quashing the rebellion, and the empress dowager is overseeing things—she's responsible for coordinating and managing personnel on top of supervising the court itself. As she couldn't handle the hot weather, she's moved to another palace and is handling government matters from there."

Understanding dawned on Shen Qiao. No wonder the emperor was so fearless. While the tiger was away, the monkey would be king. "If the empress dowager finds out about this, might she not take it out on the emperor but transfer the blame to us instead?" asked Shen Qiao.

"It's no matter," said Daoist Master Zhang. "I've already made thorough inquiries. Though the empress dowager is from a Confucian background, she rejects neither Daoism nor Buddhism—she's different from Ruyan Kehui, that stubborn old fogey. He can't wait to wipe out all traces of Buddhism and Daoism within Chen's borders. Now that we've received the emperor's favor, as long as we remain prudent with our words and actions, nothing should go wrong."

He wasn't a bad person, and he was very straightforward with Shen Qiao. However, even if the empress dowager wished to find a scapegoat to blame, she couldn't prevent the human heart's weakness to the temptations of wealth and glory. The Donghai Monastery's priests had only just been expelled, but a single summons from the emperor was enough to fill up every single seat.

Of course, there was one fake Daoist here.

Shen Qiao couldn't help but shoot another look at Yan Wushi. The man was the picture of seriousness, looking straight ahead as he sat quietly. He really did give off a bit of the air of an enlightened Daoist.

After a while, the attending eunuch called out, then a slightly bewhiskered young man walked out from behind the folding screen.

Everyone rose and bowed.

The Lord of Chen's pace was neither fast nor slow as he walked with the carefree, leisurely grace exclusive to aristocrats. This special gait had a long history behind it, and it brimmed with the charm and rhythm of the two Jin Dynasties. In the eyes of those who advocated for the gentry system, this was the bearing a leader should possess.

Unlike Shen Qiao, the other Daoists didn't have that much on their mind. When they saw the emperor arrive, they all began racking their brains, hoping that they'd be able to win the emperor's favor today and thus propel themselves a step higher.

After the Lord of Chen sat down, he first addressed all the Daoists. "I have read all the classics. Confucianism places great emphasis on righteousness and Buddhism on reincarnation. Only Daoism attaches importance to the current life. What wise opinions do all you Daoist masters have on this?"

The closer their seats were to the emperor, the more the emperor valued them. Thus everyone began to answer according to their seats.

One Daoist, with the surname Lin, said, "Buddhism speaks of three lives. However, when it comes to one's past and future lives, can one really perceive the effect of 'the merits from my past life leads to wealth and fortune in my present'? Daoism does not agree with this. Similarly, Your Majesty sits upon the royal throne because Your Majesty is the reincarnation of Polaris. Since Your Majesty is the Emperor Star itself, what is there to discuss of past or future lives? Therefore this humble Daoist believes those Buddhist statements to be absurd! With Your Majesty's heavenly talents, as long as you cultivate them diligently, why wouldn't you be able to ascend to heaven and return to the ranks of immortals?"

The Lord of Chen was intrigued. "Then, in this Daoist Master's opinion, how must I cultivate in order to return to the ranks of immortals?"

"Oh, Daoist cultivation is based on internal martial arts techniques. When supplemented with precious elixirs, the cultivator will naturally be able to attain the Dao and become immortal. This humble Daoist has much knowledge related to refining elixirs and is willing to work hard for Your Majesty."

"Good, good," said the Lord of Chen. "Then those internal martial arts techniques that you mentioned...where does one find them?"

"This humble Daoist is ashamed to say that this isn't my area of expertise," said Daoist Master Lin awkwardly. "My strength is in refining elixirs, and I don't know much about internal martial arts. However, Xuandu Mountain and Qingcheng Mountain are Daoist sects with legacies extending hundreds of years. If Your Majesty dispatches someone there, they'll be sure to have everything you need."

Shen Qiao was completely speechless at the way Daoist Master Lin dragged everyone into hot water with him.

However, the Lord of Chen snorted coldly. "Xuandu Mountain has already accepted noble titles from the Northern Dynasty. I heard they're even building a monastery in Chang'an. As a dog of the Northern Dynasty, how could they have any great talent to speak of? Though it's worth sending someone to take a look at Qingcheng Mountain. If Yi Pichen is truly a capable man, there's no harm in copying what they did with Xuandu Mountain. I'll bestow him a noble title and have him serve in our court!"

But suddenly, a chuckle rang out within the room.

Chen Shubao glared angrily and yelled, "Who dares to laugh?!"

Yan Wushi put down the cup of wine in his hand, completely unconcerned with how he'd enraged the emperor. Slowly, he said, "I was laughing at Your Majesty's inability to recognize gold when it's right before you. There are clearly eminent masters here, so why neglect them to seek help from distant places? Yi Pichen's reputation is undeserved. He lost to Hulugu; which part of him is impressive?"

Chen Shubao sneered. "Oh? In that case, the eminent master you speak of is yourself?"

"No, not at all."

Chen Shubao was the son of the empress, and thus had been designated the crown prince from birth. His entire life had been an easy road. Other than the fright he'd suffered during his ascension, he'd never had to deal with any obstacles or frustrations, so it was natural that he considered everything beneath himself. Furthermore, he was the emperor, so it was completely normal that he had this kind of attitude.

Yan Wushi didn't give him the time to rage, though. He pointed in Shen Qiao's direction. "The eminent master the emperor seeks yet fails to recognize."

Shen Qiao was once again dumbstruck.

He finally understood why Yan Wushi had snuck himself into this meeting. What other reason could there be beyond creating trouble out of nothing and messing up someone else's place!

Could Shen Qiao's avoidance of him hurt so much that he needed to do this in revenge? Shen Qiao's thoughts couldn't help but turn in this direction, and a thread of melancholy swept through his heart.

But sure enough, the Lord of Chen's attention had been diverted. He followed Yan Wushi's finger and looked at where Shen Qiao was sitting.

With this look, he involuntarily made a sound of surprise.

Shen Qiao was sitting by the entrance, and because the light had been too bright, the emperor hadn't paid too much attention to him. Now he scrutinized him carefully and realized that the man appeared outstanding, with a noble character.

The Lord of Chen couldn't help but inquire, "Who are you and which monastery do you cultivate in?"

At this point, Shen Qiao couldn't pretend he'd heard nothing, so he stood and bowed with cupped hands. "This humble Daoist thanks Your Majesty for the question. This humble Daoist is Shan Qiaozi, and he's traveled here from the north. Currently, he's staying in Baimen Monastery."

By now, the Lord of Chen's anger from Yan Wushi's arrogant attitude had completely vanished. Instead he looked at Shen Qiao with a pleasant expression, a smile upon his face. "Since you were so highly recommended, Daoist Master, I trust that you must be a man of illustrious renown in the world, and it's just that I've never heard of you?"

Shen Qiao said, "Your Majesty is too kind. This humble Daoist is simply one who wanders the wilderness, who has neither renown nor importance. He also doesn't know why his Daoist comrade recommended him."

He'd kicked the ball right back into Yan Wushi's court.

But the Lord of Chen ignored it since he'd already lost all interest in Yan Wushi. "Does the Daoist Master have any insights on refining elixirs?"

Shen Qiao shook his head. "This humble Daoist is not an adept alchemist. He only cultivates one path."

"Which path?" asked the Lord of Chen.

"The path of affection," answered Shen Qiao.

This was the same nonsense he'd told the palace envoy, and now he was using the same explanation for the emperor, completely unchanged.

"What is the path of affection?" asked the Lord of Chen, curious.

"When cultivating the Dao, most people emphasize purity and abstinence, believing one can only attain the Dao through distancing themselves from the dust of the secular world. But my path of the heart requires one to be immersed in the red dust of the secular world, to review the luxuries and riches of the world and carefully indulge themselves within, in order to attain the Dao."

Since he looked completely serious and proper, his expression solemn, no one suspected him of spouting nonsense. They only began to doubt themselves, wondering why they'd never heard of such a path.

Smiling brightly, Yan Wushi took another sip of wine. He thought, *My A-Qiao has learned to lie without batting an eyelash.*

The Lord of Chen was delighted. "Is this not the path I've been seeking for so long? I invite the Daoist Master to stay long-term in the palace and educate me!"

Shen Qiao said, "This humble Daoist wanders the four seas without any fixed destination. I only entered the palace this time because of Your Majesty's deep interest in the Dao, so that I could resolve Your Majesty's doubts a little."

The Lord of Chen chuckled. "The Daoist Master is contradicting himself somewhat. Since you cultivate the path of the heart, you'd naturally love the wealth and luxuries of the secular world. I can bestow upon you the ultimate riches, so why do you reject it instead? Or are you playing hard to get and refusing when you actually want it?"

Though this young emperor disliked governance, preferring a life of pleasure, this didn't mean that he was dull-witted—it was the exact opposite. He had significant achievements in music, weiqi, calligraphy, art, song, dance, and poetry. Compared to the ranks of emperors as a whole, he was brilliantly talented, with a far greater array of strengths than Yang Jian.

Shen Qiao's face betrayed nothing. "Your Majesty's words are incorrect. The path of the heart isn't a path that can only be cultivated while inside the imperial palace. Why not go out for a taste of the red dust of the secular world? With all its brothels and taverns, places in which you can cultivate are everywhere. Furthermore, today this humble Daoist was blessed with the chance to gaze upon Your Majesty's heavenly visage, and that is enough. However, I have some words that I must say."

The Lord of Chen raised an eyebrow. "Speak."

"The path of the heart isn't only about the riches within the secular world, it's also about the well-being of all people: clothes, food, shelter, and transportation. Though everyone clings the former, as Your Majesty is the ruler of a nation, you must not forget the latter either."

The so-called path of the heart was nonsense Shen Qiao had randomly come out with in order to test the emperor. He hadn't expected that the emperor would be so delighted at the idea, and he couldn't help but be somewhat disappointed. Hence, he came up with these words to admonish him.

But the Lord of Chen didn't take it to heart. "The Daoist Master worries too much. Someone with as divine as an appearance as yours wandering outside is a waste of heaven's gifts. If you wish to remonstrate with me, you can stay here, and we can discuss the Dao together every day."

By the end of this line, his tone was deeply deliberate, eliciting many thoughts.

Shen Qiao thought these words somewhat strange, but he didn't at all think that the emperor had seen him that way. Instead, he only thought that the emperor of Chen was unworthy of his reputation. Though Chen was based in the south, its territory wasn't smaller than the north's. Yet Chen Shubao wasn't Yang Jian's equal at all. The north was noisily whetting their knives as Yang Jian busied himself with stabilizing the situation with the Göktürks and imperial court. Yet Chen Shubao hadn't gone to quash the rebellion; instead he grew interested in immortality and elixirs. Looking at this trend, within a few years, who'd come out on top between the north and south would be easily decided.

The two of them continued, each question followed by an answer, while everyone else was left ignored. The Daoists who'd been anxiously seeking to distinguish themselves had long been unsatisfied. One after another, they began chiming in. Some spoke on the emperor's behalf, accusing Shen Qiao of being unable to recognize heavenly grace and favor, while others hurried to recommend themselves to the emperor, claiming that they were far more capable than he was.

Suddenly, Yan Wushi chuckled. "A-Qiao, do you understand now why I don't think much of Southern Chen?"

Shen Qiao didn't have the chance to respond before someone else did. "I didn't realize that Sect Leader Yan and esteemed Daoist

Master Shen had graced us with your presence. We've been remiss with our welcome; please forgive us."

A woman walked out as she spoke these words, surrounded by a great number of maidservants.

The Lord of Chen paled and quickly rose, putting his hands together. "Greetings, Mother Empress!"

The newcomer was Chen Dynasty's empress dowager Liu Jingyan, Ruyan Kehui's shimei.

Epilogue–Part Six

THOUGH LIU JINGYAN was the empress dowager, she wasn't a lady who'd been sheltered in the women's chambers, ignorant of the outside world. She came from an illustrious background and had entered Linchuan Academy when young. Linchuan Academy's rock-solid standing within Southern Chen these years was due in no small part to Liu Jingyan's efforts.

Back when Yuwen Qing and company had traveled to the Southern Dynasty with the alliance treaty, Yan Wushi and Ruyan Kehui had fought a duel. Liu Jingyan had left the palace in disguise then, so she naturally recognized Shen Qiao and Yan Wushi.

She'd been busy helping the emperor with managing court affairs when news came of the emperor summoning a group of Daoists. Caught off guard, she quickly rushed over to intervene.

Shen Qiao had exploited this favorable situation and slipped in with the rest simply for the purpose of meeting Chen Shubao. He didn't possess any ulterior motives, but having his identity exposed still caused him some embarrassment.

"This humble Daoist came here without any ill intentions. I've been terribly rude; I beg Your Highness's forgiveness."

He was willing to continue explaining, but Yan Wushi said nothing. He simply sat there, completely at ease. It was as if, to him, there was no difference between a lavish palace and a crude commoner's house.

Liu Jingyan could demonstrate her displeasure with the Lord of Chen, but she couldn't speak so bluntly to Shen Qiao and Yan Wushi. Not only did she show no anger, she even returned Shen Qiao's greeting with the decorum of an empress dowager, warm and gentle. "Esteemed Daoist Master Shen is too courteous. Despite how busy he is, he was willing to spare the time to instruct my son. That is my son's great fortune."

She couldn't address Shen Qiao as "Sect Leader." For one thing, it would make Chen's lack of hospitality clear. For another, the fact that Shen Qiao and Yan Wushi were here, yet Chen had been caught unawares, would be terribly embarrassing for them. Liu Jingyan choosing to call him "esteemed Daoist Master" instead, another address that demonstrated great respect for Shen Qiao, was a very wise decision.

She then said to Yan Wushi, "Sect Leader Yan is a grandmaster of his generation and an incredibly important person while Daoist Master Shen is also of extraordinary character and prestige, revered by everyone. My son is too blind to recognize Mount Tai, and so he was unable to receive you two with the proper courtesy and neglected you. I ask our honored guests not to hold it against us. I'll make reparations on his behalf."

Everyone had already been surprised to see the lofty empress dowager acting so polite toward Yan Wushi and Shen Qiao. When they heard their identities, they were completely stunned—most of all Chen Shubao.

By now, he of course realized that he'd been tricked. Fury exploded through him, turning his face bright red. "These scoundrels concealed their identities and deceived the emperor. Why does the Mother Empress treat them with such courtesy? Where are the guards?! Seize them at once!"

Anger immediately rose to Liu Jingyan's face. "No one dare make a move!"

With the emperor and empress dowager's orders contradicting each other, the guards all looked at each other, trapped in their dilemma. Some of them had already begun to move, and now their feet were frozen mid-step. It was terribly awkward.

Yan Wushi stood, sneering. "Empress Dowager Liu is any man's equal. No wonder my venerable self once heard that the previous academy master of Linchuan Academy had intended on giving his mantle to you—but then you married into the imperial palace, and that's how Ruyan Kehui got his hands on the position so easily. Looking at things now, if you'd succeeded Linchuan Academy instead, perhaps their influence would've already spread far and wide through the jianghu, to permeate even the northern court and suppress Buddhism instead of dragging their feet in the Southern Dynasty like today!"

Liu Jingyan knew very well that these were words of provocation, yet no anger showed in her expression—she even smiled. "I'm grateful for Sect Leader Yan's concern, but Ruyan-shixiong's martially more skilled than I am, and he's more learned as well. Hence, it was only natural that he'd succeed the academy master's position and promote Confucianism to greater heights.

"I've already ordered my servants to prepare a banquet in another palace. If the two of you don't mind, might I trouble you to attend and allow me to host you personally?"

Liu Jingyan's words were polite and respectful. She didn't rely on her own lofty status to intimidate them, nor did she castigate them for entering the palace in disguise. Shen Qiao was unwilling to make things difficult for her, so before Yan Wushi could say anything unpleasant, he replied, "Then we will be troubling the Empress Dowager."

The Lord of Chen leapt to his feet. "Mother Empress, these two treated the imperial palace as their own playground, somewhere they can enter and leave as they please. How can you let them off so easily?!"

Yan Wushi didn't even spare him a glance. Instead, he smiled at Liu Jingyan and said, "My venerable self met the late emperor Chen Xu once. He knew the right time to make the right moves and was a ruler who carried forward the accomplishments of his predecessors. The parents are both dragons and phoenixes, yet the son they birthed was so mediocre! The saying that a 'tiger cannot be the parent of a dog' is truly not to be trusted!"

Chen Shubao was the great and lofty emperor. Hearing Yan Wushi rebuke him to his face, he instantly flew into a rage. "How presumptuous. Imperial guards, seize them!"

This was the second order from the emperor; the imperial guards dared not hesitate any further. They came forward and surrounded Yan Wushi and Shen Qiao both, weapons in hand.

Seeing this, the Daoist priests who'd originally been sitting near Shen Qiao and Yan Wushi dared not get involved, lest they be seen as rebels. They fled one after another, terrified that they'd end up as collateral damage.

But as things happened in a blur, everyone had yet to react properly when those guards who'd rushed Shen Qiao and Yan Wushi were sent sprawling across the floor before they could even blink. Weapons clattered to the ground and shouts of pain rose and fell. Meanwhile, Shen Qiao and Yan Wushi had remained completely motionless, calm and composed in whatever they were doing. The sleeves of their clothes didn't so much as tremble.

Liu Jingyan really couldn't take it anymore. She said coldly, "His Majesty hasn't fully recovered and should spend more time resting.

How can His Majesty be allowed to hear such stressful words? Guards, send these Daoist priests out of the palace!"

She'd wanted to say "expel them from the palace," but on second thought, Shen Qiao was also a Daoist, and she didn't want any misunderstandings with him, so she chose to be more courteous.

Only now did Chen Shubao realize that whom he'd once considered his finest soldiers were completely insignificant before the martial experts of the jianghu.

Ruyan Kehui had taught him since he was young, but since he was the future emperor, no one had thought that he ought to pursue martial arts and become a master within the jianghu. Besides, Chen Shubao was more interested in artistic pursuits. Hence, though there were many excellent martial artists around him, he'd been completely disconnected from the jianghu. However, the once-distant jianghu now suddenly seemed very close at hand.

He watched his mother expel the Daoist priests, then invite Shen Qiao and Yan Wushi to leave with her. Yan Wushi hadn't paid him any heed whatsoever, yet his own mother had never sought out his opinion at all—instead, she'd completely disregarded his dignity as an emperor.

"Would Your Majesty like to return to Chengxiang Hall?" an attendant came forward and timidly asked.

Chen Shubao shot him a look. "Go. Why aren't you going? Dare you defy the Empress Dowager?"

The attendant didn't dare speak.

"Bring me some wine," said Chen Shubao. "I wish to compose a song and choreography! I won't be able to write anything without wine!"

The attendant awkwardly said, "But the Empress Dowager..."

Chen Shubao's stare cut him off, and he didn't dare speak further.

"Are you my subordinate, or the Empress Dowager's? If you're this loyal to her, why not go and become her lackey instead?!"

The attendant quickly replied several times that he didn't dare, then withdrew in a hurry to look for wine.

Meanwhile, Liu Jingyan had invited the two into a separate palace—the fine wines and delicacies had already been prepared. She dismissed her maids, but they hesitated to leave.

Liu Jingyan smiled at them. "Sect Leader Yan and esteemed Daoist Master Shen are both so powerful that killing me would be simpler than snuffing out a candle. They'd need not wait until now and use such an underhanded tactic. You may leave."

Once the maids had left, Liu Jingyan said, "My son lacked manners; I've embarrassed myself before the two of you. What important reason did you have for entering the palace today? If it's something even a woman like me can assist with, please tell me, and I will lend all the help I can."

"This humble Daoist indeed wandered here from the north and is currently staying at Baimen Monastery," Shen Qiao replied. "He just happened to see His Majesty summoning Daoists to the palace, and out of curiosity, he accompanied them into the palace—that was all. The Empress Dowager need not worry about it so much. We harbor no ill intent."

Liu Jingyan was a little surprised. Considering their extraordinary statuses, she'd been certain that they'd entered the palace with some objective in mind.

"So it's like that," she said. "Is it the same for Sect Leader Yan, then?"

"If I wanted to kill Chen Shubao," said Yan Wushi, "I wouldn't have needed to wait until now."

Liu Jingyan also smiled slightly. "If anyone else said such words,

I might not believe them, but I fully believe Sect Leader Yan, for who in the world is able to match him? I heard that Sect Leader Yan defeated Hulugu on Banbu Peak—a momentous event for our Central Plains. I am full of deep admiration for Sect Leader Yan and only regret that my identity prevented me from witnessing it in person. Now I have the fortune to meet you, so please accept this wine as a token of my respect."

She watched as Yan Wushi raised his cup. Though he didn't drink, this action also expressed his attitude, so she finally relaxed.

"Though those Daoists just now weren't knowledgeable about the classics and of insufficient learning, they didn't do anything immortal or unethical," Shen Qiao said. "They only entered the palace for an audience with the emperor out of their profound admiration for him. So I ask the Empress Dowager to please spare their lives this time, on my humble self's behalf."

"This incident happened because of the emperor," said Liu Jingyan. "I'm very much aware of this myself, and I won't scapegoat the innocent. The esteemed Daoist Master Shen should be at ease."

She then sighed. "The emperor was born inside the palace and has never experienced any hardships. Instead, he clings to luxuries and pleasures, completely uninterested in national affairs. Neither I nor the late emperor expected this—we've really shown you something laughable this time."

She was being so reasonable and understanding that Shen Qiao actually felt somewhat guilty. He consoled her, "His Majesty is brilliantly talented; it's only that he's too young, so he's unwilling to turn his mind to the right path. If he receives proper guidance, he might suddenly perform amazing feats. When a songbird that's been quiet all its life begins to sing, it is sure to astound everyone."

Those words clearly struck at the core of Liu Jingyan's thoughts, for she solemnly said, "If someone like the esteemed Daoist Master Shen could accompany the emperor, I would be completely at ease!"

Shen Qiao was about to answer when Yan Wushi took the chance instead. "The Chen Dynasty already has the Confucian discipline," he said coolly. "Ruyan Kehui sees this little territory of his as his greatest treasure. No one else can step in. Shen Qiao is softhearted. Your Excellency should keep your esteemed thoughts to yourself."

His words had stabbed right into her thoughts, leaving Liu Jingyan a little embarrassed. Yet she didn't grow angry and instead maintained her warm expression. "I was too forward. I ask the two of you to forgive me."

"You're clever," said Yan Wushi. "You continue to cling to the common views of this world, but I find you much more agreeable to the eye compared to Ruyan Kehui."

Liu Jingyan smiled. "I'm grateful for Sect Leader Yan's favor."

She knew that though she was an empress dowager, the other party had no need to be careful about her feelings. Thus, she'd adjusted her attitude and reactions, and to an impressive extent.

Those who walked different paths must go their own separate ways. The three of them didn't have much to talk about, so Shen Qiao took the initiative to bid her farewell. Liu Jingyan didn't persuade him to stay. Instead, she personally escorted the two of them to the gates, then had her personal handmaidens take them out of the palace, telling them to be respectful and courteous.

In the end, Liu Jingyan said, "The two of you are guests of honor. The next time you wish to enter the palace, you can have the guards notify me; I'll come receive you with the utmost courtesy. If you hide your identities like this again, you'll be treated unfairly."

"You don't have to test us," said Yan Wushi. "My venerable self only entered the palace this time to look for someone. Since I've already found him, I naturally won't come here again."

Liu Jingyan was confused. "Who was the person you were looking for?"

Yan Wushi suddenly laughed. "Other than Daoist Master Shen Qiao, who else in the entire Chen palace would be worth me looking for them?"

Shen Qiao couldn't help but add a few words. "Sect Leader Yan and I went our separate ways in Funing County. He traveled south looking for me, and he must've heard outside the palace that Daoists were being summoned into the palace. Knowing that I would attend, he entered as well to investigate the situation. We never expected that we'd disturb the Empress Dowager like this; we beg your forgiveness."

"The esteemed Daoist Master is too courteous," said Liu Jingyan. "Since that's the case, I won't get in the way of your reminiscence. Sect Leader Yan, esteemed Daoist Master Shen, goodbye. Until we meet again."

Though she hadn't interacted much with Yan Wushi in the past, she'd also heard that he was an arrogant and egotistical man. Seeing him today, she could tell that reputation was truly deserved. In contrast, Shen Qiao was very polite and restrained. Only after saying a few more pleasantries to Liu Jingyan did he finally take his leave.

Outside the palace, Yan Wushi again went back to mostly ignoring Shen Qiao. Helpless, Shen Qiao could only quicken his pace to catch up to him.

"Did you really enter the palace to look for me?"

Yan Wushi didn't speak.

"How could you be so sure I'd visit the palace?"

Yan Wushi continued to ignore him.

Feeling helpless, Shen Qiao had no choice but to grab his sleeve. "Yan Wushi, I have something I need to say to you."

By now, the two had already arrived at the city moat. The willow leaves swayed in the air, green and tender, looking like clusters of dangling jasper. Ripples dimpled the moat's surface—it was truly a lovely, balmy day.

The two men were dressed in Daoist robes, their faces the picture of handsome beauty. Who knew how many young maidens' eyes were drawn to them, their gazes affectionate and full of yearning.

Unfortunately for them, these two Daoist masters didn't bother glancing back even once.

Yan Wushi finally responded to Shen Qiao; he stopped his steps, then pretended to be confused. "Was Daoist Master Shen calling me?"

"Yes."

"Then say it," said Yan Wushi. "Afterward I need to get on my way."

"Where are you going?" asked Shen Qiao.

"Say what you wanted to first."

Shen Qiao was rather self-conscious. Even if those thoughts had churned within his heart hundreds of thousands of times, the moment they made it to his tongue, he could never spit them out. So instead, he could only change the topic.

He looked left and right, then asked hesitantly, "There are so many people here; it's not a good place to talk. Can we speak elsewhere?"

Yan Wushi's face revealed his impatience. "If you're not saying anything, I'm leaving."

Then he turned right around and left.

Shen Qiao rushed to grab his hand. "You... You stay right there!"

Shen Qiao couldn't see due to the angle, but the corner of Yan Wushi's mouth lifted slightly—but this hint of a smile instantly vanished without a trace. When he looked back, he was frowning.

Shen Qiao kept his head lowered for a long time before he finally tossed out a sentence. "Have you been doing well?"

Yan Wushi was silent.

This question didn't feel right, so Shen Qiao thought long and hard before trying again. "Do you enjoy eating tangren?"

Yan Wushi gave a cold laugh. "Xie Ling does!" Then he turned and made to leave again.

Sure enough, Shen Qiao had misspoken again. He struggled helplessly with himself—knowing his feelings were one thing, but saying them out loud? No matter what, he couldn't do it.

He gritted his teeth, then simply dragged Yan Wushi away. He strode quickly until they found a small and deserted alley.

Yan Wushi didn't put up any resistance and let Shen Qiao drag him there. However, his face grew a little bit colder. "I helped extricate you from a predicament in the palace," he said. "This is how Daoist Master Shen repays me?"

What do you mean, extricate?! It's obvious that you wanted to enter the palace to watch the show yourself!

Shen Qiao leveled this silent criticism at him, then made up his mind. He cupped Yan Wushi's face without a second word, then lightly pecked him on the mouth, no more than a dragonfly's touch upon the water.

Yan Wushi's expression froze, and all at once, that cold severity he'd purposely condensed there dissipated like smoke.

Epilogue–Part Seven

S HEN QIAO HAD BEEN about to push him away, but then the arm on his waist tightened, and his entire body was spun around. The next instant, he was pinned against the nearby stone wall.

Yan Wushi naturally wouldn't give him any chance to fight back. They were pressed tightly together, so close that their shadows on the ground had merged into one. Shen Qiao had still yet to realize what was going on when his legs were forcibly spread, a single leg of Yan Wushi's now locked tightly in between them, leaving Shen Qiao unable to move.

Shen Qiao instantly found himself baffled. He suddenly felt like he'd been a bit too impulsive. But it was too late now. Yan Wushi used his lips and tongue to silence Shen Qiao's words, swallowing every noise he made.

These deeply invasive actions made him blush all the way to his ears. It was like Yan Wushi had tasted some sublime dish; his tongue was plunged madly into Shen Qiao's mouth, staking his ownership. Then he slowed his movements, as if he were taking his time to savor the food, thoroughly enjoying this delicacy down to its very essence.

In comparison to Shen Qiao, Yan Wushi obviously had a far vaster repertoire of experience. Perhaps it was because he'd been through all sorts of ups and downs in life that he'd been able to

slowly but surely strengthen his position. He'd meticulously planned his strategy until, at last, Shen Qiao had been lured into delivering himself to his door, allowing him to claim this delicacy for himself, inside and out. Now that he sampled it, its flavor naturally became even more arresting, its taste lingering and unforgettable.

He pried open Shen Qiao's lips and teeth, grasping the other man's jaw in his hand as he heartily swirled his tongue around inside his mouth. After Shen Qiao's initial confusion finally lifted, he began to follow the movements of Yan Wushi's tongue, clumsily trying to mimic him. However, Yan Wushi didn't give him any chance to learn or follow his example. There was a slight hint of malice as he decisively withdrew, then changed to biting on Shen Qiao's chin. He suckled gently with the tip of his tongue before slowly moving downward.

As his mouth explored, so did his hands. The hand that had originally been grasping Shen Qiao's wrists, pinning him to the wall, began to caress Shen Qiao with thumb and forefinger, playing with him and lingering in sensitive spots.

Due to practicing martial arts, the joints of Shen Qiao's hands were clear and well defined, but not bony enough to jab. Instead, they felt like a sculpture carved from the loveliest of mutton fat jade, smooth and silky, though a tad warmer than an actual jade sculpture. It was a truly priceless treasure that even thousands of gold coins wouldn't be able to purchase.

Yan Wushi's hand slid into one wide sleeve of Shen Qiao's robe and began to make its way up, all the way until it reached his elbow, where he grabbed it. His other hand caressed and fondled along Shen Qiao's waist, yet without wrinkling his clothes at all. His actions were truly beyond description—Shen Qiao, someone who lacked any experience with worldly affairs whatsoever, was provoked and teased until his face flushed crimson. The corners of his eyes sparkled with tears, and his entire body had fallen limp.

"Do you know what I currently regret the most?" Yan Wushi suddenly asked.

Shen Qiao looked back at him in confusion. His thoughts seemed to have been churned into paste by an invisible hand; even his gaze overflowed with bewilderment, and his hair was mussed from all the fondling. He was the perfect picture of an innocent, guileless little creature, just waiting for some evil-intentioned person to ravage him.

"If I'd known this would happen," Yan Wushi said, "I'd have bought all the residences within this alley."

What does buying residences have to do with regret? Shen Qiao wondered in a daze. His Adam's apple was held in place and sucked on, sending a numbing ache throughout his body. He wanted to resist, but his strength wasn't quite there—despite raising his arm, all he could do was slowly place it on Yan Wushi's shoulder, which made him look like he welcomed it and was only pretending to reject him.

Yan Wushi gave a light chuckle. He'd seen plenty of pure and innocent people, but none of them had been like Shen Qiao, capable of moving him and stirring up fondness from the depths of his heart.

He longed to just cocoon Shen Qiao within his arms, to keep him close and protect him, meticulously nestle him away until no one else would be able to see Shen Qiao, so that only Yan Wushi could look at him.

However, Shen Qiao wasn't so fragile and delicate. He was an expert capable of standing at the summit with the world's strongest. He was soft on the outside but hard inside, and within his bones was a valiant strength that no cruel torture nor howling tempest could ever break. He had his own set of moral principles and was willing to continue forging boldly forward for those very same principles; he would never look back.

Yan Wushi did not agree with his principles, for in the past couple of decades of his life, not only had he always held such kindness and gentleness in contempt, he even enjoyed maliciously kicking these kinds of people when they were down. But this attitude of his had met a wall when it came to Shen Qiao. Only Shen Qiao could make him compromise willingly—even if he didn't agree with his ideals, that didn't mean he hated them.

But his increased indulgence was only for the exception known as Shen Qiao.

"Mm, there's someone there..."

Shen Qiao's ears were exceptionally sharp. He'd heard the light smattering of footsteps coming from outside the alley. They were still distant, but not so much so that it stopped him from coming to his senses a little. He reached out to push Yan Wushi away with some force, and a noise resembling a groan escaped his mouth. He jolted then, suddenly startled by how different his voice sounded.

Yan Wushi grunted in response, but he didn't restrain his actions in the slightest. Now that he was willing to employ all the patience in the world to tease, the person being teased could only surrender, letting Yan Wushi play as he liked.

Especially when it was a "pure and innocent" Daoist like Shen Qiao.

Very quickly, Yan Wushi's skillful ministrations had Shen Qiao almost forgetting about the footsteps entirely.

But only almost.

After another moment, he grabbed Yan Wushi's hand, his face flushed crimson as he said, "In broad daylight..."

Yan Wushi said, "Here in broad daylight, Daoist Master Shen took advantage of me."

Shen Qiao was speechless.

"But I refused to submit even under pain of death," Yan Wushi continued, "and resisted with all my might. I was able to go on the offensive, thus forcing the lecher Daoist Master Shen to surrender himself for capture."

Then he really did grab Shen Qiao's hands and twist them behind his back. "I never thought that Daoist Master Shen, who looks so dignified and virtuous, was secretly someone who'd lose control of himself in the face of a beauty."

Shen Qiao didn't respond. On one hand, he was stunned by Yan Wushi's remarks and his ability to twist black into white—never had he imagined that a person this shameless could exist in the world. On the other hand, thanks to the skillful ministrations of this man's wandering hands, more than half his mind had already shut off—and the remaining portion was naturally no match for Yan Wushi.

The footsteps grew closer and closer. A young man dressed in a short coat seemed to have just returned home from work, carrying some meat pastries he'd purchased at the street corner. He'd planned on taking a shortcut, not expecting that there'd be other people in this tiny alley, and came face-to-face with the pair.

Well, perhaps "face-to-face" wasn't accurate—after all, more than half of Shen Qiao's body, including his face, was hidden by Yan Wushi. Only Yan Wushi lifted his head from the crook of Shen Qiao's neck, neither fast nor slow, then deliberately turned his head to shoot the newcomer a glare.

The man gasped, and the first thought that floated to his mind wasn't: *How can these two Daoist priests do something so vulgar in broad daylight?* Instead, it was: *That man's eyes are terrifying!*

That piercing glare sent him stumbling back three steps. He didn't even say anything, just turned on his heels and fled.

Yan Wushi turned back to Shen Qiao and said, "Look, victory without bloodshed."

Shen Qiao did want to reply, but at this moment, he lacked the capacity to say anything.

Yan Wushi also felt that their current location was too inconvenient. Though doing this in the open also brought with it a thrilling sense of taboo, surely they couldn't just start going at it against the wall.

He picked Shen Qiao up in his arms like a princess and leapt into the air with a tap of his foot. Sweeping across the rooftops as if he were treading on flat ground, he ran in the direction of the nearest inn.

Lately, the innkeeper had been worried. Due to the Prince of Shixing's rebellion, the official roads were all being used for transporting grain and supplies while the roadside had grown a little less safe. As a result, the number of merchants entering the capital to do business had also decreased, and so this inn, which hadn't been making much money in the first place, had grown even more desolate.

When Yan Wushi brought Shen Qiao inside, the innkeeper was standing by the entrance, arms crossed as he agonized over these things.

Suddenly, a refreshing breeze blew past him, and before he could pull himself out of his thoughts, he heard the concierge make a sound of surprise. "Do these two gentlemen wish to stay? Our humble inn has some luxury rooms available. Is the gentleman in your arms ill? Would you like this lowly one to call a doctor..."

The concierge's prattling was interrupted by Yan Wushi. "Where are the empty luxury rooms?"

The innkeeper's thoughts had finally caught up, and he quickly said, "They're on the second floor. We have four rooms available; you can pick whichever you like. The rates are a bit more expensive— it's one hundred and fifty for a single night..."

He was a little uneasy as he said those words, as their inn wasn't very large, and yet the rates for rooms weren't particularly cheap compared to other places.

But before he could finish his sentence, he felt a weight hit his chest. The innkeeper subconsciously grabbed it. He looked down and saw that it was a round of silver, sizable and heavy.

With this, they could stay for at least half a month!

Overjoyed, the innkeeper looked up, but the stranger had already drifted off to the second floor, still carrying the other man in his arms.

The concierge leaned in and asked, "Should we call a doctor or not?"

The innkeeper hesitated for a moment. "They didn't ask for one, so we shouldn't be too nosy. Prepare some hot water, then cook some dishes and keep them warm. Once our guests need them, we can send them up at any time!"

Upstairs, Yan Wushi carried Shen Qiao into the luxury room. Sure enough, these interiors were much more spacious than a standard bedroom and well cleaned. Even the bed was larger than the ones in an average inn, with a soft mattress that still carried the faint fragrance of sandalwood incense. It was clear a fair amount of money had gone into this room—no wonder it wasn't cheap.

But with this little escapade, Shen Qiao had finally returned to his senses. He braced himself against Yan Wushi's chest, flipped himself away and down, then backed up two steps. He mumbled, "In my opinion, we should just forget it..."

Yan Wushi sneered. "You kissed me, and now you wish to throw me away after you're done with me?"

Shen Qiao was speechless.

"Throw me away after you're done with me"...didn't seem like it should be used in this situation.

He collected himself and said, "It's still early..."

Yan Wushi raised an eyebrow. "So you're saying that if it were nighttime, it'd be fine?"

Shen Qiao blushed. He likely hadn't even noticed that his collar was slightly open, and there were even two red marks imprinted on his collarbone. Half-exposed, half-concealed. The main act hadn't even begun, yet Shen Qiao's allure was already beyond compare.

Some people only had to blush and smile to send other people's hearts into a flurry, leaving them unable to control themselves. Though Yan Wushi wasn't at the point of losing control, he was still willing to indulge his desires and thoroughly appreciate this beauty, and his gaze followed Shen Qiao's every shift in expression.

Shen Qiao didn't know how he'd gone and kissed Yan Wushi with such confidence earlier. Deep down, he'd already thought about doing that hundreds of thousands of times, but he was a reserved person—normally, going through with it would have been impossible. Now that Yan Wushi was closing in aggressively, he was once again trying to retreat into his shell.

Of course, Yan Wushi wouldn't let him.

He reached out, making to grab Shen Qiao's hand, and Shen Qiao instinctively tried to block. The two of them exchanged several blows, but after executing a couple of feints, Yan Wushi managed to grab his waist sash and dragged him into his arms. With a yank, Shen Qiao's sash fell to the ground, and then he was pinned to the table with Yan Wushi looking down at him from above.

What followed was a scene of bridal candles and spring tents, of brocade laid upon a bed in rippling red waves.

"Inn... Innkeeper? What's that sound coming from the second floor?" The concierge could hear what sounded like an insistent rattling, but it quickly fell back into silence. "When those two came in just now, wasn't one of them being carried... How did they end up fighting instead? Should I go up and take a look? What if someone ends up dead!"

The innkeeper was performing calculations on an abacus; he didn't even look up. "When immortals are fighting, stay out of their business!"

"'Immortals are fighting,' my ass. Sounds more like demons fighting to me!" the concierge muttered to himself.

Young Again—Part One

SHIWU STOOD OUTSIDE the door, hesitating over whether he should knock.

By this time, Shizun should have long woken up, either to teach them the sword or to help them practice writing. Even when Sect Leader Yan had been there, that hadn't changed; the routine was never broken. Shen Qiao would never be like this.

"Shizun, are you awake?" After standing there for a long time without hearing any noises from inside, Shiwu grew a little worried despite himself, and he couldn't help but call out.

There was a thump, followed by muffled noises. It sounded like somebody had fallen.

Shiwu hesitated no longer; he quickly pushed open the door and entered. "Shizun, are you all right..."

When he circled around the folding screen and saw the situation within the bedroom, the expression on his face, originally full of anxiety and worry, transformed into dumbfounded shock in an instant. So much that he couldn't even finish speaking.

His shizun wasn't on the bed, and beneath the bed, covered by clothes, was only a struggling, flailing...child?

"Who are you?!" Shiwu blurted out.

The child was only wearing a single-layered shirt and a pair of pants. He seemed to be trying to put himself in Shizun's clothing, though he ultimately failed.

It was obvious that Shiwu's arrival had frightened him quite a lot. He stared blankly at him for a moment, doing his best to appear calm and composed, but his crisp, childish voice exposed the tiny tremble within it, so it wasn't too effective.

"This one is Shen Qiao. May I ask who this distinguished master might be? Where is this place?"

What, you're Shen Qiao? Then where's my shizun?

Shiwu stared blankly back at him, and the two gazed at each other for a while, both at a loss. The child's body was still swamped in that oversized robe, and it was like he'd been fixed in place, for he didn't move a muscle.

Last night, Shiwu remembered very clearly that, since it'd been Qilang's birthday, everyone had been full of cheer. Shizun had specially asked for several dishes to be made at the foot of the mountain, then delivered up here. Everyone had drunk quite a bit of wine, only retiring after they'd thoroughly enjoyed themselves. Hence, everyone had woken up a little later than usual.

However, Shen Qiao hadn't said that they could rest today, so Shiwu, Yuwen Song, and the rest still rose the way they usually did. But no matter how long they waited, Shen Qiao never showed up...

Still, Shiwu could have never predicted this kind of comical farce. He collected himself and took a couple of steps forward. The child hurriedly retreated a few steps, then ended up tripping on his robes, his entire body falling backward. Shiwu nimbly reached out to grab the child, holding him in place.

"Don't be scared. I'm not a bad guy. I'm a disciple from Xuandu Mountain: Shiwu!"

The child's eyes widened. "You're also a disciple of Xuandu Mountain? How come I've never seen you before?"

Shiwu skipped right over this question. "Do you know where my shizun went?"

"Who is your shizun?"

"The Xuandu Mountain Sect Leader."

The child's eyes grew even rounder. "My shizun is also the Xuandu Mountain Sect Leader."

"My shizun is Shen Qiao," said Shiwu.

"I am Shen Qiao," the child said, completely innocent.

Shiwu feebly held his forehead. "Then who's your shizun?"

The child was young, but he wasn't stupid. "You called yourself a disciple of Xuandu Mountain, so why wouldn't you know who my shizun is?"

A rather improbable idea slowly floated to Shiwu's mind. "Qi Fengge?"

The child's expression told Shiwu that his answer was correct.

Shiwu wanted to cry, but he had no tears right now. He carefully asked, "Then... Then, how old are you this year?"

For some reason, even though the child didn't recognize Shiwu, he felt a kind of innate closeness toward him.

"I'm almost seven."

So he was only six years old.

My god, my shizun turned back into a six-year-old overnight! Can he even return to normal? What if he can't?! What will we do then?! This thought struck Shiwu like a bolt from the blue, and for a short time, he couldn't collect himself, but only stared dumbly at the child.

Shiwu had wondered before if this entire thing was just one enormous hoax, but for one thing, his shizun would never make this kind of joke; for another, with his shizun's martial prowess, no one could have managed to kidnap his shizun without notice. And for yet another thing, this child's face really did resemble his shizun's, by seven or eight parts out of ten.

It was clear that this was a miniature version of his shizun!

Seeing that Shiwu hadn't spoken for a very long time, little Shen Qiao panicked and yelled, "I'm going to go find Shizun!"

And then he tried to run outside.

Shiwu hurried to stop him. Little Shen Qiao moved to attack, but as he currently was, he was far from being Shiwu's match. A few seconds later, Shiwu had sealed his acupoints.

Little Shen Qiao was horrified to realize that, though he didn't recognize this person at all, his every move and stance indeed belonged to Xuandu Mountain.

His little mouth pursed, and his eyes, like black grapes, quickly became glossy and moist. "I want to find my shizun!"

Shiwu felt his nose tingle with the urge to cry. "I want my shizun too! Give my shizun back to me!"

Little Shen Qiao was unable to reply.

The news that the sect leader had transformed into a child quickly spread through the entirety of Xuandu Mountain. After everyone had faced the same emotional ups and downs as Shiwu, they finally accepted this almost fantastical reality.

Little Shen Qiao, however, was unable to accept it for now. He hugged the stuffed rabbit that Gu Hengbo had found on the mountain, his expression lost but innocent. Every time he opened his mouth, he'd ask for his shizun.

Otherwise, though, little Shen Qiao was unusually well behaved: he didn't cry or fuss, and he didn't require anyone to soothe him.

Due to his extremely adorable appearance, other than finding the situation utterly unbelievable, everyone on Xuandu Mountain refused to pass over this chance to observe their sect leader as a child.

They all found various excuses to show up in front of little Shen Qiao and stroll around; they even brought him all sorts of presents.

Of course, everyone was also racking their brains for a way to restore Shen Qiao to normal. The elders even tried channeling their internal energy into him, but strangely, little Shen Qiao's body was like a bottomless pit—any true qi they poured into him was like mud sinking into the deep sea, vanishing without a trace.

"Shishu, why did your esteemed self go and find Shi...little Shizun a rabbit?" Shiwu asked Gu Hengbo. "Did Shizun love rabbits as a child?"

"When Si-shixiong and I first entered the sect, Er-shixiong was already much older than he seems to be now, so his personality was completely different," she replied. "He could even teach us on Shizun's behalf, so naturally he wouldn't spend the entire day hugging stuffed animals. I only heard about this from Shizun, myself, but his esteemed elder once gifted Er-shixiong with a stuffed rabbit, and Er-shixiong was ecstatic. He'd hold it even while sleeping."

Not far off, little Shen Qiao was sitting quietly, his hand intermittently patting the large white rabbit. He saw that they were talking, but he only kept on watching curiously without interrupting them.

But letting things continue like this really wasn't a solution!

Shiwu held his forehead and asked, "Does Shishu have any ideas?"

Hesitant, Gu Hengbo said, "I've already sent Liuli Palace a letter of inquiry; Liuli Palace's disciples are incredibly knowledgeable, so perhaps they have a method. However, they're far away and beyond the sea, so we won't receive a reply for a while. Why don't we send a letter to Sect Leader Yan?"

Yan Wushi had left the mountain for Chang'an only a few days ago. Shiwu didn't dare to imagine what his reaction to this incident might be.

Would he fly into a rage and take it out on them?!

Shiwu was trembling with fear a little, but the idea of his shizun staying this way forever, unable to recover, terrified him even more.

"I'll write a letter at once!"

Yan Wushi's reaction was not what they'd expected.

Not at all.

When he first saw little Shen Qiao, he too froze for a fair amount of time. But a grandmaster was a grandmaster, after all—he quickly recovered his senses. "If a person didn't cause this, perhaps it was just a chance occurrence, and he'll naturally return to normal when the time comes," he suggested.

Shiwu was dumbfounded. "What if he doesn't return to normal?"

Yan Wushi glanced at him. "Your shizun has taught you for so long, and you're his eldest disciple, yet shouldering the sect's responsibilities is too much for you?"

Shiwu was ashamed. "Thank you, Sect Leader Yan, for your instruction. Shiwu understands."

"Mm." Yan Wushi sounded satisfied. He approached little Shen Qiao.

Naturally, Little Shen Qiao didn't recognize Yan Wushi. He watched as this handsome man strolled toward him, and his gaze was filled with the usual wariness one would show strangers, but also a hint of curiosity.

"I'm Yan Wushi." He got straight to the point. Unexpectedly, little Shen Qiao's eyes grew round.

"Shizun said that you fought him once," said little Shen Qiao.

"That's right."

Little Shen Qiao canted his head and squinted at him, finding something a bit odd. "But...but Shizun clearly said that Yan Wushi was a very young man..."

"Am I not young?" said Yan Wushi. "Have you forgotten? Who was complaining on the bed a couple days ago that I had far too much energy and asked me not to take so long?"

He'd spoken these words practically right into little Shen Qiao's ears—Shiwu didn't hear them.

Bewilderment was written all over Shen Qiao's face. He didn't understand at all.

Yan Wushi suddenly thought that Shen Qiao staying this way for a while wouldn't be too bad. At least he was amusing and easy to trick. Once he recovered and recalled all of this, he'd probably try to crawl into a hole in the ground while blushing to his very ears.

"I'll take you down the mountain to play," said Yan Wushi.

Little Shen Qiao shook his head. "I'm staying here."

He hadn't seen anyone he was familiar with these past few days, but no matter what, he knew that this place was Xuandu Mountain and that the people on the mountain treated him well, without any malice to speak of. So, naturally, he was unwilling to go anywhere else.

Yan Wushi smiled. "That's not up to you."

He wasn't like Shiwu and Gu Hengbo and the others, who'd spend half the day coaxing him with sweet words. Instead he simply knocked Shen Qiao unconscious.

Shiwu was speechless at first, but seeing how Yan Wushi had picked up the boy, ready to leave, he quickly ran up to stop him. "Sect Leader Yan, where are you taking Shizun?!"

Yan Wushi swept him a glance. "It's time for you to be tested. Don't betray your shizun's efforts in teaching you. My venerable self will be taking him down the mountain for fun; once he returns to normal, I'll bring him back."

He was willing to offer Shiwu this explanation on account of Shen Qiao. This was already a tremendous amount of favor to show him.

Little Shen Qiao had never imagined that he'd wake up to find himself no longer on Xuandu Mountain. He looked around at his unfamiliar surroundings, and combined with how he'd only just met Yan Wushi, panic and confusion immediately welled up inside him. In an instant, his eyes were shining with tears.

Yan Wushi was well prepared. "If you start crying, I won't take you back again. You know that I've fought your master before. I'm a bad person."

Little Shen Qiao forcibly held back his tears. He didn't dare cry, but he couldn't help retorting, "Shizun didn't say that you were a bad person. He said that you had extraordinary aptitude and that you were certain to achieve great heights in your martial arts studies in the future."

With how young little Shen Qiao was, Yan Wushi hadn't expected the boy to be capable of maintaining such fluency of speech before someone like himself. He adored Shen Qiao to a ridiculous degree, but this kind of adoration was usually expressed through teasing and bullying.

The present was no exception.

When he saw little Shen Qiao's eyes well with tears, Yan Wushi held him in his arms and said gently, "All right, I'm taking you elsewhere to play. I'll send you back in two days."

Still holding back tears, Shen Qiao tugged on Yan Wushi's sleeves, his face full of grievances. "Sect Leader Yan, can...can you take me to see Shizun? I miss him."

"All right," said Yan Wushi.

Little Shen Qiao's expression immediately filled with joy. The radiance beaming out from his little face was practically visible to the naked eye.

The two of them got off the carriage—they were in a marketplace. It was boisterous beyond comparison as people came and went.

In the end, children were children. When there were fresh new things to look at, they'd temporarily forget their sorrows. Little Shen Qiao looked left and right, his face filled with curiosity.

Yan Wushi carried him to a tangren stall.

"How about we have him mold you a Shizun?"

Shen Qiao looked at the lifelike tangren in all different colors and nodded joyfully.

The peddler smiled. "What kind of person does this little gentleman want me to mold? How tall is he? What kinds of clothes does he wear?"

Shen Qiao earnestly gestured with his hands. "He's this tall, and he likes wearing blue. He carries a sword on his back..."

The peddler was quick and skillful; soon, the tangren was finished. "Look at this, little sir. Does this look like him?"

Shen Qiao nodded repeatedly, his eyes completely fixed on the tangren. When it was placed into his hands, he clutched at it, completely unwilling to let go.

Yan Wushi smiled. "I didn't lie to you, right?"

Little Shen Qiao froze, and his small mouth hung slightly open. He looked at him, then looked at the tangren. His eyebrows scrunched as he struggled with himself for a long time. He seemed deeply upset, but in the end, he swallowed it down again.

Even Yan Wushi couldn't help but admire his self-restraint a little. After all, this wasn't a ten-year-old Shen Qiao, and certainly not a fifteen-year-old Shen Qiao. He wasn't even seven years old, and he'd been suddenly transported into a foreign world within the span of a night. There wasn't a single familiar person around him, but he still managed to hold on to some basic sense. It was truly remarkable.

But no matter how he endured, when little Shen Qiao's voice rang out again, it was slightly nasal. "Sect Leader Yan, your esteemed self knows where my shizun is, right? May I trouble you to help me find him?"

"He's left you with me for now," said Yan Wushi. "He'll naturally appear when the time is right. Someone as powerful as he is will never have any problems."

His gentle consoling helped relieve some of little Shen Qiao's panic. The boy sniffled, then wrapped his arms around Yan Wushi's neck and nodded.

But the next moment, Yan Wushi lowered his head and opened his mouth, then bit half the tangren's shoulder right off.

Little Shen Qiao was dumbfounded. Unable to take it anymore, he burst right into tears with a wail.

Young Again—Part Two

I N AN INSTANT, many denouncing gazes landed on Yan Wushi from all directions, including from the peddler. He looked like such a proper gentleman, but to think he went as far as to steal a tangren from a child! He'd even bitten off such a huge piece of it. What child wouldn't cry?

The peddler also had two daughters himself. Seeing Shen Qiao's reaction, his heart ached, and he quickly said, "Uncle will mold you another one. Don't cry!"

Hearing this, little Shen Qiao really did stop crying and raised his sleeves to wipe at his tears. His voice was very nasal as he said, "Thank you, Uncle. One is already enough."

He looked again at his "shizun," who was now missing a shoulder, and he couldn't help but feel choked again. He quickly fought to hold back his tears, looking both pitiful and adorable. It was more than enough to move women overflowing with maternal instinct; even the peddler couldn't help but want to mold him a few more tangren to make him smile.

Some passersby were feeling indignant and wanted to rebuke Yan Wushi, but when they met his cold gaze, they were so intimidated by his aura that they swallowed down their words, too afraid to speak, and their faces flushed red.

Yan Wushi said to little Shen Qiao, "All right, I was only joking with you earlier. Let him mold you another one. You can give me the crippled Qi Fengge."

"Shizun isn't a cripple!" said little Shen Qiao angrily. "You bit it off!"

Yan Wushi smiled. "If you continue being so ferocious, I'll take you away, and you'll never see Qi Fengge again."

"Shizun..." Little Shen Qiao pursed his lips as he struggled not to cry, his eyes filled with tears. "I want Shizun!!!"

The emotions he'd repressed for so long spilled forth all at once, and Shen Qiao transformed right into a weeping mess. Now even ten tangren wouldn't be able to silence him.

Yan Wushi hugged the boy, his temples and the corners of his mouth twitching as he finally tasted distress, entirely by his own doing. For the first time, Sect Leader Yan, who'd always been the willful and unreasonable one, found himself completely helpless.

If the person in his arms hadn't been Shen Qiao, he of course would've had a hundred ways of getting them to shut up, but in his eyes, everything Shen Qiao did was adorable. It was just that Yan Wushi's method of expressing his adoration was different from everyone else's, and he'd also forgotten about the age gap between little Shen Qiao and the actual Shen Qiao. In a moment of carelessness, he'd gone overboard with the teasing.

• • •

Everyone thought that Shen Qiao had become a child overnight, but in reality, that wasn't the case.

Shen Qiao opened his eyes, then realized right away that something was off.

True, there were soft blankets beneath him, and above his head were the familiar ceiling beams. But beyond the windows was pitch-dark night, with a bright moon suspended high in the sky.

There wasn't anything wrong with a dark night. What was wrong was that the five senses of all martial arts practitioners were incredibly sharp, and under normal circumstances, they'd never sink into such deep slumber. If his sleep had been deeper than usual, it should have been morning right now.

He didn't need any candlelight. Using only the moonlight, Shen Qiao surveyed the room around him, then realized something strange: this place was indeed Xuandu Mountain, but instead of waking up where he was supposed to be living, he'd found himself in the house he'd lived in as a disciple.

The feeling of strangeness grew stronger and stronger—but Shen Qiao wasn't little Shen Qiao, after all. Though he was a bit disturbed, at the same time, a certain idea appeared within his heart.

Was he dreaming about the past?

As he considered this, he rose and pushed open the door, then walked outside. The night was silent. Shen Qiao raised his head to look at the sky, then left and right around him.

What he saw instantly froze him in surprise.

Currently, he was standing in the front area of a small building. And this small building was where Qi Fengge and his disciples had lived. After Shen Qiao had become sect leader, he was unwilling to continue occupying his shizun's residence, and he'd moved to a nearby house instead.

Right now, his surroundings were pitch-black. The only exception was the faint light seeping from Shizun's old room. The candlelight swayed; it seemed someone was inside.

Shen Qiao's heart pounded with emotion for a moment. He went up the stairs and slowly headed for the room where the candlelight shone. Even though it felt like a dream, he was also afraid of being disappointed by the dream. He made no attempt to hide the sounds of his footsteps; the person in the room quickly discovered his presence.

"Who's outside?" The other party didn't stand to open the door. His tone was casual and gentle, as if he were reading via the candlelight. It was tremendously familiar, something Shen Qiao had heard innumerable times.

He was unable to control his quickening heartbeat. His eyes burned and his vision instantly blurred.

"Who is it?" When the other party failed to hear a response, he thought it strange. Thus he finally stood and came to open the door.

The moment the door opened, the two men stood face-to-face, and the countenance that Shen Qiao had recalled countless times in his memories was now right before him. Shen Qiao's entire body seemed to have frozen in place; he couldn't move even half a step. He stared at the other man, unwilling to even blink.

"You're..." Qi Fengge paused, then continued, "Who is this distinguished master? What business brings you to Xuandu Mountain?"

At this time, Qi Fengge was in his prime, the hair at his temples an inky black. It seemed that he'd just bathed, for his hair was tied up, still damp. He wasn't an outstandingly handsome beauty. At most one could call him somewhat good-looking, but his features were bright and confident. The polish of the ages, his abundant experience, as well as the breadth and depth of his knowledge and moral character, all imparted to him a share of indescribable charisma. If there was a type of person in this world with the power to make others trust him on sight, then that description would undoubtedly refer to Qi Fengge.

Shen Qiao remembered very well the time when Shizun had failed to break through. Just as he was about to pass away where he was sitting, Shen Qiao had been ordered to go in and see him for the final time. By then, Qi Fengge had already lost the unchanging appearance that he'd maintained for several decades. Instead, his complexion had been ashen, his temples peppered with strands of frosty white. Even his gaze had turned dim and lifeless. Hence, when Shen Qiao once again saw Shizun as he'd been in the past, nostalgia and sorrow both suddenly surged within his heart. He could no longer control his tears—they rapidly brimmed over, streaming right down his cheeks.

"Shizun..." Shen Qiao choked through sobs. Realizing that he was forgetting his manners, he quickly lowered his head and wiped away his tears before raising it again. "Shizun, this disciple is Shen Qiao... I'm...the Shen Qiao from twenty years in the future. This disciple doesn't know what happened either; I woke up already back in the past. Perhaps by saying this, your esteemed self finds it inconceivable, but this disciple isn't harboring any evil intentions..."

"I believe you," said Qi Fengge.

Shen Qiao's words cut off, right there, and he stared at Qi Fengge with some surprise.

Qi Fengge smiled. "I believe you, because even though you've turned...grown bigger, your features are still the same, and there's the way you speak, the way you walk, along with all sorts of other things—your old self is visible within all them. How could I fail to recognize you?"

Then he extended a hand and gently patted Shen Qiao's head. "So this is how A-Qiao looks once he's grown up."

Shen Qiao only felt a momentary warmth upon his head, and he couldn't stop the choked feeling from returning once again.

"But what manner of divine occurrence is this? You said that you're A-Qiao from twenty years in the future, then what happened to the six-year-old A-Qiao?"

As expected of Qi Fengge, he'd gotten to the root of the situation right away.

Shen Qiao frowned. "This disciple doesn't know either. I was meditating, then I somehow fell asleep. When I woke up, I discovered that I'd gone back twenty years into the past."

Qi Fengge seemed quite fascinated. "Then where is this master, twenty years in the future?"

Shen Qiao was silent.

Qi Fengge understood. "I'm already dead by then."

"Shizun..."

Qi Fengge was amused. "Birth, aging, illness, and death... These are all normal things. Martial arts practitioners may live longer, but their life spans can't compare to that of the heavens. Why does A-Qiao make such an expression? Could it be that you've spent twenty years of growth in vain, seeing as you still can't move on from this?"

Shen Qiao sucked in a deep breath. "This disciple has received guidance."

"Who's the sect leader of Xuandu Mountain at that time?"

"This disciple is."

Qi Fengge didn't look particularly surprised. Instead he smiled and nodded.

"Many events happened in between; it's a long story," said Shen Qiao. "Does Shizun want this disciple to give a detailed report?"

Qi Fengge shook his head. "No need to say more. The things that should happen are already predestined. Knowing them gives no benefits, and it might even make things worse."

Any ordinary person who received the chance to learn about their future would find it impossible to curb their curiosity. But Shen Qiao was unsurprised by Qi Fengge's answer; that was simply how wise and considerate his shizun was.

"I'm not sure how long this divine occurrence can last," Qi Fengge said. "This master has received such a rare chance in getting to meet a grown-up A-Qiao, but you can't waste all your time here. It's the Lantern Festival tonight, and your martial siblings have all gone down the mountain to play. Would you like to head down for a stroll as well?"

"Of course this disciple is willing," said Shen Qiao joyfully.

The two of them descended the mountain, one behind the other. Qi Fengge used his qinggong, his figure drifting like a wandering immortal's. Shen Qiao realized that in this dream, not only did everything in his surroundings feel completely real to the touch, even his martial arts hadn't been diminished in the slightest. It really didn't feel like it was actually a dream.

Qi Fengge had just stopped when he saw that Shen Qiao was already standing next to him, and he couldn't conceal his pleasure. "The disciple surpasses the master! Xuandu Mountain has a worthy successor!"

Shen Qiao smiled. "Shizun is too kind. My martial arts is still inferior to yours during your peak. Yan Wushi, however..."

Right after he spoke this name, he realized there seemed to be an inexplicable force restraining him, preventing him from talking about various things pertaining to the future.

Qi Fengge didn't notice any peculiarities. "Yan Wushi? It seems that in twenty years, his strength will reach another level!"

Shen Qiao found himself unable to elaborate, so he only nodded his head.

Qi Fengge also didn't pursue the matter further. His gaze fell on the festive and noisy scene before them, the people coming and going. He smiled and asked, "I trust that Xuandu Town will also be livelier, twenty years in the future?"

Lanterns as far as the eye could see, in colors rich and varied. From time to time, the sound of children laughing and playing drifted over. It was truly an exuberant and lively Lantern Festival.

"I think it's about the same," said Shen Qiao.

He'd already calmed down completely. It wasn't any hardship to be unable to talk about the future. Spending a night together with Shizun like this was already the greatest and happiest surprise.

Qi Fengge brought them to a stall for guessing lantern riddles, where he joined in and answered a riddle correctly, winning a rabbit lantern in the process. Then he handed the rabbit lantern to Shen Qiao, joking, "When you came down the mountain last year, you also took a liking to this rabbit lantern. But Yuan Chun wanted it too, so you let him have it. You didn't come down with him this year, so you're getting this rabbit lantern at quite a bargain!"

Shen Qiao no longer remembered what had happened when he was six, but he found the sincere and cherishing love Shizun showed him impossibly warm, and he clutched at the rabbit lantern, completely unwilling to let go.

The candlelight shone from within the rabbit's belly, bringing with it a faint warmth.

Twenty years in the past, and twenty years in the future.

A living person, and an icy tomb.

Moisture welled up in Shen Qiao's eyes, and, worried that Shizun would think him weak, he quickly blinked it away. Only then did he smile. "Thank you, Shizun."

Qi Fengge patted his shoulder, his gaze full of tender love. He didn't say anything, but he seemed to have understood everything.

As they passed through the alleyway, the clamor and activity gradually quieted down. Before their eyes, the river gently flowed past. Many lanterns had been placed on paper boats, and they drifted down from upstream, the wishes and dreams of many all entrusted within them.

The two rested beneath a tree for a while. Qi Fengge saw Shen Qiao still carrying the rabbit, unwilling to put it down. He couldn't help but smile. "Why is my A-Qiao still so childish when he's all grown up?"

Shen Qiao smiled as well. "Because it's what Shizun gave me."

Just looking at the lantern made him feel like Shizun was by his side, accompanying him. Shen Qiao didn't want to believe that this was only a dream, and perhaps the existence of this rabbit lantern could make his own existence feel more real.

Qi Fengge took the lantern from him, then used a slender twig to draw out the wick inside. He made it a little longer so that it could burn for a little longer as well. He then returned the lantern to Shen Qiao. "I'm sorry."

Shen Qiao started. "Why does Shizun say that?"

"Twenty years from now, you'll become the sect leader," said Qi Fengge gently. "I trust that at that time, you were the only one among all the disciples who could shoulder such a heavy burden. You're humble and kind by nature, and you dislike the limelight. So it was this master who pushed you into it."

Shen Qiao laughed softly. "I am a Xuandu Mountain disciple. I wish for Xuandu Mountain to be peaceful, so if Shizun believes I can do well, I must devote all my efforts to it as well."

Though he'd taken a detour in the beginning and paid some horrifically heavy prices, in the end, he felt he had not betrayed those expectations.

The two of them chatted beneath the tree for a long time. Shen Qiao couldn't remember when, but he'd grown tired and ended up falling asleep.

In his dream, his head rested on Qi Fengge's thigh, and held in his arms still was the rabbit lantern, already extinguished. A small smile was on his lips. One hand gently patted his head, over and over again, just like it had when he was a child.

Shen Qiao was awakened by the piercing rays of sunlight.

He opened his eyes. Sunlight was pouring down between the cracks of the foliage, dappling his body. There was another person next to him, leaning against the tree trunk. Yet it wasn't Qi Fengge but Yan Wushi.

Yan Wushi opened his eyes and rubbed his temples. He was preoccupied with trying to work out why, even with his martial prowess, he couldn't remember when he'd fallen asleep, but when he saw Shen Qiao, he jolted slightly. "You're back?"

The two of them compared their tales down to the tiniest details. Shen Qiao suddenly realized that it might not have been a dream but that he'd truly switched places with the seven-year-old Shen Qiao for a short while and returned to the past.

"But I don't remember having any memory of this from when I was six," he said.

"Perhaps because it happened in the past," said Yan Wushi. "That's why your old self naturally forgot everything."

Shen Qiao thought hard about it some more. It seemed that this was the only possible answer.

Yan Wushi suddenly bent at the waist to lean over; with most of his upper body pressed on top of Shen Qiao's, he reached over to pull something out from behind him.

Shen Qiao looked. To his surprise, it was that rabbit lantern.

Side Story One

BEHIND THE FOLDING SCREEN, there was a bed. On top of the bed lay a beauty. More precisely, the beauty's eyes were tightly shut, and he was in a deep slumber. Next to him sat a man who was currently watching the beauty.

Yan Wushi stared at him for a long time, then gently placed his hand on Shen Qiao's eyelashes, brushing his fingers over them. Shen Qiao's eyelids reflexively fluttered, and then he knit his brows, just a little bit. It was rare for him to sleep so soundly. On an ordinary day, even the slightest movement within his surroundings would jolt Shen Qiao awake never mind Yan Wushi running his hands over his face. It was clear that Shen Qiao was much too tired.

The corners of Yan Wushi's mouth pulled up in a satisfied, relaxed smile. If anyone else had been here, they were sure to suffer a shock great enough to send goosebumps to ripple through their body. This smile of his was far too gentle; so gentle that it shouldn't have appeared on his face at all. Even Yan Wushi himself probably hadn't noticed the appearance of this refreshing smile upon his face.

His fingers moved from Shen Qiao's eyelashes to the spot right between his eyebrows, then slowly slid down from there until he reached the tip of his nose. Then, he made to gently pinch that nose.

Yet before he actually did it, he seemed to change his mind and continued to sweep downward. He pinched Shen Qiao's lips into a flat line, and this lovely picture of a sleeping beauty during spring immediately took on a comical touch—Shen Qiao's upper and lower lips had been squished together, and now it looked like he had a duck's beak.

Shen Qiao remained completely unaware. Perhaps he simply had no guard when it came to the person next to him, and he was content to continue wandering within his dreams.

Sect Leader Yan had finally realized that his actions were a bit childish. He smirked as he let go, then lowered his head to kiss Shen Qiao's mouth. From the corner of his eyes, he glimpsed the specks of green and purple patterning Shen Qiao's neck and shoulders. The corner of his lips curved as he yanked the blankets up so that the man's neck was snugly covered.

A knock sounded at the door and Yan Wushi rose and left the bed to answer it. He didn't blush when the concierge outside saw his languid appearance, complete with a draped outer robe and mussed hair, but that concierge turned bright red.

"Good morning, sir. The kitchen downstairs has been lit, and the innkeeper had this lowly one come up to ask if the two of you needed anything?"

As he asked, he furtively tried to peek inside. Several hours ago, they'd heard rattling noises while downstairs. They hadn't dared to come up and ask at the time, but now he was naturally checking whether they'd broken anything.

Yan Wushi had wanted to decline at first, but then he reconsidered. "What food do you have?"

The concierge smiled. "We have Western-style baked cakes, roast chicken, grilled duck, okra, and so on. Our humble store has some of the best cooking in the area; generally, we'll be able to fulfill any order you wish to make."

"Then let's have some buttermilk barley congee and pork trotters simmered in garlic. The trotters should be stewed until they're extra tender, and no need to hold the sauce. I'll be sure to reward you properly after. Prepare some fresh fish too; it doesn't matter which kind as long as it's fresh. Nothing fancy, just steam it and add some scallions and garlic. As for the rest, prepare some vegetable dishes and send them over."

Accompanying his words, a silk pouch landed in the concierge's arms. It was heavy, and the concierge guessed that it was full of silver nuggets.

Yan Wushi rattled off that long list without even a blink. The concierge was left secretly astounded as he thought that this guest really knew how to eat. It seemed like he was a rich nobleman buried in luxuries. Just this man's receipt for today alone could match three or five days of the inn's regular business earnings.

"Yes, yes, whatever this gentleman wishes for, our inn has it all," the concierge said attentively. "This lowly one will go and make the preparations right now. Please wait a moment, and this lowly one will send some hot water over first!"

Yan Wushi also bid the concierge go to the bookstore and purchase a couple of scrolls for light reading. With such a generous reward at hand, the concierge was naturally willing to do anything for him, and he quickly completed each task one by one.

•••

It was the fragrance of food that woke Shen Qiao up. The moment his eyes opened, he felt his stomach rumble with hunger. It'd been such a long time since he'd had this feeling, he found it somewhat unfamiliar and disorienting.

Shen Qiao blinked, then slowly scanned the room, his eyes moving from the table behind the folding screen, covered in dishes, to the silhouette sitting by the desk and reading. In an instant, his vision transformed from confused and blurred to wakeful clarity.

As there was only a folding screen between them, Yan Wushi had naturally noticed his noises and movements. "A-Qiao is awake?"

He put down his book, stood up, then circled around the screen. He was a little regretful that he'd been one step too slow to catch the sight of Shen Qiao waking up. But the next moment, Shen Qiao yanked the covers over his head, and he burrowed into the nest of blankets. The covers suddenly bulged into a massive dome.

Yan Wushi was silent. A single glance at the covers as they shifted around told him that Shen Qiao must be putting on his clothes beneath them. Yan Wushi's stomach was almost cramping from laughter, but he kept his expression flat as he faked concern: "Are you all right?"

Shen Qiao's muffled voice came from beneath the covers. "I'm fine..."

Yan Wushi came forward a few steps and pressed a hand to the covers. "A-Qiao, are you injured? Come out and let me see?"

"I'm really fine..."

The rustling beneath the covers grew terribly fierce. Yan Wushi guessed that he must be looking for his pants. Smiling, he said, "A-Qiao, I forgot to tell you."

"Mm?"

"Your underpants were soiled last night, so I had the concierge head out to buy a new pair. He hasn't returned yet."

The covers were suddenly flung aside, and a slightly reddened face poked out. "How could you let a stranger buy that?!"

"Then, should I go and personally buy them?"

Shen Qiao held his forehead, then mumbled somewhat incoherently, "That's not what I meant. You... How did he know my measurements..."

Yan Wushi smiled. "I told him, of course."

Shen Qiao didn't ask how Yan Wushi knew. It was obvious how. Yan Wushi must have measured last night while he was feeling him.

Recalling the mad frenzy from last night, Shen Qiao desperately wished to just crawl into a crack in the ground and hide there. Up to just now, in fact, when he had the covers over his head, he could still smell that thick, strong scent within his own breaths.

He gave a dry cough, feeling awkward, but he couldn't not answer. "Sect Leader Yan..."

Yan Wushi interrupted him, his brows knit in displeasure. "We're this intimate now, yet you insist on calling me Sect Leader Yan?"

"Then what should I call you?" Shen Qiao asked, his words faltering.

"Yan-lang. You called me that many times last night, didn't you? You were even crying at the same time!"

Shen Qiao's entire face was flushed crimson. "Stop talking!"

Yan Wushi sighed and sat down on the edge of the bed. "We've now had intimate relations. If we were a man and a woman, I'd have already asked you to go through all the traditional marriage etiquette with me, like the three matches and six appointments. Then I'd marry into your family and you could bring me over the threshold. Unfortunately, you're not..."

"Wait!" Hearing this, Shen Qiao felt like something was off. "Why are you marrying into mine?"

Yan Wushi raised an eyebrow. "Unless you want to marry into mine instead?"

Shen Qiao said, "No, of course not..."

"My venerable self likes you; I don't care about dignity or reputation. Of course I'd have no objections if you'll let me marry you. That way, bystanders won't start criticizing or gossiping about the great and lofty Xuandu Mountain sect leader. I don't have any reputation to speak of. If it's for your sake, any grievance is no grievance at all."

These words might have sounded egotistical, but there was still a hint of grievance within them as well.

Shen Qiao didn't know whether to laugh or cry. "That's not what I meant."

"Then, will you take responsibility or not?"

Shen Qiao was speechless.

Ultimately, what happened last night had been completely consensual. With Shen Qiao's sincere personality, it was impossible for him to push the entire responsibility onto the other person. Yan Wushi was banking on this, hence he'd lured Shen Qiao forward, bit by bit, then let him leap into the pit he'd long dug beforehand.

Sure enough, Shen Qiao's brows pinched for a long time before, finally, he arduously spat out two words: "I will..."

Yan Wushi smiled slightly, then leaned over to kiss his cheek. "Shen-lang."

Shen Qiao shuddered.

Yan Wushi said gently, "Shen-lang, you still haven't put on your underpants. Aren't you cold?"

Shen Qiao's face flushed red, and he clutched at the covers, refusing to let go.

By this time, the concierge had purchased the underpants and returned. He knocked on the door, and Yan Wushi went to answer it, then brought the underpants back with him.

"Shen-lang, how about I help you dress?"

Shen Qiao couldn't take it anymore. "Just continue calling me A-Qiao!"

Yan Wushi had a look of utter helplessness. "You refuse to call me Yan-lang, and you won't let me have this satisfaction either?"

Shen Qiao would not let him continue this twisted teasing. He snatched up the pants and continued to dress, pulling them on beneath the covers. Only then did he remove the covers, get off the bed, and prepare to fasten his sash.

It would have been fine if Yan Wushi didn't look. The moment he did, he couldn't stop himself and burst out laughing. "My dear A-Qiao, you've put your pants on backward!"

Shen Qiao was speechless as he flushed as red as a fully cooked shrimp.

Side Story Two

THE GATES to the Daoist monastery had been left unlatched. The osmanthus flowers were in full bloom. A refreshing breeze blew, and the clouds were sparse. The sky looked like colored glaze, as clear and bright as ice.

Cluster after cluster of pale yellow and silvery-white clasped the branches, weighing them down so much they were almost overloaded. There were even several small birds hopping about on them. The branches swayed gently, causing petals to flutter down with every motion. They scattered all over the head of the deer standing below. The deer tossed its head several times until it couldn't help but let out a sneeze.

On a low table to the side was a cup. No tea had been poured yet, but quite a few petals had made their way inside. There was a teapot simmering away on low heat, its aroma wafting and mingling with the fragrance of osmanthus. The rich, refreshing scent was balanced in a marvelous equilibrium, and anyone who passed by would find comfort permeating throughout their entire body.

The petals fell and tea brewed, the Daoist monastery tranquil and quiet. It was undoubtedly a scene pleasing to the heart and eye both, something to be painted. But Yang Guang was focused on something else.

He was looking at the man brewing tea.

The man in question wore a Daoist robe, his hair pulled back into a bun. It was a simple manner of dress that couldn't have been more ordinary, but Yang Guang was forced to admit that the simpler the dress, the more it enhanced how outstanding the man himself was.

How long had it been since the first time he'd laid eyes on this person? Yang Guang didn't think too hard about it, but he'd aged from a youth into a young man since then, so it must have been a fair number of years. Yet this man was truly like an immortal, for he showed no signs of aging.

Of course, Yang Guang knew that once someone's martial arts reached a certain level, they'd maintain their youth indefinitely, just like this man. It was said that such people weren't uncommon in the jianghu, but because this man's looks were exceptional, every time they met, Yang Guang couldn't help but glance at him a few more times. The man had made a deep impression on Yang Guang.

"Our backyard is too humble to properly receive guests. If Your Highness is here to ask about immortality, please head to the front door."

The voice, clear yet mild, rang out from behind the door. Yang Guang felt slightly awkward and couldn't help glancing at the man next to him.

The man's eyes were lowered, a slight frown upon his face. But his expression was tranquil—even though he'd been waiting together with Yang Guang for a while now, he showed no sign of impatience, nor any hint of embarrassment at being called out. It was as if he were truly only here to accompany Yang Guang on his visit, keeping his own presence as low-profile as possible.

Since he'd been discovered, Yang Guang simply chose to laugh and push open the gates to enter. "This prince noticed how quiet and beautiful the monastery was, so he decided to tour the area in passing and unexpectedly ended up here. I've disturbed the perfected master's peace; I beg your forgiveness."

Though he said this, he had no plans of leaving. Instead, he boldly walked in, completely certain that the master of the monastery couldn't refuse him.

Yang Guang's life had been smooth sailing since he was young. His parents' doting ensured that he encountered no dissatisfactions or imperfections along the way, so his personality had naturally become rather self-important.

"So it was the Prince of Jin. Please come in."

Shen Qiao gave a slight smile, showing absolutely no hint of displeasure. Yang Guang thought that the man didn't dare to show any—if Xuandu Monastery wished to hold on to its place in Chang'an, it needed the support of the imperial court.

As he'd been peeping in from outside, he'd inevitably committed some discourtesies. At this moment, Shen Qiao didn't rise to greet him, and Yang Guang wasn't shameless enough to fuss about it. He simply lifted the hem of his robe and sat down across from the other man, then he took the initiative on behalf of the host and gestured for the person accompanying him to sit as well.

"Just now, I smelled the tea the perfected master was brewing and couldn't help but stop because of it. I trust that the perfected master won't be offended by our sudden visit?"

Shen Qiao smiled. "Of course not. But who is this guest with you?"

Yang Guang pretended to be annoyed at himself. "I forgot to introduce him to the perfected master. This man is Great Master Zhizhe's disciple, the Buddhist monk Yuxiu. To elaborate, he's also my father's shidi!"

Buddhist Master Zhizhe was from Tiantai Sect—a martial brother of Fayi and Xueting. Two years ago, in order to bring the

Buddhist discipline under control, Yang Jian had willingly tossed aside his dignity as an emperor and acknowledged Buddhist Master Zhizhe as his master, demonstrating just how much he valued Buddhism. Once news of this incident spread, Buddhism's reputation and standing had exploded, their limelight bright beyond compare.

However, though Buddhist Monk Yuxiu had no hair whatsoever, he was dressed in common wear rather than a monk's robes; hearing his identity, Shen Qiao couldn't stop surprise from coloring his expression.

"I've brought a Buddhist monk to a Daoist monastery. Is the perfected master unhappy?"

Shen Qiao smiled. "Of course not. All who come are guests. If the Prince of Jin and the Buddhist master don't mind, please have a taste of this humble Daoist's coarse tea."

Yang Guang gave a carefree smile. "Since it's tea that the perfected master personally brewed himself, I must have a taste. Then I can go home and boast to my parents later!"

He and Yuxiu took the teacups and lowered their heads to give the tea a sip.

It was indeed a coarse tea. Though it carried the fragrance of osmanthus blossoms, that couldn't conceal the bitter astringency of the tea itself. Yang Guang was completely unaccustomed to drinking something like this—after one small sip, he frowned and put down his bowl, then glanced at Yuxiu. The monk was quietly holding his cup in both hands, taking sip after sip of tea, neither fast nor slow. Soon, he'd finished the entire cup.

"It seems that I'm the one who doesn't understand tea," said Yang Guang self-deprecatingly. "It was a waste to gift it to me."

"The Prince of Jin speaks too seriously," said Shen Qiao. "The tea leaves have already been brewed; it is meant to be drunk. Whether the Prince of Jin or someone else drinks it makes no difference. The tea exists regardless of whether it's in your stomach, so there's no waste to speak of."

Yang Guang started. For a moment he didn't know how to respond.

Instead, it was Yuxiu who spoke. "The perfected master's words reflect the will of Buddhism."

Shen Qiao gave a slight smile. "Buddhism and Daoism share many common points. It seems that the Buddhist master is rather compatible with Daoism."

Yuxiu also smiled. "People say that the perfected master isn't good with words and that's why he refuses to open public lectures to speak of the Dao. But this humble monk sees that it's untrue—the perfected master knows the art of debate very well!"

His appearance had always been refined and delicate, yet this smile was as bright and charming as a flower. It left a strong impression.

"While Master Yuxiu was apprenticed under Great Master Zhizhe, he also learned martial arts from his shibo, Great Master Fayi," said Yang Guang. "They say that he's a genius who only appears once every couple of decades, that his aptitude is even higher than that of Xueting's, but I was born too late to witness how formidable Buddhist Monk Xueting was. Could I have the fortune of watching Yuxiu seek some martial guidance from the perfected master?"

Shen Qiao swept his gaze over both of them before it landed on the teacup in front of him. "With Buddhist Master Yuxiu's aptitude, he'll likely see great achievements within a couple of years. This humble Daoist is incompetent; how could he carelessly offer pointers?"

This was rejection.

Yang Guang was deeply unhappy. He'd wanted to make friends with Shen Qiao and Yan Wushi, but news of the latter's whereabouts came and went, and even when they did meet, Yan Wushi never gave Yang Guang any face. Once, unable to contain himself, Yang Guang had gone and tattled to his parents. But he hadn't expected that the parents who'd always indulged him would react opposite to how they usually did—they didn't take his side, which left Yang Guang even more frustrated.

As for Shen Qiao, Yang Guang had attempted to visit him several times. Each time, he'd been met with either the cold shoulder or polite rejection. Shen Qiao seemed wholly uninterested in associating with the Prince of Jin. Even if he remained courteous, he was also distant. For someone like Yang Guang, who was the pride of the heavens, this was undoubtedly equivalent to slapping him in the face multiple times. More than once, it had made Yang Guang so furious that he'd returned to his sleeping quarters and smashed things. But this only made him more unwilling to give up; instead, he'd developed an obsession with what he couldn't obtain.

His only consolation was that Huanyue Sect and Xuandu Mountain, while demonstrating no signs of accepting him, showed no intentions of growing close to the crown prince either. As he looked at Shen Qiao's handsome and gentle profile, Yang Guang felt somewhat defeated and resentful.

Shen Qiao had saved his life, and Yang Guang knew it. That year, the traitor Chen Gong had held him hostage as he left the palace, and Shen Qiao had rescued him. But Yang Guang thought that his parents had given Xuandu Mountain enough over the years to repay the favor of Shen Qiao saving his life, so deep within his heart, Yang Guang actually held little gratitude toward Shen Qiao.

More than anything else, this connection was an excuse to build a closer relationship, to pull Xuandu Mountain over to his side.

Unfortunately, Shen Qiao was always the same: neither cold nor warm. It matched the distance that Xuandu Mountain kept from the Prince of Jin.

But it was one thing to think this—Yang Guang didn't dare reveal any trace of rudeness or disrespect in his expression. "The perfected master is too modest. If we consider seniority within the jianghu, Yuxiu is even your esteemed self's junior. It's a given that he should receive your guidance. However, if you're unwilling, we naturally can't force you. In a few days, it will be the Double Ninth Festival. I've also reported to His Majesty that we'll be holding a banquet in the spare villa on Cuihua Mountain. Would the perfected master do us the honor of attending? This prince warmly welcomes you, naturally!"

Now that he'd said this, he was afraid that Shen Qiao would think the venue too crowded and be unwilling to attend, so he made sure to add some more: "The banquet won't have any unconcerned persons—there will only be famed literati from the schools of Daoism and Buddhism. We're following the example of the scholarly discussions from the Wei and Jin Dynasties; it certainly won't be a lowbrow affair!"

Shen Qiao looked apologetic. "It's most unfortunate; this Daoist is about to set out for Xuandu Mountain today. He fears that in a few days, he'll be on Xuandu Mountain and hence unable to attend the banquet. He begs the Prince of Jin's forgiveness."

Fury swept across Yang Guang's face, but he quickly recovered his smile, then picked up his teacup and drank everything in one go. "I was the one asking something impossible. The perfected master need not be concerned!"

After Yang Guang and Yuxiu left, someone spoke from behind the colonnade with a leisurely voice. "You really offended him."

Shen Qiao didn't turn his head but simply sipped a few mouthfuls of tea as he said, "Sect Leader Yan was cowering within his house like a turtle, so I was forced to play the villain."

Yan Wushi laughed. "Who made Daoist Master Shen so compassionate and kind? If I'd come out instead, that Yuxiu probably wouldn't even be able to leave the gates of Xuandu Monastery!"

Shen Qiao sent him a pointed look, but he said nothing.

Yan Wushi bent at the waist and brushed his lips over the side of Shen Qiao's face, leaving a trail of heat from his breath in his wake before he finally stopped at Shen Qiao's ear. "This venerable one originally planned on returning to celebrate Qixi with you. I didn't make it in time, but at least I won't miss the winter solstice."

Shen Qiao's face was a little red. It was unclear whether he had been warmed by Yan Wushi's breath or if he was blushing from shyness. "Your trip was rather long this time."

Yan Wushi gave a low chuckle and continued to tease him. "So Daoist Master Shen missed me?"

Blasted by these words, Shen Qiao's face grew even redder. "You know I wasn't asking about this..."

"Then what were you asking about?" Yan Wushi seemed to take great enjoyment in teasing him, and he also appeared very interested in Shen Qiao's ear. He took it into his mouth and refused to let go. He licked from the lobe to the shell, until it was wet from his tongue all over. Shen Qiao had gone completely stiff, as if he'd been immobilized by a martial technique. He was unable to move at all.

"Did you..." he arduously mobilized his willpower, "...enter the heart of the Khaganate?"

"No, I went to Goguryeo." Yan Wushi even rattled off a few

sentences in fluent Goguryeon as his hands reached deep into certain unspeakable places, roaming freely about.

"Goguryeo? What...did you go there for?"

"Ginseng is plentiful there, so it's a trade location for Huanyue Sect. I passed through the Eastern Khaganate on the way there, so I took the chance to look around. Duan Wenyang is currently doing quite well there; he's even been elevated by the Tulan Khagan, Yongyulu. He's practically become Hulugu the Second now."

Shen Qiao shook his head. "As his heart isn't on the martial path, he'll never become a second Hulugu. I find that monk Yuxiu from earlier much more interesting."

"What?" said Yan Wushi. "Is having me not enough for you? You want a monk too?"

Shen Qiao's face instantly flushed red, his mouth falling open as he stammered. He was angry and wanted to refute Yan Wushi, but he didn't know where to start. It made for a pitiful and lovable sight. Yan Wushi couldn't help but burst out laughing. He picked Shen Qiao right up like a princess and carried him inside.

Side Story Three

I T WAS THE NIGHT of the winter solstice. The lanterns had
been hung. Tiny specks of firelight glistened beneath the eaves.
Shining through thin sheets of red paper, together they formed
a line of crimson that illuminated the entire courtyard.

The snow continued to fall in drifts, neither great nor little. Yet it
was enough to turn the whole world white: it blanketed the rooftops,
the ground, and trees all the same.

Martial arts practitioners did not fear the cold. The door to the
house was open, but there was no wind, so no snow fluttered inside.
Sitting within the house, they could use earth dragons for warmth
and even enjoy the snowy scenery—two birds with one stone.

This wasn't Xuandu Monastery, but the former junior preceptor's
residence in Chang'an, now known as the Duke of Wu's residence.

After Yang Jian succeeded, he'd done as Yuwen Yong had and
named Yan Wushi the junior preceptor, then made him a state
duke. In truth, everyone knew that this was only a title and nothing
more: it didn't matter what Yan Wushi was called. Even if he'd been
declared a general or marquis, Yan Wushi would remain the same
Yan Wushi, and Huanyue Sect the same Huanyue Sect. No one
could affect his standing.

Compared to Yuwen Yong, Yang Jian had a deeper understanding
that the emperor alone was unable to call all the shots: there were

many rich and powerful families, all with long-established histories and influence, which meant that even rulers were forced to heed their opinions. Seeking to break free from the power held by such families, he proclaimed a new system of imperial examinations, completely different from the Nine Ranks System that had been in place since Wei and Jin. This allowed numerous scholars from humble families to propel themselves upward by passing the exams.

But this meant that the authority that had originally belonged to the officials responsible for selecting new ministers no longer existed, instead being reclaimed by the emperor. Scholars from humble backgrounds were naturally delighted, but the noble families were not. Therefore, in order to contend with their immense power, it was impossible for a long time for Yang Jian to toss Huanyue Sect aside.

As for Xuandu Mountain, the current cornerstone of Daoism, it was better to win them over instead of throwing them away. As the founding emperor of a dynasty, Yang Jian naturally understood this. His preferential treatment toward Buddhism was a given, but he didn't forget to indulge the Daoists with various favors either, wanting to maintain a balance between the two schools. Meanwhile, he also put great effort into supporting Confucianism, establishing Sui as an equal competitor to Southern Chen and pulling their talents over.

The disparity in strength between the north and the south grew clearer with each passing day. Seeing that a battle between the two was inevitable, people's hearts gradually began to waver, and indeed, quite a few of the south's scholars traveled north to Chang'an to take the Northern Dynasty's imperial examinations.

With how bright the Northern Dynasty's future was, everyone thought the same: that if things went as expected, the Central Plains that had been fragmented since Wei and Jin would once again see unification in the future.

However, at this moment, the man sitting within the junior preceptor's residence and facing the snowy courtyard did not look happy at all.

The reason was thus: in front of him was a bowl of dumpling soup.

More precisely, it was a bowl of dumpling soup made using lamb broth as the base, with tangyuan mixed in. Shen Qiao gave a slight frown. Staring at this bizarre medley, Shen Qiao had no idea what expression he should make.

A man stepped out from behind the screen, saw his expression, and smiled. "The winter solstice is equally important as New Year's. The north eats dumplings, the south tangyuan, and in the riverlands they drink lamb soup. Now all three have been assembled, allowing you to experience a gathering of all the lands. Why are you unhappy?"

Shen Qiao shook his head. "I don't enjoy eating them this way. Tangyuan should be a sweet food, so why is it mixed with lamb soup? Did someone come up with this to please the emperor?"

Yan Wushi lightly clapped. "You guessed correctly! At the winter solstice's banquet this year, the Prince of Jin came up with this method to please the emperor. He even named it the 'Soup of Unity,' meaning that the entire world will be united as one. Yang Jian was delighted and handsomely rewarded him right there. The crown prince was on the scene as well, and his expression was quite spectacular!"

The banquet for the winter solstice had been held yesterday, when Shen Qiao was away from the capital. He hadn't needed to attend, but Yan Wushi had gone. To him, it was the same as going to watch a good show.

Shen Qiao lightly exhaled, letting out a puff of white. "When someone grows up, their thoughts grow complex as well. The Prince of Jin is much more eloquent than the crown prince, so his parents pamper him more; this is reasonable. But I've seen darkness lurking within his expression, and there's a certain malice in his eyes. I fear he won't be satisfied remaining the Prince of Jin for long."

Yan Wushi gave a slight sneer. "Weren't his thoughts already complicated as a child?"

Hearing this, Shen Qiao couldn't help but cast his mind back to that time, when Yang Guang had viciously stabbed Chen Gong.

"Does the emperor intend to appoint a new crown prince?" he asked.

Others would have been horrified at this topic, but to them, it was something trivial and ordinary, nothing to take seriously.

"Not now, perhaps, but it's hard to say in the future," Yan Wushi replied. "If everything proceeds as expected, there'll be a southern campaign to Chen next year. If Yang Jian and Lady Dugu truly preferentially favor Yang Guang, they will definitely make him a marshal to let him have some military exploits."

He sat down next to Shen Qiao and wrapped his arms around his waist, then lowered his head to take a bite as he scooped up a dumpling. "The taste isn't bad at all. Here, shall this husband feed you?" Yan Wushi made to hold out the wooden spoon to Shen Qiao, and sure enough, received a glare for his troubles.

"Sect Leader Yan, please have some dignity."

Though several years had passed, this man's skin remained as thin as paper, unable to take the slightest bit of teasing. But the more he saw this, the more Yan Wushi loved teasing him.

"Dignity? But you didn't seem to be so worried about my dignity last night?"

Before Shen Qiao could say anything to spoil his fun, Yan Wushi grabbed his chin and passed him a mouthful of soup. For a moment, everything fell silent. There was only the faint rustling of falling snow outside, punctuated with the soft sounds of lips and tongues meeting within the house.

It was some time before Shen Qiao finally shoved away the man who was glued to him. "We're talking about serious matters!" he panted. "Don't just start fooling around!"

"This is called 'having some fun'!"

It was obvious that Shen Qiao did not approve of this kind of "fun." And contorting his expression further was the lingering taste of lamb soup in his mouth.

This kind of lamb soup, mixed with tangyuan and dumplings... He really had to excuse himself.

He thought about the winter solstice banquet, where quite a few people must have struggled to appreciate this "Soup of Unity"—but with the emperor's enthusiasm hanging over them, who would have the nerve to say so?

Shen Qiao sighed. "As an emperor, Yang Jian is indeed wise, so I feel like my choice was correct. It's only when his children are involved that he becomes somewhat foolish. Now that it's already decided which son will be king and which will be subordinate, he shouldn't flaunt his favoritism for his second son so much in public. What kind of position does that put his eldest in?"

Yan Wushi tried to grab him, but then he saw Shen Qiao nimbly tuck his hand back into his sleeve, and some regret came over his expression. "This isn't hard to understand," he said. "Many brilliant people will have a blind spot when it comes to a certain subject. Yang Jian and Lady Dugu are the same. If this continues, sooner or later, a tale of discord between brothers will play out. 'There are no siblings within the imperial family.' That has been true all throughout history; it isn't uncommon."

"The crown prince's personality is a bit weak, but should he ascend the throne, I trust that he'd be able to follow in his father's footsteps," said Shen Qiao. "However, it's hard to say the same for Yang Guang. When I try reading his features..."

He shook his head and didn't continue. Instead he said, "Sometimes, it's not good to be too clever. Those who are clever believe that they're the only person in the world who matters. This makes them even more isolated and lonely, which will eventually result in a great deal of anguish and trouble. In the end, they become a burden to both themselves and others. Changing the crown prince would bode poorly for both the Yang family and the world itself."

Yan Wushi burst out laughing. "A-Qiao, are you talking about me?"

Shen Qiao shot him a look. "Are you like this, Sect Leader Yan?"

"Not at all," said Yan Wushi. "After all, I'm much cleverer than Yang Guang."

Shen Qiao couldn't keep a straight face. He laughed, and his eyes curved into crescents—a sight to melt the heart. Even if a tempest raged around them, as long as someone saw this smile, no challenge would feel too great, and the world around them would seem to warm. That was what Yan Wushi thought.

"That Yuxiu isn't as simple a character as he looks," Shen Qiao said.

Yan Wushi, with this beauty in his arms, had already moved on to considering tonight's plans—which location should they choose in order to deepen their passion? "Of course he isn't," he said carelessly. "I've already had Bian Yanmei investigate him. Currently, the news I received says that he's the same as Duan Wenyang: a child with both Göktürk and Han blood."

"He has Göktürk ancestry?"

Yan Wushi nodded. "This matter is most intriguing. Someone with Göktürk ancestry enters a Buddhist sect, becoming a disciple of Buddhism, yet he also accompanies the Prince of Jin, their relationship murky and ambiguous. The relationship between the Sui Dynasty and the Khaganate is also an ugly one, yet there's a half-Göktürk monk by the Prince of Jin's side. What do you think he means to do? Isn't this incredibly intriguing?"

This was quite a shock to Shen Qiao. "You're saying...that Yuxiu and the Prince of Jin...have that kind of relationship?"

Yan Wushi countered, "Did you seriously fail to realize?"

Shen Qiao was still digesting this information. "I really never thought in that direction..."

Yan Wushi sputtered a laugh. "If you didn't notice, clearly you lack experience."

Shen Qiao stared at him.

"There's nothing for it—this venerable one has no choice but to wear myself out once again. I'll use my body to instruct you properly."

Shen Qiao could say nothing.

Side Story Four

S HEN QIAO WASN'T SURE if Yuxiu was really in an illicit relationship with the Prince of Jin. Perhaps Yan Wushi had simply disliked him on sight... But these were all minor, inconsequential details. What was truly important was that Yan Wushi's words had revealed a key piece of information—one that linked the Khaganate, the Buddhists, and the Prince of Jin into one—and from this, Shen Qiao discovered an issue he'd never noticed before.

The current crown prince, Yang Yong, didn't hold Buddhism in high esteem. He preferred to debate and discuss with Confucian scholars on their classics and principles. The Buddhist sects didn't wish for their influence to end with Yang Jian's generation, though, so they took a gamble on the next and sent an outstanding disciple from one of their sects to foster good relations with the Prince of Jin. This wasn't strange—if Shen Qiao hadn't disliked the Prince of Jin himself, he might have been pleased to see Shiwu and Yuwen Song grow friendly with him as well.

The strange part was Yuxiu's Göktürk ancestry, and it was very possible that the Buddhist discipline themselves knew nothing of this. It really made one's imagination run wild.

Shen Qiao sank into contemplation as he murmured, "Could it be a coincidence?"

"Yuxiu lost his mother when he was five, and he entered Tiantai Sect at seven," said Yan Wushi. "There's only a wall separating Ronghe Village from the lands beyond the Great Wall, so the Göktürks plundered them year after year. Yuxiu's origins were not secret. When he turned six, a great drought descended upon Ronghe Village and killed many people. The survivors were forced to leave, and because of that, Bian Yanmei was able to follow those faint trails and learn about this.

"What's even more interesting is that by the time the drought arrived, he'd already disappeared from Ronghe Village."

Shen Qiao knew that the story didn't end there, and he quietly waited for Yan Wushi to continue.

"After his mother's death, the villagers ostracized him," Yan Wushi went on. "He vanished one night. Even after the drought came and left, he never showed up again, so the villagers all assumed that he'd either left and starved to death or been carried off by some vicious animal.

"Such a young child was able to travel thousands of miles from the north to the south and arrive safely at Tiantai Sect. That should be all but impossible—unless someone was helping him throughout the journey. And the person who helped him was a Lady Yuwen."

"Which Lady Yuwen?" asked Shen Qiao.

"Princess Dayi."

Shen Qiao was stunned.

Princess Dayi was once an honored princess of Northern Zhou. During that time, she'd married into the Khaganate and became the wife of Ishbara Khagan. With her encouragement, the Khaganate and the newly established Sui Dynasty had warred with one another, and the Khaganate was defeated. After Ishbara Khagan's death last year, in accordance with Göktürk customs, she'd married Tulan Khagan. Even now, she was still a Göktürk Khatun.

"Lady Yuwen sees Yang Jian as the traitor who toppled the Zhou Dynasty, so she's eager to get rid of him. However, since she doesn't have enough power, she can only bow her head to Yang Jian for now while plotting for the future. This Yuxiu is one of the secret pawns she's prepared."

Lady Yuwen bore a deep-seated grudge toward Yang Jian, born of grievances over her family and nation. Though her plans of instigating the Khaganate into going to war with the Sui Dynasty had fallen through, she was unwilling to drop the matter since she still had connections to Yuxiu. In fact, she'd even changed her strategy, using more covert methods to destabilize the Sui Dynasty's foundations.

The Sui Dynasty was currently in excellent condition. Even if they declared war on the Chen Dynasty and marched their army southward, their victory would be just around the corner. The time for the Sui Dynasty to unify the lands was imminent now that the Göktürks were suffering from civil strife and thus incapable of fighting back. However, Sui's internal affairs weren't entirely devoid of weaknesses either. For example, the issue between Yang Jian's two sons. Yang Jian and Lady Dugu's favoritism for their second son, together with Yang Guang's own burning ambitions, meant that a dispute over the position of crown prince was inevitable.

If Yuxiu could counsel Yang Guang, helping him to conquer the throne, he would be sure to obtain Yang Guang's trust. Then he could slowly, bit by bit, impose his influence upon him.

Reasonably speaking, the lands should see unification within Yang Jian's generation, so the next emperor's task would be to secure the fruits of Yang Jian's victory, consolidating the various powers. But with Yang Guang's temperament, it was unlikely that he'd be satisfied with being a ruler who only maintained his predecessor's achievements. If someone fanned the flames when his time came, it wasn't difficult to imagine how the situation would develop.

Shen Qiao's experiences over these past years had affected him—it was rare to see him grasp such tortuous affairs with perfect clarity. As he pondered this matter, he couldn't help but gasp in surprise. "Every step has been planned out and reinforced! A strategy that will come to fruition as easily as waters flowing through a canal!"

On the outskirts of the capital was Cuihua Mountain. Two people stood at its treacherous summit, facing the wind as they gazed down at the capital.

The location was jagged and craggy, the terrain slanted. Even if the scenery on Cuihua Mountain was beautiful, officials and nobles still preferred to build their villas at the foot of the mountain, or the halfway point at most. As such, there was little human presence here, but the dense forests and faint birdsong prevented it from feeling desolate.

The winding landscape of the mountain's foot was exquisite. Ever since Yang Jian had ascended the throne, Chang'an had grown more prosperous by the day. They saw that the golden age was imminent, yet Shen Qiao and Yan Wushi could already anticipate what would happen ten years, or even decades, into the future.

Yan Wushi stood with his hands behind his back. "Lady Yuwen's plot is no small one," he said coolly. "Unfortunately for her, even if she topples the Sui Dynasty, what does it matter? The Yuwen family no longer has any talents who can take back their country. What can a single woman who was married into the distant Khaganate do? It's laughable and pointless, that's all!"

Shen Qiao sighed. "But this bit of peace for the common folk didn't come easily. I really don't wish to see it destroyed."

"Yang Jian is an outstanding ruler. Unfortunately, the Sui Dynasty's good fortunes won't last long. They won't continue beyond the second generation."

"Why are you so certain?" asked Shen Qiao curiously.

Yan Wushi asked in return, "A-Qiao didn't object. Doesn't that mean you agree with my words?"

"Xuandu Mountain has hundreds of years of legacy as a Daoist sect, and they've dabbled in fortune-telling through facial features. I have observed Yang Yong's face—he is excellent in wealth and honor but has none of the signs of a ruler. Meanwhile, Yang Guang overflows with auspicious qi, and he's also blessed with the Nine-Five orientation, the sign of an emperor. Yet..."

He shook his head and didn't continue.

Yan Wushi smiled. "In truth, there's no need for you to perform divinations or read their features. You see, if anyone wished to topple the Sui Dynasty, they'd find a way to enthrone Yang Guang. His personality is diametrically opposed to Yang Yong's—if he became emperor, he'd strive to achieve something grand. It wouldn't matter if it was Yuxiu or some other random person—when the time came, they'd only need a single foreign war, draining the common folk's resources and creating dissatisfaction in the lower levels. Furthermore, Yang Jiang's adjustments to the bureaucracy and establishing the imperial examinations have already offended the gentry. Once it happens, the aristocrats and commoners will oppose the emperor together. A lucky break won't be able to save this dynasty—it's inevitable it will be replaced."

Shaken by the scene Yan Wushi had described, Shen Qiao was quiet for a long time. Though his words were enough to shake all of heaven and would have astounded anyone, that didn't mean they were impossible.

The dynasty hadn't granted Yan Wushi any official position, but few people in the world could match his views in viciousness. Now, the more profound Shen Qiao's cultivation grew, the more proficient his divination became. The tiny glimpses of heaven's design that he'd seen confirmed everything Yan Wushi had said.

"First destiny, second luck, and third feng shui," he said. "These are the factors that determine one's life. A person's destiny might be predetermined and inevitable, but luck comes from the Houtian, after birth. It may still be possible to turn things around."

"If Yang Guang is willing to behave himself and rid himself of his malice toward us, Huanyue Sect can continue collaborating with him even if he ascends to the throne," said Yan Wushi. "However, if he nurses a grudge toward us for our unwillingness to befriend him and seeks an opportunity for revenge, then all those lurking threats around him will become crises that will backfire on him in the future."

Understanding dawned on Shen Qiao. "So that's why you didn't touch Yuxiu!"

Yan Wushi smiled. "That's right. When you look at it this way, what does Yuxiu's background have to do with us?"

Shen Qiao released a slow breath, then returned his gaze to the distant scenery.

Currently, Huanyue Sect took orders from Yang Jian, but theirs was a relationship of cooperation, not subordination. Yang Jian knew this very well, so his collaboration with Yan Wushi was a pleasant affair. Yan Wushi, in turn, was happy to remove troubles and threats for him. But if Yang Jian's successor failed to understand this, there was no way someone with Yan Wushi's character would keep old affections in mind.

If possible, Shen Qiao would naturally wish for the world to remain peaceful, for the chaos of war and the agony of separation to never again appear. For the common people to enjoy their lives in peace.

But he also knew very well that this was impossible.

Just as every person possessed a life span, dynasties too had their own destinies. Perhaps it was the Sui Dynasty's destiny to last a hundred years or maybe only fifty. Such things weren't determined at the founding of the dynasty, but would change as each ruler made their decisions, accumulating blessings and fortunes both that would intertwine and offset each other. Thus, they'd influence the rise and fall of that dynasty.

The lingering blessings Yang Jian had left for his descendants... how many years could they buy for the Sui Dynasty?

Shen Qiao couldn't help but wonder.

He thought that he'd finally supported a wise ruler onto the throne, but perhaps it'd only been the beginning. He felt that it was a pity, but then he also quickly grew relieved.

The tides rose and fell, the clouds gathered and scattered, the flowers bloomed and withered. It'd always been this way, from the genesis of the world. As long as one could face this fact with a peaceful mind, they would remain undefeated.

"What are you thinking?" asked Yan Wushi.

Shen Qiao smiled. "I was considering heading south in the next couple of days. I heard that there are many fantastical mountain landscapes, the kind you'd imagine at the ends of the sky and seas. Such impressive scenery is worth a look, and one can even watch the vast and magnificent ocean tides. I trust that it'll be beautiful beyond words."

Yan Wushi raised an eyebrow. "Daoist Master Shen is going alone?"

"Would Sect Leader Yan be willing to accompany this humble Daoist?"

"This venerable one shall consider it."

Shen Qiao couldn't help but find this amusing, and the corners of his lips stretched upward.

In the distance, the heavens stretched high and far, brimming with vitality, while the mountains and rivers sprawled forth, endless and exquisite.

This was the dawn of a new dynasty, as well as the dawn of a new era.

Perhaps there was chaos within, but there was also an even greater radiance.

• • •

Twenty-five years ago.

Xuandu Mountain.

"I'm older than you, so you must call me Shixiong!" Yu Ai was holding onto Shen Qiao's robe, preventing him from leaving. While Shen Qiao struggled to continue walking forward, Yu Ai trailed behind him like a little duckling, and the two of them entered the main hall, one in front of the other.

"I won't! Xuandu Mountain's rankings are based on time of entry! I'm the Shixiong!" Though little Shen Qiao was gentle, he refused to budge a single bit when it came to this.

There was a ripping noise. Yu Ai had used too much force and torn Shen Qiao's robe.

The two of them were instantly dumbfounded.

When he saw Shen Qiao's reddening eyes, Yu Ai scrambled, at a loss. "I... I didn't do it on purpose!"

Shen Qiao sniffled. "Shizun gave me this robe..."

A warm palm rested on his head and gave it a pat, then its owner crouched down and pulled both Shen Qiao and Yu Ai into his embrace. "What's wrong?"

As if he'd seen his father, Shen Qiao buried his head into the newcomer's shoulder and sobbed, "Yu Ai ripped my robes..."

Knowing that he was in the wrong, Yu Ai lowered his head and was quiet.

Qi Fengge consoled them both. "It's fine, it's only a hole, that's all. This master will patch it for you later. Today, the disciple of your Lin-shibo, Zhou-shixiong, is about to head down the mountain for training. You can send him off on this master's behalf. Dry your eyes, quickly!"

Shen Qiao was a good child. Hearing this, he quickly raised his sleeves to wipe at his eyes. Then he raised his head and asked, "Will it be dangerous for Zhou-shixiong to head down the mountain?"

"Not at all," said Qi Fengge. "Your Zhou-shixiong's martial arts are enough for him to protect himself. Though our Xuandu Mountain doesn't involve ourselves in outside affairs, if a disciple takes the initiative and asks to descend the mountain for training, they will naturally be allowed to do so. We don't insist that they must always stay and practice on the mountain."

Hearing these words, Shen Qiao and Yu Ai couldn't help but show expressions of envy. In their eyes, being unable to descend the mountain for training meant that they'd attained a certain level in their martial arts.

"Shizun, in the future, will we be able to do the same as Zhou-shixiong and head down the mountain for training?"

Qi Fengge smiled. "Of course you can. Once you turn fifteen, you can head down the mountain yourselves. After leaving the mountain, what do you want to do?"

Yu Ai snuck a glance at Shen Qiao, then averted his eyes at top speed. "I want to go down and earn money so I can purchase a tangren for A-Qiao. Make him happy so that he won't be mad at me anymore."

Truly the words of a child. Qi Fengge burst out laughing. "Then what about A-Qiao?"

Shen Qiao thought for a moment. "I'd probably use the martial arts Shizun taught me to help good people and beat off the bad ones. But can I return after only a month?"

How could one determine who was good or bad? Again, the words of a child. But Qi Fengge didn't douse his enthusiasm and instead gently asked, "Why only a month?"

Shen Qiao was a bit embarrassed. "Because I don't want to leave Shizun and my siblings for too long. I wish that everyone can be happy together, for a very long time."

The wind blew past, rustling the trees and flowers, preserving these words of his within the ages.

Though the grass and trees are silent, feelings linger forevermore.

The End

Wish

OVER TWO HUNDRED MILES of golden sand, stretching as far as the eye could see. The Gobi Desert seemed as though one could walk for their entire life and never reach its end.

The noisy wind battered his face. It was painful.

Yin Chuan had already gone a full day and night without any water. Sand blew into his mouth and nose with every breath, and his throat ached as if it were being scraped with a knife.

But still, he had to keep going. If he didn't, and his pursuers caught up to him, all that awaited him would be death.

He didn't how long he'd been walking—stretching far ahead and into the distance was the same expanse of yellow.

Yin Chuan was almost in despair. The sword on his back felt abnormally heavy, impacting his pace and breathing. It was so heavy he longed to unfasten and fling it far away.

But he couldn't do such a thing. The sword existed with the man. When the sword perished, the man did as well. Yin Chuan's family was owed a blood debt, and they were waiting for him to collect it.

His sweat trickled down his forehead, dripping into his eyes and blurring his vision. As the wind howled around him, Yin Chuan thought he could still hear his own panting. Though his body had already reached its limits, almost unable to keep going, one thought remained in his heart, preventing him from giving up, stopping him from collapsing.

From the distance came the sound of hoofbeats.

Yin Chuan didn't know if he was really hearing pursuers or if he was already exhausted to the point of hallucination. But they once again drove his survival instincts to take over: somehow his legs filled with strength, and he even quickened his steps.

"This gentleman was once so handsome, a jade tree in the wind. Yet after a few days of rushing about, he's become so wretched! Just seeing him makes my heart ache!"

The gentle, lovely voice elicited no surprised joy or curiosity within Yin Chuan. Instead, it was like he'd seen a ghost—his face filled with terrified shock.

The reason was simple: just now, there'd clearly been no one nearby, yet the voice had suddenly exploded within his ears. Unless something had gone wrong with his hearing, this meant that the other party's martial arts vastly outstripped his.

Yin Chuan summoned all the strength within his body and sped up even more, yet that voice clung to him like his shadow, following him without pause.

"Why does the gentleman ignore me? Is my beauty not enough for you to stop?"

Yin Chuan's hands trembled faintly. His legs no longer seemed to be his own—they were aching and sore to the point of numbness. His Dantian was completely empty, his true qi utterly exhausted. Finally, he couldn't hold out any longer, and he collapsed right to the ground.

That voice sputtered a laugh, then said sweetly, "Oh my! This gentleman, so pitiful! This one will lend you some help!"

A hand, so soft it seemed almost boneless, gripped Yin Chuan's shoulder, before effortlessly lifting him right off the ground and placing him beneath a tree.

Yin Chuan gasped a breath, then scrubbed away the sweat on his brow. His vision gradually cleared, and he saw a young woman dressed in red, with a pretty face, standing in front of him. She was staring at him, smiling as she played with her hair.

The days he'd spent fleeing had transformed Yin Chuan from a wealthy young master who knew nothing of dangers and hardships to a man full of vigilance at all times, both as he slept and woke. Even with the girl's harmless appearance, he dared not underestimate her. "Why was this maiden following me?" he asked, incredibly cautious.

The girl smiled. "Naturally, it was because you're handsome!"

Yin Chuan took a gulp of water from waterskin he'd been carrying on his person. This soothed his throat somewhat. "Many thanks for the maiden's kind words. I'll be leaving now. May we meet again in the future."

For a girl in the spring of her youth to appear in the Gobi Desert and to even follow a man she'd never seen? Yin Chuan pretended that he hadn't noticed anything strange. Once he felt that his strength had returned somewhat, he quickly stood and made to leave.

But the next moment, a single line from that girl stopped him dead in his tracks.

"I heard that the lord of the Yin family had a veritable host of concubines, indulging himself nightly. So why does the young master act like a nestling who's never seen a woman before?"

So she had known his identity, and she'd come with something in mind!

Yin Chuan's gaze instantly turned wary, and his hands silently tightened around his sword.

Seeing this, the girl laughed. "You can't even defeat me. What's the point of putting on such an act?"

Yin Chuan only saw a blur; in an instant, his sword had already flown from his hand, landing nearby, and his acupoints had also been struck, leaving him unable to move.

"Who exactly are you?!" Yin Chuan was both furious and panicked.

"I'm called Liu Xufei," the girl introduced herself with a face wreathed in smiles. "I know that someone's pursuing you. If you're willing to enter Hehuan Sect, I can guarantee your safety."

The Yin family had no martial arts background; Yin Chuan himself was only a mediocre practitioner. Otherwise, she wouldn't have been able to subdue him so easily. But he still knew about Hehuan Sect.

Under the leadership of the sect leader, Bai Rong, their power and influence was expanding with each passing day, especially now that they'd received the favor of the current emperor. Rumor had it that they, together with Buddhism, had divided the emperor and empress's support between them.

"I'm not a member of the jianghu," said Yin Chuan. "This Yin can only accept the maiden's kind intentions."

Liu Xufei didn't grow angry at his rejection, and only continued to smile. "An ordinary man bears no sin, but holding a precious stone will cast him as a sinner. Most of your family's wealth has been hidden, and only you, the next head of the Yin family, would know where it is. The people of Tuyuhun are eager to restore their country, so they'll never let you go. Yet you lack the ability to protect those things. Sooner or later, you will fall into their hands. Instead of letting this happen, why not join Hehuan Sect and receive our protection? We won't gobble up the Yin family's entire fortune, at least—we'd split it half-and-half with you. What does Yin-langjun think?"

Four years ago, Yang Guang had ascended the throne and subsequently launched a war against Tuyuhun. He annihilated Tuyuhun in one fell swoop, then turned upon the Yin clan, the wealthiest family in Tuyuhun. The Yin family suffered a massacre, and Yin Chuan alone had managed to escape. After the Yin family's destruction, the court ferreted out quite a fortune, but it was a far cry from the legends that had claimed the Yin family possessed enough wealth to rival a country's. Thus, a rumor had quietly spread, claiming that the key to the Yin family's treasury was hidden on Yin Chuan, and only he knew where that treasury lay.

As a result, Yin Chuan, who'd yet to recover his senses after his clan's massacre, found himself the target of pursuit from all directions. The Sui Dynasty's imperial court, the remnants of Tuyuhun's power, both were looking for him. And now even Hehuan Sect had come knocking.

Yin Chuan forced a smile. "I won't lie to the maiden. I've never had such a key, and the Yin family has no treasury. Though my ancestors amassed a large fortune, my father squandered everything long ago, and the imperial court has already looted the rest. I have nothing at all."

Liu Xufei naturally didn't believe him.

The Yin family had hosted a great number of guests; everyone knew their members drank from cups made of glaze, that even their chopsticks were made of gold and inlaid with jade. The crafty hare keeps three burrows—who'd believe that the Yin family would fail to leave themselves a way out?

Liu Xufei said sweetly, "From what I know, the people of Tuyuhun aren't only after your fortune—they're after your life. Hehuan Sect only wants half of your family's wealth, and we'll even guarantee your safety. Is Yin-langjun incapable of weighing his options and making the correct choice?"

"My only fear is that once I fall into your hands, the decision won't be mine to make."

Liu Xufei was somewhat astonished. She hadn't expected that this tender and pampered youth would be capable of thinking this deeply.

She gave a small smile. "You've considered this quite thoroughly, but isn't there one thing you've failed to realize? The decision isn't yours, even now."

She stretched her arm forth, and her red sleeve fluttered with an airy fragrance, bringing to mind the charming scene of Jiangnan in late spring, gentle and exquisite. Already immobilized, Yin Chuan could only helplessly watch as that hand drew closer—there was nothing he could do.

Yet in the end, the hand of that girl in red never touched Yin Chuan. The next instant, a blur swept before him, and then she was fighting a man.

Yin Chuan didn't rejoice that he'd been saved. Instead, his complexion grew worse.

He recognized this man.

This man was the reason he'd spent the past few days fleeing for his life—Cheng Lugui, the disciple of Tuyuhun's state preceptor, the Kosa Sage.

The two parties' robes flapped and danced as their internal energy swept forth, pouring out in vigorous waves. Only the immobile Yin Chuan found himself suffering, as from time to time the waves would assault him.

Needless to say, he was rather dejected.

Yin Chuan thought that the two of them were like dogs biting and tearing at each other over a chunk of fatty meat. And his unlucky self was that meat, left to the mercy of others. No matter who won here, it would do him no good.

Liu Xufei was clearly vastly superior to Cheng Lugui in martial arts—Cheng Lugui was quickly reduced to wretchedly defending himself, and Liu Xufei smiled all the while.

"This young gentleman didn't practice his martial arts properly. You should return to your shifu's bosom to drink a few more years' worth of milk. Why did you show up here, just to embarrass yourself?"

She was so delicately pretty, yet her words were so harsh and venomous, they'd make a person wish they could crawl into a hole out of shame.

Cheng Lugui was furious, his face flushed crimson. In halting Han speech, he said, "You should mind your own business! This isn't the Central Plains, and it's certainly not your Hehuan Sect's territory! If you stick your hand in too far, careful that it doesn't get lopped off!"

Liu Xufei smiled brightly. "I would love to be lopped, but I fear you lack the ability!"

"Would this venerable one have the strength, then?" A voice carrying a hint of age suddenly rang out. Though it sounded unremarkable, Yin Chuan suddenly fell to the ground. Buzzing filled his ears, and a muffled pain woke in his chest. He almost coughed up a mouthful of blood.

Liu Xufei, who'd been holding victory in her grasp, suddenly went pale. Being faster to detect danger compared to Yin Chuan, her red robes drifted backward, her movements as graceful as a butterfly's, and she alighted on a tree branch.

A person was standing upon that flimsy tree branch, yet it only swayed a little.

Liu Xufei wiped away her look of shock, her bright smile returning. "So it was the state preceptor of Tuyuhun. This little girl apologizes for her disrespect!"

The Kosa Sage wore a kasaya, yet it wasn't in the style of the Central Plains' Buddhists—instead, he was dressed like a monk from beyond that territory. His face was average, his brows arched toward his temples, and his eyes were both narrow and dull. He appeared only around forty years of age.

If not for Lu Xufei exposing his identity, Yin Chuan would never have guessed this man to be one of the world's foremost martial arts masters, as famous as the likes of Huanyue Sect Leader Yan Wushi and Xuandu Mountain Sect Leader Shen Qiao.

In front of this man, Liu Xufei had to be exceedingly careful. Even if her face was smiling, it couldn't conceal the wariness within.

"Is your esteemed sect's Sect Leader Sang doing well?" asked the Kosa Sage.

Liu Xufei started, but she instantly recovered her smile. "I fear that it's been too long since the Sage has visited the Central Plains, and he's grown a bit muddled. Currently, for us, Sect Leader Bai is in charge."

"Is that so?" said the Kosa Sage coolly. "When I was in the Central Plains in the past, Bai Rong was merely a little girl, still wet behind the ears. Now she's even posing as the sect leader, and her disciples too have no aptitude to speak of. Truly, each generation is inferior to the last."

Liu Xufei's expression stiffened slightly. Though she was enraged, she dared not voice it. "The Sage speaks too seriously. With our leader running things, Hehuan Sect has become larger and stronger than ever, far more than when Sect Leader Sang was around. If the Kosa Sage is willing to travel to the Central Plains and visit us as a guest, Hehuan Sect will extend to him the warmest of welcomes."

The Kosa Sage laughed loudly, yet the sound was uniquely cold and apathetic. "A sect whose leader earned her spot through her woman's charms, enchanting an emperor of the Central Plains, dares to call itself strong? Don't think that this venerable one is unaware of all your two-faced dealings!"

As he spoke, his entire person rose into the air, seemingly without pushing off anything, completely spontaneous. In the blink of an eye, he was in front of Liu Xufei, his robe and sleeves sweeping toward her as if blown by the wind.

Liu Xufei paled with shock. She knew without a doubt that if his palm strike connected, she'd instantly suffer broken bones and a mouthful of blood.

There was no time to think more, let alone concern herself with the nearby Yin Chuan. She flung herself backward straight away, letting herself fall.

Right before she brushed the ground, her palms landed first and patted it slightly. With that, her entire body flipped and turned—in an instant, she'd retreated dozens of steps.

Even so, it was clear that Liu Xufei didn't dare to pause for a moment. She turned and ran right after landing, never sparing a single glance back. In the twinkling of an eye, she'd vanished without a trace.

"The sage is a noble and virtuous man!" A sweet voice drifted over to them from afar. "Xufei had the fortune of meeting him today and was overjoyed! I will not forget to return to tell my master and elders and come again when invited. I'll leave that kid for the sage to deal with!"

Confused, Cheng Lugui asked, "Shizun, why didn't we just capture that demoness?"

"She and Bing Xian are Bai Rong's favorite disciples. Capturing them doesn't benefit us and would only start a feud with Hehuan Sect. That isn't our goal."

That was enough to stop Chen Lugui from speaking.

Yin Chuan watched as Liu Xufei left, leaving only master and disciple, the Kosa Sage and Cheng Lugui. His heart couldn't help but despair. He'd thought that they'd fight—when two tigers fought, one would inevitably fall, giving him the chance to escape. Instead, Liu Xufei had lost and retreated with such speed, dashing his hopes. Now that he'd fallen into the Kosa Sage's hands, he feared what awaited him would be a fate worse than death.

While his thoughts were spiraling, Cheng Lugui had begun walking in his direction. He grabbed Yin Chuan's shoulder, then viciously flung him to the ground.

"Didn't you still want to run? Run! Let's see where you can run to!"

Yin Chuan gritted his teeth and endured the pain.

"Benefactor Yin, Tuyuhun was destroyed by the Sui Dynasty's Yang clan, and they also exterminated your family. We should be working together. If you're willing to hand over your family's belongings, once the revival is complete, Tuyuhun will dispatch troops to attack the Sui Dynasty and your blood debt can be repaid. This way you can kill two birds with one stone, so why must you be so stubborn?"

This wasn't the first or second time Yin Chuan had heard such words. The other party simply refused to believe that the Yin family's vast riches had been squandered completely. Yin Chuan didn't feel like arguing, so he simply closed his eyes and remained silent.

Cheng Lugui sneered. "Shizun, this brat is far too stubborn. I'll make him open his mouth."

He extended two fingers and pinched Yin Chuan's shoulder, then slid them downward. As he did, cracking noises rang out along the arm, and Yin Chuan could withstand it no longer: he began to scream in pain.

"Rending muscle from bone? Why go so far?"

In the middle of this extreme agony and torture, Yin Chuan seemed to hear that voice sigh. However, he was completely incapable of sparing the attention to recognize it—he even thought he'd heard wrong.

A stone flew toward Cheng Lugui's wrist. The Kosa Sage gave a cold sneer, raising his sleeve to slap it to the ground.

However, Cheng Lugui could no longer continue with his torture of Yin Chuan—it seemed that someone had secretly struck him from behind. He only felt a pain along his back; his acupoint had also been struck, leaving him unable to move.

At the same moment, the Kosa Sage realized that something was wrong with his disciple. He immediately freed Cheng Lugui's acupoint but paid no further attention to Yin Chuan. Instead, he was both shocked and furious.

He was furious at how his opponent had feinted, then struck from elsewhere, and at how their sneak attack had succeeded right beneath his nose. And he was shocked at how audacious this person was, at their supreme confidence. Clearly, they were terrifyingly strong.

The other party had no intentions of lurking out of sight. After that strike, they emerged from behind a tall boulder, not too far away.

Fluttering Daoist robes; a face that was serene and handsome. He looked like an immortal.

The Kosa Sage was in no hurry to strike. Once one lived to his age, they'd naturally develop the ability to assess all kinds of things.

Though the man looked young, he possessed incredible martial prowess; one couldn't determine his age based on his appearance.

A list of people within the jianghu with reputations on par with his own quickly surfaced within his mind—it wasn't difficult for him to identify the man in front of him.

"To think that the great and lofty Xuandu Mountain Sect Leader would perform a surprise attack on his junior, like a coward. He truly fails to live up to his reputation!"

Shen Qiao smiled. "Yet the Kosa Sage tolerates his disciple hurting a junior. That doesn't seem too just and upright of him either, now does it?"

His tone was gentle, without even a trace of provocation or anger.

Enduring immense agony, Yin Chuan opened his eyes to stare blankly at Shen Qiao. He didn't know whether this man's arrival meant his salvation or another fresh round of suffering.

Inwardly, the Kosa Sage was frowning. Their current location wasn't a lively one, and yet first Hehuan Sect had shown up, and now it was Xuandu Mountain. It was clear that the Yin family's situation was known to all now. To prevent further delays from causing future problems, he had to quickly lead Yin Chuan away.

"There's history between our Tuyuhun and Yin Chuan, and he's taken things that should belong to Tuyuhun, so my venerable self must naturally take him away. I ask Daoist Master Shen to mind his own business!"

Hearing this, Yin Chuan was stunned. Unable to concern himself with anything else, he shouted, "Save me, esteemed Daoist Master Shen! I didn't take anything that belongs to Tuyuhun!"

Shen Qiao cast a glance at Yin Chuan, then said to the Kosa Sage, "He isn't the sage's disciple, so could the sage give me some face and allow me to take him away?"

The Kosa Sage sneered. "Daoist Master Shen, your words are terribly bizarre! On what grounds must my venerable self hand someone of mine to you?" Once these words fell, he ignored whatever reply Shen Qiao might have had and simply struck at him.

Qi surged forth, like the wind wailing through forests and mountains, sweeping through the cloud-cloaked peaks. It rose and fell as it swept out, and Yin Chuan only felt an enormous pressure bearing down on his head, which immediately began to throb as nausea overcame him. Shen Qiao promptly acted—he raised his sleeve and severed the Kosa Sage's qi, reversing it right after. Kneading the true qi into an orb, he flung it back to the original sender.

The Kosa Sage's robes billowed upward as one—he was no longer in his original spot. But Shen Qiao didn't raise his head; instead, he swept forward. The instant he moved, a figure appeared in the spot where he'd been standing.

It was the Kosa Sage!

Yin Chuan watched with round eyes, shock and terror intertwining. Only now did he grasp the true profundity of the Kosa Sage's martial prowess. The only reason he'd been able to run so far before was because Cheng Lugui's shifu had never personally shown up.

The moment he swept forward, Shen Qiao grabbed his sword, and Shanhe Tongbei emerged from its sheath. He leapt into the air and performed a reverse downward slash. Wherever the sword glare reached, sparking lights closely followed—its majesty resonating with both heaven and earth.

The Kosa Sage's expression shifted slightly. He dared not receive this blow, but he instead chose to withdraw and fell back. But the moment he drew back, he realized with a shock his own lack of will to fight—that he even wished to retreat in the first place. Even if his abilities should have been on par with Shen Qiao's, this momentary slip would ensure his defeat.

Sure enough, the sword glare followed him in hot pursuit. Shen Qiao's figure didn't pause for even a second—his sword qi surged forth, slicing a section of the Kosa Sage's sleeve right off.

Shen Qiao used this chance to pull Yin Chuan behind himself. Only then did he stop and stand tall with his sword.

The Kosa Sage's complexion shifted erratically. "The Xuandu Mountain Sect Leader is indeed worthy of his reputation!"

"The sage is too kind," Shen Qiao said generously. "If you'd gone all out, I fear that I too wouldn't have gotten off easily."

Hearing these words, the Kosa Sage's heart eased a little, but as he'd just watched the duck he'd cooked fall into Shen Qiao's hands, he was naturally unwilling to let this matter rest.

"I heard that after Yang Guang ascended to the throne, he renounced the relationship Yang Jian previously had with Daoism and went to support Buddhism instead. Logically speaking, Tuyuhun's desire to revive our nation shouldn't conflict with Daoist Master Shen's interests at all. On the contrary, we can work together instead. If Daoist Master Shen is willing to hand over Yin Chuan, my venerable self can cede half of the Yin family's fortunes to him."

Shen Qiao shook his head. "The sage has a couple things wrong. The Daoist discipline's collaboration with Yang Jian has never been a relationship of the supporter and supported. Yang Guang's closeness with the Buddhist discipline is his own concern. For all things in the world, as long as they can move with the flow, they'll naturally thrive. Daoism is this way, and dynasties are as well. I passed through this area returning from the Western Regions back to the Central Plains, and my intervention just now is wholly unrelated to anyone's wealth. Besides, even if the Yin family possessed immense wealth, that belongs to the Yin family. Since Yin Chuan is unwilling to give it to the sage, why does he demand it by force?"

The Kosa Sage sneered. "As expected of the head of Daoism. Wholly pompous and full of sanctimonious nonsense. So what if my venerable self demands it by force?"

"It's important to be self-aware, you bald old donkey."

Shen Qiao hadn't said these words, and it was even more absurd to imagine they could have come from Yin Chuan. They seemed to have emerged out of thin air.

The Kosa Sage's expression twisted drastically. When Shen Qiao had arrived on this scene, he was preceded by hints of his presence, but there was no trace of this new speaker to be found. The Kosa Sage had no idea where this other man was hiding, or even how long he might have been eavesdropping. He hadn't noticed at all.

"Who is it?!" Cheng Lugui yelled as he scanned all around him. "Enough with the tricks!"

Then they saw a man leap down from the nearby tree, one that was practically bare and had few leaves left. Before now, there'd been no one on the tree.

Seeing the newcomer, Shen Qiao revealed an expression of helplessness. "Didn't I tell you to wait for me at the inn? Yet again, you came to stir up trouble."

The man's temples were faintly white, but his face was terribly handsome as he smiled. "There's nothing to do around here. I didn't expect to see something so entertaining."

The new man's appearance was so striking, the Kosa Sage was instantly able to guess his identity.

"Yan Wushi?!"

Now his expression had finally changed completely. A single Shen Qiao was already a thorny problem for him, and now the world's foremost martial arts master was here as well. He'd immediately lost all chance of victory.

It was almost as if the name possessed a magic power: all who heard it would pale with horror. Cheng Lugui held his sword across his chest, his guard incredibly high. Even so, this action was of little use.

Yan Wushi raised an eyebrow as he regarded the Kosa Sage. "I heard that in last year's top ten rankings, you placed fifth, advancing by several ranks. My venerable self's heart has been restless ever since—why don't we have a spar?"

The Kosa Sage's mouth twitched. "My venerable self still has some important matters to attend to. I'll keep this incident with Yin Chuan in mind for now and seek martial guidance from the two of you another day."

With that, he grabbed his disciple and left. His qinggong had long reached the stage of transcendence—within a few steps, he was already dozens of yards away from Shen Qiao and Yan Wushi.

Yan Wushi had no desire to give chase. Instead, he said to Shen Qiao, "I scared him off."

Shen Qiao thought this somewhat comical, but also couldn't help but say, "The Kosa Sage has been in secluded meditation for many years, so his martial prowess is naturally extraordinary. When I exchanged blows with him just now, I discovered that his strength was not inferior but rather comparable to mine. Alas, he's too anxious to revive his country, so he stumbled on his own inner demons."

Yan Wushi gave a light humph. "No need to concern ourselves with him. Let's go eat."

He tugged at Shen Qiao and made to leave.

Yin Chuan suddenly realized that he could move. Seeing Yan Wushi's actions, he tossed aside the agony his arm was in and threw himself over, wanting to cling to Shen Qiao. But with a flick of Yan Wushi's sleeve, he was sent tumbling back again.

"This one is Yin Chuan! He asks the esteemed Daoist Master Shen to accept him as a disciple!"

"I'm stronger than he is," said Yan Wushi curiously. "So why are you asking him and not me?"

Yin Chuan dared not say anything like, "I heard that you were mercurial and erratic," so he could only answer, "My late father held the esteemed Daoist Master Shen in great esteem, and there were those who received his kindness among the Yin family's guests as well. So this junior admires the esteemed Daoist Master Shen's demeanor greatly and hopes that he can serve at his side. Even cleaning and odd jobs would be a great honor!"

Yan Wushi bluntly sneered at him. "Isn't this just seeking protection from the capable? By clinging to A-Qiao, you'll no longer be hunted down."

Those words flayed Yin Chuan's intentions wide open. His face grew a little red, but fortunately he'd tanned quite a bit while he'd been fleeing for his life these days, so it wasn't too obvious.

"Do you wish to learn martial arts to take revenge?" asked Shen Qiao.

Yin Chuan shook his head and smiled bitterly. "This junior will be honest; my personality was slothful, and the couple of masters who taught me martial arts in the past all said that I lacked talent. Most of the time, I was only interested in calligraphy and painting. If I weren't so useless, I wouldn't have been unable to save my family and ended up as the only survivor. Furthermore, it's true that the reason the Yin family was eradicated was that the tallest trees attract wind, but we ourselves held some culpability as well. This was the result of a cycle of karma."

Shen Qiao gave a slight smile. "A straightforward person indeed. You're not untalented, but you're unsuited for Xuandu Mountain, as well as Huanyue Sect."

Yin Chuan only thought the other party was politely declining him. Though he was disappointed, having the fortune of encountering a martial arts grandmaster in the first place, and even being saved by him, was already a blessing. It would have been truly inappropriate to grow resentful, so he respectfully said, "This junior understands."

Shen Qiao laughed. "I didn't finish. Though we won't take you as our disciple, there's one person who is very suited to be your shifu."

A light at the end of the tunnel. Yin Chuan's spirits soared.

"Linchuan Academy's Zhan Ziqian," said Shen Qiao. "Though he's only above average in martial prowess, he's a renowned master painter of these times. However, I can only take you to him—whether he's willing to accept you will depend on himself."

Yin Chuan was overjoyed. "Everyone knows of Master Zhan's name! If I can become his esteemed self's disciple, this junior could die a hundred deaths without regrets!"

Yan Wushi, however, was unhappy. "You're going to drag this load back with us to the Central Plains?"

Shen Qiao smiled. "It's no trouble at all. If I can help someone, I will. The most that will happen is that I return with you to Huanyue Sect after taking him to see Zhan Ziqian. How about it?"

Yet Yan Wushi deliberately questioned him. "Oh? Didn't Bai Rong invite you to attend a spring outing banquet? You're not going?"

Shen Qiao shook his head. "Currently, Hehuan Sect is too involved in Yang Guang's interests, so I'm unwilling to see her. We'll meet again in the future."

Yan Wushi sneered. "The mountains and rivers are easier to change than one's character. Hehuan Sect has always been this way. Don't relapse into your annoying habit of getting all tender and soft!"

Shen Qiao was at the end of his rope. "You—!"

The two of them walked as they conversed. Though their pace didn't seem fast, they flowed as smoothly as the clouds and rivers—in a moment, they were already far away.

Yin Chuan panted and gasped; he was about to fall behind. But then he saw that Shen Qiao had already stopped and was waiting for him with a smile.

Seeing that he'd be able to see the person he'd admired his entire life, Yin Chuan felt his body fill with inexhaustible energy, and he quickly ran to catch up.

There would always be hope ahead.

Ren Ying

THE WINTER WINDS were bitterly cold, their chill piercing straight to the bone.

A roaring whistle sounded, and an arrow grazed right by his ear.

Ren Ying's chest and lungs burned in pain; each breath he drew felt like knives gouging into his flesh, but he had no choice except to run.

If he didn't, he'd be dead.

Ever since childhood, he'd toiled away in the lowest of jobs. He might have had little else, but his legs were fairly good at running.

But his pursuers drew closer and closer, yelling as they hefted their torches. They were even full of good food and drink, well satiated, while Ren Ying hadn't eaten for a full day and night. He was running entirely on his last dregs of willpower as he cut through the forest, then past a hill. If he continued running like this, he'd ultimately suffer capture and a sound beating.

In the end, it'd only been because he'd been starved to desperation and stolen a cloth bundle from a household. It was heavy and filled to the brim with flatbread—he could even smell the aroma!

Ren Wing made his decision. Even if they captured him, he'd hide the bundle, or at least toss it far away. He'd never let these people have it.

As these thoughts flashed through his mind, he saw a glimmer of light before him.

It was a night without stars or moon. That tiny, feeble light flickered, and beneath the cover of the mountain forest, it seemed dimmer and more obscure than ever. But to Ren Ying, that tiny speck of light was akin to the stars or moon, shining brilliantly. He sprinted toward it without a second thought.

Once he made out the scene before him and realized that the light was coming from a broken-down temple, he was suddenly filled with regret.

This shabby temple was utterly isolated; it must have been something like eight hundred years since someone had last worshipped or made offerings there. Why would there be a light? Could it be his pursuers' companions? If there was no back exit, wouldn't he soon find himself completely trapped?

Ren Ying was but a boy in his adolescence, after all. He wavered, thinking that he'd made the wrong judgment, but it was too late to turn back. He could only barge inside.

A pile of burning firewood entered his vision—this was the source of the light he'd seen.

However, behind the wood pile sat a man, currently warming himself by the fire. The man looked like a Daoist priest. His head was lowered, and he was half-hidden in the shadows; the pattern of the Eight Trigrams upon his robes was already vague and indistinct.

Though the wind blew fiercely outside, the fire had been raised in a corner, shielded by the door as it opened, and it hadn't been extinguished.

Ren Ying quickly swept him a glance. He saw that the man's clothes were ragged, and he looked fragile and weak—not at all involved with the people relentlessly pursuing him. Thus, Ren Ying paid him no further heed and began searching for a back exit.

This broken-down temple was letting in drafts from all sides, but a glance was enough to survey the entire thing. Even the buddha statue was mottled and dilapidated, missing half its body—it was impossible to tell which buddha it was supposed to be. Ren Ying ran several laps around the statue like a headless chicken, his heart despairing and panicked. The footsteps behind him grew closer and closer, and Ren Ying whipped his head back. A large swathe of firelight had swiftly arrived, and seven or eight men were blocking the door. There was no escape!

He should have never entered this temple!

The early spring nights were cold, but Ren Ying's clothing was drenched in sweat. He clutched at the bundle in his arms and involuntarily took two steps back.

"Brat, where are you going to run to next?!"

"You think you're tough? Keep running!"

Voices rose all at once, their gazes like knives, practically chopping him into various pieces.

The man in front stepped out and extended his hand. "Give us the parcel."

Ren Ying gritted his teeth, reluctant and unwilling, but he hurled it toward the man.

The other person was holding a torch. Using only his free hand, he caught the angrily flung bundle. Rather than shoving it at his subordinates, he carried it himself. "Have you opened this parcel?" he asked Ren Ying.

It wasn't an accent from the Central Plains, but one couldn't call his Mandarin imprecise, just somewhat strange.

When would Ren Ying have had the time? He'd run right after stealing the bundle, terrified of being captured. The aroma of food would waft out from time to time, but despite how starved he was, he'd forcibly endured it.

But before the contemptuous stares of these men, he subconsciously refused to admit defeat. He straightened himself and retorted, "I opened it. So what?"

As he was speaking, Ren Ying glanced at the nearby window out of the corner of his eye. He thought that, if these men came up to gang up on him, he'd jump right out the window and flee. The sounds of trickling water came from outside. He was a strong swimmer; perhaps he still had a way out.

But before he could realize these thoughts, the man was already grabbing at him. "Whether you've opened it or not, you'll be leaving your life behind today!"

The man's movements were terrifyingly swift. Thoroughly shocked, Ren Ying couldn't help but lift his chin and stumble back.

When he'd been working for his boss, Ren Ying had learned a couple of moves. He considered himself nimble—otherwise, he could have never held on for so long while so starved.

But these men were supremely skilled, far beyond what Ren Ying had imagined. No matter how quick his reflexes were, he couldn't compare to that man's grab.

A chilling aura and pressure engulfed him from the front and his throat was tightly grasped. At that moment, murderous intent surged, and Ren Ying grew dazed from suffocation, his hands and feet losing the strength to struggle.

As he watched the other party's mouth stretch maliciously, he suddenly realized something: these people were clearly exceptionally skilled. The entire way, they'd only hunted instead of capturing him.

They'd let him exhaust himself before drawing in the nets, much like a cat would toy with a mouse between its paws. However, all he'd stolen was a parcel filled with food. If he hadn't been so hungry, if a little brother and sister hadn't been waiting at home for him, Ren Ying would have never taken the risk of provoking these men. They had enough to eat and drink; they didn't look like people who'd lack for one missing parcel of food, so why must they drive him to his death? In such tumultuous times, were the poor truly doomed to be unable to survive?

Jumbled thoughts surged within his mind, and the hand around his throat tightened more and more. Out of the corner of his eye, he glimpsed the others, who'd turned to interrogating the man behind the fire. They thought that he was together with Ren Ying.

Ren Ying opened his mouth; he wanted to tell the man to hurry up and leave. But he could no longer make any noise. His vision gradually darkened, and even his limbs had gone stiff and numb.

"Since he never opened it, why must you be so ruthless?"

Dimly, Ren Ying thought he heard a voice, both near and far, but he was unable to tell where it was coming from.

Perhaps he was only hearing things before his death, he numbly thought. He knew that his death was imminent, that there lay a vast gap between their abilities. He'd already given up all struggle. But then the pressure on his body vanished and there was a scream, one that hadn't come from his mouth.

Ren Ying opened his eyes in a muddle and saw a man fly backward and land heavily upon the floor.

The Daoist priest by the fire rose and dusted himself off. His clothes were disheveled, in a wretched state, yet his movements were as smooth as drifting clouds and flowing waters or a cool breeze kissing the moon. There wasn't a mote of dust on his face.

Even those men had never imagined that someone so formidable would have appeared within this broken-down temple.

"He might have stolen something, but that's not a crime that warrants death," the stranger said. "In your belief that someone was plotting after your things, you took him as bait. Now you've realized that it was only happenstance, why not let him go?"

The Daoist wasn't at all flustered at the intrusion from these uninvited guests. He was as steady as a mountain, showing neither anger nor surprise.

All who wandered the jianghu knew that the more inconspicuous a person seemed, the less one could afford to provoke them. But this group seemed to have subconsciously concluded that he was the instigator behind Ren Ying. They instantly shot back with a sneer. "Let him go? Then you can take his place?"

The man in front attacked first while his men behind him split into two groups surrounding the Daoist—they'd wordlessly arranged themselves into a sword formation.

Ren Ying didn't understand martial arts, but he could tell that the Daoist was in danger. Seven or eight men drew their swords, their sword qi interweaving. For a moment, it was difficult to determine who was near or far. Ren Ying only felt a pressure slamming into his face from the front. He tried to back up, but he was stopped by a pillar. All he could do was flatten himself against it. He saw the Daoist surrounded, and he couldn't resist blurting out, "Careful!"

He'd just said this with a bright laugh rang outside the temple. "An insignificant little sect from Yamato,[5] and you're strutting about in the Central Plains?"

Those words had exposed their identities—hearing them, the faces of those seven or eight men fell. Just as they were thinking

---

5   Ancient name for Japan.

that they'd finish off the Daoist before heading out to deal with the newcomer, the Daoist suddenly shook his sleeves and spread them. The men's sword formation instantly collapsed, and the shock waves caused two of their swords to shatter and fly from their owners' grasps. A couple of men reeled back several steps, disbelief written all over their faces.

At this time, the laughter from outside drew closer and a man strolled inside, his robes fluttering, his demeanor calm and composed.

"It's only been about a dozen days since I last saw you. How did our Sect Leader Shen end up this wretched?" The newcomer clicked his tongue twice, a smile on his lips. As he scanned his surroundings, he seemed to be looking at everyone, yet he also seemed to consider them beneath his notice. In the end, only the Daoist had been calmly accepted into the boundary he drew around himself.

The Daoist seemed familiar with him; hearing those words, the man shook his head, but didn't explain any further. Instead, he turned to the group of people. "Still going to fight?"

The leader had heard the words "Sect Leader Shen," and an ominous feeling surfaced within him. For a moment, his suspicious, wary gaze wavered between Shen Qiao and the newcomer.

Shen Qiao didn't wait for them to figure out what was going on. He followed up with: "If you're not going to fight, it's my turn."

Before the leader could react, he felt an all-encompassing pressure before him, enough to topple mountains and overturn the seas. He instantly found himself unable to breathe, and before he could return the attack, he was forced to fall back. Unfortunately, he was still a step too slow: his subordinates could only helplessly watch as their leader was seized by Shen Qiao, completely unable to move.

"What are you doing? Let go!"

"How brazen!"

Some of them had grown angry in their panic, even shouting in Japanese. Two of the men were about to rush forward, but they'd scarcely taken half a step when Shen Qiao forced them back with a flick of his finger.

The man beside him, who was dressed like a distinguished scholar, never intervened even once. He simply watched from the sidelines, his face full of smiles. But though he was only watching, those men from Yamato also felt an immense pressure from him.

A single Shen Qiao was already too much for them, never mind the thought of adding another.

"Infiltrating the Central Plains and browbeating the common folk. To think that the great and mighty Shinbu Sect, the foremost sect of Yamato, could do something so dishonorable."

When he heard Shen Qiao's words, the leader paled right away. He subconsciously still wanted to struggle, but then a wave of agony pierced through his restrained shoulder, completely unexpected. He couldn't help but yell in pain as he slumped down, but because his shoulder was still in Shen Qiao's grasp, he could only forcibly support himself on his weak, limp legs.

"This one is Asano Taku, disciple from Shinbu Sect. May I ask if this distinguished master is Sect Leader Shen of Xuandu Mountain, the world's foremost Daoist sect? Everyone says that Sect Leader Shen is benevolent and generous beyond compare, so why are his actions so ruthless? It's heavens and earths apart from his reputation, so please forgive me for failing to recognize you!"

His face was contorted in pain, yet he'd still remembered to probe Shen Qiao using psychological tactics.

The man watching from the side suddenly burst into laughter. "Showing mercy when the other side clearly bears ill intent?" he scoffed. "You're describing an idiot, not Sect Leader Shen. Though our A-Qiao is a little foolish, thanks to my teachings these past few years, he's at least able to weigh and judge things somewhat."

His tone was frivolous, as if he was flirting with some uptown lady. But Asano Taku dared not underestimate him at all, because he could feel an invisible and terrifying presence emanating from the man. It was something impossible to describe—one could only feel it from grandmasters who'd achieved the summit of martial arts. Though Yamato had quite a few martial arts practitioners, there were practically none on the level of the two men in front of him.

It also looked like the man was well acquainted with Sect Leader Shen, for the latter sent him a glance, yet remained completely silent.

With two great martial artists on the scene, Asano Taku dared not act so unbridled—he could only endure the pain while explaining what was going on.

According to Asano Taku, the Shinbu Sect had only ended up in the Central Plains by chance. Originally, they'd been tracking down a missing token from their sect. They arrived in Goguryeo, where they'd clashed with the premier sect in Goguryeo: Dungjeou Sect. Quite a few members of Shinbu Sect had been killed or injured, and disagreements emerged within Asano Taku's party. Some of them proposed returning to their sect first to report, then lay down a plan for the future since they'd suffered such heavy casualties. But others insisted that they should continue investigating until they found the token so that they had something to bring back to the sect.

Asano's group was the latter.

They'd followed the faint trail all the way from Goguryeo to the Central Plains and discovered the token's whereabouts nearby. After a difficult and bloody battle, they managed to retrieve it, only to find themselves heavily surrounded, for many sects were also eyeing that token of theirs. Asano and his men had become like birds startling at the twang of a bow—they took everyone who approached them as thieves. Even if they knew that Ren Ying's skills were mediocre, that he couldn't even qualify as a member of the jianghu, they still couldn't help but suspect that there was someone behind him, so they'd wanted to use him to lure out the "big fish."

Yet they never expected that Ren Ying was really someone without any background or history, merely a starving thief—instead, it was Asano and his party who'd charged headlong into a mighty mountain.

No, two mountains.

After haltingly explaining the ins and outs of his tale, Asano forced a smile to his face, acting humble and submissive.

"Though we possess eyes, we failed to recognize Mount Tai when it was right before us. We ask the two masters to forgive us, and avoid lowering your esteemed selves to our level."

"A trivial sect token had all the sects hunting you down covetously?" Shen Qiao said. "You've been avoiding the important matters the whole time—not once have you explained what that token is. Do you think we're that easy to fool?"

Shen Qiao disliked causing difficulties for others, but if not for his intervention, a boy would have died at their hands. Though Asano had detailed all their troubles, Shen Qiao still had no intentions of letting them off easily. Who knew if they'd attack someone else once he left?

Sure enough, Asano revealed a reluctant expression and stammered.

"Why not let me guess?" Yan Wushi paced over slowly, his tone filled with the schadenfreude of one watching a grand show that had nothing to do with him. "A while ago, I heard that some disciples from Dungjeou Sect defected after carrying out a massacre within their sect, causing great chaos within Goguryeo for some time. Later, people from Goguryeo and Yamato showed up again and again within the Central Plains; even Tuyuhun and the newly born Tibet ended up drawn into this matter. Ultimately, it was all due to the Mitake sword that found its way out of Dungjeou Sect. Legend says that the sword was blessed by the divine, and thus the wielder would be protected by a divine light, making them indestructible like the Vajra. Furthermore, the sword blade is carved with mountains and rivers, indicating the location of a treasure. Several groups have been vying for it without end, and now even the sects of the Central Plains have caught wind of this and joined in one after another. Inside that parcel of yours is Mitake, right?"

Asano's expression had flickered several times throughout Yan Wushi's speech. Though he gritted his teeth and refused to utter a sound, that in and of itself was a tacit confirmation.

Ren Ying only half understood what was going on. He was completely confused, but he still knew that the parcel he'd stumbled upon and stolen was actually a precious object that the jianghu was fighting over. At once, he couldn't prevent his face from turning ashen.

If someone hadn't suddenly popped up to save him, he would have died here.

Ren Ying subconsciously hid behind Shen Qiao, his hand gripping Shen Qiao's sleeves. Yet he felt a faint prickling sensation upon his back and instinctively turned to look. He only saw the man who'd spoken earlier, who was standing behind the firelight, cast his gaze toward him, and there was an invisible threat hidden in that gaze. Ren Ying shrank away and quickly withdrew his hand.

Asano was worried that Shen Qiao and Yan Wushi were also here to steal Mitake. He could scarcely imagine that the two were wholly uninterested in the object, for they spoke no further. Instead they continued to stoke the fire, preparing to rest. Yan Wushi even pulled out a small flask of shaojiu from his lapels. He handed it to Shen Qiao, who smoothly received it and took a swig, then returned it to Yan Wushi. Then he procured a couple of pieces of flatbread and dry rations, giving them to Ren Ying to allay his hunger.

Ren Ying thanked him repeatedly. He was clearly ravenous, yet he ate the food slowly. Even after a long time had passed, more than half of the palm-sized flatbread remained.

"The bread isn't poisonous. You can be at ease," said Shen Qiao gently.

Ren Ying shook his head, then awkwardly explained that his younger siblings at home had nothing to eat. He was terrified that the noble person before him would think that he was asking for more and failed to notice that Shen Qiao's expression had gentled further.

"I still have some dry rations here," said Shen Qiao. "Though I can't give them all to you. You're alone and won't be able to hold on to so much food. Afterward, bring your siblings over. This place isn't far from Guyang City. You can settle them here for a while, then look for some work opportunities within the city."

Ren Ying had considered entering the city before, but his siblings had been too hungry to walk. Left with no other choice, he could only set out alone in search of food, which was how he'd run into Asano's cohort.

Asano was anxious and apprehensive, and he dared not make rash movements. But there were people in his party who didn't know Shen Qiao and Yan Wushi's illustrious reputations and sought a chance to escape. One of them had just risen under the cover of darkness and taken two steps when his waist was struck twice. It'd been soundless and quick as lighting—the man hadn't even noticed what was going on before he fell sideways, collapsing to the ground and twitching ceaselessly.

"These years, no one in front of me has ever dared to come and go freely without my permission." Yan Wushi remained completely calm, and his gaze upon Asano's group was filled with ridicule, as if he were a cat toying with a mouse.

Asano did possess the capacity for sound judgment, and so he could endure. But the people around him couldn't—they immediately burst out with a yell and raised their weapons, slashing at Yan Wushi.

Since Shen Qiao had done most of the attacking before, Asano's subordinates assumed that Yan Wushi would be easier to deal with—they aimed to take him hostage.

This was truly an example of digging one's own grave—death-seeking behavior. One man had just raised his weapon over his head when he was sent flying. His sword shot out of his hands and toward the wall behind the buddha statue, where the blade stabbed halfway in!

Asano looked at his motionless subordinates and felt his mind crack completely. The feeble desire for resistance within him had already evaporated. He grew completely docile and obedient, fearing that even the slightest hint of disrespect would lead to him sharing that man's fate.

Within Yamato, the Jinmu Sect's power was such that they could do as they pleased. Being used to this, Asano had thought quite highly of himself—even after arriving in Goguryeo and the Central Plains, at times he'd developed the mistaken impression that the foreign martial artists were below his notice, all because he'd never encountered any of the top martial artists. Now he completely understood that a mistaken impression was just that: a mistake. The reason he'd never encountered any rivals was because he'd never met any top experts. Then Shen Qiao and Yan Wushi, the two great mountains, had come crashing down before him. Unable to scale them, he was left in sudden despair.

He thought that today would become the day of his death, but then Yan Wushi airily let them all go.

"Get out. Don't let me see you ever again."

Shen Qiao supplemented his words with his own. "If your lot dares to seek revenge on this young friend of mine, Xuandu Mountain will become your enemy."

"Sect Leader Shen's threats are so lackluster," Yan Wushi commented in a chilly tone. "Just tell them that you'll hunt them down to the edges of the world to punish them, that they'll be unable to die in one piece. Wouldn't that settle everything?"

Having witnessed how terrifying these men were, Asano dared not doubt the truth of Yan Wushi's words. He repeatedly kneeled and bowed, then stumbled back, swearing that he'd never dare take any kind of revenge on Ren Ying, thus showcasing completely their tendency to fall apart before the strong. Only afterward, when their group was a long distance away from the temple and they were certain Shen Qiao and Yan Wushi really had let them go did they finally allow themselves to sink to the ground.

Meanwhile, inside the broken-down temple, Ren Ying had managed to survive a disaster. He stared blankly at Shen Qiao, as if he were in a trance. In the aftermath, a belated fear surged within him, and his eyes reddened.

"Shen… Shen-xiansheng, I'm worried about my siblings. Can I go pick them up first? I wish to thank and kowtow to these two gentlemen for their great kindness together with them."

He'd moved his siblings to a broken-down kiln earlier. It let in the cold air from all sides, and the two children's stomachs rumbled with hunger. They lacked even the strength to truss a chicken; anything could happen to them at any time.

"I'll go with you." Shen Qiao volunteered, then turned his head to say to Yan Wushi, "I must trouble Yan-xiong to wait here a moment. I'll leave with our young friend, and we'll soon be back."

Yan Wushi prodded at the flames before saying icily, "By the time you get back, my venerable self might be gone already."

He'd put on great airs, yet Shen Qiao laughed in response. "Then, Sect Leader Yan, you'll have to stoop to waiting a moment."

Yan Wushi gave a slight snort but spoke no further.

Ren Ying was anxious and fearful. He didn't know who Yan Wushi was, but the man's presence scared and intimidated him on an instinctual level. He had no idea that, at this moment, Yan Wushi had already restrained himself quite a bit. One could even call his disposition pleasant.

With Shen Qiao there, Ren Ying's reunion with his siblings went smoothly. The two children were so starved they seemed barely human—they could scarcely open their eyes. Ren Ying dared not feed them too much at once; he could only have them eat a bite at a time, waiting for them to gradually recover their strength.

Only then was Shen Qiao able to ask about Ren Ying's brimming resentment and frustrations.

"When I was young, I heard my parents say that Emperor Wen replaced Zhou and vanquished Chen, unifying the lands," said Ren Ying. "We thought that us common folk would be able to enjoy good days ahead. It's only been a few years since the emperor and court changed, so how did things end up this way? A great drought, followed by a great flood. Our family lost everything and my parents passed away. Our house and farmlands were flooded too; our chickens all died. It's… It's fine if I starve to death, but what about my siblings? Where is the hope for us commoners? Will we still be able to survive?"

Even if he were nimble and had learned a little martial arts, within these troubled times, he was little more than a leaf adrift on the wind with nothing he could rely on.

There were thousands and thousands of people just like Ren Ying.

Shen Qiao sighed. "Before, I also believed that Great Sui, with Emperor Wen, would at least be able to enjoy several hundred years of peace. Looking at things now, it seems Yan Wushi was truly correct!"

Ren Ying was confused. "What are you saying, sir?"

Shen Qiao burst out laughing. "I'm saying that I know a little fortune-telling. But unfortunately, in all my divinations about the future, I'd failed to account for the human heart."

Who would have thought that Emperor Wen and Empress Dugu, who'd been wise rulers their entire lives, would stumble in choosing their heir? Yang Guang indeed surpassed the emperor's other sons when it came to talents and intelligence, but when the entire world was already within one's hands, the key lay not in how nimble those hands were, nor in what miracles they could perform, but in how stable they were. And Yang Guang's hands were indeed more than nimble, but they were lacking in stability.

He held great and lofty ambitions surpassing dozens of emperors who came before him. The sole things he'd missed were the hearts and resources of the people.

An eastern expedition, a transportation canal, and separating the military from the aristocracy and offending the powerful families. These three things were enough to topple his throne, and enough to cause the already short-lived nation to sway, on the verge of collapse.

Though Yang Guang still sat on the throne today, Shen Qiao could already see the crisis brewing beneath the facade of prosperity.

Ren Ying knew nothing of this. He couldn't stand that high nor see that far; he only knew that his family and home had perished from natural disasters, and yet the court didn't care. Or perhaps the court lacked the ability to care. Ren Ying couldn't see any hope of survival, but for his siblings, he could only hold on bitterly. One day, if even his sole concern was gone, people with similar experiences to Ren Ying might simply grit their teeth and turn to the life of an outlaw. Perhaps then he'd gain some riches as he licked the blood from his sword, or perhaps he'd lose his life beneath the glint of blades.

On this trip, Shen Qiao and Yan Wushi were just returning now from their wandering journey of several years to the Western Regions. Along the way, they'd witnessed the violent changes that had befallen the Central Plains, which was ready to retread the fate and mistakes of the Northern and Southern Dynasties. The hearts of the people wavered, and the jianghu and court were irrevocably interlinked. Few of the world's sects were at peace; they seemed restless and poised to cause trouble, with each hatching their own plots.

"This was the way of the world. Those long divided must be united, and those long united must be divided."[6] The only pity lay in the Sui Dynasty's rough destiny: the unity had been too brief. Turbulence had arisen again in a flash. One could only sympathize with the innocent common folk, who could do nothing but drift along with the tide, lacking any agency.

Thinking about this, Shen Qiao was at a loss.

---

6   天下大勢, 分久必合, 合久必分. *The first line of the historical novel,* Romance of the Three Kingdoms.

He could lead Xuandu Mountain and even bring his sect to great heights, and he was unable to share these benefits with the world.

A single person's strength was limited. No matter how skilled a martial artist they were, they could only protect the people around them. It was impossible to protect all the people in the world.

Only good timing, good terrain, and the support of the people could give birth to an era of peace and prosperity. And how long this prosperity could be maintained depended on how clear-minded the ones in charge were.

"If you have nowhere to go, why not come with me to Xuandu Mountain?" Shen Qiao suggested. "There's a village at the foot of the mountain, and there are few bandits there. They were also fortunate enough to not suffer natural disasters this year. Your siblings can spend their days working while studying; it's much safer than wandering about outside."

This was the method Shen Qiao had come up with to ensure that Ren Ying could settle down safely. Perhaps he was incapable of saving everyone in the world, but as long as he had the ability to help, it was impossible for him to watch from the sidelines.

Ren Ying thanked Shen Qiao.

Shen Qiao still felt that the youth's heart was heavy with worries and his spirits low. But his own mind was buzzing with thoughts, so he said nothing more. The four people walked silently back, all the way until they reached the broken-down temple and saw the faint glow of fire gleaming through the holes in the window paper. With this, the slight disappointment within Shen Qiao's heart too inexplicably scattered.

An aroma wafted out along with the fire's glow. Ren Ying and his siblings' stomachs growled as one.

Yan Wushi sat cross-legged behind the fire, playing with a long pole he held in his hand, his head lowered as he carved something upon it. Even when he spoke, he didn't look up. "A-Qiao, if you wish to have these three eat some roast chicken, then guess what I'm doing right now."

Ren Ying and his younger siblings all looked at each other, then stared at Shen Qiao.

The corner of Shen Qiao's mouth twitched. "You wish to carve a fake Mitake sword?"

Yan Wushi was all smiles. "Sect Leader Shen knows me well. Here, this roast chicken is yours."

From beginning to end, he hadn't made any excessive displays of power, but for some reason, Ren Ying and his siblings still held an instinctive fear and awe toward him. Hearing this, they looked at Shen Qiao. Only after Ren Ying saw him nod did he carefully shift himself over and thank Yan Wushi in a small voice before picking up a piece of roast chicken.

Shen Qiao politely declined the food Ren Ying was trying to share with him and had the three of them move to the side, where they could warm themselves while eating. Then he sat down next to Yan Wushi.

"No matter how dexterous Sect Leader Yan's hands are, a simple bamboo pole can never become the true Mitake. What kind of ruse are you plotting this time?"

"Do you know the origins of the Shinbu Sect's name, and why the Mitake sword is called Mitake?" Yan Wushi asked, instead of answering.

"It's said that the first emperor of Yamato was called Emperor Jinmu, and Shinbu Sect claims that they're his direct and legitimate descendants. That must be the reason for their namesake. As for Mitake, it's probably related to their belief in Shinto."

"A-Qiao is indeed a man of great learning and ability. Now here's another test question: what does Mitake look like?"

"This, I have no clue. Has Sect Leader Yan seen it before?"

"A-Qiao, didn't you realize? The Mitake sword Asano's cohort had in their possession was also a fake."

Of course Shen Qiao had noticed.

Asano had allowed Ren Ying to run off with the parcel containing Mitake before giving chase. This was surely in hopes of reeling in a larger fish using a longer line. If the sword had been real, there was no way he'd be able to stand using it as bait.

"The real Mitake sword was never in Asano's hands at all. Them running about with a fake sword on their back is probably only a cover for the people with the real sword." Yan Wushi took the bamboo pole, polished and glossy, and wrapped it in silk. As he played with it, it really did look like it could be the genuine article. "If I release some news saying that I chanced upon the real Mitake sword, what do you think those who hear of this will do?"

"Many people will believe it to be true, and they'll employ all sorts of techniques, hatch all sorts of plots, to obtain this bamboo pole from you."

He'd specially emphasized the words "bamboo pole."

Yan Wushi's smile was full of malice. "At that time, I'll find another reason to have this object end up in Asano's hands, then let the whole world know the truth. Then he won't be able to clear his name even if he leaps into the Yellow River."

Shen Qiao was silent for a moment. "They offended you today; I trust that they'll end up drowning in regret in the future."

"You happened to be here tonight. If that wasn't the case, this youth would have lost his life, and his siblings their protection, and they too would have died one after the other. Knowing this, can you still pity that bunch?"

"I've never been able to outtalk you," Shen Qiao said.

Yan Wushi smiled brightly. "Then you should listen to me. The cold nights are long, and I've already warmed the wine. Only when he's full of food and drink can our Sect Leader Shen have the strength to cherish the world's people."

Though his tone was mocking, if one listened closely, there was a hint of coaxing to it, like he was speaking to a child.

Shen Qiao watched as he fished out a flask of wine and uncorked the stopper. The aroma of wine immediately fanned out, wafting toward his nose.

Shen Qiao took the flask, then tipped his head back and took a large gulp. His movements seemed somewhat urgent, and the wine trickled out from the corners of his lips, meandering down his throat and Adam's apple. When he lifted his eyes again, he saw Yan Wushi gazing at him. And though their relationship was already far from ordinary, Shen Qiao still felt a little embarrassed.

"That bamboo pole..."

Shen Qiao had already vaguely guessed what Yan Wushi wished to do.

It wasn't as simple as Yan Wushi finding Asano and his group disagreeable and wanting to vent his frustrations. This man had always enjoyed spoiling other people's schemes—even if no wind blew, he'd still find a way to stir up waves. And with the world showing signs of latent chaos, poised to reenact the scenes of confrontation between Northern Zhou and Southern Chen, he was bound to involve himself, secretly guiding the situation while fanning the flames, all so that he could profit from the chaos.

And before he could determine what Yan Wushi would actually do, Shen Qiao decided to bide his time, to watch and wait.

After all, even if the man known as Sect Leader Yan sometimes held wicked intentions, it didn't necessarily mean that he'd do wicked things.

He had to concede that when it came to insight into the state of the world at large, his own still lagged behind Yan Wushi's.

"Either the wine isn't good, or I'm too ugly," Yan Wushi said. "Otherwise how could your mind wander off in my venerable self's presence?"

A hand reached out unexpectedly, catching Shen Qiao off guard as it grabbed his cheeks.

The great and lofty leader of the world's foremost Daoist Sect, who'd appeared as steady as Mount Tai, enigmatic and unfathomable, vanished in an instant. All it took was the blink of an eye, and he'd transformed from refined and cultured to lovable and adorable.

Seeing this, Ren Ying was so stunned, he even forgot about eating the chicken wing in his hand.

Naming

I T WAS AN AUTUMN DAY.

The autumn winds whistled over thousands of miles of desolation and destruction, stretching as far as the eye could see. The land could never be restored to its original appearance.

Qi Fengge led his horse to the Yellow River and stopped.

Last year, the Yellow River had burst through the dikes, flooding countless acres of farmland and leaving thousands of people homeless. And today, both riverbanks were laid bare. Even though there were villages, they were scattered all about.

The waters surged and the winds wailed, whipping up his hem and sleeves. Even his sigh scattered on the winds.

Last year, a flood. This year, a drought. Standing before the Heavenly Dao, humans were utterly powerless.

For the sake of allowing the horse to rest a while longer, Qi Fengge was not in a hurry to mount and gallop off. Instead, he slowly proceeded on foot. Quite a few refugees passed him in twos and threes. When they saw the well-fed horse behind him, their eyes flickered with hunger and their mouths filled with saliva. They were only deterred from rash action by the longsword in his hand. The few that were starved to desperation and had lost their reason paid that no heed either, and they rushed toward him to take the horse. Naturally, Qi Fengge knocked them to the ground with a flick of his sleeve.

In the beginning, when Qi Fengge had encountered these types, he'd shown them great kindness and shared his food with them. But he'd slowly come to realize that, though he could save one person, he couldn't save them all. And even if they could fill their bellies this time, without a reliable source for next time, or the time after that, they'd still end up starving to death.

After watching this scene play out enough times, even the most compassionate of hearts would grow cold and hard.

Qi Fengge didn't pay them any further heed. He leapt straight onto his horse and galloped off, leaving roiling dust in his wake.

There were still a few days' worth of travel before he'd reach Xuandu Mountain. Qi Fengge wasn't in a hurry to get back, so he found a temple, intending to stay the night.

The temple had been deserted for many years—the buddha statue had toppled to the ground, and its head had somehow vanished. The emperor of Liang had believed in Buddhism, yet the buddhas and bodhisattvas had failed to save his people. In the end, he too had starved to death.

Qi Fengge lit a fire and boiled some water. He'd almost achieved inedia,[7] so eating was of little importance. As long as there were tiles above his head, he could spend the night meditating, and that would be all the rest he needed.

A faint noise came from behind the pillar.

Someone else might not have noticed, but Qi Fengge was somewhat astounded. With his hearing, he should have discovered the person the moment he'd entered, so either their breathing was too feeble or this hidden person was a powerful martial artist.

"This one is Qi Fengge. May I ask which Daoist friend is there?"

---

7   In wuxia, after reaching this level of internal cultivation, martial artists can subsist on very little food.

After a period of silence without receiving an answer, Qi Fengge rose and walked over. There he realized that behind the pillar was a large clay jar.

He lifted the limestone slab covering it, and his gaze just happened to meet another pair of eyes.

The other party was a child.

Qi Fengge gentled his voice. "What's your name?"

No response.

Qi Fengge reached in, wanting to carry the child up and out, when pain suddenly flared in the back of his hand. The Xuandu Mountain Sect Leader, whom unrelated parties weren't even able to approach, had been bitten by a child.

He didn't know whether to laugh or cry. The bite had drawn blood on the back of his hand. Threads of blood oozed out, and a fiery pain filled his hand.

Qi Fengge sealed the child's acupoints, then lifted him out. He realized that the boy was at most four or five years old, and he was small and skinny. His entire face was smeared in grime—even his hair was unbound and matted. Fear was clear in his eyes.

"Don't be afraid. I'm not a bad person."

He didn't know if the boy was listening, but Qi Fengge was in no hurry to unseal his acupoints. First, he tore off a corner of his robe, then poured some hot water so he could wash it. After wringing out the cloth, he used it to wipe the boy's face.

As the boy's face grew cleaner bit by bit, Qi Fengge couldn't help but make a sound of surprise. Though the child was frail, judging by that fair face and tender hands, which had never seen a day of labor, it was evident that the child must have been from a good background.

"What's your name? Do you remember where your house is? I'll take you back to find your parents."

Perhaps Qi Fengge's attitude had placated the boy, for even after he undid his acupoints, the child didn't scream or flee. He simply remained quiet, never replying to any of Qi Fengge's questions, right up until he took the flatbread he was offered and nibbled it. Only then did he weakly say, "Water..."

"So you do know how to talk." Qi Fengge smiled and passed him some water. "Drink slowly and be careful not to eat too quickly or you'll get bloated."

The boy was very well behaved. Even though he'd been hungry for a long time, he still left more than half of the flatbread and returned it to Qi Fengge. Qi Fengge surmised that the child must have come from a well-off home, and his heart melted a little more. "You can keep it. Eat it when you grow hungry again."

The night grew deeper and the dew heavy. The child involuntarily leaned closer to the fire, and Qi Fengge removed his outer robe and draped it over his small body, yet the boy tried to avoid it as he whispered, "Dirty..."

Qi Fengge swaddled him in the outer robe, then simply picked the boy up, holding him in his arms. "I don't mind being dirty."

This warm embrace was something the boy hadn't felt since leaving home, and now it was as if he'd returned to his parents' arms. He almost thought he could hear the faint sounds of his mother's loving teasing. He unknowingly dropped his guard and closed his eyes, then slipped into the land of dreams.

"There's a broken-down temple here! Come quick! Now we can take shelter from the wind! Shit, these stinking heavens. It's not even winter yet and the winds are already this fierce!"

"Fierce winds are no matter. What's really eerie is that there's nowhere to eat for dozens of miles around us! We don't even know if we'll make it in time if we keep going!"

"The three demonic sects are holding a meeting. This is really unprecedented! Perhaps we can also…"

The voices drew closer, waking the child. He shrank into Qi Fengge's arms and peeked out. Two large men walked in, one after the other. A puff of wind whirled in with them from outside, sending the flames into a frenzied dance.

They'd already seen the fire glow from outside the temple and knew that there were people inside; that's why they'd deliberately come. People meant food.

Inside was a Daoist priest with a timid little child. Seeing this, the two men were overjoyed. Though they could tell that this Daoist was someone from the jianghu, he was only one person—and being only one person meant that he'd be weak.

The two men strode in. "It's too windy outside, so we came in for shelter and to warm ourselves by the fire. The Daoist master wouldn't mind, right?"

"I don't own this place," said Qi Fengge. "Please, go ahead."

Looked like this person was easy to persuade as well. The two men shared a glance, then sat down.

Wu Wenguang said, "Dozens of miles lie ahead of us, and there are but a few villages around. Is the Daoist master heading somewhere in particular?"

"I was about to head home," Qi Fengge replied. "I'm only passing through this place."

Ji Chunzhai laughed. "So the Daoist master isn't heading to the assembly of the three demonic sects?"

Qi Fengge smiled but didn't respond.

The two new arrivals' stomachs growled in hunger. Seeing as they were unsuccessful in procuring any information on Qi Fengge's background, they stopped beating around the bush. "We were searching our entire journey, but we saw no kitchen smoke from any of the villages' chimneys. If the Daoist master has any rations, could he share them with us? In the future, we will definitely pay you back double."

Qi Fengge coolly replied, "I have none."

He no longer needed to eat; he was practically capable of surviving on only wind and dew like an immortal. He'd given the only flatbread he'd had on him to the child in his arms.

Ji Chunzhai rolled his eyes. Instead of looking disappointed, he smiled instead. "Looking at this young boy, he doesn't seem like the Daoist master's disciple or a relative. Was he someone you chanced upon along the way? How about we strike up a deal: sell the child to us, and we'll pay you amply in silver."

He pulled out a silver round from his sleeve and tossed it over. It landed right in front of Qi Fengge. Qi Fengge didn't even glance at it. "What do you want with him?"

"That's none of your concern!" said Wu Wenguang impatiently.

Qi Fengge raised his brow. "Are you going to make him into hegulan?"

Consuming humans for food wasn't uncommon during such tumultuous times. When it came to the victims, or "two-legged sheep" as they were called, the flesh of children was tender and easy to cook, their flavor superior, hence the name "hegulan," or "gentle and tender bones."

It was unclear whether the boy could understand them or if he was simply afraid of these two malicious men. He clutched at Qi Fengge's arms tightly, his face pressed into Qi Fengge's robes, too fearful to raise his head.

Qi Fengge gently reassured him. "Don't be afraid. I won't hand you over."

Wu Wenguang gave a cold humph. "Think this through carefully. Boys like this are everywhere. Antagonizing our Hehuan Sect for his sake—is it really worth it?"

"Back then even Cui Youwang dared not speak to me like this," Qi Fengge said coolly. "It seems like Riyue Sect truly just regresses with everything they do. Not only have they fragmented, they continue to wane, accepting anyone and everyone!"

In the beginning, when he'd been reticent, he'd only looked like an ordinary Daoist priest. At most, perhaps his demeanor seemed a little special. But when he spoke these words, his aura suddenly grew strong and imperious.

Unfortunately, Wu Wenguang and Ji Chunzhai's surprise only lasted a short moment, and they failed to be intimidated by his words. Instead, they barked out an ugly laugh. "You have guts! Then there's no need to waste more words on you. We'll seize and cook the two of you today. This even saves us some money!"

They were still speaking when Wu Wenguang's figure drifted in front of Qi Fengge. He moved in a flash, with extraordinary speed, crooking his fingers into claws like an eagle after its prey, and brought his hand down on Qi Fengge's head.

The little boy in Qi Fengge's arms only felt an ill wind blowing. He was about to raise his head, but it was like a thousand pounds were crushing him from above—he couldn't lift his head an inch.

"Don't be afraid."

It looked as though Qi Fengge was about to lose his life to Wu Wenguang's "Netherworld Talons," yet he still had the leisure to comfort others! In Wu Wenguang's eyes, Qi Fengge was already a dead man.

His fingertips had almost touched Qi Fengge's topknot.

But it was only "almost."

White light flashed before his eyes. Wu Wenguang hadn't even been able to discern what was happening when a pain was burst in his chest. The next instant, his body was sent flying back, completely beyond his control. A mere moment later, he crashed heavily to the ground.

Agony tore through his back, and his face was still frozen in his earlier expression of horrified surprise. He hadn't even had the time to change it.

The nearby Ji Chunzhai, who'd been prepared to leisurely watch the show from the sidelines, now realized that things weren't looking right. He immediately drew his sword and swept toward Qi Fengge.

His movements were swift, his figure like smoke, as his sword glare arced like a rainbow. If the people from Liuli Palace in Fangzhang Isle were to rank his swordplay, they'd say that, though his skills were insufficient for the top ten, he'd still be a contender for a sword masters' ranking. It was obvious that Ji Chunzhai was no mediocre swordsman.

Ji Chunzhai was indeed quite satisfied with his swordplay. He thought that although this stab of his didn't use his full power, it'd used around nine-tenths of it, and that it was more than enough to deal with the Daoist in front of him.

But his smile suddenly froze upon his face.

Because just as his sword glare was about to touch the other man's clothes, it suddenly halted in place. Or perhaps it should be said that his entire body, along with his sword, was being locked in place by some invisible force.

It lasted only an instant, but it was enough for Ji Chunzhai to look like he'd seen a ghost.

The next moment, like Wu Wenguang, he too had been sent flying back and a stabbing agony emanated from both his wrists.

Qi Fengge rose. He carried the young boy in one arm while sheathing his sword with the other. "You don't deserve to use the sword," he told Ji Chunzhai.

Ji Chunzhai was filled with both loathing and anger—he was practically about to vomit blood. "The...the tendons... My hand!"

With the tendons of his hands severed, even if they could be reconnected, he'd never regain the same agility. This meant that he could never again seek the summit of swordplay.

At this time, Wu Wenguang was also drowning in regret. Had they known this man would be that difficult to deal with, they'd have never entered this broken-down temple!

"We were too blind... We beg the Daoist...the Daoist master to please have mercy!"

Qi Fengge handed the sword to the child in his arms. The child accepted it as if it was second nature to him, holding it in his arms as if it were precious. Freeing his other hand, Qi Fengge brought his hand down on Wu Wenguang's head with a light slap.

Wu Wenguang's eyes went round. He'd assumed that the man would kill him, but a moment later, his terror transformed into extreme rage. "You dared to destroy my martial arts?!"

Qi Fengge said, "The two of you wish to eat people," Qi Fengge said. "But since you were unsuccessful this time, I've destroyed your martial arts so that you can't commit more evils in the future."

As he spoke, he moved to destroy Ji Chunzhai's martial arts as well when an airy chuckle drifted in from outside. "He's a mediocre martial artist. Only his sword skills are somewhat acceptable. As Sect Leader Qi has severed the tendons of his hand, that should be enough. Why do something unnecessary?"

A cool breeze blew forth along with those words, shoving Ji Chunzhai back several steps and causing Qi Fengge to miss.

The boy's eyes went round as he watched the young man who'd seemingly appeared from nowhere suddenly begin exchanging blows with the priest who was carrying him, their robes flapping and dancing. He lay between the two and watched, thoroughly dazzled. He couldn't tell at all what either of them were doing. A short while later, both men suddenly separated and landed solidly upon the ground.

The young man spoke his praise. "Sect Leader Qi is carrying a child and his sword unsheathed, yet I couldn't gain the upper hand at all. If not for this child dragging you down, we could have dueled to our heart's content."

"When I was around Yan-gongzi's age," said Qi Fengge, "I didn't possess even half of his strength. With time, the new generation will replace the old. The world's jianghu will depend on your generation then."

"Xuandu Mountain is the world's foremost Daoist Sect, yet you're stuck in your old ways, focused only on guarding your gates. What's the point of your number one position?" He snorted. "Even I'm feeling dreary for your sake!"

Yan Wushi was an incredibly handsome man, his features almost beautiful, but he carried about him a sense of sky-high arrogance. This made his radiance even more awe-inspiring, and even more exceptionally forceful.

Qi Fengge smiled. "To each their own."

He'd already realized that this man's personality, combined with his astounding talents, would likely make him a character capable of shaking the world.

The path to a buddha, the path to a demon. Only a fine line separated the two. This person was from the demonic discipline, so naturally he couldn't become a buddha. But right now, the Buddhist discipline was embroiled in their interests that involved the courts and mortal world, so they weren't that noble and virtuous either. With the addition of this type of character, these tumultuous times would only grow more troubled, and the common folk would only suffer more.

Qi Fengge inwardly sighed.

Yan Wushi said, "In the past, Ji Chunzhai was somewhat involved with Cui Youwang. Since I owe Cui Youwang a favor, I'd like him to keep his life."

Qi Fengge nodded. He had no intentions of making things difficult. "I've already severed his tendons. If he can guarantee that he won't attack innocent civilians in the future, I won't do anything more to him."

By now, from their conversation, Ji Chunzhai had already realized just who Qi Fengge was. In his view, he and Wu Wenguang were truly beyond unfortunate, otherwise why would they run into the world's strongest martial artist? Though they couldn't afford to provoke him, they could at least hide from him. They were already lucky to be able to escape with their lives; how were they still in a position to bargain? He immediately swore an oath to the heavens, pledging that he'd never again take another person's life.

Yan Wushi gave a faint smile. "Many thanks to Sect Leader Qi for saving me this face. If some day one of your disciples ends up in trouble, Huanyue Sect will also offer them our help—once."

How could the disciples of the world's foremost Daoist sect end up in trouble so easily? But Yan Wushi had said it in a way that made it sound completely reasonable.

Qi Fengge was a bit astonished. "I heard from them just now that there were three demonic sects, and I was confused as to when a new one had appeared. So Yan-gongzi has already established his own sect. Congratulations."

Yan Wushi had never known the meaning of the word "modesty." Hearing this, he nodded. "Many thanks."

With no common topics, there was no point in further conversation. Qi Fengge and Yan Wushi were chance acquaintances with no relationship to speak of. Qi Fengge looked up at the first glimmers of dawn, then made to leave, still carrying the boy.

"If there's a chance in the future, I will definitely come to seek guidance from Sect Leader Qi." Yan Wushi sent a leisurely glance at the child in his arms. "The boy has remarkable aptitude. If Sect Leader Qi doesn't wish to accept him as his disciple, why not hand him to me?"

Qi Fengge raised a brow. After spending a night with the boy, he'd already grown very fond of him and harbored thoughts of taking him in as a disciple. Now that someone was trying to take what he loved, he was naturally displeased. "There's no need for Sect Leader Yan to go to the trouble of meddling. Farewell."

"Take care, Sect Leader Qi."

Yan Wushi smiled, his hands behind his back as he watched Qi Fengge leave. Then he withdrew his smile as his gaze fell on the pair who'd tried to attack Qi Fengge.

Meeting his frigid gaze, the pair felt their hearts chill. Though this man was young, all demonic practitioners knew of Yan Wushi's name. No one dared to look down on him.

Meanwhile, Qi Fengge carried the boy out of the temple. After a night of fierce gales, the wind had finally stopped. A faint radiance peeked through the layers of clouds, as if promising that this coming day would be a brightly shining one.

Seeing the way the boy was gripping his lapels, his gaze rapt and unblinking, Qi Fengge couldn't help but laugh. "Fear not; I won't abandon you. Would you like to go back with me? I live atop the mountain. You'll have many shixiong and shidi around your age there, and you can accept me as your master and call me Shizun."

"Shizun!" The child crisply addressed him without the slightest hesitation.

"Good boy." Qi Fengge patted his head. "I almost forgot to ask. Do you still remember your name?"

"Shen..."

"Shen and?"

The child thought hard, finger in his mouth. "Qiao..."

Qi Fengge was incredibly patient. "Which 'Qiao'?"

The child shook his head, bewildered. He was still young, and he'd suffered through a long period of wartime chaos, so he didn't remember.

Qi Fengge put him down. With his arm around the boy, he dragged his sword across the ground, using the sheath to write the character, "Qiao."

"Then we'll use this one. How about it?"

The boy's expression was perplexed and conflicted. "Too hard..."

Qi Fengge laughed. "It's not hard. Here, I'll teach you."

He held the boy's hand and showed him each and every stroke. The character "Qiao" was etched there upon the sand, straight and neat.

"'The hundred gods does he placate, the peaks and rivers all partake.' In the future, I hope you'll become someone like the peaks and summits, a man broad in both mind and heart."

The Past

A CERTAIN NUMBER OF YEARS AGO, when Yan Wushi wasn't yet Yan Wushi, he was called Xie Ling. At that time, though Xie Ling held the radiance of the Chen Commandery's Xie family, he wasn't a particularly popular person within the Xie family. Many of them looked down on him behind his back, yet because all who'd attempted provoking him to his face had received a thorough lesson, none would dare. He disliked the Xie family, and they disliked him as well. Both sides loathed the sight of the other.

The Xie family thought that someone like Yan Wushi, who held no respect for the law, the gods, his parents, nor his superiors, would eventually drag the Xie family into a situation beyond redemption. This noble family of the Chen Commandery had suffered many setbacks; though the clan itself was still there, they'd long lost the dignity they'd possessed in the past. In these troubled times, they could only protect themselves by being exceedingly careful.

Yan Wushi thought that the Xie family was too small, without the room to foster his talents. He scoffed at their behavior, like quails cowering away. He found it utterly intolerable—in his eyes, the Xie family would be finished sooner or later if they continued on this path.

The Xie family couldn't accommodate him, and he also had no interest in becoming a savior who'd weep for their sake. So Yan Wushi left.

Within the sword trial circles of Jiangnan, there was a grand martial arts conference. Though there were no top-ranked grandmasters in attendance, there was no lack of rising stars, tender sprouts who'd just begun peeking out, from all sects. Among them, there was no lack of favored successors, or head disciples from major sects. Decades from now, the jianghu would invariably belong to the people present here.

As Yan Wushi was passing by the location, he coincidentally encountered this conference and thus entered to watch. No one paid any attention to this nobody; though this youth's fair face was enough to draw their gazes, establishing yourself in the jianghu required ability, not appearance.

To Yan Wushi, this was a new frontier. Before this, all he'd seen were the noble families related to Chen Commandery's Xie family. The clans in decline, and those just emerging, had to vie for status and voice; even as they suppressed each other, they were forced to support each other as well.

Above those noble families, there was the imperial court that changed dynasties again and again, along with an emperor who extolled peace through singing and dancing. Below those noble families lay the territories separately governed by the north and the south, along with the hearts of starving people, stretching for thousands of miles.

Just like a vast river, the noble families were a gulf that divided heaven from earth. As for the martial arts world, that was another world entirely, beyond the natural moat that encompassed all this.

He'd thought himself a passing guest—never had he expected to become the main character.

Yan Wushi's stepping stone to fame was the "Thunderclap Sword," Cheng Renmei. He was a swordsman from Qingcheng Mountain, the head disciple of the Chunyang Monastery Master. With his talent and reputation, it was highly likely that he'd inherit the position of the Chunyang Monastery Master in the future.

Within the Jiangnan sword trial circles, he'd indeed achieved five victories without any losses. The opponents he'd faced were all top experts from the younger generation, and each and every one of them had been young dragons and phoenixes with outstanding martial skills. Thus, the Thunderclap Sword had built his own reputation and ability on top of theirs.

The reputation of Chunyang Monastery on Qingcheng Mountain was also one that resounded as loudly as thunder, shocking everyone who heard it. They even compared the Thunderclap Sword to the likes of Qi Fengge and Cui Youwang, saying that in ten years, there'd be a position for Cheng Renmei within the world's top ten rankings. The talk grew increasingly exaggerated. No matter how modestly Cheng Renmei acted, he'd ultimately still benefit from it.

But there were always people who refused to recognize the obvious and insisted on becoming a roadblock. Yan Wushi was that kind of person.

At that time, everyone looked at this arrogant young man, and for a while, the scene was as quiet as a grave. It wasn't because he'd crushed everyone with his presence, but because no one had expected someone to be so ignorant as to come forward and provoke Cheng Renmei even after his demonstrations of strength.

"Where did this young hero come from?" Cheng Renmei asked. "Which sect do you belong to; what weapon do you use?"

Yan Wushi was empty-handed. What weapon was there? He looked left and right, his gaze shifting from a spirited young man to a young girl who was an obvious novice. Men, and especially hand-some men, undoubtedly had a much easier time borrowing things from women than they did from men.

"Could you lend me your sword?" he asked the girl.

His tone was flat and indifferent, but after being glanced at by those eyes, she somehow found herself unfastening her sword and handing it over.

Yan Wushi smiled at her, then weighed the longsword in his hand as he said to Cheng Renmei, "Then I'll use the sword."

Even his weapon had been obtained impromptu? How could this madman be fit to be an opponent?

Cheng Renmei was indignant, and so he decided to teach Yan Wushi a lesson.

"Then please make your moves. I'll let you have three."

Yan Wushi didn't restrain himself either. He drew his sword and flew forward, then struck at his opponent three times.

And with these three taps, Cheng Renmei found himself almost breaking his word. Once the third strike came, he launched a counterattack—at least he'd managed to persist. The sword tip of the opponent's sword had already touched his face, poised to pierce his brow. He could no longer keep up his attitude of modesty and quickly slashed back with his sword. The two blades met and crossed, emitting a deafening clang.

Surrounded by spectators who couldn't even follow the scene, the two of them exchanged over two hundred moves. In the end, Cheng Renmei won by a small margin: the match finished with Yan Wushi's sword being sent flying.

Cheng Renmei had won. That was the natural conclusion. He came from an extraordinary sect, and he was supremely talented. He'd already stepped halfway over the threshold to becoming a grandmaster, having glimpsed the supreme martial arts upon the path.

But the problem arose here: Cheng Renmei was that strong, yet he'd only eked out a small victory over a pure nobody. Over time, once the other party became proficient with swords and his internal energy grew more profound, would this tiny guarantee of victory still exist?

Cheng Renmei couldn't conceal his shock. He couldn't help but ask, "Which sect is this young hero from?"

The fellow holding the sword thought for a moment—it seemed like he was pondering his name. Finally, he said, "Yan Wushi. I have no sect."

Cheng Renmei didn't believe him at all. Though his swordsmanship was unfamiliar and stiff, great skill lay within, almost to the point of simplicity. True ingenuity was unassuming. How could someone achieve this without the guidance of a master?

Yan Wushi saw that Cheng Renmei didn't believe him, but he didn't deign to explain further either. He tossed the sword back to its original owner, then said to Cheng Renmei, "Next time...I'll use a different sword. For our fight."

The "different sword" he spoke of was Tai'e, which he hadn't had the time to bring, having left home in a hurry this time.

The bewildered Cheng Renmei hesitated, then gave a nod. "I'll be waiting for Yan-shaoxia at Qingcheng Mountain."

However, Cheng Renmei never had the opportunity to fight Yan Wushi again. Despite this, Yan Wushi's name truly spread to every corner of the world due to his battle with Cui Youwang after joining Riyue Sect.

Cheng Renmei could have never imagined that the astonishingly talented genius who'd appeared from nowhere, a youth whose background and sect were unknown, would abandon the righteous path of his own volition and join the demonic discipline.

Thinking about how the other person's every move had been filled with grace and elegance, Cheng Renmei subconsciously came up with all sorts of difficulties Yan Wushi may have faced to justify his actions. But in truth, Yan Wushi joining the demonic discipline involved no difficulties, nor was there an inside story. He'd joined simply because he liked the demonic sect's atmosphere.

That's right—Yan Wushi took to the demonic sect like a fish to water, or a bird to trees. He felt that the demonic sect had no constraints, that he was free there and could do as he pleased. He was allowed to do things most people found disagreeable, and even some things that confused the other demonic practitioners.

There were many people who disliked him in the demonic discipline. Cui Youwang's disciple Sang Jingxing had longed again and again to make Yan Wushi disappear from this world, but in the end, not only did he fail to kill him, he'd driven himself halfway to death from rage.

But what truly established Yan Wushi's footing within the demonic discipline was Huang Yangfeng's death. Though most people in the jianghu saw Riyue Sect as the demonic sect, its internal factions were no different from all the other sects of the world: they fought hard with each other, attacking anyone who disagreed with their views. At most they were just more blatant and bloody about it.

Huang Yangfeng had been an elder within Riyue Sect—he held an incredibly powerful position within the sect, second only to the sect leader Cui Youwang. And, naturally, he hadn't held this position because of his age and qualifications, nor was it even entirely due to his martial arts. Rather, it was his methods and his brain. To put it bluntly, the man's ways were cruel and savage, and few other people could compare. From time to time he'd come up with unexpected ideas, leaving Cui Youwang with no choice but to rely on him.

Naturally, his martial prowess was also outstanding within the demonic discipline.

Sang Jingxing had never fought Huang Yangfeng, but he'd believed himself and this old fogey to be evenly matched.

And yet such a person had died at the hands of Yan Wushi.

"Why did you kill him?"

By the time Shen Qiao asked this question, it'd already been a great many years since the incident.

His shimei, Gu Hengbo, had returned, and Shen Qiao's birthday was close. Though he didn't intend to do anything grand for it, he couldn't stop Xuandu Mountain in their desire to have some fun. Even Yang Jian, who was far away in Chang'an, had somehow learned the news and sent people to bring many congratulatory gifts. He'd even had his eldest son, Yang Yong, personally bring them up the mountain to offer his congratulations. As such, no matter how badly Shen Qiao wanted to keep a low profile, it was impossible.

However, while the others were handling arrangements, the main character of the day had actually run to hide in the back mountain and relax. The person who'd encouraged him to do so was sitting opposite Shen Qiao, lazily drinking wine as he placed a weiqi piece.

"Naturally, I had to establish my prestige," said Yan Wushi lazily. "I entered the demonic discipline as a person with no connections, without any master above me or backer behind me. I was alone, and everyone wished to stomp on me and take me as their disciple. Even Cui Youwang asked me if I wished to acknowledge him as my master."

"You rejected him."

"If I didn't reject him, wouldn't I have to change my name?"

Shen Qiao couldn't help but laugh. It would indeed be terribly awkward for Yan Wushi to change his name to "Yan Youshi."[8]

"I heard from Shizun once that Cui Youwang lived up to his name—he was also an egotistical man. How did you manage to enter the demonic discipline after rejecting him?"

Yan Wushi narrowed his eyes, and his gaze turned dangerous. "A-Qiao, you said 'also.' What's that supposed to mean?"

Shen Qiao didn't reply.

"'Also,' which means 'as well.' Are you saying that I'm the same as Cui Youwang—egotistical, with no conception of the vastness of heaven and earth?"

Shen Qiao was just about to nod when he saw Yan Wushi suddenly leaning toward him, reaching out to grab him by the nape of his neck, roiling with murderous intent. Startled, he subconsciously tried to back away, raising his hand and sweeping at him. In an instant, they'd exchanged dozens of blows.

"All right, I'm just playing with you," said Yan Wushi as he withdrew his hand.

At those words, Shen Qiao also stopped.

But he didn't expect that Yan Wushi would grab his wrist right after, then take the chance to kiss him while his guard was down.

It was a long, lingering kiss, to the point that Shen Qiao, the simple and honest man he was, almost couldn't take it anymore. He wanted to escape but couldn't; their breaths were short and their passions high as their lips met again and again.

They'd disturbed the weiqi board somewhat with their knees and clothing, and Daoist Master Shen caught a glimpse of it. He was about to speak up to stop them, but the moment he opened his

---

8   晏有师, "Youshi" means "has a master," as opposed to Wushi's meaning of "has no master."

mouth, Yan Wushi's tongue took the opportunity to invade even more deeply. Even the skin around his collarbone was stained with a dark blush. His breaths came in heaves, beyond his control.

Yan Wushi didn't forget to tease him. "If it'd been someone else who was full of malice, they'd never let you off so easily."

The person with the most malice is you!

With difficulty, Shen Qiao managed to push him away, gasping for breath, and he couldn't help but defend himself. "You only succeeded because you took advantage of my lack of guard toward you."

The pieces on the board were in disarray, but Yan Wushi remembered each and every move and replaced each piece once more, calm and leisurely.

"So what if I did? The means aren't important, only the result." Yan Wushi raised his eyebrow, his expression screaming "you can't do anything to me." "But you're right," he said. "I'm just as egotistical as Cui Youwang, to the point that I know nothing about where the heavens and earth are whatsoever. These types of people all share a characteristic: when they meet someone supremely talented or strong, not only will they not mind any discourtesies, they'll even hope to gain a new opponent."

Shen Qiao felt that Yan Wushi wasn't so much talking about how great men like Cui Youwang would appreciate other great men as he was simply praising himself as a heavenly genius.

"Then how was this connected to you killing Huang Yangfeng?" he asked.

"Huang Yangfeng was very close to Sang Jingxing," Yan Wushi replied. "They even shared their women with each other. Sang Jingxing wanted to get rid of me, but he didn't want to rashly take action himself, so of course he had to borrow Huang Yangfeng for it.

Huang Yangfeng gifted me a woman—but if I slept with her, I'd be poisoned by the gu."[9]

"Gu?" When he heard this last word, Shen Qiao was finally a little astonished. "Love gu?"

"Heartbreak gu. It requires a special elixir that can alleviate the suffering you feel when it activates."

Shen Qiao understood. If Yan Wushi fell into that trap, someone else would be holding his life in their hands.

"But that woman was a demonic practitioner? And you killed her?"

Yan Wushi clicked his tongue. "A-Qiao, oh A-Qiao, I've finally seen through you. Having heard about that vicious gu poison, not only are you not concerned about me, you worry about an outsider instead. Could you be looking forward to my death? Will it be easier for you to cuddle up with some other random person that way?"

Shen Qiao pretended that he hadn't heard any of Yan Wushi's nonsense and simply inquired about the woman's fate a second time.

Yan Wushi sneered. "I know you've always felt soft and tender toward the weak and downtrodden. However, that woman was also a demonic practitioner. Since Huang Yangfeng had brought her there, of course it wasn't only due to her beauty. She was also well versed in the path of harmony and in pair cultivation."

Shen Qiao's heart thumped. "That girl...could she have been Yuan Xiuxiu?"

"She was Yuan Xiuxiu's shimei. Her name was Yang Yun."

"What happened afterward?"

"Afterward," Yan Wushi said lazily, "while they were holding their meeting, I went right up to their doors and killed Huang Yangfeng in full view of everyone."

---

9   蛊. A type of poison, said to be crafted by sealing venomous animals in a jar and letting them prey on each other.

He still vividly remembered the onlookers' gobsmacked expressions—especially Sang Jingxing, because Sang Jingxing had also been very fond of Yang Yun. Even when Huang Yangfeng had wanted to gift her away, Sang Jingxing was quite reluctant. However, he'd never expected that Yan Wushi would not only fail to take the bait, he'd actually be audacious enough to kill Huang Yangfeng directly.

Huang Yangfeng wasn't some piece of meat on the chopping board that anyone could hack apart. Though he wasn't as strong as Cui Youwang, he was still a top-ranked martial expert—yet Yan Wushi had disregarded all that and simply butchered him, right in front of all of them!

Sang Jingxing had been stunned and held some misgivings—but in the end, he hadn't taken action. Others had their own axes to grind, so they'd really just watched as Huang Yangfeng was killed.

After this battle, Yan Wushi's name spread far and wide within the demonic discipline. Whenever a demonic practitioner wished to provoke him again, they'd have to first consider if their skull was as hard as Huang Yangfeng's.

And another little interlude had happened after.

Though Yang Yun had failed to complete her mission of poisoning Yan Wushi with the gu, she seemed to have fallen in love and insisted on following him.

"She said I was lonely." When he said this, Yan Wushi's face showed no traces of lamentation at all. Rather, his expression showed that he found this terribly bizarre and hilarious.

Yang Yun had said to Yan Wushi, "Wherever you drift, you're alone. Even if you're part of the demonic discipline, you need someone who knows your heart, who remembers your birthday and the things you like. Who remembers your seasons and where you wish to go."

Shen Qiao gave his assessment: "They're very touching, romantic lines."

It wasn't that the demonic discipline had no sincere people whatsoever; rather, most of them just wouldn't easily show their sincerity.

He suddenly thought of Bai Rong.

Yan Wushi gave a slight snort. He must have noticed what Shen Qiao was thinking because he reached out to grasp his chin, forcing his thoughts back.

"Then, do you think I'm lonely?"

"Even if everyone else in the world became lonely, Yan Wushi would not." Shen Qiao slapped his hand aside. "All human hearts are unpredictable, while the martial path is endless. To you, such things are the same as eternal entertainment."

The man known as Yan Wushi had never needed anyone's approval.

And as for like-minded people who walked the same path as him, asking the same questions? He needed them even less.

"Sect Leader Shen knows me well." Yan Wushi laughed. "I'm indeed not lonely, but I've changed my mind."

Shen Qiao didn't understand. In the past, Yan Wushi would have never taken anyone's birthday to heart. Even when it came to his own, he considered it unimportant. As long as he desired it so, any day could be a birthday.

But from start to end, Shen Qiao was different.

Yan Wushi knew everything about this man as well as the back of his hand, but he still wanted to explore him further. It would never be enough. Even Shen Qiao's birthday had become something worthy of special attention to him. "It's almost the first day of autumn."

"To be honest, even I can't remember my true birthday." Shen Qiao held no attachments to such things. The first day of autumn was when Shizun had found him, so it later became his birthday.

Shen Qiao liked the meaning behind the day, but it wasn't because of his birthday. It was because, from that day forth, his destiny had become unequivocally intertwined with that of Xuandu Mountain and his shizun.

As for Yan Wushi, originally, the first day of autumn had been something plain and unremarkable, yet now it'd become the day in the year most special to him.

The same was true for everyone on Xuandu Mountain.

A faint clamor came from outside, at first distant but growing closer. It must have been the disciples calling them for dinner.

"The first day of autumn. It's a good day," said Yan Wushi.

Shen Qiao said nothing as he placed his final weiqi piece.

New Year's Eve

YAN WUSHI RARELY DREAMED. But on this New Year's Eve—perhaps because it was his birthday tomorrow—he dreamed a rare dream.

Within the dream, it was also New Year's Eve. He was walking on a long street, alone. It was almost midnight, and the crackle of firecrackers could be heard from each house, unceasingly. From time to time, happy chatter and laughter came from the other side of the courtyard wall. The candlelight flickered warmly while the cold moon stood on guard, waiting for the New Year.

But these hints of liveliness had nothing to do with him.

Yan Wushi himself was very aware that he was dreaming. He even knew that this was the year when he'd left the Xie family and began wandering the jianghu.

The word "wandering" was terribly apt here. This journey that took him throughout the land had been for the purpose of broadening his knowledge and experience. He was in no hurry to establish a name for himself.

But it was the unknowingly planted willow that brought shade. When he'd injured and defeated the Yang family's three brothers, the "River-crossing Dragons," then made a caustic comment to them afterward, his words made one of them so angry that he'd suddenly grown ill and died. Yan Wushi's mouth became famous in the jianghu before his martial arts did.

Gradually, many people in the jianghu came to know that Yan Wushi—this young man who bore a strange name—could be fought with, but one absolutely shouldn't attempt to provoke him or anger him with your words. If you fought, getting injured and dying was just the consequence of being weaker. However, if you provoked him verbally, you'd only end up raging half to death—you'd never be able to gain any advantage over him in a battle of words.

Couplet scrolls and fortune characters had been freshly pasted on the doors of many houses.

Regardless of whether one had money, one had to return home for the New Year. Though the end of the year could be difficult, this had always been the case. Even for the wanderers who were drifting far from their hometown, if they could manage to make it home in time, they'd always return to reunite with their loved ones.

From the moment Yan Wushi left home, though, he'd broken off all connection with his old family. Henceforth, his surname was only Yan, not Xie.

Even right now, when he was walking alone on the streets, his clothes flimsy as he drifted like rootless duckweed, Yan Wushi didn't feel lonely or unhappy in the slightest. Instead, he listened to the noises from each household with great interest.

Some had three generations living together, with the harmonious sounds of the grandfather spinning a top for his grandson to play with. Some were arguing; it seemed like the father was disciplining his son while the mother came forth to protect him. The parents began arguing as the child bawled, and now everything was in chaos.

And some were young couples calculating their spendings for the year, almost unable to make ends meet. They longed to break their copper coins into multiple pieces for their expenses—disagreements arose, and they quarreled quietly for a while. Before long, the wife began to sob in understanding while the husband sighed and pulled her into his arms to comfort her. Though it was a heartwarming scene, the fact remained that they were newlyweds yet also impoverished. Their situation would persist, unchanging—as the saying went, for poor couples, everything was a cause for lament.

As these subtle sounds reached Yan Wushi's ears, the slight curve of his lips suddenly froze, and he stopped in his tracks next to a manor with green walls and red roof tiles.

Two lanterns had been hung high, and the words "Hong Residence" came into view—gilded and set against a black background. One could see how well-off the household was.

Behind the door, it was far too quiet.

It was said that wealthy families were particular about many things, but that was no explanation for the complete silence behind these gates. Besides, this Hong residence still paled in comparison to that of Jiangnan's Xie family.

Ding.

A very faint sound. Most ordinary people would have a hard time noticing it.

But Yan Wushi heard it. That was the final sound a sword tip made as it entered its sheath.

Drip, drip.

This wasn't the sound of rain. How could it be? It wasn't raining.

That was blood. The sound of blood droplets hitting the ground.

Yan Wushi narrowed his eyes.

He quietly entered—naturally, by vaulting over the wall.

All was silent, save for the rustle of falling leaves.

The stench of blood spread from within the house, impossible to conceal, and assaulted his nostrils.

This wasn't an ordinary murder but a planned massacre.

He pushed open the unlatched gates. Inside, around a dozen people were sprawled on the ground: men, women, the elderly, children. All of them faced upward, their eyes wide open in death.

Any traces of the killer had already vanished.

It seemed like the culprit was another martial expert. Just now, when Yan Wushi heard the click of a weapon entering its sheath, the other party had detected him in turn and left straight away.

Of all the corpses on the ground, only one was still slightly breathing—even if it was almost inaudible, a mere feeble wisp. If he did something now, the person could be saved.

But why should he involve himself in something unrelated to him?

Yan Wushi looked across the room, following the faint sound of breathing. Beneath the body of an old woman, there was indeed a youth there, still alive. Even without approaching, Yan Wushi could see that this person was on the verge of death.

If Yan Wushi chose to withdraw and ignore him, this youth would undoubtedly die. And if Yan Wushi chose to reach out and help him, he might still be able to live. But why should Yan Wushi save him? Was anything about this youth worth him saving?

As if he'd sensed Yan Wushi's attention, the youth with the bloodstained face struggled to open his eyes, his lips trembling as he said something.

Save me...beg you...martial arts...fortunes...

Yan Wushi understood.

What the youth meant to say was that the Hong family had amassed a hidden fortune, and they also possessed secret cultivation manuals that no one else knew about. Because of this, they'd drawn the covetous glances of the evildoers who'd massacred the entire Hong family. But in the end, they hadn't found anything. As long as Yan Wushi was willing to save him, this boy was willing to give it all to him.

Yan Wushi smiled faintly. Things had become even more interesting.

The youth looked at this smile of Yan Wushi's, and he too felt as if he had hope to survive.

The scenery within this dream wasn't a coherent construction. These were things that had already happened, and sometimes the order of events would fragment or jump around.

In the end, Yan Wushi really had saved that one lucky survivor of the Hong household, Hong Wen. He was the eldest grandson of the Hong family's fourth-generation master, and immensely talented. Ever since he was young, he'd been the pride of his family. But now the entire clan had been wiped out, leaving only him. If Yan Wushi hadn't just happened to pass by and channel some timely true qi into him, he too would have left to see the Hong family's ancestors.

But this story would not develop into a tale about repaying kindness with virtue, or evil with vengeance. Three days later, Hong Wen left Yan Wushi's place without a farewell, his whereabouts unknown.

Three months later, at the grand martial arts conference, Hong Wen made a shocking appearance. To the other members of the jianghu, he accused Yan Wushi, who was also present, of taking advantage of the Hong family's tragedy to steal his family's martial techniques and treasures.

There, the dream came abruptly to an end, and Yan Wushi woke up.

His forehead itched a little. He opened his eyes and saw a frond of willow leaves swaying above his head. And the one holding those willow leaves...

A deer's face loomed close, with Yan Wushi's face reflected within its glossy eyes. Yan Wushi sneered a little, then pushed the deer's head aside.

Since the deer posed no threat, he'd failed to notice it for a moment. The fawn was naturally completely oblivious to Yan Wushi scoffing at it. It swallowed the willow leaves it'd been chewing, then spat out the twigs. Right as Yan Wushi was picking up a twig to poke the fawn's ear, Shen Qiao returned.

Daoist Master Shen's sleeves were rolled up, and he carried a large bamboo basket in his arms. He didn't have a bit of the poise expected of a sect leader and martial expert.

Yan Wushi looked up just as he was about to put down the basket—it was filled completely with pears.

"It's been a poor harvest for the pear farmer at the foot of the mountain this year on account of the heavy rains, so I'm purchasing some to help him."

Shen Qiao had taken the initiative to explain before Yan Wushi could even ask. As he spoke, he casually took the willow twig away, lest the fawn suffer more.

"Due to his overflowing kindness, our Sect Leader Shen always loves doing pointless things." Disapproving, Yan Wushi stood and stretched. "Even if you purchase this basket of pears, he won't earn much more. And he'll think that he has a crutch to rely on—when natural disasters come again in the future, he won't think about working harder but hope for a solution from you instead."

He offhandedly picked up one of the pears from the basket and turned it over. As expected, it was rotten. Then he picked up another one from deeper down. Again, there was a small, blemished area. As he picked and chose, around nine-tenths of the pears were spoiled, and even the good ones didn't look too impressive.

Yan Wushi raised his eyebrow at Shen Qiao, the expression saying, *See? I wasn't wrong.*

Shen Qiao smiled. "When I took this basket, I already knew that these pears were spoiled," he said. "I know the farmer who sells them. He has a son and a daughter, and his wife recently passed away. It isn't easy to make a living. Since I can help, I helped him."

This was where the two of them differed.

Shen Qiao had always been this way, and Yan Wushi knew this already.

Human hearts were unpredictable, and Yan Wushi delighted in this fact. He often made bets with Shen Qiao, most of which he won. But every single time, Shen Qiao was willing to bet. He didn't know if it was because Shen Qiao was simply too stubborn or because he really did firmly believe that everyone was good at heart.

Yan Wushi placed the pears back into the basket. "What should we bet this time? And Sect Leader Shen shouldn't be too stingy."

Shen Qiao shook his head. "I'm not betting this time."

"Afraid now?"

Shen Qiao thought, *I'm afraid that you'll come up with some new method to retaliate against me even harder if you lose. With how vengeful you are, Sect Leader Yan, you're always able to concoct twisted ideas that no one else can, so there's no way to guard against you.*

But ultimately, these words were too difficult for him to say because if he enraged or embarrassed Yan Wushi, the unfortunate one would always end up being Shen Qiao.

Yan Wushi snorted a laugh, but he showed no intentions of persisting.

"Speaking of which, I had a dream just now about some old events. They're very interesting, and they pertain to the human heart."

"If you can call them interesting, then you must not have suffered any losses."

"Oh, this time, you're wrong," said Yan Wushi. "Not only did I lose, I lost big."

Then he began talking about that time within his past.

When the story reached the point of the conference and he was telling Shen Qiao about how Hong Wen had suddenly accused him, Yan Wushi became exactly like one of those frustrating tea house storytellers—he suddenly stopped, and there was that loathsome sense of "To find out what happens next, please listen to the next installment."

But Shen Qiao knew that Yan Wushi wouldn't stop at a climax for no reason. If he was stopping here, that meant an unexpected twist had occurred.

To think that even the young and reckless Yan Wushi had once stumbled due to rescuing others.

Shen Qiao thought for a moment. "After you saved him, did you search the Hong family's manor?"

"I did, but I didn't find anything," said Yan Wushi. "There was a hidden room inside the study in the main courtyard, but it'd already been opened, and there wasn't anything inside. Everything had probably been taken away already."

Shen Qiao furrowed his brow. "So did you just let yourself be condemned in front of everyone, and allow public opinion to twist the truth?"

No, Yan Wushi was absolutely not this kind of person. He'd destroy Hong Wen's reputation before the latter could join up with others and attack him.

Could it be…

Shen Qiao blurted out, "That Hong Wen conspired with outsiders against his own family?!"

"I didn't expect Sect Leader Shen would manage to think of this, with the way he always assumes the best of people," Yan Wushi mocked him.

The entire Hong family had met with tragic fates. When even Hong Wen's uncle Hong Tao, a first-rate martial artist, had been unable to survive, how could Hong Wen have managed it?

With Hong Wen's identity, combined with his youth and energy, the killer would have certainly focused on him the moment something went wrong. The killer had even made sure to murder women and children, each and every one. How could they have let Hong Wen live? Surely they wouldn't deliberately leave a survivor and witness who could cause them a great deal of trouble in the future?

When Yan Wushi had discovered that Hong Wen was still alive, he'd also realized this logical flaw.

The killer couldn't have purposely spared Hong Wen, and Hong Wen had indeed been alive. Therefore, even if Yan Wushi hadn't happened to pass by and enter just in time to lend a hand, Hong Wen could have survived.

Which was to say, in the case of this massacre, Hong Wen was suspected of conspiring with the murderer in harming his own family.

That made the entire thing even more interesting.

Despite knowing that it all might have been a conspiracy, Yan Wushi had still chosen to save Hong Wen.

"After Hong Wen woke, he left without bidding farewell because he thought I was only a green and kindhearted person. He never expected that I'd follow after him and see the murderer with whom he'd conspired to have his family killed."

Yan Wushi recounted this in a leisurely fashion. He remembered these events especially clearly—he'd seen countless examples of human treachery within his lifetime, but this event was the first he'd encountered after entering the jianghu, which also just happened to confirm his original beliefs. Ever since then, his demonic core had grown increasingly stable, which greatly helped his martial arts.

Though Hong Wen was the pride of his family, he carried a burdensome secret. He was secretly in love with his own younger sister, but because they were related by blood, his wish could never come true. Instead, he'd been denounced when he attempted to bring it up to his mother.

If the matter had ended there, then nothing else might have happened. Unfortunately, his sister's fiancé was also from a famous family within the jianghu, and not only was he handsome, his martial prowess also surpassed Hong Wen's. When comparing the two, even if one cast aside Hong Wen's shameful thoughts, did he have anything that could match up to this man?

Hong Wen had been pampered since childhood. When he wanted the wind, he got it. When he wanted the rain, he got that too. How could he tolerate the gap between them? His wish could never come true, and his martial arts refused to progress. As the flames of jealousy burned higher and higher, they gradually twisted his mind, completely transforming it into a blazing inner demon.

When inner demons were born, misfortune lay only a step away.

The opportunity soon arrived.

While Hong Wen was training outside, he'd encountered a fellow martial artist with the last name of Cui. As he was the tenth son, they called him Cui-shilang. Hong Wen and Cui-shilang became friends straight away, and they regretted that they hadn't met sooner. They grew so close that all they were missing was a vow of brotherhood. There was nothing the two of them couldn't talk about, and Hong Wen even confided some of his secret to him while drinking. Cui-shilang had consoled Hong Wen, saying that he could help fulfill Hong Wen's wish.

There must have been magic within Cui-shilang's words, or perhaps Hong Wen had already harbored those twisted intentions in the first place. They laid down their plan: Cui-shilang would pretend to be a robber and kill the entire family, leaving Hong Wen's sister as the only survivor, then he could take her away. Henceforth, the woman known as Lady Hong would vanish from the world, and that sister would naturally find herself without any support, so Hong Wen could do as he wished.

But the plan went a little awry. On New Year's Eve, the younger sister, who'd been married off and had just returned to visit her parents, saw them being killed, and she ran straight over to take a slash for her mother. She died right there, and all of Hong Wen's conspiring went to waste.

However, Hong Wen had still gained something: the Hong family's wealth and martial arts, which from then on would naturally become his alone. He'd locked onto Yan Wushi, who'd "inadvertently" saved him, planning to pour all the blame onto this rube so that he could make a smooth return to the jianghu. That way, he could walk the jianghu with spotless hands.

Having listened up to this point, Shen Qiao couldn't help but frown. "This Cui-shilang," he said, "why do his actions sound so much like a demonic practitioner's?"

Yan Wushi was all smiles. "You guessed correctly. For that was your dear old acquaintance, Cui Youwang!"

Shen Qiao was speechless.

No matter what, Cui Youwang was still considered a grand-master of the demonic discipline. These acts of banditry didn't befit his standing much. But everyone had been young once. Besides, instigating and bewitching people were indeed the kinds of things demonic practitioners loved to do.

"Then how did you rid yourself of the suspicions?" he asked.

"What could a weak pushover of a young man like me have done, other than desperately plead my innocence?" Yan Wushi sighed. "Hong Wen had painted many pictures of his sister and hidden them within the secret room I mentioned before. There were all sorts of poses. I displayed them all in public."

One could imagine how Hong Wen must have reacted seeing all those paintings being unwrapped, one after another, right in front of him. Those hidden paintings that should have never seen the light of day...

Panic, rage, helplessness. He probably longed to kill Yan Wushi right then and there and destroy all those paintings.

But he'd been in full view of everyone. How could he have dared?

Yan Wushi then said, "Fortunately, I was completely clean and innocent, as the sun and moon could attest to. Even Cui Youwang was so moved, he came out to testify. He admitted that he'd been invited by Hong Wen to massacre the entire Hong family, and that it had nothing to do with me."

Shen Qiao could say nothing. With the kind of man Cui Youwang was... Even if you wiped his memory a hundred times, he'd never have performed an act of charity like this.

Yan Wushi met Sect Leader Shen's doubtful gaze with a small smile. "I made a trade deal with him."

Back then, Yan Wushi had received a set of martial arts techniques for pair cultivation. He personally looked down on that kind of path while Cui Youwang enjoyed it tirelessly, so they each took what they needed and thus got along straight away.

To Cui Youwang, Hong Wen had been merely a toy to amuse himself with. After he used him, he threw him away. Betraying a friend had nothing to do with it. Even if he admitted it in front of everyone, he could still walk away unscathed; no one could do anything to him.

The only unlucky one was Hong Wen.

And Hong Wen had even assumed Yan Wushi to be a weak, soft persimmon he could push around. He'd never imagined that the man he'd encountered was actually a great demon with boundless prospects.

As the saying went, all things had their weakness. Only evil people could torture other evil people.

Hesitantly, Shen Qiao said, "But I suddenly thought of a phrase."

Yan Wushi's smile turned dangerous. "I advise Sect Leader Shen to consider things carefully before speaking."

Naturally, Shen Qiao would follow good advice. He instantly clammed up.

It was a two-word phrase. If he said it out loud, he'd definitely offend this Sect Leader Yan, who was incredibly intolerant.

They were still talking when the pear farmer from the foot of the mountain showed up to visit Shen Qiao, having been led here by the Daoists from the sect.

"Daoist Master Shen, that clearly wasn't the basket I gave you!" The farmer was hunched over with his hands on his knees as he complained, his face soaked in sweat. "Why did you bring the spoiled ones here? No matter how I called out to you, you never looked back. Because of this I had to chase you the entire way, but I still couldn't catch up!"

He and the pear farmer were old acquaintances. "I already said, you can still sell the good basket and earn a little money," Shen Qiao said helplessly.

"I can't let your esteemed self suffer any losses either!" cried the pear farmer. "You already treat us so well. How could we complain, never mind take from you?! I've already left the good ones in your back kitchen. Give them to your disciples! If they're tasty, your esteemed self can simply buy more next year. I'll take the spoiled basket away. You must not do this in the future, or our hearts will never be able to rest!"

He didn't wait for Shen Qiao to reply, just slung his bamboo basket onto his back and left.

Shen Qiao watched the pear farmer go, then suddenly recalled something and turned to look at Yan Wushi. "I refused to bet just now because I was afraid you'd renege. So you should be thanking me now, shouldn't you?"

Yan Wushi was surprised. "My venerable self's word is as good as gold. Why would I renege? Since I lost, my venerable self will let Sect Leader Shen do as he wishes. I won't resist at all. Come."

He relaxed his limbs and opened his arms, adopting the pose of someone who was allowing a king to take as he pleased.

Shen Qiao just looked at him for a long moment.

"Pretend I said nothing."

Then he turned and left straight away, swift and decisive.

But then something suddenly tugged on his sleeve. Caught off guard, Shen Qiao stumbled back a little.

The fawn cocked its head, then idly wandered off.

Weibo's Mini Extras

MINI EXTRA ONE

IT WAS EVENING. Wind and snow pelted down, and the sky was dim.

All the passersby rushed into the roadside teahouse for shelter, desperately wishing that they could shrink even further inside and stop the bone-piercingly cold winds from brushing their skin.

Only one person continued to sit at the roadside, completely unperturbed. The teahouse owner walked over and advised him kindly, "The winds and snow are fearsome! This gentleman should take shelter inside!"

The man shook his head and sighed. "I'm afraid that they won't be able to find me when they arrive."

The owner was confused. "Who?"

The man shot him a glance. "My sweetheart."

So he was the infatuated type. No wonder the hair beneath his hood was completely white; was it because he missed his wife too much?

Sympathy immediately welled up within the teahouse owner, but then he noticed out of the corner of his eye that the tea within the cup the man was holding was actually still steaming with vapor.

The owner froze a little. For a moment he couldn't tell if the tea was so chilled it was spewing cold vapor or if really had managed to remain hot.

If it was the latter...

He couldn't help but shoot the man another glance. The profile beneath the hood was astonishingly handsome—nowhere near as old as he'd previously thought.

Before the owner could react, another horse came galloping swiftly along the official road from afar. The horse stopped by the teahouse, and the rider removed his hood before walking over.

It was a Daoist priest.

And it was a Daoist priest with the poise of an immortal, his features incomparably delicate and refined. *Looks like the gentleman is about to be disappointed,* the owner thought.

But unexpectedly, the man laughed, delighted. Then he fished out a small clay jar of wine from his lapels and waved to the Daoist. "Quick, A-Qiao, over here! I've warmed this wine to perfection using my own body! Have a sip to rid yourself of the chill!"

The teahouse owner was speechless.

MINI EXTRA TWO

IN HIS LIFE, the word "regret" didn't exist.

It'd been true that year he'd left the Xie family. And it'd been true when he'd changed his name to "Wushi." Later, when he battled Cui Youwang, it'd still been true.

The heavens and earth were vast, and he saw no lords, no fathers, and no masters.

The heavens and earth were vast, and no one had ever been able to leave a mark within his heart.

Shen Qiao wouldn't be that exception.

When he'd first met Shen Qiao, to Yan Wushi, he was only "Qi Fengge's disciple and pride." The lingering dissatisfaction he harbored from his duel with Qi Fengge from back then...perhaps he could resolve it through Shen Qiao.

But he quickly realized that he'd been mistaken.

Shen Qiao was only a blind man, with barely any martial arts left. If he were tossed onto the streets somewhere, no one would spare him a single copper. The former Xuandu Mountain sect leader was already finished.

Yan Wushi sneered in the depths of his heart as he contemplated this, full of malice.

During his life, Qi Fengge had been a hero of heroes, but his eye for disciples was truly nothing special. Since Shen Qiao couldn't be his opponent, then Yan Wushi could only make him his toy.

Being a sanctimonious sect leader, if his hands were stained with the blood of innocents, could he still retain his original pure and lofty self? Surely, it was impossible. At most, this was an amusing distraction with a foreseeable conclusion, Yan Wushi had thought.

Instantly, it became boring.

But he'd never thought that there'd come a time when he'd predict incorrectly. That blind man really managed to persevere, time and time again. He'd been faced with his martial siblings' betrayal, and as Yan Wushi looked at his expression, he almost thought that the man would cry. But Shen Qiao didn't.

"Everyone said that you are wrong, and you were betrayed by the ones you were closest to. Do you still not despair?" he'd asked Shen Qiao.

But the blind man hadn't answered. Instead he turned his head to face the unceasing drizzle outside the window, to face the beautiful withered flowers. But Yan Wushi knew that the man couldn't see any of it.

"There is nowhere for you to advance, and nowhere you can retreat. You're alone and surrounded on all sides. It'd be easier if you just died," Yan Wushi said lightly while gazing at the blind man. "Don't you agree?"

"No." The man gave a quiet sigh, and concealed within this sigh, of all things, was a trace of compassionate sorrow. "If I'm wrong, I'll correct it. But I won't die. I fear I'll have to disappoint Sect Leader Yan."

Is that so? Yan Wushi snorted a soundless laugh. *That's only because you've yet to arrive at true despair.*

When he'd fought with Cui Youwang in the past, Yan Wushi's Taihua had been taken away. For many years, he never retrieved it. After Cui Youwang died, Taihua had subsequently fallen into the hands of his disciple, Sang Jingxing.

But Yan Wushi's martial arts had already blazed a second path. Whether he had Taihua or not made little difference to him.

Sang Jingxing didn't know this; he only assumed that losing his sword had been a great shame and humiliation to Yan Wushi, so he deliberately had someone pass a message to Yan Wushi: that he'd exchange Taihua for the *Zhuyang Strategy*.

Of course Yan Wushi would never do that, but he thought of an even better idea. He'd use Shen Qiao—the former leader of the world's foremost Daoist sect—to make the exchange. To Shen Qiao, this wasn't just an extremely treacherous situation, it was also the ultimate humiliation. For the great and lofty sect leader of Xuandu Mountain to be worth no more than a dispensable Taihua sword.

Yan Wushi's fingertips landed on Shen Qiao's forehead, then lightly meandered down to his chin. His pale complexion exposed his illness, and that slender, graceful neck looked like it'd break with just a light squeeze. But beneath this appearance, this person possessed a steely core that would never yield.

He knew Sang Jingxing, and he knew what things Sang Jingxing might do to this kind of Shen Qiao. *So, Shen Qiao, what will you do?*

The choice he made would be very interesting.

As Yan Wushi knocked on the gates of Bailong Monastery, he'd already begun to ponder what the answer might be. *Shen Qiao, will you choose to bend, or would you rather break?*

It was a moonlit night.

Shen Qiao frostily gazed at Yan Wushi as well as Sang Jingxing, who stood not too far away. Or perhaps it wasn't frosty, and it was only the moon's silver light spilling upon his face that bestowed his whole face with a sense of coldness.

Looking at his serene expression, a sliver of regret suddenly welled up within Yan Wushi's heart. But this hint of regret wasn't enough to make him change his mind.

"You're too soft and weak, A-Qiao." He bent at the waist, then gently tucked the loose hair at Shen Qiao's temple behind his ear, the motion as tender as the willows of spring. "The soft and weak will never make anything of themselves, and they're even less qualified to be my opponents."

Shen Qiao only looked at him without speaking.

"I hope that you can survive." Yan Wushi laughed. "However, if you become a Shen Qiao who simply lingers on half-dead, who bows to others, you'll become no more than an ordinary person without any remarkable aspects whatsoever. Isn't that right?"

He threw Shanhe Tongbei into the man's arms, then lightly clapped his shoulder. "I wish you good luck."

Then, he rose. And left. His qinggong was capable of traversing vast distances as if they were mere inches, but today, he didn't employ it. Instead, he walked away, step by step. From behind him he could hear Sang Jingxing chuckling at Shen Qiao, his voice carrying a thick tone of mockery and contempt.

As for Yan Wushi, he never looked back.

MINI EXTRA THREE

1

ON THE BACK SIDE of Xuandu Mountain, Shen Qiao discovered a clay jar of wine.

The wine lacked both name and label. He asked around the disciples of Xuandu Mountain, yet no one claimed it. However, when he unsealed the wine, a familiar aroma wafted toward him. Then Shen Qiao knew: his late master had personally made this wine himself.

The esteemed Daoist Master Qi was celebrated by all for his aspirations in martial arts, and he also bore the glory of Xuandu Mountain's sect leader. However, few people knew that he was also proficient when it came to sewing clothes, cobbling shoes, making wine, cooking—all of it. Whenever rips appeared in his disciples' clothing, their shift would be the one to patch them up.

This jar of wine stirred not only Shen Qiao's long-distant memories but his longing for his shizun as well. Thus, with some encouragement and persuasion from Yan Wushi, the pair drank the wine together, down to the last drop.

Sect Leader Shen woke up the following day with a splitting headache.

He'd never expected that Shizun's wine would be strong enough to knock him out. As he held his forehead and tried to remember what had happened, he found the words "little brat" kept echoing within his mind; it felt like someone had scolded him after they'd started drinking.

In all of Xuandu Mountain, who'd dare to scold him?

Thus Shen Qiao went to ask Yan Wushi.

Yan Wushi, then looked at him with a tenderly affectionate gaze. "You're always very mindful of yourself when you're sober, so I didn't expect that the moment you got drunk you'd start dwelling on the past and all your old mistakes. You even took me for your shifu; you clung to my thigh and begged me for a scolding. What was I to do? I could only satisfy you."

Shen Qiao was speechless. He was sure that he'd never do such a thing, but his memories of last night were completely fragmented, so he could only let Yan Wushi rattle off his nonsense.

"After I scolded you, you even started weeping and wailing. You cried that your shizun was right to yell at you, and that from now on, you'd be good and listen to everything he said, that you'd never go west if he told you to go east, and that if you were asked to chase a dog, you'd never chase a chicken."

With that, he beckoned to Shen Qiao, as if he were calling over a bewildered fawn or lamb. "Come, let me hear you call me Shizun."

2

BIAN YANMEI HAD BEEN practicing his martial arts. Yan Wushi brought him to a bamboo forest behind the villa and had him closely observe his surroundings, to try with all his might to comprehend and break through his bottleneck.

The young and ignorant Bian Yanmei stared at every little thing around him with eyes as round as lanterns. He didn't let himself miss even a mosquito. Finally, he noticed something: all the bamboo within this forest had been arranged in a specific pattern. With his location as the epicenter, they were planted in rings that spread outward. Additionally, the distance between each ring seemed to be precisely identical, without the slightest variation.

Bian Yanmei felt that there must be some sort of profound secret here, and that must be what Shizun wanted him to comprehend yet couldn't tell him.

He stayed in that bamboo forest for three days and nights, feeding three days and three nights' worth of mosquitoes—until the once-tiny mosquitoes were so full they could barely fly anymore. In the end, finally unable to take it anymore, he fled the place and went to ask Shizun for advice, his scalp tingling and numb.

Yan Wushi looked surprised at his question. "The real cultivation manual that can resolve your bottleneck is buried beneath one of the bamboo of the third ring. There are fakes buried under the rest of the bamboo. I wanted you to closely observe and see which bamboo had the manual beneath it. What have you been looking at these past three days?"

Bian Yanmei's eyes were dull and lifeless, the bags beneath them dark and heavy. "Then why are the bamboo all spaced equally from each other? Why are all the distances exactly the same, ring after ring, like an array?"

Yan Wushi raised an eyebrow. "Don't you think it looks better that way?"

Bian Yanmei had no words.

Many years later, Bian Yanmei took Yu Shengyan to the bamboo forest behind the villa.

"Observe carefully, let yourself learn and experience things with all your might; perhaps you'll be able to break through your bottleneck here."

Bian Yanmei stood with his hands behind his back, emanating the very picture of an eldest disciple.

MINI EXTRA FOUR

1: OBSESSIVE-COMPULSIVE DISORDER

ALL HUMAN BEINGS have their own temperament. Some are combative, others mild. Some people are carefree, others miserly. Having spent so long with him, Shen Qiao had gained a fair understanding of Yan Wushi's temperament.

He himself was a fair and mild person. As long as he was capable of tolerating something, he'd do his best to do so. However... Yan Wushi had certain habits that even someone as tolerant as Shen Qiao would sometimes find unbearable.

For example...

The two of them were eating at a restaurant, and the owner brought them a bowl of noodle soup. Yan Wushi took one look and paused his chopsticks.

Seeing this, Shen Qiao was confused. "What's wrong?"

"There are scallions in the soup," said Yan Wushi.

"You don't eat scallions?"

Yan Wushi grunted in confirmation.

"Then just pick them out."

"Won't the taste of scallions remain?"

Shen Qiao was disinclined to see someone wasting food, so he took the bowl and picked out the pieces of scallion one by one, until none were left.

"Eat," he said.

Yan Wushi reluctantly gave the bowl another look. "Why are there sesame seeds too?"

"Only three or four," said Shen Qiao.

"I won't eat that either." An unspoken hint lay within those words.

Shen Qiao slapped his chopsticks down hard against the table. "Then your esteemed self doesn't need to!"

2: TRUE NATURE

WHEN IT CAME TO wildly disparate temperaments, there were probably no people in the world who differed more than Yan Wushi and Shen Qiao. However, those two had their own unique ways of getting along.

Whenever he sighted an injustice, or the weak in distress, not only would Shen Qiao lend a helping hand straight away, he'd tail them in secret after, checking to see if they were truly safe.

As for Yan Wushi, he'd remain indifferent and observe coolly from the sidelines, to see just how wretched the person would end up: would they put up a death struggle or would they fight back with everything they had? Perhaps he might even toy with them the way a child would a cricket, poking it with a stick.

One person was good by nature, and the other evil.

When one really got down to it, only one thing had changed. Within the decades of life that Yan Wushi had spent strutting around, there was now the addition of Shen Qiao, whom he was a little more willing to rein in his nature for.

But when it came to other people, his nature hadn't changed a bit.

Guang Lingsan looked at the game of weiqi in front of him. He'd lost by half a move. Only half a move. But a loss was a loss. He gave a slight sigh, unable to tamp down on his dissatisfaction. He could only abide by the agreement and tell Yan Wushi a piece of news.

"If all goes as expected, the new crown prince should be the Prince of Jin."

Yan Wushi raised an eyebrow. He had his own eyes and information sources within the capital, but Fajing Sect had decidedly closer ties to the imperial palace: they could obtain some news before even the officials in the capital.

Watching him, Guang Lingsan was suspicious. "I recall that Huanyue Sect is quite friendly with the emperor," he said. "Everyone knows that the Prince of Jin is a difficult man to deal with. The current situation might be detrimental to the Sui Dynasty in the future, and it might even become a blight to the emperor. Why do you look happy instead?"

Yan Wushi gave a laugh. "Change gives birth to chaos, and chaos brings renewal. The new will replace the old, and the young will supplant their elders. If the Sui Dynasty grows unstable, the world will undoubtedly see the rise of great men everywhere. Once that happens, won't it make for a marvelous and gripping show?"

Guang Lingsan was speechless.

He'd almost forgotten this old scoundrel's true nature.

Characters and Associated Factions

CHARACTERS
AND ASSOCIATED FACTIONS

The identity of certain characters may be a spoiler; use this guide with caution on your first read of the novel.

A sizable portion of *Thousand Autumns'* cast are based on real-life historical figures, though they have all been fictionalized to some degree. The names of those with real-life counterparts but without an entry of their own are indicated by **bold text**.

MAIN CHARACTERS

Shen Qiao (沈峤)

TITLE(S): Sect Leader of Xuandu's Violet Palace

CHARACTER BASIS: Fictional

As the chosen successor of the legendary Qi Fengge, and the reclusive leader of the land's foremost Daoist sect, Shen Qiao seemed to have it all: first-rate talent, a world-class master, a loving family, and a kind heart devoted completely to the tenets of Daoism. But a duel atop Banbu Peak changed everything for him.

The *qiao* in Shen Qiao's name is a rare character, referring to a tall and precipitous mountain peak. He was named after a verse in "Ode to Zhou: On Tour" (周颂·时迈), recorded in the *Shijing*—a song written in commemoration of King Wu of Zhou. The verse extols how he traveled the land after vanquishing the Shang in 11th century B.C.E. He offered sacrifices to the many gods, including those in the rivers and tallest mountains.

Yan Wushi (晏无师)

TITLE(S): Huanyue Sect Leader, Junior Preceptor of the Crown
Prince of Zhou (former), Demon Lord

CHARACTER BASIS: Fictional

The egotistical and capricious leader of the demonic Huanyue Sect.
A terrifying martial artist who some sources claim was on par with
Qi Fengge, Yan Wushi is also ambitious, shrewd, and above all,
a committed misanthrope. In Yan Wushi's eyes, there are no good
people, only evil people disguised as good people. As far as he's
concerned, anyone who thinks otherwise is either a liar or a fool.

Or at least, so he thought.

Yan Wushi's personal name means "has no master." The *ling* in his
old name, Xie Ling (谢岭), means "mountain range."

XUANDU MOUNTAIN (玄都山)

The world's foremost Daoist sect, located on the border intersection
of Northern Qi, Southern Chen, and Northern Zhou. Sect Leader
Qi Fengge built their legendary reputation, but despite this prestige
and influence, he chose to seclude Xuandu Mountain away from
the world, closing its gates and withdrawing from all outside affairs.
After his death, his mantle passed to Shen Qiao, who held fast to
his shizun's isolationist stance. When Shen Qiao fell during his duel
with Kunye, Yu Ai took the reins as Acting Sect Leader and made
the dangerous decision to collude with the Göktürks.

Officially, Xuandu Mountain is a location—the actual sect is
called Xuandu's Violet Palace (玄都紫府, *xuandu zifu*), named after
Taishang Laojun's abode on the mythical Daluo Mountain. *Xuandu*
("black city") refers to Daluo Mountain's immortal realm, while *zifu*
("violet residence") refers to the Bajing Palace supposedly located

within it. The sect leader of Xuandu's Violet Palace is known as the *zhangjiao* (掌教), a term more specific to Daoism compared to *zongzhu* (宗主), which is how Yan Wushi is addressed in Chinese.

Qi Fengge (祁凤阁)

TITLE(S): Sect Leader of Xuandu's Violet Palace, World's Number One Martial Expert

CHARACTER BASIS: Fictional

The number one martial artist in all the land before his passing and Shen Qiao's master, Qi Fengge is held in high esteem by the entire world to this day. Two decades ago, he won a duel with Hulugu of the Göktürks. In lieu of a reward for his victory, he made Hulugu swear to stay out of the Central Plains for the next twenty years. He had five disciples in total: Tan Yuanchun, Shen Qiao, Yu Ai, Yuan Ying, and Gu Hengbo.

Yu Ai (郁蔼)

TITLE(S): Acting Sect Leader of Xuandu's Violet Palace

CHARACTER BASIS: Fictional

One of Qi Fengge's disciples and Shen Qiao's shidi, though two years older than him. Originally the closest to Shen Qiao out of all his martial siblings, he collaborated with Kunye to poison Shen Qiao, which led to Shen Qiao's crushing defeat on Banbu Peak. Afterward, he took over leadership of Xuandu Mountain and involved the sect in the ongoing power struggles of the current regimes, cooperating with Göktürk Khagahate.

Tan Yuanchun (谭元春)

CHARACTER BASIS: Fictional

The first of Qi Fengge's disciples and one of the current elders of Xuandu Mountain. Despite being the eldest, Qi Fengge passed him over for the position of sect leader in favor of Shen Qiao. Indecisive and dislikes conflict.

Yuan Ying (袁英)

CHARACTER BASIS: Fictional

The fourth of Qi Fengge's disciples. Has a weak and introverted personality due to a lifelong speech impediment.

Gu Hengbo (顾横波)

CHARACTER BASIS: Fictional

The youngest of Qi Fengge's disciples, though she was primarily taught by Shen Qiao. Forthright, with a strong sense of justice.

Shiwu (十五)

CHARACTER BASIS: Fictional

Shen Qiao's eldest disciple who he accepted after Shiwu's master's death. Sweet and gentle. His fellow disciples include Yuwen Song and later Duan Ying.

HUANYUE SECT (浣月宗)

One of the three demonic sects, established and led by Yan Wushi after the collapse of Riyue Sect. Though wealthy and influential, they tend to keep a low profile and are the key supporters of Yuwen Yong's rule in Zhou. Like the rest of the demonic sects, their final goal is to reunite the sects of the demonic discipline. After Yuwen Yong's death, they have been driven into hiding by Yuwen Yun.

Yu Shengyan (玉生烟)

CHARACTER BASIS: Fictional

Yan Wushi's youngest disciple. A quick-witted and charismatic young man.

Bian Yanmei (边沿梅)

CHARACTER BASIS: Fictional

Yan Wushi's first disciple. Shrewd and insightful, he's a key to Huanyue Sect's continued survival under Yuwen Yun's regime.

HEHUAN SECT (合欢宗)

One of three demonic sects born from Riyue Sect's fall, Hehuan Sect specializes in charm techniques and parasitic cultivation, where the practitioner drains qi and energy from their sexual partners to strengthen their own martial arts. Hehuan Sect was established and led by Yuan Xiuxiu, but her lover Sang Jingxing is known to hold great power within it as well. Once highly influential in Qi, after Qi's downfall and Yuwen Yun's ascension, they gained his favor and great power in Zhou, replacing Huanyue Sect.

Bai Rong (白茸)

CHARACTER BASIS: Fictional

One of Hehuan Sect's most prominent disciples under Sang Jingxing. Cunning and devious. Though deeply fond of Shen Qiao, she has her own goals for herself: becoming the next leader of Hehuan Sect.

Yuan Xiuxiu (元秀秀)

TITLE(S): Hehuan Sect Leader

CHARACTER BASIS: Fictional

The leader of Hehuan Sect, rumored to have gotten her position due to her relationship with Sang Jingxing. Despite this, they do not get along, but constantly seek to undermine—even kill—each other.

Sang Jingxing (桑景行)

CHARACTER BASIS: Fictional

An exalted elder in Hehuan Sect, Cui Youwang's disciple, and Yuan Xiuxiu's supposed lover. A twisted martial artist with a horrific reputation, as well as an appetite for beauties and parasitic cultivation. He was grievously injured by Shen Qiao when the latter destroyed his own martial arts to take him down and loathes both Shen Qiao and Yan Wushi.

Xiao Se (萧瑟)

CHARACTER BASIS: Fictional

Yuan Xiuxiu's disciple, but seeks to earn favor with Sang Jingxing. Specializes in fighting with fans.

Bing Xuan (冰弦)

CHARACTER BASIS: Fictional

A disciple who joined Huanyue Sect after Bai Rong rescued her.

FAJING SECT (法镜宗)

One of the three demonic sects born from Riyue Sect's fall. Unable to compete with the other two branches, the sect now primarily operates within Tuyuhun, though they still hold ambitions for the Central Plains. Their sect leader is Guang Lingsan.

Guang Lingsan (广陵散)

TITLE(S): Fajing Sect Leader

CHARACTER BASIS: Fictional

The leader of Fajing Sect, who moved their operations to Tuyuhun ten years ago due to overwhelming pressure from Huanyue Sect and Hehuan Sect. A master of the zither who uses music to harm and confound his opponents. Freely switches between enemy and ally with Yan Wushi.

RIYUE SECT (日月宗)

The origin of the "Noble Discipline" (demonic discipline to outsiders). Once located in Fenglin Province, it vanished after splintering into three: Huanyue Sect, Hehuan Sect, and Fajing Sect. Their last sect leader was Sang Jingxing's master, Cui Youwang.

Cui Youwang (崔由妄)

CHARACTER BASIS: Fictional

A martial arts grandmaster, known to be one of the strongest in the world when he was still alive. Like most demonic cultivators, he was pragmatic, self-serving, and ruthless.

CHUNYANG MONASTERY (纯阳观)

The powerful Daoist sect led by Yi Pichen, one of the top ten martial artists in the world. Their sect shares close ties with Bixia Sect.

Yi Pichen (易辟尘)

TITLE(S): Abbot of Chunyang Monastery

CHARACTER BASIS: Fictional

The leader of Chunyang Monastery. Calm and stolid.

LINCHUAN ACADEMY (临川学宫)

The leading Confucian sect and the main force backing the Emperor of Chen. Their leader is Academy Master Ruyan Kehui, one of the world's top ten martial artists.

Ruyan Kehui (汝鄢克惠)

TITLE(S): Linchuan Academy Master

CHARACTER BASIS: Fictional

The leader of Linchuan Academy. A powerful and cultured martial artist who ranks in the top ten, he believes wholeheartedly in the superiority of Confucianism and the Han's right to rule, and therefore sought to undermine Yuwen Yong's Zhou Dynasty.

LIULI PALACE (琉璃宫)

A famous but reclusive sect located on the isolated island of Fangzhang Province. Their members are not skilled martial artists but possess extraordinary knowledge of the jianghu and uncanny powers of observation. They produce the official rankings for the jianghu, including the highly revered "World's Top Ten Martial Artists." Their young palace mistress, Yuan Zixiao, is next in line to inherit the leader's mantle.

LIUHE GUILD (六合帮)

One of the largest martial arts organizations in the Central Plains, whose reach extends both north and south of the Yangtze River. Led by guild leader Dou Yanshan and deputy leader Yun Fuyi, they deal in all kinds of business, from escort missions to spy work, and they were a key player in the group ambush on Yan Wushi. However, friction has been growing between the two heads.

ZHOU DYNASTY (周朝)

The country that occupies the region northwest of the Yangtze, also known as Northern Zhou. Its capital is Chang'an (now known as Xi'an). Though it was established by **Yuwen Tai** before his death, for years his nephew **Yuwen Hu** held power as regent, killing off Yuwen Tai's puppet-ruler sons whenever he perceived them as a threat. The third such son, **Yuwen Yong**, managed to feign obedience for years before finally ambushing and killing Yuwen Hu, officially seizing back his imperial authority.

After Yuwen Yong's death, his son **Yuwen Yun** has taken over. With his unstable, mistrustful personality and deep grudge toward his father, his influence has rapidly driven Zhou into a decline.

Yuwen Yun (宇文贇)

TITLE(S): Emperor Xuan of Northern Zhou

CHARACTER BASIS: Historical

Yuwen Yong's son, who grew up under the harsh discipline of his father and loathed him greatly. An erratic hedonist who makes little attempt to govern and even instated his own son as a puppet ruler. Deeply mistrustful of his father-in-law, Puliuru Jian.

Puliuru Jian (普六茹坚)

TITLE(S): Duke of Sui

CHARACTER BASIS: Historical

A learned, high-ranking official of Zhou whom Shen Qiao met at an earlier birthday banquet. A talented statesman of no small ambition and influence, which draws Emperor Yuwen Yun's ire and mistrust. Currently working together with Huanyue Sect.

Empress Tianyuan (天元皇后)

CHARACTER BASIS: Historical

Puliuru Jian's eldest child and Yuwen Yun's official empress, though her position has been heavily undermined by her husband. Yuwen Yun held her and her younger brothers hostage to use against Puliuru Jian. Careful and modest.

Xueting (雪庭)

TITLE(S): State Preceptor of Zhou (former)

CHARACTER BASIS: Fictional

One of the top ten martial artists of the world and a former member of the Buddhist Tiantai Sect. Originally heavily favored by Yuwen Hu, who honored Buddhism, the late emperor Yuwen Yong's oppressive anti-Buddhist stance led to him taking drastic measures to eliminate him and his supporter Yan Wushi. One of the participants in the group ambush.

With Yuwen Yun's ascension, he and Buddhism have regained their previous glory in Zhou.

Chen Gong (陈恭)

TITLE(S): Duke of Zhao

CHARACTER BASIS: Fictional

Once a homeless youth who Shen Qiao met in Funing County, he was later bestowed the title of county duke by Gao Wei, then grand duke by Yuwen Yun. Opportunistic and possesses the outstanding ability to remember everything he hears and reads.

SUI DYNASTY (隋朝)

The dynasty replacing Northern Zhou after Puliuru Jian's revolt succeeds and he usurps the throne. One of the most influential dynasties in Chinese history due to their founding emperor's achievements in governance and his role in reunifying the Central Plains, ending the large-scale turmoil that began with the Uprising of the Five Barbarians.

Yang Guang (杨广)

TITLE(S): Duke of Yanmen Commandery (previous), Prince of Jin
CHARACTER BASIS: Historical
Puliuru Jian or Yang Jian's second son. Heavily favored by his parents over his own brother, the crown prince, and is opportunistic and ambitious. Possessed a ruthless personality even as a child.

Yuxiu (玉秀)

CHARACTER BASIS: Fictional
A monk from Tiantai Sect who follows Yang Guang.

CHEN DYNASTY (陈朝)

The country south of the Yangtze River, founded by **Chen Baxian**, also called Southern Chen. Unlike Qi and Zhou where most of the upper class are of Xianbei descent, the Chen Dynasty is dominated by the Han. Its capital is Jiankang (modern-day Nanjing).

Chen Shubao (陳叔寶)

TITLE(S): Emperor Fei of Southern Chen
CHARACTER BASIS: Historical
The new emperor of Southern Chen after his father Chen Xu's

passing. Though talented, he's more interested in immortality, elixirs, and the arts than in ruling his country.

Liu Jingyan (柳敬言)

CHARACTER BASIS: Historical

The reigning empress dowager and mother of Chen Shubao. Was trained in Linchuan Academy and is Ruyan Kehui's shimei. Troubled by her son's antics.

GÖKTÜRK KHAGANATE (突厥)

A powerful Turkic empire north of the Great Wall, led by **Taspar Khagan**. Their people have been at odds with the nations of the Central Plains for years—relations between them are uneasy and tinged with hostility.

Hulugu (狐鹿估)

CHARACTER BASIS: Fictional

Once the most powerful martial artist of the Göktürk Khaganate, he was narrowly defeated by Qi Fengge twenty years ago. Qi Fengge then made him swear not to set foot in the Central Plains. Though falsely thought dead thanks to Duan Wenyang's lies, he proves to be very much alive and dangerous.

Duan Wenyang (段文鸯)

CHARACTER BASIS: Fictional

Hulugu's disciple and Kunye's shixiong, a shrewd and ambitious whip user. An active agent in spreading the Khaganate's influence in a bid to earn his own place in their society as a person of mixed descent. Extremely loyal to Hulugu.

OTHER CHARACTERS

Characters who aren't associated with any major factions, regardless of where they live.

Escort Guard Liu (刘镖师)

CHARACTER BASIS: Fictional

One of the guards escorting the Li family to Jiankang. Shen Qiao runs into them, and they end up traveling together. Contributed greatly to Shen Qiao's understanding of romantic relationships.

Yin Chuan (殷川)

CHARACTER BASIS: Fictional

A youth from Tuyuhun and the sole survivor of the Yin family massacre. On the run from the many factions who have their eye on the Yin family's fabled fortune.

Kosa Sage (俱舍智者)

CHARACTER BASIS: Fictional

A resident of Tuyuhun and one of the top-ranking martial arts grandmasters in all the land. His disciple is Chen Lugui, who he pursues Yin Chuan with.

Ren Ying (任婴)

CHARACTER BASIS: Fictional

A poor orphaned youth with younger siblings to feed. An unfortunate soul who attempted to steal food from the Jinmu Sect, drawing their murderous ire.

Asano Taku (浅野泽)

CHARACTER BASIS: Fictional

A disciple of the Jinmu Sect from Yamato. Claims to be chasing Ren Ying due to him stealing their prized sword.

PRONUNCIATION GUIDE

Mandarin Chinese is the official state language of mainland China, and pinyin is the official system of romanization in which it is written. As Mandarin is a tonal language, pinyin uses diacritical marks (e.g., ā, á, ǎ, à) to indicate these tonal inflections. Most words use one of four tones, though some (as in "de" in the title below) are a neutral tone. Furthermore, regional variance can change the way native Chinese speakers pronounce the same word. For those reasons and more, please consider the guide below a simplified introduction to pronunciation of select character names and sounds from the world of *Thousand Autumns*.

More resources are available at sevenseasdanmei.com

NOTE ON SPELLING: Romanized Mandarin Chinese words with identical spelling in pinyin—and even pronunciation—may well have different meanings. These words are more easily differentiated in written Chinese, which uses characters.

CHARACTER NAMES

Qiān Qiū

Qiān, approximately **chee-yen**, but as a single syllable.
Qiū, as in **cho**ke.

Shěn Qiáo

Shěn, as in the second half of ma**son**.
Qiáo, as in **chow**.

Yàn Wúshī

Yàn, as in **yen**.

Wú, as in **oo**.

Shī, a little like **shh**. The **-i** is more of a buzzed continuation for the **sh-** consonant than any equivalent English vowel. See the General Consonants section for more information on the **sh-** consonant.

Qí Fènggé

Qí, as in **chee**se.

Fèng, a little like **fun**, but with the nasal **ng** one would find in so**ng**.

Gé, a little like **guh**.

Bái Róng

Bái, as in **bye**.

Róng, a little like the last part of chape**rone**. See the General Consonants section for more information on the **r-** consonant.

GENERAL CONSONANTS

Some Mandarin Chinese consonants sound very similar, such as z/c/s and zh/ch/sh. Audio samples will provide the best opportunity to learn the difference between them.

X: somewhere between the **sh** in **sh**eep and **s** in **s**ilk

Q: a very aspirated **ch** as in **ch**eat

C: **ts** as in pan**ts**

Z: **ds** as in su**ds**

S: **s** as in **s**ilk

CH: very close to **c-**, but with the tongue rolled up to touch the palate.

ZH: very close to **z-**, but with the tongue rolled up to touch the palate.

SH: very close to **s-**, but with the tongue rolled up to touch the palate. Because of this, it can give the impression of **shh**, but it's a different sound compared to the **x-** consonant.

G: hard **g** as in **g**raphic

R: partway between the **r** in **r**un and the **s** in measure. The tongue should be rolled up to touch the palate.

GENERAL VOWELS

The pronunciation of a vowel may depend on its preceding consonant. For example, the "i" in "shi" is distinct from the "i" in "di," where the first is a buzzed continuation for the sh- consonant and the latter a long e sound. Compound vowels are often—though not always—pronounced as conjoined but separate vowels. You'll find a few of the trickier compounds below.

IU: as in **yo**-yo

IE: **ye** as in **ye**s

UO: **war** as in **war**m

Historical Primer

HISTORICAL PERIOD

While not required reading, this section and those after are intended to offer further context for the historical setting of this story, and give insights into the many concepts and terms utilized throughout the novel. Their goal is to provide a starting point for learning more about the rich culture from which these stories were written.

The following segment is intended to give a brief introduction to the major historical events featured in *Thousand Autumns*.

THE JIN DYNASTY

In 266 C.E., at the close of the tumultuous **Three Kingdoms** era, the central plains were finally united under Sima Yan, founder of the **Jin Dynasty**, also known as **Western Jin**. But when Sima Yan passed away in 290 C.E., his son and heir was deemed unfit to rule. Conflict broke out among members of the imperial court who vied for the throne. This became known as the **War of the Eight Princes**, after the eight members of the Sima royal family who were the principal players.

UPRISING OF THE FIVE BARBARIANS AND THE SIXTEEN KINGDOMS PERIOD

Over a period of fifteen years, the repeated clashes and civil wars greatly weakened the Western Jin Dynasty. During this time, most of the royal princes relied on non-Han nomadic minorities to fight for them, in particular Xiongnu and the **Xianbei**. The Han lumped them together with other foreign ethnicities like the Jie, Di, and Qiang, collectively designating them the **Hu**, sometimes translated as "barbarians." As the Jin Dynasty's control over these minority tribes slipped, instances of rebellion combined with local unrest to usher in the **Uprising of the Five Barbarians** in 304 C.E.

Although it began as a revolt spearheaded by the Hu, the Uprising of the Five Barbarians soon led to the complete collapse of Western Jin as its Han upper class fled south of the Yangtze River. This was the mass **southward migration of the Jin** referenced in *Thousand Autumns*. When the old capital of Chang'an fell, the new emperor reestablished the seat of government in Jiankang, heralding the start of the **Eastern Jin Dynasty**. At the same time, north of the Yangtze River, the Di, Qiang, Xiongnu, and Jie each established their own dynastic kingdoms. Thus began a time of great upheaval known as the **Sixteen Kingdoms** period.

During the turmoil of the Sixteen Kingdoms, regimes formed and collapsed in the blink of an eye as they warred with each other and the Eastern Jin. The strife finally abated when the **Northern Wei Dynasty** conquered the other northern kingdoms in 439 C.E. and unified the lands north of the Yangtze. Meanwhile in the south, Liu Yu usurped the emperor of the Eastern Jin Dynasty and founded the **Liu Song Dynasty**. This marked the beginning of the **Northern-Southern Dynasties** period, during which *Thousand Autumns* is set.

NORTHERN-SOUTHERN DYNASTIES

For a period of almost ninety years, Northern Wei held strong. The first half of their reign was focused on expansion, but when Tuoba Hong rose to power in 471 C.E., he championed the dominance of **Buddhism** and Han culture, going so far as to ban Xianbei clothing from the court and assigning one-character family names to Xianbei nobility (Tuoba Hong himself changed his family name to Yuan).

South of the Yangtze, the regime changed hands three times—from Liu Song to **Southern Qi** to **Liang**, before the **Chen Dynasty** that ruled during *Thousand Autumns* was finally established in 557 C.E.

A rift slowly developed in Northern Wei between the increasingly Han-acculturated aristocracy and their own armies who adhered more to the traditional, nomadic lifestyle. A series of rebellions escalated into all-out revolt, and by 535 C.E. the kingdom had split in half. **Western Wei** was ruled by Yuwen Tai, and **Eastern Wei** by Gao Huan. In the space of a generation, they would depose the last of the old leadership and become the kingdoms of **Northern Zhou** and **Northern Qi**. In the Zhou Dynasty to the west, rule favored the Han-acculturated nobles, while in the Qi Dynasty to the east, the traditional tribes came into power.

Qi's military superiority over both Zhou and Chen began to diminish due to corruption and incompetence in the ruling class, and particularly that of the emperor's grandson, **Gao Wei**. After a politically turbulent period of regency in Zhou, **Yuwen Yong** took power in 572 C.E. and made a point of bolstering state administration and military affairs.

By 575 C.E., where *Thousand Autumns* begins, a new maelstrom is already brewing...

THE THREE SCHOOLS OF THOUGHT

This section hopes to provide some basic context as to the major schools of thought that inform the background of *Thousand Autumns*, so that readers may explore the topic in more depth on their own. Note that with their long period of coexistence, the schools have all influenced each other deeply, and their ideals have become rooted in Chinese culture itself, even among non-practitioners.

Daoism (道)

Daoism revolves around the concept of **Dao**, or "Ways": the courses things follow as they undergo change. Though there are many Dao a human can choose from, there is one primordial "great Dao" (大道), the source of the universe and origin of all things—the void of infinite potential. The course all things in the universe follow is the "heavenly Dao" (天道), the natural order.

According to Daoist principles, by imposing constraints and artifice, humanity strays from the primordial Dao and stagnates. In particular, the rigid social roles enforced by society are seen as unnatural and an example of degradation. For humans to flourish, they must revert themselves, disengaging from these tendencies in order to return to the primordial Dao. This is sometimes known as "becoming one with heaven" (天人合一). The method of disengaging is called **wuwei** (无为), sometimes translated as inaction or non-interference.

Expanding on this idea, Daoism has the concepts of **Xiantian** (先天, "Early Heaven") and **Houtian** (后天, "Later Heaven"). The prenatal Xiantian state is closer to the primordial Dao, and thus is both purer than and superior to the postnatal Houtian state. The Houtian state is created at birth, along with the **conscious mind** that thinks and perceives and which in turn suppresses the primordial mind. This is what gives rise to sources of suffering: anger, worry, doubt, desire, and fatigue.

The goal of *wuwei* is to reverse the changes brought on by Houtian and return to the primordial state of Xiantian. To conflict with nature is to stray from it, and to intervene in the natural order—as society does—is to perpetuate degradation. Disengaging from all of these influences requires rejecting social conventions and detaching from the mundane world altogether, so seclusion and asceticism are common practices. Emptying oneself of all emotion and freeing oneself from all artifice is the only way to achieve union with heaven and surpass life and death itself.

When it came to politics, Daoism was often seen as a justification for small, *laissez-faire* governments—in fact, *laissez-faire* is one of the possible translations of *wuwei*—supporting low taxes and low intervention. The anti-authority implications of its philosophies were not lost on its followers, nor on their rulers. As a result, it wasn't uncommon for Daoism to struggle to find its footing politically, despite its cultural pervasiveness.

Buddhism (佛/释)

Founded by Gautama Buddha in India, Buddhism only arrived in China during the Han Dynasty, well after Confucianism and Daoism. Despite early pushback and social friction, its parallels with Daoism eventually helped it gain widespread influence.

Buddhism is rooted in the concepts of reincarnation, karma, and **Maya**—the illusion of existence. Attachment to Maya keeps living beings rooted in the cycle of reincarnation, where they are beholden to the principle of karma that determines their future rebirths. Buddha claimed that this eternal cycle is the root of all suffering and that the only escape is through achieving **Nirvana**, or enlightenment. To achieve enlightenment is to fully accept that all things within existence are false. It then follows that any emotions, attachments, or thoughts that one develops while interacting with and perceiving the world are equally false. This philosophy extends to the attitude toward karma—the ideal Buddhist does good deeds and kind acts without any expectation of reward or satisfaction, material or otherwise.

Despite these selfless ideals, it also wasn't uncommon to see Buddhist temples amass land, authority, and wealth through donations, worship, and the offerings of those seeking better futures or rebirths. Combined with the men who'd leave their homes to join these temples as monks, this sometimes made the relationship between Buddhism and rulers a tricky, precarious one.

Confucianism (儒)

Unlike Buddhism and Daoism, Confucianism focuses on the moral betterment of the individual as the foundation for the ideal society. The founder Confucius envisioned a rigidly hierarchical system wherein the lower ranks have the moral duty to obey the higher ranks, and those in superior positions likewise have the moral responsibility to care for their subordinates. This social contract is applied to everything from the family unit to the nation itself—the emperor is the father to his people, and they in turn must show him absolute obedience.

To foster such a society, Confucians extol the **five constant virtues** (五常): **benevolence** (仁), **righteousness** (义), **propriety** (礼), **wisdom** (智), and **integrity** (信). Paragons who embody all five virtues are called **junzi** (君子), sometimes translated as "gentlemen" or "noble men," while their direct opposites are *xiaoren*, literally "petty people," and sometimes translated as "scoundrels."

Throughout most of history, mainstream Confucians believed in the goodness inherent in humanity, that people can better themselves through education and learning from their superiors. The ideal ruler must be the ultimate *junzi* himself and lead by example, thereby uplifting all of society. In the same vein, Confucius expected officials to be virtuous parental figures, held to a higher moral standard than ordinary citizens.

Due to its emphasis on social order, Confucianism was easily the most influential and politically favored of the three schools throughout history. Its social contract was so absolute that even dynastic takeovers had to be performed in a way that did not "break it." Usurpers who acted otherwise ran the risk of being seen as illegitimate in the eyes of the people. Famously, the old emperor had to offer the new emperor his position multiple times, with the new ruler declining three times (三让) before finally accepting.

Bonus: Legalism (法)

Though not regarded as one of the "big three" and although it received far less overt support, Legalism was enormously influential for one key reason: it served as the foundation for the entire Chinese government tradition for two thousand years, regardless of dynasty.

Unlike the three schools, which are each in pursuit of an ideal, Legalism is entirely utilitarian and concerned only with efficacy.

This is reflected in its Chinese name, the "house of methods." Core to its beliefs is the idea that human nature is selfish and evil, and so people must be motivated through reward and punishment. Morality is inconsequential, the ends justify the means, and the most effective administration must minimize corruption by restricting its subordinate administrators as much as possible.

It was with these tenets that the first unified Chinese empire, the Qin Dynasty, dismantled the existing feudalist system and established in its place a centralized government overseen by the emperor. After the Qin's collapse—brought about in part due to how harsh a fully Legalist regime was on the people—the succeeding Han Dynasty under Emperor Wu of Han made sure to suppress Legalism as a philosophy. However, they inherited the entire Legalist government structure mostly unchanged, though their policies were softened by a push toward Confucianism. This trend of furtively repackaging Legalist tendencies within the leading school of thought (usually Confucianism) continued almost uninterrupted for this period of two thousand years, and rulers continued to study Legalist texts like the *Han Feizi*.

OTHER IMPORTANT CONCEPTS

DAOIST CULTIVATION, THE ZHUYANG STRATEGY, AND THE POWER OF FIVE

In real life, the scholar Tao Hongjing compiled the famous, three-volume *Concealed Instructions for the Ascent to Perfection* (登真隱訣, translated in the novel as "Dengzhen Concealed Instructions"). For *Thousand Autumns*, Meng Xi Shi invented an extra associated manual, called the *Strategy of Vermillion Yang* (朱陽策, translated in the novel as "Zhuyang Strategy") after the real-life Monastery of Vermillion Yang on Mount Mao where Tao Hongjing secluded himself.

The *Zhuyang Strategy* draws heavily from classical concepts of Daoist cultivation and pulls together many ideas from Chinese culture. Primarily, they are based on the *Wuqi Chaoyuan* (五气朝元, roughly "Returning the Five Qi to the Origin"). The first lines of each of the *Zhuyang Strategy*'s five volumes correspond exactly to the *Wuqi Chaoyuan*'s five principles:

1. The heart conceals the mind; Houtian begets the conscious mind, while Xiantian begets propriety; once emptied of sorrow, the mind is settled, and the Fire from the Crimson Emperor of the South returns to the Origin.
2. The liver conceals the soul; Houtian begets the lost soul, while Xiantian begets benevolence; once emptied of joy, the soul is settled, and the Wood from the Azure Emperor of the East returns to the Origin.

3. The pancreas conceals the thought; Houtian begets the deluded thought, while Xiantian begets integrity; once emptied of desire, the thought is settled, and the Earth from the Yellow Emperor of the Center returns to the Origin.

4. The lungs conceal the anima; Houtian begets the corrupted anima, while Xiantian begets righteousness; once emptied of rage, the anima is settled, and the Metal from the White Emperor of the West returns to the Origin.

5. The kidneys conceal the essence; Houtian begets the clouded essence, while Xiantian begets wisdom; once emptied of cheer, the will is settled, and the Water from the Black Emperor of the North returns to the Origin.

The traditional Chinese worldview includes the **Five Phases**, the **Deities of the Five Regions** (also known as the **Five Emperors**), the five constant virtues, the **Five Spirits**, and the five major internal organs. The *Wuqi Chaoyuan* links all these ideas together, unifying them into a doctrine that explains how one can achieve immortal status or "godhood." For those who are interested, we provide here a brief introduction to several of these concepts in hopes that readers can further appreciate the world of *Thousand Autumns*.

THE FIVE PHASES

The **Wuxing** (五行), sometimes translated as Five Agents or Five Elements, are a cornerstone of Daoist philosophy. Unlike the Four Elements proposed by Aristotle, the Five Phases—**Metal** (金), **Wood** (木), **Water** (水), **Fire** (火), and **Earth** (土)—are seen as dynamic, interdependent forces. Each phase can give rise to another (生), or suppress another (克). As Daoism dictates that all entities are bound by the natural order, the Five Phases can be seen as an overarching rule set that governs all aspects of nature. Most things are regarded as corresponding to a certain phase, including but not limited to planets, seasons, cardinal directions, organs, colors, and types of qi.

FIVE EMPERORS, FIVE REGIONS, FIVE COLORS

In Daoism, the **Wufang Shangdi** (五方上帝), or High Emperors of the Five Regions, are the fivefold manifestation of the **Supreme Emperor of Heaven** (天皇大帝), or simply **Heaven** (天). As they correspond to the Five Phases, each emperor has an associated cardinal direction, as well as a color that informs his namesake.

FIVE SPIRITS, FIVE ORGANS

The traditional Chinese conception of the spirit divides it into five separate aspects: **mind** (神), **soul** (魂), **thought** (意), **anima** (魄), and **will** (志). These classifications may not be a perfect match with their western definitions. For example, the will—which arises from the **essence** (精)—is responsible for memory, as well as discernment and judgment. A strong will is generally associated with clear-mindedness. In another example, the anima governs instincts, impulses, and reflex reactions, and is said to dissipate on death, unlike the soul.

Each of the five aspects is said to reside in one of the five major internal organs—heart, liver, pancreas (includes the spleen), lungs, and kidneys, which in turn also correspond to the Five Phases. The *Wuqi Chaoyuan* claims that part of ascending to immortality is learning how to "return" the true qi of each aspect to one's Dantian, or "Origin."

THE FOUR OCCUPATIONS

The 士农工商 classification of citizens as *shi* (eventually **gentry scholars**), *nong* (**farmers**), *gong* (**artisans**), and *shang* (**merchants**), was a cornerstone of ancient Chinese social hierarchy strongly associated with both Confucianism and Legalism.

As the upper class and decision-makers, the *shi* naturally ranked the highest, followed by the peasant farmers who were valued as the backbone of the nation. Merchant businessmen were seen as agents of exploitation who profited from price fluctuations, so they were placed lowest.

In practice, these hierarchical rankings shaped cultural attitudes more than they dictated political clout. Even though merchants were looked down upon, the much-needed cash flow they provided made them far more influential than the artisan and farmer classes. This created a curious situation—merchants were both sought after and derided by the *shi* in charge of governance. In later dynasties some merchants went so far as to purchase positions within the imperial court, making them honorary *shi* and granting them legal protections.

Though the *shi* remained firmly at the top of the social hierarchy regardless of the period, the membership of the class changed over time. Originally, the *shi* were warrior aristocrats not unlike western knights, but they became obsolete when the Warring States period mobilized the common folk for warfare. With the rise of philosophy, the warriors slowly gave way to scholars. Later, during the harsh Legalist regime of the Qin Dynasty, the emperor began assigning administrative responsibilities to learned scholars who showed promise and merit. To weaken the authority of the noble class, he dismantled the existing feudalist system in favor of a centralized bureaucracy of dedicated officials.

Though the Qin's system of governance persisted well after the dynasty's collapse, the importance of family lines meant that prominent scholar-officials effectively became the new aristocracy. Their wealth and influence almost always guaranteed their descendants the resources to land their own positions within the imperial court. *Thousand Autumns* includes examples of powerful clans like the Su and the Xie; one talented ancestor could elevate their entire family for generations to come. It wasn't until the Tang Dynasty that a true merit-based system was introduced—the civil service exams—that would give capable commoners the chance to find their place in governance.

Glossary

GLOSSARY

GENRES

DANMEI (耽美, "INDULGENCE IN BEAUTY"): A Chinese fiction genre focused on romanticized tales of love and attraction between men. It is analogous to the BL (boys' love) genre in Japanese media and is better understood as a genre of plot rather than a genre of setting. For example, though many danmei novels feature wuxia or xianxia settings, others are better understood as tales of sci-fi, fantasy, or horror.

WUXIA (武侠, "MARTIAL HEROES"): One of the oldest Chinese literary genres and usually consists of tales of noble heroes fighting evil and injustice. It often follows martial artists, monks, or rogues who live apart from the ruling government. These societal outcasts—both voluntary and otherwise—settle disputes among themselves, adhering to their own moral codes over the law.

Characters in wuxia focus primarily on human concerns, such as political strife between factions and advancing their own personal sense of justice. True wuxia is low on magical or supernatural elements. To Western moviegoers, a well-known example is *Crouching Tiger, Hidden Dragon*.

NAMES, HONORIFICS, AND TITLES

Diminutives, Nicknames, and Name Tags

A-: Friendly diminutive. Always a prefix. Usually for monosyllabic names, or one syllable out of a two-syllable name.

DA-: A prefix meaning "eldest."

LAO-: A prefix meaning "old." A casual but still respectful way to address an older man.

-ER: A word for "son" or "child." When added to a name as a suffix, it expresses affection.

XIAO-: A prefix meaning "small" or "youngest." When added to a name, it expresses affection.

GE/GEGE: A word meaning "big brother." When added as a suffix, it becomes an affectionate address for any older male, with the -gege variant expressing even more affection.

Cultivation Sects

SHIZUN: Teacher/master. For one's master in one's own sect. Gender-neutral. Literal meaning is "honored/venerable master" and is a more respectful address, though Shifu is not disrespectful.

SHIXIONG: Older martial brother. For senior male members of one's own sect. When not bound by sect, speakers may also append "-xiong" as a suffix for names, as a friendly but courteous way of addressing a man of equal rank.

SHIJIE: Older martial sister. For senior female members of one's own sect.

SHIDI: Younger martial brother. For junior male members of one's own sect. When not bound by sect, speakers may also append "-di" as a friendly suffix to names, with "-laodi" being a more casual variant.

SHIMEI: Younger martial sister. For junior female members of one's own sect.

SHIZHI: Martial nephew or niece. For disciples of the speaker's martial sibling.

QIANBEI: A respectful title or suffix for someone older, more experienced, or more skilled in a particular discipline. Not to be used for blood relatives.

Other

DAFU: A general but respectful address for court officials.

DAOYOU: An address used by Daoists, usually for fellow Daoists.

GONGZI: A respectful address for young men, originally only for those from affluent households. Though appropriate in all formal occasions, it's often preferred when the addressee outranks the speaker.

LANG/LANGJUN: A general term for "man." "-lang" can be appended as a suffix for a woman's male lover or husband, but it can also be used to politely address a man by pairing it with other characters that denote his place within a certain family. For example, "dalang," "erlang," and "sanlang" mean "eldest son," "second son," and "third son" respectively. "Langjun" is a polite address for any man, similar to "gentleman."

NIANG/NIANGZI: A general term for "woman," and has the same pairing rules as "lang." "Niangzi" is a polite address for women, both married and unmarried.

SHAOXIA: Literally "young hero." A general way to address a younger martial artist from the jianghu.

XIANSHENG: A polite address for men, originally only for those of great learning or those who had made significant contributions to society. Sometimes seen as an equivalent to "Mr." in English.

XIAOYOU: An address for children, meaning "little friend."

XIONGZHANG: A very respectful address for an older man the speaker is close to. Approximately means "esteemed elder brother."

TERMINOLOGY

FACE (脸/面子): A person's face is an important concept in Chinese society. It is a metaphor for someone's reputation or dignity and can be extended into further descriptive metaphors. For example, "having face" refers to having a good reputation and "losing face" refers to having one's reputation damaged.

INTERNAL CULTIVATION (内功): Internal cultivation or *neigong* refers to the breathing, qi, and meditation practices a martial artist must undertake in order to properly harness and utilize their "outer cultivation" of combat techniques and footwork. As Daoism considers qi and breathing irrevocably linked, a large part of internal cultivation centers on achieving the advanced state of **internal breathing** (内息). Practitioners focus on regulating and coordinating their breaths until it becomes second nature. This then grants them the ability to freely manipulate their qi with little effort or conscious thought.

In wuxia, the capabilities of internal cultivation are usually exaggerated. Martial artists are often portrayed as being able to fly with qinggong, generate powerful force fields, manipulate objects across space without physical contact, or harden their bodies and make themselves impervious to physical damage.

JIANGHU (江湖, "RIVERS AND LAKES"): A staple of wuxia, the jianghu describes the greater underground society of martial artists and associates that spans the entire setting. Members of the jianghu self-govern and settle issues among themselves based on the tenets of strength and honor, though this may not stop them from exerting influence over conventional society too.

MARRIAGE: In Chinese culture, the woman traditionally marries into the man's family when she takes his surname. Because of the importance placed on lineages and ancestors, this concept remains even if either side has lost, disowned, or never knew their family at all.

MERIDIANS: The means by which qi travels through the body, like a bloodstream. Some medical and combat techniques target the meridians at specific points on the body, known as acupoints, which allows them to redirect, manipulate, or halt qi circulation. Halting a cultivator's qi circulation prevents them from using their internal cultivation until the block is lifted.

NAMES: When men and women came of age in ancient China, they received a new name for others of the same generation to refer to them by, known as a **courtesy name**. Use of their original or **personal name** was normally reserved only for respected elders and the person themselves—using it otherwise would be very rude and overfamiliar.

Using an emperor's personal name was even more disrespectful. Rulers were usually addressed by the dynasty they led, and they each had a formal title to distinguish themselves from their predecessors or successors. For example, Yuwen Yong's official title was "Emperor Wu of Northern Zhou" (北周武帝).

PAIR CULTIVATION (双修): Also translated as dual cultivation, this is a cultivation practice that uses sex between participants to improve cultivation prowess. Can also be used as a simple euphemism for sex.

PARASITIC CULTIVATION (采补, "HARVEST AND SUPPLEMENT"): The practice of draining life energy and qi from a host to strengthen one's martial arts. As the bodies of men are believed to hold more *yang* qi while women hold more *yin* qi, the person in question will often "harvest" from the other sex to "supplement" themselves, which gives the practice its association with sexual cultivation.

QINGGONG (轻功): A real-life training discipline. In wuxia, the feats of qinggong are highly exaggerated, allowing practitioners to glide through the air, run straight up walls and over water, jump through trees, or travel dozens of steps in an instant.

SECLUSION (闭关): Also known as "closed door meditation," seclusion or secluded cultivation is when a martial artist isolates themselves from the rest of the world to meditate and further their internal cultivation for the purpose of healing injuries or taking their martial arts to the next level.

TRUE QI AND CORES: True qi (真气) is a more precise term for the "qi" commonly seen in Chinese media. In Daoism, one's true qi or life force is believed to be the fusion of Xiantian qi and Houtian qi.

True qi is refined in the lower Dantian (丹田, "elixir field") within the abdomen, which also holds the foundations of a person's martial arts, called the core. In *Thousand Autumns*, Daoist cores and demonic cores are mentioned, differentiated by the discipline (and hence Dao) the practitioner chose. All internal cultivation and breathing builds off these foundations—losing or destroying them is tantamount to losing all of one's martial arts.

In wuxia, a practitioner with superb internal cultivation can perform superhuman feats with their true qi. On top of what is covered under internal cultivation above, martial artists can channel true qi into swords to generate sword qi, imbue simple movements and objects with destructive energy, project their voices across great distances, heal lesser injuries, or enhance the five senses.

YIN AND YANG (阴阳): In Daoism, the concept of *yin* and *yang* is another set of complementary, interdependent forces that govern the cosmos. It represents the duality present in many aspects of nature, such as dark and light, earth and heaven, or female and male. *Yin* is the passive principle, while *yang* is the active one.

WARRING STATES PERIOD: An era in ancient Chinese history characterized by heavy military activity between seven dominant states. The rise of schools of thought like Daoism, Confucianism, and Legalism was partially in response to the extreme turmoil and suffering that were rampant during this time. It lasted from around 475 B.C.E. to 221 B.C.E., when the Qin state annexed the rest and established the first unified Chinese empire: the Qin Dynasty.

WEIQI (围棋): Also known by its Japanese name, *go*. Sometimes called "Chinese chess," it is the oldest known board game in human history. The board consists of a many-lined grid upon which opponents play unmarked black and white stones as game pieces to claim territory.

ZOROASTRIANISM: A religion from ancient Persia founded by the prophet Zoroaster.

Afterword

JIANGHU, or "rivers and lakes," is a term specific to the Chinese language.

It's not just a simple combination of rivers and lakes, but rather it uses rivers and lakes as an analogy for a greater setting. Here you'll find the flash of swords and sabers, deception and blackmail, and of course, elegant and valiant martial arts, together with the temptation offered by the fame and fortune of becoming number one in the world.

Within it, the sides of humanity number hundredfold, and there's also a chivalric spirit distinct from what we see in real-life society. We feel a sense of distance between us and the world of the jianghu, but it's also a distance that isn't too vast. From it springs forth a hazy beauty, one that attracts us, blazes our blood, and makes us relive it endlessly.

Thousand Autumns is exactly this kind of jianghu.

And Shen Qiao and Yan Wushi, as well as the other characters, are the elements that thoroughly complete this jianghu.

Even though the curtains have already fallen on the novel's main story, they will continue to joyfully wander that jianghu, living out their lives to the fullest.

With the passing of hundreds of thousands of years, the only thing that stays eternal is the never-ending beauty preserved within our hearts, along with the brilliance of human nature.